# SHADOWMAN

# SHADOWMAN

SHOLA ADEDEJI

BLACK STONE PUBLISHING

Published in 2025 by Blackstone Publishing
Cover artwork provided by Valiant Entertainment
Cover layout by Candice Edwards



Printed in the United States of America
Originally published in hardcover by Blackstone Publishing in 2025

First paperback edition: 2025
ISBN 979-8-228-64746-6
Fiction / Horror

Version 1

Blackstone Publishing
31 Mistletoe Rd.
Ashland, OR 97520

www.BlackstonePublishing.com

*To my Family, near and far, blood or not.*

*Uno absurdo dato, mille sequuntur*—Admit but a single absurdity, you invite a thousand.

—Matthew Henry

# CHAPTER 1

Baron Samedi sat on his throne.

Although the eye sockets of his skull seemed empty, the skeleton god watched as his fellow Lwa conversed among themselves.

As with all the major deities, the realms housing the seat of their rule always reflected some aspect of their authority. Seeing as Samedi was the Lwa given dominion over death and the grave, it was no surprise his realm was not the most welcoming.

It was not like the dazzling underwater palace of Met Agwe's domain, nor was it surrounded by the brilliant flora and fauna that made up Grand Bois's.

Known as the Deadside, the baron's domain bore an appearance worthy of the title. It was a perverted replica of the mortal world, lacking the characteristics and features indicative of life.

In essence, a dead world.

There were edifices and buildings, to be sure, but these decrepit structures were merely the twisted reimaginings of Liveside equivalents. Towering monuments, with foundations too narrow to support the bloated and misshapen configuration of their upper levels, created a landscape of teetering buildings seemingly poised to collapse at the slightest gust of wind.

Routinely commissioned by the baron, these eyesores were cobbled together by the realm's monstrous inhabitants. There was an aura of resentment and despair emanating from the hollow structures, traits inherited from their undead architects.

However, Baron Samedi's abode, the Manse Ghede, was different.

For one, it was structurally sound, and while not a grotesque husk of some Liveside counterpart, it was in need of a new paint job. Its symmetry, an architectural necessity taken for granted in the land of the living, was a mark of distinction in these parts. When considered in human terms, the mansion's appearance could be likened to that of a haunted house, and seeing as it was currently housing godly guests of the spectral realm, such a description would prove exceedingly accurate.

These gods of voodoo, known as the Lwa, had come to celebrate the anniversary of Baron Samedi's marriage to Erzulie Freda, the goddess of love. Despite her title, there was no such sentiment involved in their union. It was solely transactional.

For the better part of a century, the Lwa had been steadily falling out of human memory. Due to a mix of syncretism and the distracting nature of technology, this downward trend had touched the renown of nearly all of the Lwa pantheon.

Freda, however, had experienced an *increase* in eminence, at least on the mortal plane.

Several of her divine peers dismissed this as merely the result of the emotional and covetous nature of human beings, which unfairly guaranteed the deity a consistent supply of mortals seeking her favor.

Regardless of the reason, Freda's rise in fame could not be denied.

So, in an act of divine acknowledgment of her worshippers, Freda promised through a prophesying priestess a period of no less than twelve years in which all unnatural deaths and bloody violence would cease in the land in which they resided, New Orleans.

For such an unprecedented phenomenon to occur would require the cooperation of the Ghede branch of Lwa. And so, determined to fulfill this lofty promise and prove herself true, Freda sought the aid of her most senior husband, the sky father known as the mighty Damballa.

Who, resenting Freda's attempt to manipulate his authority over something so trivial, responded with a plan.

As the most ancient Lwa of the pantheon and fully aware that newlywed grooms were honor bound by tradition to grant their brides one request, the serpentine Damballa made a proposition: If Baron Samedi would take Freda's hand in marriage, he would grant the god of death an audience with their creator, the all-powerful Gran Met.

Although this proposal came as a rather unwelcome surprise to some, neither Maman Brigitte, the baron's first wife, nor Freda's remaining husbands, Agwe and Ogun, dared voice any disapproval.

Baron Samedi seized the opportunity and it was not long before the two were wed.

For any Lwa besides Damballa, the opportunity to stand in Gran Met's presence carried the same enthusiasm as the humans had toward their idols.

Immediately, Freda made known her wish that the baron, as ruler of the Ghede branch of Lwa, use his authority to lawfully suspend the march of violent death and bloodshed until the prophesied twelve years were completed.

Samedi's indignation was short-lived. All things considered, the promise of a much-coveted audience with Gran Met was more than worth it.

And his fellow Lwa knew it.

So, on the same day for the past eight years, these gods of voodoo gathered themselves at the Manse Ghede to commemorate the baron and Freda's marriage. As expected, the transactional union proved to have a profound effect on the land of the living.

With the aid of his subordinate Ghede, the baron quickly initiated a new system of roles and responsibilities to govern their behavior and progressively limit their actions in the mortal realm, ultimately stunting Ghede influence altogether.

Some of the more bloodthirsty Ghede Lwa, like Nibo and Criminel, frequently expressed their dissatisfaction with the new order. However, the more diplomatic baron repeatedly reminded them that his eventual meeting with Gran Met would yield fruits exclusive to their branch.

As for the few non-Ghede Lwa who shared Nibo and Criminel's resentment, it had been anticipated that New Orleans's rapid decrease in violence and death would come with unforeseen societal consequences.

But to their dismay, the unprecedented change and its effects seemed to go unnoticed by most in the land of the living.

---

It was nearly noon as a yawning Jack Boniface began gathering the scattered pages of his completed assignment off the dorm room table. He had stayed awake just shy of morning to ensure his professor would deem his work flawless.

It had been over two months since he left his hometown of New Orleans for New York University. In the time leading up to his departure his parents had made it clear that their allowing him to attend NYU was not a gift to be wasted. Additionally, Jack was well aware that his father, Josiah, considered Jack's academic aspirations to be somewhat misguided.

While Josiah was not completely devoted to the superstitious culture of New Orleans, he was still at odds with Jack's unwavering adherence to what the lad proudly labeled intellectualism. Josiah often expressed skepticism toward his son's thought processes and conclusions but never went as far as outright belittling them. In fact, Josiah was the one who most encouraged Jack's academic pursuits for distinction.

Though grateful for his father's unexpected support, Jack felt certain there was an ulterior motive. Josiah's behavior was likely just a ploy, ultimately designed to coerce his son into bearing witness to what he often referred to as "institutionalized intelligence."

Despite having no proof for this theory, Jack made sure his parents understood his resolve and confidence. Aside from mailing his graded assignments to them weekly, he kept correspondence with his parents to a minimum, choosing instead to completely immerse himself in the college experience.

While Jack was not immune to bouts of homesickness, his transition was still easier than he anticipated. He had already begun dating and generally found no difficulty fitting right into his new surroundings.

However, it was not for the reasons he had hoped.

New Orleans's reputation as a dangerous place was widespread. Similar to the "juice" Jack had inherited from his father as a youth, the city's infamy granted him an aura of respect and intimidation. This, despite Jack speaking without any slang and conducting himself as a truly diligent student, resulted in a confounding sense of admiration among his fellows.

Letting out the final bits of his yawn, Jack felt compelled to check his work a final time.

Due to an oversight on his last assignment that he initially considered trivial, he had fallen short of the perfect grade. Guided by intense dissatisfaction, Jack was forced to accept the hard truth that his blunder was not only significant, but resulted from his own hubris. The determination to redeem himself was the driving force behind Jack's thorough attention to detail.

Though this same meticulousness had caused him to oversleep, Jack was not worrying as much as he normally would. Fortunately, slightly over an hour remained until class, which left him ample time to meet his current crush, Carmen, as promised.

As he searched his pocket for his phone, his roommate, Warren, called out to him.

"Jack, you're up! Check your phone cuz that girl came around looking for you. I told her you weren't here, by the way."

"What?! Why would you tell her that, man?"

Although Jack had only been dating her a short while, he already understood why his father had advised against a relationship so soon. Despite the increased workload and expectations that came with attending a university more prominent than the local college he had transferred from, Carmen was quickly becoming Jack's primary focus.

The young woman initially showed intense interest in him but recently had begun expressing some doubts. Jack took it upon himself to prove these reservations misguided rather than give them honest consideration.

Warren calmly unwrapped his pastry snack and proceeded to place it in the microwave. "Well, you were studying all night, and you haven't got a good night's sleep for a while, and, no offense, she's the main reason why. You said you were gonna meet up with her today anyway, so I figured just let the man sleep."

Feeling the uncomfortable tingle of panic, Jack immediately began searching for his phone. Now smirking into the microwave, Warren gave a slight shake of the head as he finished his reply. "She wasn't mad, bro. Matter of fact, she seemed cool about it."

Jack ignored him to continue the search but froze at a sudden and unfamiliar feeling of displacement.

*What is this?* he thought, standing still. *Am . . . am I high right now?*

Stunned, Jack thought back to the night before to determine if he had taken something, but being acutely aware of every passing second, he quickly dismissed the possibility.

*No*, he continued, unwilling to allow any further distraction. *I'll just deal with this later.*

Composing himself with a forceful shake of the head, Jack returned his attention to his missing phone. Looking at his notebook from a new angle, he could see a gap between its closed pages. Quickly throwing it open, he sighed with relief upon finding the phone inside.

His hands somewhat slippery against its slick exterior, he clumsily tried to grab the phone without crumpling the notes it was set on. "How long ago was she here?"

"I don't know, it was like . . . eight, maybe?" Warren replied.

Jack started toward the door. "Damn . . . well can't do anything about it now."

"Oh!" Warren grabbed a coat from the back of a dining room chair and flung it toward him. "And here's your jacket. Thanks for letting me borrow it."

"Yeah."

Catching the coat, Jack stopped in his tracks as he realized his phone felt uncharacteristically hot. He looked at the screen and immediately groaned at the battery icon. Its barely noticeable sliver of red blinked slowly as if to mock him.

"The phone has been on the whole time?!"

Warren emitted a lazy giggle in response. "Rookie mistake, bro," he replied. "You gotta put it on battery saver so it cuts off in case you knock out."

Jack nervously began swiping through the stream of notifications that had collected on the screen during his slumber, the majority of which were from Carmen. Too numerous to be previewed, he was forced to open the messaging app.

"I know that, man," he finally replied. "I turned the saver off because the screen kept dimming and cutting off while I was using it to study."

"I don't know what to say, bro."

Jack groaned again as Carmen's messages appeared on the screen, their disappointment increasing progressively as one unanswered text appeared after another, before ultimately ending with one of acceptance. "You're too busy and that's okay. There's nothing wrong with taking a break."

Jack began frantically typing his response, only to be thwarted as the screen froze before suddenly going blank. "Dammit!"

"Battery died?" Warren asked, his eyes still fastened to the spinning pastry.

Jack began searching for the charger. "Any other day, there are chargers all over the place. Now that I'm actually in need, I can't even find *one*?"

"I got you, bro, hold on . . ."

Finally removing his gaze from the pastry, Warren casually strolled to his bed. He gingerly peeled back the blanket and placed the pillows on the carpet. His chronic marijuana use rendered him incapable of displaying any sense of urgency. "I have no idea where it is," he stated. "Here, use my phone instead."

Jack gritted his teeth as he considered what to do. The

messages were now marked as read on Carmen's phone, and he knew she would see it as suspicious if he suddenly switched to Warren's phone to reply. *Why is everything so difficult?*

Deciding to cut his losses, Jack hastened to the door. "Don't worry about it," he said, "I'll just find her."

Carmen's residence hall was on the other side of Washington Square Park. Situated just outside his own building, the popular park served as a constant source of wonder for his dorm mates, especially for those from out of state.

Despite being from New Orleans, Jack did not share their admiration. Counting it among his long list of trivialities, he considered the scenic park an unnecessary distraction from his goal of academic distinction.

Warren often teased him about this. The carefree New Yorker found it amusing that Jack, who was otherwise very perceptive, denied himself the simplest of enjoyments for the sake of his academics yet had no qualms about getting a girlfriend.

Jack began jogging toward Carmen's dorm when the strange displacement from earlier returned, forcing him to consider any explanations as he made his way through the scarcely populated park.

While it was true he had just woken up, the sensation was different from mere grogginess. It seemed situated more in Jack's mind than his body. The way he interpreted visual stimuli felt altered somehow. As Jack took passing glances at his surroundings, colors seemed to emanate from objects like rays from the sun. And while this subtle change was enough for him to notice, it was insufficient to cause worry.

Jack opened the door to the residence hall and walked inside.

He was immediately recognized by the middle-aged man stationed at the security desk, who gave him a nod of acknowledgment.

"Stood her up again, huh?" the guard asked.

Trying to keep his altered state unnoticed, Jack managed a brief smirk in response, casually rubbing his eyes as he passed by. With the security guard now behind him, Jack began blinking to see if this was all due to watery eyes.

The door beeped as he passed through and the intensity of the sound revealed this simplistic hypothesis to be impossible. The tone seemed to skip his ears, instead sounding directly in his mind.

Unlike with the visual phenomenon, Jack found this one to be unsettling.

Initially stunned, he composed himself despite the jarring mental echoes and strolled casually down the hallway. Although the door had fallen silent, its sound was still in his head, exhibiting a Doppler effect as it lingered.

*Am I dreaming?*

Jack's confusion only intensified upon discovering the effect the sound was having on his already altered vision. Eerily synchronized with the auditory distortion, the lights and colors lining the hallway aggressively loomed toward him. Their movements seemed designed to catch his attention.

Recoiling, Jack stepped backward to avoid the seemingly sentient visuals, totally oblivious to the fortuitously empty stretch of hallway.

Feeling his shoulder graze the wall, Jack clenched his eyes shut and leaned against it. *I can't let her see me like this*, he thought. *Whatever is going on there's no way I'm gonna be able to hide it.*

He groaned through clenched teeth, more frustrated than frightened. *Whether I leave to let this trip pass or continue to meet her, I'm screwed—*

Jack stopped his thoughts and slowly opened his eyes as

the sound in his head ceased. Met with the sight of a relatively normal-looking hallway but no time to consider its explanation, he promptly made his way to Carmen's apartment near the end of the narrow hall. He knocked on the door and listened for a response.

Hearing nothing, Jack was about to do it again but was stopped by the faint creak of the apartment's bathroom door.

"Hello?" Carmen said loudly. "Did someone just knock?"

"H-hey," Jack replied. "It's me."

He heard the sound of footsteps approaching from within and nervously patted his face for sweat.

"Jack?" Carmen began from behind the door. "Is that you?"

Expecting to be sent away, his response came out like a sigh. "Yeah . . ."

To his surprise, he heard the dead bolt quickly disengage.

Wrapped in her towel, Carmen stood at the door while combing her hand through her hair. Already smiling, she tilted her head to the side before giving the strands a vigorous shake.

"When you're swamped," she began, "it's easy to lose track of time."

Free from any signs of amusement or relief, Jack's face conveyed inordinate levels of fear and shock. Carmen's dimples disappeared as she stood upright, her gracious expression ultimately giving way to one of concern.

Jack was frozen in terror as he stared at her. The water from her recent shower dripped down her yellowish-bronze skin and was replaced by what he could only assume was blood.

But the liquid's hue was an otherworldly dark, a black deeper than any ink and lacking the lustrous quality of a liquid.

Furrowing his brow, Jack tempered the look of terror as he continued to observe the remainder of her figure. Saturating her towel, the liquid marred its bright pink color, resulting in what looked to be a grisly shawl of flesh splotched with blood and gore.

He began breathing heavily, fighting the compulsion to continue staring at the nightmarish image.

Carmen calmed down and resumed shaking her hair. "I guess you're trying to be funny?"

Her question fell upon deaf ears as Jack fell backward.

His sights having reached her head, he was suddenly faced with what appeared to be a horned demon glaring at him. Its red eyes shined with the kind of feral aggression that seemed impervious to reason.

It cocked its head to the side and seemingly began wringing out a horn, the sound of the sprinkled drops of blackened blood echoing in his head.

Momentarily paralyzed as he lay on the floor, Jack tried to make sense of what was happening. It was all too good to be a prank.

"Jack!" Carmen shrieked.

Without any effort on his part, the fear that seemed ready to consume him suddenly dissipated and his vision returned to normal.

In place of the scantily clad demon was Carmen, her motionless hands still clutching her hair.

Jack stammered in confusion. "Wha-what?" he began. "What's going on?"

Carmen watched as he attempted to compose himself. "You weren't trying to be funny," she said, concerned. "Are you okay?"

Jack tried to get his bearings but to no avail. Instead, he remained on the ground, dumbstruck and blinking repeatedly as if in a daze.

"Did something happen?"

Jack struggled for the appropriate words to explain his hallucination as Carmen crouched down next to him. He could hear her gently sniff the air as she helped him to his feet.

"That explains it," she said softly. "You've been smoking."

He sighed defeatedly before standing to his feet. *Dammit, Warren*, he thought, only now noticing the stench wafting off the jacket.

"Look," Carmen began, "I get that weed may help you tackle your responsibilities or whatever but I'd rather you just be honest with yourself. It's unrealistic to assume you can quit when you've got so much on your plate. It's better if we just go our separate ways until you're at a place where quitting is actually a possibility." Jack began shaking his head as she spoke. "Besides, getting lied to over weed just isn't for me."

Jack was eager to clear up the misunderstanding, but as he opened his mouth to speak, he considered how unbelievable it sounded.

*It's only going to make me look worse*, he thought.

He smiled weakly at Carmen before looking down. "I guess it wasn't meant to be."

"I wouldn't say all that," she replied with a grin.

Jack looked up at her with newly widened eyes. His expression seemed more comical than sincere. "You would," he said, nodding confidently. "Trust me."

Carmen spoke through her laughter. "Okay, Jack Boniface, whatever you say."

Jack cut short his antics upon hearing the door beep at the far end of the hallway. "You should get inside," he said. "I'll see you later."

Carmen nodded in agreement and walked back into her apartment.

As Jack made his way down the corridor, he could hear her

call out to him once more. “And by the way,” she began, “you better find a new connect because that weed had you pretty messed up.”

Jack waved as he continued toward the exit. “Count on it.”

Experiencing a mix of emotions, he shook his head as the door closed behind him. *What the heck was that?*

Making his way through the residence hall, he tried to make sense of what transpired. He quickly concluded that the ridiculousness of it all, not just the hallucination, made any attempt to understand hardly worth the effort.

*I might as well get ready for class,* he thought, heading back toward his dorm. *Wish I knew things were gonna go south before I left. I would've brought my stuff with me.*

Jack remained alert, expecting the hallucinations to take hold once more as he made his way to his apartment. He thought back to the glaring demonic visage in wonder; though he could distinctly recall the unprecedented terror that had begun to take hold, he could no longer *feel* it.

Jack was certain the image was terrible enough to impart, at least, some fearful tinges in his memory.

Experiencing the original fear contained in memories was a common occurrence. After all, he had done so countless times before when remembering events far less dreadful.

It was not too long ago that the mere thought of a pissed-off girlfriend was enough to send waves of panic throughout his body, but now, even the memory of the demonic apparition was reduced to nothing.

It was as if he had become altogether numb to the fear.

Jack crossed the park feeling only a sense of intrigue, encouraging him to finally ponder the source of his hallucinations.

Apparently unable to derive any negative emotion from the memory, the emboldened youth kept the monstrous visage fixed in his mind's eye while considering the possible origins and felt a tickle at the corners of his mouth as his excitement intensified.

He examined the experience with the same attention to detail he applied to his assignments, but instead of being driven by some egoistic compulsion, this was fueled by an indomitable curiosity.

It felt good.

*Drugs or not, I've never gone through anything like this.*

Jack's expression progressed into an unmistakable smile as he scanned his surroundings with anticipation, hoping to somehow restart the sensory hallucination. *I gotta make sure to ask Warren if he has any experience with this kind of stuff when he gets to class.*

Nearing the side of the park closest to his building, Jack looked toward the dense curtain of trees at the far side.

Having deduced that no further hallucinations were to be experienced, Jack sighed through his childlike expression. Though slightly disappointed, he could not help but feel a new sense of appreciation for the visuals naturally imparted to him.

Still smiling at the line of trees, he made sure to pay particular attention to the combination of greens, reds, and golds. As a gentle breeze blew across them, the sunlit colors rippled, alternating their prominence in waves. Though not the powerful rays he saw during his hallucination, the shining colors of the leaves somehow seemed more vibrant than usual.

As if to prevent him from attributing this rejuvenation only to his eyes, Jack suddenly took notice of the varied sounds of the campus.

The chirping of birds mixed with the indecipherable chatter of people and vehicular racket, typical of a metropolitan area, were now distinctly perceived.

*Damn, it feels like I just got my ears cleaned.*

As he entered his building, Lipton Hall, Jack gave the outside one last look with a sweeping gaze.

The vestibule was alive with fellow students going about their business, some socializing while others hurriedly attempted to get things done.

Their voices sounding crisp in his ears, Jack made his way toward the elevator.

Despite his look of childish fascination, he was not self-conscious in the slightest. Feeling rather numb to the periodic glances of his peers, Jack's focus was on the clarity of his senses as he examined the vibrant glow of the elevator's call button.

Having ridden the elevator lost in his thoughts, Jack stepped out and passed by the few people on the floor as if in a trance. He stood motionless in front of his door before suddenly coming to himself and fumbling for his keys.

"Warren," he said, entering the apartment, "you still here?"

Hearing no response, Jack shrugged his shoulders as he hurriedly grabbed his belongings and headed to class.

# CHAPTER 2

Despite what most would consider an extremely bad start to his day, Jack sat patiently in the lecture hall, alone and untroubled. The confounding tranquility from earlier had never left him and, considering his lack of sleep, the empty hall made it all the more difficult to stay awake.

Jack began scanning his notes in a desperate attempt to avoid falling asleep, but, if anything, the activity pushed him further toward dozing off. Just as his mind started morphing the words on the page into unreadable garble, Warren arrived.

Noticing his roommate rhythmically nodding above the open notebook, Warren quickly approached. "What's good, gangsta?"

Jack jumped with a start, the sudden address snatching him from his stupor. "Hey, man . . ."

Warren fell into the seat beside him. "We didn't have any assignments for this class, right?"

Jack rubbed his face, vigorously massaging away any signs of sleepiness. *Is this guy serious?* he thought, smiling through his shuffling hands. *He saw me working on it all night.*

Before he could reply, Jack was suddenly overwhelmed by the scent of marijuana. He lazily fanned the air before turning toward Warren. His blue irises were in stark contrast to the general redness surrounding them. The stoned young man had been patiently staring at Jack the whole time, waiting for a response to his question.

Jack huffed through his smile as he gazed back at his notes. "Wow, man."

Already paranoid, Warren's face fell. "Nooo . . . !" He sniffed at his sleeve before shifting upright. "I'm loud?"

"What?"

"Loud," Warren replied. "It's slang for when—"

Jack unintentionally cut him off as he hissed a chuckle through his teeth. "I know what it means," he said. "My answer was meant to be a confirmation, not a question." Warren abruptly bowed his head and began laughing onto the top of his desk. "Yeah, man, you reek."

Jack returned to his notes. The fact that his friend's restrained laughter would be the first thing noticed by those entering the lecture hall did not bother him at all. Warren, however, seemed embarrassed upon seeing their remaining classmates arrive one after the other.

He cleared his throat as he fully lifted his head off his desk. "Why do you always sit in the front, bro?"

"Because it's a lecture," Jack replied. "Where else am I gonna sit?"

"Fair point." Warren turned around and checked the ascending rows of desks at their back. "I'm too loud to sit here though."

Jack began smiling again. "If you care about that kind of thing, why smoke before class?"

Warren started to reply but stopped upon their professor's

entrance, and promptly stood to begin climbing toward the back rows.

Jack scoffed in pity at his fleeing friend. *No reason to move now*, he thought. *You're just drawing attention to yourself.*

Their professor began class, either because he failed to detect the odor coming from Warren or because he was unwilling to address it.

Attentive to the ensuing lesson, Jack was taking notes in his customary style, thorough but brief.

At least initially.

The professor's tone had a steady drone to it, paving the way for Jack's sleepiness to return. Eventually noticing that his notes were becoming illegible, he pinched himself.

Wearily examining his surroundings, Jack finally appreciated how exposed he was and regretted sitting in the front.

Though he had just forced himself awake, the state was woefully short-lived. He didn't even know when he fell asleep.

Seamlessly and without warning, he was immersed in total darkness. Although he could not see his extremities, Jack felt no fear.

The one thing he *could* feel, however, was the dark.

Its depth was palpable, though how it was made so was entirely unfamiliar. An unprecedented sixth sense.

Mentally feeling his way through the doughlike void, Jack discerned it to be doing the same with him as visions of his life began playing through his mind unbidden. He chuckled as he recognized the fleeting image of him eavesdropping on a group of conspiracy theorists at a bus terminal back in New Orleans several months earlier.

Intrigued, Jack began walking through the darkness, consciously aware it was a dream.

*Am I moving or what?*

Intending to experiment his way to an answer, he suddenly broke into a run, confirming the expected sensations within his limbs and core. However, no matter how hard he pushed himself, or for how long, exhaustion never came.

Jack could feel the beginnings of a modest smile forming on his face.

There certainly was some enjoyment to be derived from the experience but since it took place in utter darkness, he lacked external indicators of speed or distance.

The novelty began to wane the moment he understood this, and while it was true that he had not experienced any nightmare vibes, the dream itself started to feel pointless.

Cognizant that he dozed off in clear view of his professor, Jack began to feel more concerned about his state in the real world; the time spent in the dream had approached nearly an hour.

Unsure what to do, he ceased his infinite sprint and called out to the dark.

"Hello?"

Feeling foolish in waiting for a response, he began impatiently pacing about before calling again, this time with a shout. "HELLOO—"

Though still not afraid, Jack froze upon hearing an otherworldly sound within the darkness.

*What in the world was that?*

Appreciating the fact that such a noise would surely send any normal person into immediate panic, he calmly sought an explanation.

*The noise was so deep and rumbly, I can't tell if it was a sigh or a groan . . . whatever it is, it definitely ain't human. Probably a figment of nightmares or something like that.*

Devoid of any hesitancy or concern, he instinctively engaged the darkness with his newly acquired sixth sense and was struck by how natural it felt. *It's literally a phantom limb without the pain.*

Although it was invisible, Jack could still perceive it and so paid close attention to how its movements felt against the doughy dark.

*Doesn't move like a limb, though, more like a tentacle or some kind of appendage.*

As he continued palpating the void, the visions of his life started up again.

He had already suspected this phenomenon was indicative of some kind of invasive inspection, but now he was able to confirm it. He observed in wonder as long-forgotten memories, coupled with past experiences utterly unknown to his consciousness, flew through his mind.

Though initially feeling violated, Jack noticed that the frequency of the imagery would fluctuate based on the intensity of the appendage's probing.

In defiant response, he proceeded to clutch at the dark with increased vigor. *No shame in my past, buddy, rifle through it as much as you want.*

In a moment, Jack was forced to relive soiling his pants in the fifth grade before the visions switched to him losing his virginity. Considering the dream had access to these shameful events, the coercive manner in which they were being utilized was very telling.

He wondered if this truly was a dream, but quickly dismissed any alternative explanations, deeming such considerations more superstitious than intelligent.

Kneading through the void, Jack was able to feel the outline of an entity sharing the darkness with him. Before he could examine further, the entity shrugged him off like an irritant.

"Is someone there?" he asked. "Show yourself!"

The void responded once more.

The sound was still gravelly, more of a sigh than before, hesitant and not malevolent.

"Well?"

The young man rolled his eyes as everything became strangely quiet, as if the entity was stealing time to consider things. Just as Jack was about to complain, another reluctant sigh broke the silence.

"Well played, Josiah," the unseen entity stated.

Though the voice would still send any normal person into a panic, it now had a distinct tone of acceptance.

"Wait," Jack began, "I'm not Josiah."

"I know who you are."

"All right . . . but why did you mention my dad's name?"

"Jack . . ." The entity paused to let out another sigh before speaking. "Your father is dead."

The normally stoic young man hesitated as he felt an unfamiliar surge of emotion flooding his chest. No sooner had he sensed this than it began rising to his head with ridiculous pressure.

Instinctively searching for a release, Jack channeled the brimming fury and screamed himself awake.

"BUUULLLSHIIIIII—"

The only thing restraining Jack's outrage was the awareness that he was in class, and he managed to hold his tongue. The strange insensitivity he felt while strutting through his dorm had not faded, rendering him unable to feel shame or embarrassment.

Breathing deeply, he scanned the stunned faces in the classroom, ultimately locking eyes with his professor.

"Jack, are you all right?"

Feeling a scowl unwittingly set upon his brow, Jack widened

his eyes as if recovering himself and swiftly adopted a look of embarrassment.

"I just had a nightmare," he explained. "It was the most vivid thing I . . . I . . . I'm so sorry about that."

Jack remained unaffected by the uncomfortable tittering from his classmates and continued to gaze innocently at his professor.

"It's fine," he replied. "This is quite unlike you, so I'll give you a pass."

Jack gave a quick nod of gratitude. "Thank you, Professor."

The man motioned toward the door. "Would you like to be excused? Exceptions are included with every pass, so if you like, I can have someone send you their notes."

Envious gasps sounded from the seats in the back.

"No, sir, that isn't necessary, as it won't happen again."

The other students murmured in disappointment at his rejection of the never-before-seen offer.

Outwardly giving the professor his undivided attention, Jack strangely found it all too easy to disregard the entity's unsettling message. But just before dismissing the entire experience outright, Jack flexed as he did in the dream, curious as to whether it would result in anything now that he was in his right mind. Without warning, his eyes began widening. The look of extreme surprise caused his professor to stop abruptly once more.

Utterly astounded, Jack maintained his expression as he palpated through the unmistakably doughy texture of the dark.

# CHAPTER 3

Standing patiently in the main hall of the Manse Ghede, Baron Samedi pondered his predicament.

Initially, he had no reason to be concerned by the report of Freda's disappearance. She was not his wife in the traditional sense, so she technically was not his responsibility.

Though it seemed perfectly sensible at the time, as he waited for Damballa to manifest inside his personal abode, this rationale's appeal was significantly reduced.

But before the baron could think of more appropriate excuses, he spied the subtle twinkle of ethereal light that characterized the sky father's imminent arrival.

Swiftly raising his ivory-colored hand, the skeleton took hold of his ornate top hat and braced it firmly atop his skull. With the other hand, he readjusted the dark glasses covering his seemingly empty eye sockets as the various charms and ornaments of death adorning the hat began to rattle.

As if on cue, the main hall was rocked by an explosion of pressure. The baron didn't move as his intricate long coat flapped violently in response to the rush of wind.

The tempest ended as abruptly as it began and there, shining with a near-blinding brightness and occupying the majority of the space, was Damballa.

Upon manifestation, the giant snake had his head positioned directly in front of the baron and gazed knowingly at the younger deity while adjusting the rest of his body.

Graciously reducing its brightness, the serpentine titan's gleaming white trunk gathered itself in massive coils, leaving only the outermost corners of the large hall untouched.

Seeing as the bluster had ceased, the baron let go of his hat and peered back silently into Damballa's glowing eyes before subtly moving his skull from side to side.

He groaned in exasperation before finally addressing the sky father. "Good lord," he said, "I can't look you in both your eyes at the same time. Your head's too big."

The serpent's head loomed unwavering, inches away from the bespectacled god of the underworld. When he spoke, his voice maintained a delicate balance of whistle and whisper due to the subtle hiss slipped beneath his every utterance. "Out with it, Samedi," he said. "What happened?"

The baron looked surprised. Despite having no flesh or facial features, his face was quite expressive.

A slight arching of the bone above the eyes or at the sides of his mouth was usually enough to convey most emotions. And while a poker face was sinfully easy to maintain, the lack of flesh made it very difficult to feign the more nuanced and intimate emotions.

If not for this one downside, the baron would always stay in this form.

"Why," the baron began, "I was expecting you to tell me!"

Damballa scoffed and finally turned away. "Do not reply to me with nonsense."

The skeleton shuddered slightly before adjusting the front of his coat with a firm tug. "I'll be sure to avoid that," he said. "And might I add, that lisp of yours is dreadful as ever."

Damballa said nothing while his head continued to weave and sway about the hall, as if surveying its entirety. With this winding complete, he set his head atop the massive mound of shining coils that was his body and set his gaze on the skeleton once more.

The baron cleared his throat before continuing. "So . . . er, yes, it is as I said. I was under the assumption that you were apprised of her whereabouts. You're Freda's first husband. Surely, I thought she tells you things to which I'm not privy." The giant serpent remained silent. "We were married for business. I'm not her keeper. How should I have known her absence was an issue?"

Damballa seemed to take a deep breath, evidenced by the steady rise of his neatly wrapped body. "Is this within the norms of her behavior? Yes or no?"

The baron sighed, reluctantly giving his response. "Admittedly . . . no, it is not normal." He quickly shed his somber demeanor before continuing. "But neither is a pantheon-level goddess goin' missing against her will with no warning or enemies. In peacetime, to boot?"

Damballa forcefully jerked his head as if evading the response. "Bah!"

The baron shrugged his shoulders before finally gathering the strands of his hair that had been loosened from under his hat by the serpent's tempestuous entrance, his bone fingers casually twiddling the strands away from his face.

"Your insouciance is greater than your predicament permits," Damballa said.

The baron's hands became still. "I beg your pardon?"

"Assuming that you are being forthright in your claim of

innocent ignorance, this was a calculated act not just against her, but you as well. I trust you are aware of this, yes?"

"Don't believe I saw it that way initially, no."

"Indeed, for they have assuredly anticipated the rescinding of your oath to pause death and bloodletting, seeing as her absence effectively releases you from it."

"Oh bother." The skeleton god adjusted his top hat, securing the errant strands of hair. "I fear my subordinates have grown unseemly rapacious during the hiatus, so flipping the switch just like that could prove disastrous for the Liveside."

"How you do it concerns me not. I am just illustrating for you the intricacies of this plot, the one in which you haven't had a hand."

Uncertain if the elder god was being sardonic, the baron replied all the same. "I follow," he began, thoughtfully curling his finger around his chin, "but damn . . . the nullification of the oath was the furthest thing from my mind, and all the while these conspirators anticipated that I would have no choice—"

"Just as they anticipated that I would have no choice but to hold responsible the one I married her off to."

Hearing this, the skeleton lowered the brim of his hat. "I didn't anticipate that, sorry to say." His tone fluctuated as he struggled to conceal his genuine displeasure. "What's that entail, might I ask? Gran Met ain't off the table, is He?"

Like a whip, Damballa uncoiled himself and reformed so his length was stretched upward. Flexing himself rigid, the tip of his tail supported the entirety of his mass.

A gargantuan gleaming spring of serpent skin, frozen in time the moment after release.

He bore a telling similarity to the artwork adorning the ceremonial chambers of various ancient peoples, their two-dimensional depictions attempting to capture his likeness.

The baron pulled the brim of his hat a bit lower as he took in the sight.

The sky father somehow took up even more space in this position, and the tip of his snout seemed to touch the high ceiling of the main hall.

The speed of the change, coupled with its striking appearance, was enough to freeze the hearts of both mortal and immortal alike. However, the baron knew that this indicated Damballa's imminent departure, and felt relieved instead.

He firmly held his hat against his skull as the giant serpent began to shine brighter.

Damballa's brightening eyes shifted toward the lesser Lwa. "You had better stop being cute, Samedi." The deity's head remained pointing upward, unwilling to allow any imperfections within his monstrous contortion. "Find Freda or suffer the consequences as the one truly responsible."

The giant serpent's shining had intensified to a level the baron felt was oppressive. However, the imperceptible speed of the sky father's departure reduced it to a mere flash that was followed by the sudden implosion of pressure.

Stabilizing his hat against the wind that was now trying to pull it off, the baron silently considered his options.

How was he supposed to know where Freda went?

If it was indeed a conspiracy, then only his fellow Lwa could be behind it, and he would be unable to accuse anyone without solid proof. Furthermore, acquiring such evidence himself would be impossible as the conspirators would certainly know to be on their guard. He would need an intermediary hard enough to get into the nitty-gritty, yet capable of the flexibility to be unpredictable; someone they could not anticipate.

Baron Samedi waited for the bluster to cease as a plan began to form in his mind. If he had a face, he would be full-on grinning.

"This may be fun after all."

The baron suddenly shouted, his countenance shifting to one of authority.

"Papa! Nibo!"

A large, light brown square immediately appeared at his feet. While maintaining their width, the four sides of the square extended outward, each stretching in its own direction and forming a large cross splayed along the floor of the main hall.

A figure began rising out of the dirt square at the center of the conjured crossroad. Having emerged just inches away from the baron's wing tips, the entity stood before him.

The short man dusted himself off with his oversized top hat, pausing only to acknowledge his leader. "Master Saturday," he muttered. The ethereal dirt seemed to evaporate after being brushed off his tattered coat. "How can I be of service?"

"It would appear that treachery is set against the Ghede by conspirators unknown."

The short man removed an apple from his hat and began rubbing it against his coat. "Treachery against us, eh?" he said. "Well, one thing we know for certain is that they—"

The baron raised his slender index finger, silencing his subordinate. "Hold that thought, Papa." The short man took the opportunity to bite his apple. "Where is Nibo?"

At that moment, wisps of gray could be seen forming in their midst.

"Present, sire," a voice responded from the culminating cloud. It was melodious and, unlike the baron or Papa, expressed a youthful enthusiasm.

A glowing ember could be seen moving about the ever-expanding plume just as the Lwa, Nibo, stepped forth from within.

He took another puff of his cigar, revealing the source of the gray cloud.

It was clear that Nibo had a liking for a certain aesthetic. Shirtless, he wore a bright pink double-breasted sports coat that somehow complemented his tightly fitting tan odd trousers.

However, his choice of black-and-white checkerboard loafers was questionable.

The exuberant Lwa took a quick glance at their immediate vicinity. "What of Mother?" he asked. "Apologies for my lateness, by the way. Your summoning was most unexpected, requiring that I make my—"

The baron brushed away the explanation as he repeated himself. "It would appear that treachery is set against the Ghede by conspirators unknown."

"Oh?"

"Indeed, Papa was just giving me his assessment of our anonymous adversaries."

Papa, the Ghede of the Crossroads, swallowed a bite of the apple. "Yes," he replied, "I was saying that their decision to scheme against our branch indicates that they are either exceedingly stupid or hopelessly desperate."

Nibo shrugged as he let out an uncomfortable chuckle. "Okay?" he began. "So, do we have a plan of retaliation or no?"

"Without knowing the culprits there cannot as yet be a plan of retaliation." Hearing this, Nibo shrugged his shoulders even higher as the baron continued. "A plan of action, however, is most appropriate. It is a pity, though."

Papa uttered his question as he munched anew. "What is?"

"I didn't want to nullify the restriction on death and bloodshed just yet. Doing it so abruptly makes equilibrium, at least at the initial phase, damn near impossible."

"Ohhhh," Nibo said. "Like breaking the seal?"

"Perverted yet apropos," Papa replied as he looked at the baron. "Is the nullification necessary at this time?"

"Yes, as the Liveside holds the key to the first step to my plan." He let out a long groan of annoyance. "I guess it can't be helped."

"Sire?"

"Inform Shadowman that his hiatus has ended."

---

Jack wound up accepting his professor's offer to be excused.

He had been spending the day trying to contact someone from the neighborhood, as his home's landline continuously went unanswered.

*I never imagined I'd regret not giving the boys from back home my number*, he thought.

Though fully aware of the implications posed by his unanswered phone calls, Jack noticed that his actions lacked urgency. He loved his father, to be sure, and would be deeply saddened if he was truly dead.

But he was not *scared* of it as a possibility.

As much as this displeased him, he could not help it.

Jack reasoned this was due in part to his preoccupation with the appendage-like sixth sense he inherited back in the void, as he had been flexing it nonstop since class.

Unsure what these flexes were actually doing, Jack found himself in the middle of Washington Square and decided to try figuring it out.

He sat down on the nearest park bench and readied the appendage. The darkness in the dream had made it impossible to tell what he was doing. But now that he was in the real world, he could at least get an idea of where he was sending the thing.

Instead of wielding it in the same thoughtless manner as before, Jack took aim at a nearby cluster of trees and slowly drew it forth. He felt the unseen appendage graze against the leaves and started palpating his way without thinking.

Jack leaned forward and began casually rubbing the stubble on his face. "This can't be real."

He appeared to be gazing thoughtfully at the setting sun but was actually trying to contain his disbelief. Through the meticulous handling of his sixth sense, his mind was receiving an impression of the targeted trees. The transmission grew in detail the more the appendage flexed its way through, even communicating changes in movement.

Jack watched in awe as the trees responded to the wind, their sway providing visual confirmation of what his supernatural sense was transmitting.

He tried flexing the appendage in the chaotic way he had before but it felt heavier now, less quick. *I don't understand*, he thought, still examining the swaying trees in his mind's eye. *It wasn't capable of showing me anything when I was flexing in class. If anything, I should be able to move it even faster now.*

Jack stared at the waning daylight and was hit with a realization, causing him to suddenly sit back. "That's right," he said softly. "It felt like I was flexing against the dark back then. But this"—he turned toward the park's giant arch—"is different."

Stretching out the appendage toward the stone structure, Jack's mind began receiving impressions of the various sightseers positioned along its path. The transmission felt relatively fuzzy, briefly imparting vague characteristics as the people passed by.

Sensing it had reached his target, Jack pressed the appendage against the stone structure and immediately saw the images carved on the arch's exterior.

The impressions quickly vanished as he abruptly stood to his feet and began the short walk to his dorm. *No way*, he thought, shaking his head. *There's got to be some explanation.*

Upon reaching his building, however, Jack sensed this doubt begin to fade. Unfortunately, a wholehearted disbelief in the supernatural was the basic premise of his worldview, making his dwindling skepticism all the more unsettling.

*At least that freaking invisible monster hasn't shown up again*, he thought, entering his dorm room. *Still don't explain what happened with Carmen, though. Damn.*

His eyelids were heavy, and feeling mentally exhausted, Jack struggled to think up more rationalizations as he lay down.

"Maybe I got a contact high from Warren?" he mused out loud. "After all, it's been a long time since I last smoked." He rolled over in his bed. "Yeah, I'm sure there's some research that would back that up. This is fine."

Feeling satisfied with this excuse, Jack released his eyes and quickly drifted to sleep.

He opened them immediately upon hearing the unmistakable guttural tone of the entity from the void—the invisible monster.

He found himself surrounded by the deep blackness of the infinite dark, just as before, this time listening to the voice in earnest.

"Hm hm hm," the entity chuckled dryly. "You regard yourself as an intellectual of the highest caliber, eh?"

Jack, unfazed, enthusiastically received the taunt. "Yeah," he replied, grinning in the dark. "What about it?" He did not flinch as the monster roared back, apparently irritated by the young man's demeanor.

"WHAT ABOUT IT, YOU SAY?!" Its feigned displeasure

gave way to additional bursts of dry laughter. "Hm hm, take heed to my words, you ephemeral speck!"

"All ears."

"Mark that the Jack of yesterday would never entertain nor accept the sorry excuse you just summoned. Today's Jack only thought of it because of a pathetic need to explain away his dissonance, no matter the cost. And it only lulled you into an even deeper stupor!"

*What excuse is he screaming about?*

"The marijuana!" the entity replied.

"Oh . . ."

"You are a dullard for accepting it as a logical offering. Just like everyone else, you sacrificed your intellect on your pride's altar. It makes you a hypocrite. This desperate rationale proves a level of logical consistency vastly inferior to what you heard two months ago at the bus terminal."

Jack was unable to reply.

Though surprised at the phantom's reference to something so trivial, he was more stunned by how he had been taken to task.

"Particularly the theory expressed by that one local, Lou, was it? Why keep silent? It is your memory."

"Wait—How did . . . ?"

The entity let out a long groan as if bored.

"Jack, you know I have been going through your memories. You even encouraged it. 'Rifle through it' were your exact words."

Jack immediately went about kneading the dark, aggressively feeling along the entity's massive outline. "What are you?"

It responded as if in a struggle. "Y-you dare!"

Jack recoiled slightly as he felt his appendage shoved away with brute force. Sensing the subtle shifts and alterations within the doughy void, Jack could feel something moving within.

"I must say," the entity began, "regardless of your inexperience, your proficiency is noticeably superior to that of your predecessors, bound or willing notwithstanding."

Jack stopped himself from fully enjoying the compliment, given pause by its closing words. Before he could ask for clarification, two red circles appeared in the darkness.

He rubbed his eyes, unsure if he was truly seeing anything. But as he watched the circles glowing from on high, they suddenly began moving. Side by side, the two points traveled in unison, burning short-lived streaks of red through the heavy darkness as they drew near.

Squinting into the void, he followed the dancing lights while trying to figure out what he was looking at.

"You still do not see?" The entity's cadence made it impossible to determine if it was curious or condescending. Jack became still as the lights' movements suddenly ceased. "Stop the foolishness with your eyes; they are of no use here."

Unable to think of anything else, Jack closed them. "If my eyes can't help me see—" He gasped. Not only were the lights still there but they were clearer. "But," he began, "how?"

The lights commenced their movements. "Yesss," the entity said, "now you are beginning to see."

"I don't . . . what the f—"

As Jack followed the lights, the impression of something massive growing in the background became progressively more noticeable. Before he could look away, the glowing lights became the eyes of some towering monstrosity, now lumbering its way toward him.

In a state of disbelief, Jack was slow to react as the behemoth came into focus. He shook his head violently as if to cast out the image from his mind's eye.

To his dismay, this only seemed to improve its clarity.

Jack opened his eyes in one last attempt to spare himself from the sight, but it was futile. Whether his eyes were open or closed, he saw every little detail that comprised the monster's grotesque visage.

The monster was a pale purple that distinguished it from the darkness of the void. Two horns protruded laterally from its head, one on each side, their tips curving forward slightly as if to meet in front of its glowing red eyes. As for the face, it was hideous. An abominable pig composed more of bone than swine, it had a rigid snout that jutted upward from the center of its face. Scant of flesh, there were no lips to be found, making the monster appear to be angrily gnashing its teeth. Its mandible protruded outward in a massive underbite caused by the two tusks that erupted forth from the sides of its chin. More like giant ascending fangs, the tusks' converging tips somehow glistened in the void and held their position just beneath the bone snout.

It was almost too grotesque to behold.

Jack remembered the demon he saw at Carmen's. The similarities between the horror he glimpsed then and what he was seeing now were impossible to ignore.

Obviously, this was the entity behind it all.

The massive creature stopped in front of Jack, peering down at him.

It raised its head slightly, breaking its gaze, and took a mighty inhale through its bony snout. Its apelike posture rose as the sound of a rushing wind filled the void.

The creature sighed in satisfaction and looked at Jack. "Is that fear?"

Jack did not take the bait, opting instead to stare at the beast. He just could not get over its sheer size. Not quite a skyscraper but definitely bigger than any of the high-rise apartment projects back home. Beholding the monstrosity, he considered its question.

Despite his fear being somehow kept at bay, the beast's image still aroused a profound sense of foreboding.

But this was not due to any of its inherent horrifying qualities, at least not directly. Rather, it was given life the moment Jack understood the implications of its existence.

His worldview had been destroyed.

The monster roared with insensitive laughter. "That is what you fear most?" it asked. "Even more than Josiah's death, eh? You are fuller of yourself than you think, Jack Boniface."

At this rebuke, Jack felt the beginnings of the rage that erupted the last time the monster brought up his father. Recognizing it, he quickly stifled the incoming surge.

"Damn, I guess you're right," he replied.

A short silence filled the void before the apelike behemoth suddenly slammed its fists into the ground. "Well, get over it!" Jack was too disillusioned to flinch, merely watching as the monster continued its speech. "There is work to be done. And if you are already feeling defeated over a bruised ego, then we are in dire straits, and your father died in vain."

Jack remained silent for a moment, his thoughts remaining on his father.

"You keep mentioning my dad," he began. "Why should I trust what you're saying when I don't know what the hell is going on? You're not particularly trustworthy looking and I know nothing about you, not even your name."

The monster lifted its weight off its fists, unfurling to its massive height. "You don't need to know my name," it replied, "but because I sense in you a unique shred of potential, and time is not on our side, I will tell you." Jack waited expectantly. "You do not even comprehend the honor in what I just said. What a cruel joke, Josiah. Well played."

"I guess thank you for the honor then."

The monster's gaze remained on Jack for a moment before it resumed speaking. "My name is Bossu Koblamin and you are Jack Boniface, the latest in a long line of humans I dwell in by inheritance—"

"To what end?" Jack interrupted.

"Ultimately, and I have never given this answer, it is up to you."

Jack hesitated before shaking his head. "That's not what I meant, I don't think."

"Oh?"

"No, not really. I meant, like, the stated purpose of this. What do you mean by inheritance?"

"Essentially, you are to be an enforcer on behalf of the Lwa and are lawfully permitted to operate with impunity in the human world."

Jack flinched. "Lwa? So you're talking voodoo. Are you kidding?"

"You will have to shed this ignorance you so graciously view as skepticism if you are to have any chance of surviving."

"Yeah," Jack said, calmly lifting his hand as if for quiet, "I definitely don't believe you."

"I am ending this right now," Bossu replied. "I am not going to waste my time with the willfully ignorant."

"Willful?" Jack challenged. "You're making claims without proof! My doubt isn't willful or ignorant."

"Very well, I have sent forth proof. If you allow yourself to receive it as such, it will be a testament to the truth in all I have claimed thus far. For now, as I said unto you, this is ended."

"Fine by me."

---

Jack woke up in his bed feeling abnormally groggy.

Despite this dream feeling significantly shorter than the first, in reality, it was much longer. The first time, the professor had barely begun class when Jack screamed awake, but this dream had him passed out until nightfall.

Slightly parting the curtain next to him, Jack struggled to rectify the confounding phenomenon but immediately let it go upon peeking out the window.

A mass of people had formed at the edge of the park just outside his building, animatedly talking among themselves. Many had their phones out filming.

Jack noticed the multitude's attention would alternate between whatever it was they were looking at in the trees and his general location in the dorm.

They all, independently, would look one way and then the other.

Some would then make a comment or pull out their phone, but sooner or later, they all would repeat the cycle.

Jack kept still, silently watching the back-and-forth. He could tell the collective mood was not one of merriment; many looked concerned.

His curiosity getting the best of him, Jack pushed his curtain fully to the side to see what they were looking at. Immediately everyone's attention snapped directly to him.

He barely noticed this as he stared past them.

Along the grass and trees lining the park's perimeter were countless crows in an unnatural array. Definitely supernatural in origin, the swarm ignored their dumbstruck audience, collectively gazing opposite them and straight at Jack with otherworldly purple eyes. Innumerable dots of this spectral light were shining in the distant trees as well.

"Oh," Jack uttered, almost pleadingly.

Keeping the crows in view, he leaned to the side.

The crowd froze in silence as the birds, in a most disturbing manner, slowly turned their necks. Their glowing eyes twinkled knowingly as if to tell Jack that, indeed, they were looking at him.

Covering his mouth in disbelief, he returned to his original position, as did the crows. He heard himself moan in dismay as he watched the spectral lights housed in the trees glitter in response.

He quickly drew the curtain closed and pulled his knees to his chest, sitting in stunned silence. Jack started rocking back and forth to steady his sudden panting, but all this seemed to do was loosen the tears gathering in his eyes.

He buried his head between his knees just as they began to fall. "Dad," he whispered.

He could feel the rage threatening its upsurge again. This time, it was canceled by the flood of sadness overwhelming him. "My dad is dead."

The pain of this realization came in crashing waves, their intensity growing the more he thought about it.

Sobbing into his knees, he knew his paradigm had been irreversibly destroyed, but that seemed ridiculously trivial at this point. Jack's focus was only on his father.

He began to reminisce through his tears, but not wanting to draw the attention of Warren or anyone else who may have entered, he laid down with his back toward the door.

Jack cringed upon remembering several years earlier when he and his father had a slight clash over their different worldviews. He could slightly recall the amusement on his father's face as he listened to his young son explain why his outlook was "objectively superior."

Jack had hoped memories of their time together would dull

the sting of his emotions. Unfortunately, it made everything all the more piercing, but he still could not bring himself to stop. He lay motionless on his bed, unable to disengage from the cycle of recollection and sorrow.

Jack was brought back to the time he last saw his father, the depth of his emotional turmoil making it more of a hallucination than a mere memory.

# CHAPTER 4

Two months earlier, Jack was hurriedly gathering the last of his belongings from his room, his television rambling on as Josiah Boniface stood in the doorway. Jack's semester had started several days prior, but he had come back home to retrieve some things he had left behind.

Having been encouraged by his father to pursue his dream of a career in journalism, Jack wasted no time in escaping the backwardness that was New Orleans. And the news on the television seemed to confirm the wisdom of this decision.

"Alarming news from Pines Village predicts the gang violence endemic to the area will continue its upward trend with no end in sight. In addition, reports say the rates of home invasions are at an all-time high citywide. In response, Troy, the fledgling start-up already generating buzz within the tech world, has announced the unveiling of their new creation that many are hoping will bring an end to the mindless acts of violence. Mayor Goodwill had this to say . . ."

The image on the television switched to show the mayor

of New Orleans taking the time to stoke the hype for the new device during one of his many press conferences.

"Known simply as Inicio, this state-of-the-art device will be able to alert authorities whenever a crime is committed, whether installed in private homes or public spaces. When activated, Inicio seamlessly captures video and audio the moment it detects something amiss in its perimeter."

Jack was immediately struck by the man's delivery. Not only was he plainly reading a script, but his delivery was far too technical for a public servant. Jack twisted his face into an incredulous expression as he looked at his father to see if the sentiment was shared. The man knowingly shook his head, smirking before returning his attention to the television.

"In addition," Mayor Goodwill continued, "owners have the option of syncing their own device with others nearby, allowing each household or business to not only remain informed about the welfare of their neighbors, but also contribute to the capture of any *perpetrator* who attempts to flee the scene of the crime by tracking them in real time. The more Inicios in a community, the better protected . . ."

Jack sighed loudly, intentionally drowning out the report before shutting off the television.

Entering the room, Josiah smirked at his son's exaggerated display. "What is it, boy?" he asked. "Second-guessing the move?"

"Of course not, Dad," Jack replied, pulling the zipper closed on his suitcase. "I was just reminded that nothing's ever gonna change here." Shaking his head, he let out three tuts of disapproval as if suddenly discovering something shameful. "There's always something new that is presented as the solution, and it never works."

"And what does that tell you?"

"That the problem can't be fixed. The city is rotten through and through."

"Is that it?" Josiah asked, still smirking.

Jack shrugged. "What else is there?"

"Damn, son, not saying I agree, but if your conclusion is that it can't be fixed, then what do you have to say about your pundits who seem to suggest that it can?"

Jack had expected to think of a reply quickly, but nothing seemed right. He hated when his father did that, saying needlessly complicated statements that somehow left him stumped.

His father's gaze was firmly set on him. *Oh man*, he thought, *the old man is expecting an answer to this one . . . damn.*

Josiah waited as his son considered the question.

Overhearing their conversation, Jack's mother, Helena LeBreton, approached the doorway to take a look. Despite the hardship endured due to Josiah's prolonged absences, as she observed the interaction between her husband and son, she could not help but feel it was all worth it.

From Jack's perspective, his father's presence during his formative years was sporadic at best. Though the man made it a point to obsessively impart words of wisdom and gentle instruction whenever he stopped by, these visits were always marked by their suddenness and irregularity. As a result, Jack was routinely subjected to rumors claiming Josiah was a criminal.

To protect her son from any emotional issues resulting from the baseless neighborhood gossip, Helena was sure to impress upon him that his father was a good man. "Far better than most."

Fondly locked in Jack's memory was the exact moment Josiah began establishing himself as a constant presence in their home.

It had been almost seven years since that day.

---

Young Jack was awakened by the sound of his father playing the saxophone, an occurrence rarer than his visits. He had remained in bed wondering why his father would practice so early in the day; he had always preferred discretion when seeing them. Jack's eyes widened as the saxophone belted out its final note, cartoonish and off-key.

His confusion became intolerable when he heard the uncharacteristic sounds of his mother's laughter, and finally got out of bed. The scent of food filled the house as he moved toward the noises emanating from their dining room. Jack could not believe his eyes as he saw both his parents seated at the table, preparing to eat breakfast.

Jack's parents merely engaged him in conversation without explanation, like this was completely natural for them. The behavior was such that any potential awkwardness or confusion felt completely unwarranted and, eventually, foolish.

From that day onward, it continued like this without interruption. They were definitely a normal family now, and while Helena's constant reassurances were appreciated, her son had come to know his father for himself.

Even during intermittent visitations, Jack determined that his father's personality was incongruous with the rumors, and he instinctually disregarded them.

This attitude proved passive yet unwavering.

His disinterest in the town's gossip was so pronounced that his neighbors started calling him "Too Good."

The neighborhood nickname served two purposes: It accused the boy of thinking too highly of himself while simultaneously belittling him for doing so. Jack found the title humorous because it was only accurate by chance, ultimately proving to be a self-fulfilling prophecy.

While he was convinced that the culture of New Orleans

eroded the intelligence of all who had the misfortune of inheriting it, he had come to regard his father as the pinnacle of sagacity.

Josiah had consistently exhibited a standard of patience and understanding far beyond anything his son, now a young adult, could compare it to.

"Far better than most."

---

This was the reason behind Jack's careful consideration of his father's question that afternoon in his room.

"I'm not sure," he finally replied. "They're either stupid or on the take."

Josiah shrugged at this. "Take your pick, boy, either one should be enough to keep you awake at night."

Unable to summon a worthy retort, Jack winced as he grabbed the suitcase handle, silently pulling it upward in defeat. His contorted expression shifted into a strained smile as he reached out his hand.

"You got me, Dad, fair and square."

Josiah's initial look of confusion broke into a grin as he accepted the handshake. "Of course I got you, son," he said. "It's my primary responsibility, after all."

He flashed a wink at his wife, having noticed her at the door. She turned toward Jack as he released his father's hand.

"You two done saying goodbye?" she asked. "Let the boy go, Josiah. You not likely to change his mind no matter how clever you go about it."

Josiah laughed briefly as he looked back to Jack, making way for him in the doorway. "He knows that wasn't my intention," he replied. The grin was gone now, though his tone suggested he was only semiserious. "You know that, don't you?"

Jack remained silent, his smile becoming more genuine as he looked at his parents.

"It doesn't matter what you do with your life," Josiah continued, "if you're looking for Truth, you'll find It." He leaned toward Jack, eye level but not uncomfortable. "My only intention is to make damn sure you're one of the few capable of accepting Its invitation at your appointed time." He stepped backward, never taking his eyes off his son as he gently brought an arm around his wife and pulled her close. "Shit, even I failed, so trust me when I say the invitation isn't something to shake a stick at. Luckily for you, my failure also allowed me to see the answers to the test. I got you, son."

Jack gasped. "You're advocating that your son cheat?"

"Damn right," Josiah replied. "No hope of you succeeding otherwise . . ." He trailed off. "And boy, you will succeed." Placing her arm around his waist, Helena appeared primed to cut him off, but Josiah quickly began to speak again. "Remember these words: Giving up my life to ensure you become more than I can ever hope to be, that is my greatest accomplishment."

Jack saw his mother subtly pinch his father's side.

Seemingly defying her prodding, Josiah began talking again, pretending to be baffled. "Or does 'will be my greatest' sound better? They both sound good, and they're both true. Just make sure you never forget that it's better to die standing than to grovel." He tapped the side of his head. "As long as you keep that in mind, you'll be unstoppable."

Somehow sensing the beginnings of some private disagreement, Jack moved to cut it short.

"I know, Dad," he replied. "You've expressed that same idea in different ways going on forever. I won't forget it. If I wasn't absolutely sure that I wouldn't fail you, then I wouldn't pursue this." He looked at his mother and then his father. "Do you believe me?"

Josiah smiled and turned toward Helena, her face already mirroring his own. "You hear your boy?" he asked, before suddenly reaching toward Jack with an outstretched arm.

Nodding in response, Helena was swept into the embrace Josiah was giving their son. She looked at Jack's expression, his youthful face resting on her husband's broad shoulders.

Not appearing smug or annoyed, he wore a smile she had never seen before; it was more in his eyes than his mouth.

Contentment.

Jack gave his father his undivided attention as he spoke.

"I believe you, Jack," Josiah said, his voice now devoid of any humor. "After all, it is doubtful you would be able to phrase it that way if you were faking it."

Jack gasped and pulled back from the family hug.

"Exactly!" he said. "That's exactly it!" His wide eyes darted between them excitedly. "So you don't need any further convincing, right?"

Josiah shook his head in response, his stoic demeanor giving away a most subtle bit of amusement. "No," he replied. "I am convinced you are ready. If I was not absolutely sure that you wouldn't fail, then I wouldn't let you go. Do you believe me?"

Rather than finding the seriousness within his father's delivery unsettling, Jack began grinning all the more.

Josiah motioned toward the door. "Now, begone."

---

Jack's good humor was short-lived when he remembered that streetcar service had been temporarily suspended citywide, upon seeing the orange sign posted at his stop.

It was unlikely Josiah had forgotten, though.

Jack considered returning home until service resumed, but could not shake the suspicion that this was some sort of test orchestrated by his father.

Recalling his parting words, Jack snorted with amusement. *It did kinda feel like he was rushing me out the door.*

The sun already felt oppressive, prompting him to wipe the beads of sweat from his forehead as he made his way through his neighborhood, known as Black Pearl, situated about five miles from the city's main bus terminal.

Jack's slight frame progressed with a disciplined stride as he lugged the duffel bag and rolling luggage that made up the entirety of his belongings.

*One last character-building lesson, eh, Dad?*

Looking around, he saw various townsfolk gathered in the shaded portions of the sidewalk, seeking respite from the heat.

The sounds caused by the wheels of his suitcase got the attention of those nearest him.

"You leavin' already, Too Good?" one of them asked.

Jack nodded, smiling at their predictability. "Yeah," he replied. "I'm gonna miss you guys . . . sike."

The young men howled in amusement.

"Look y'all!" another exclaimed. "Too Good's bouncing on us!"

Hearing this, the group began to draw near, offering a mix of jokes and words of encouragement.

"It was only a matter of time."

"Betta not forget where you came from, Jack."

"Yeah, yeah," he replied, "I know."

Jack's childhood friend, Jester, elbowed him. "Damn, bro," he began, "you walking all the way to the bus with all this? Ya pops be doing you dirty."

Still smiling, Jack rolled his eyes and pressed onward.

Jester moved in front of him. "Nah, my fault, my fault," he said, reaching to relieve Jack of his belongings. "I was just messing witchu."

"So what are you going to do?" Jack asked, releasing the luggage's handle. "Walk with me to the Greyhound?"

"Greyhound?" Jester scoffed as he returned the handle. "Oh nah, that's all the way at the main bus terminal! I thought you was just goin' down the block."

"The trolleys are out of commish."

"The local buses still workin' though."

Though Jack had forgotten this, he was already determined to walk the whole way, unsure if his father would have eyes on him. "It's complicated," he replied.

The group stared at him in confusion.

"Of course, Too Good's too good for the bus!"

"Y'all need a car then."

Jack gently dismissed the suggestion. "It's all good guys."

"Don't nobody got a whip?" someone said, shouting incredulously.

"Stop," Jack said, fearing a prolonged send-off, "it's not a big—"

"Wait," Jester cut Jack off, "don't McMullen got a whip?"

The multitude groaned, with looks of annoyance on the faces of some.

Jester was immediately met with scoldings from every side.

"Why you gotta bring up Jamal though?" one of their neighbors asked.

"He stupid as hell, is why."

Unabashed, Jester defiantly swatted away their contempt. "What?" he asked. "Y'all still trippin' about the time he went in on Jack's face?"

Jack chuckled. Jamal McMullen had been the neighborhood tough guy for more than ten years before inexplicably deciding to become Jack's bully. Jack suspected the troubled youth had somehow become jealous of the rumors surrounding his family.

Juice is what they called it.

Being the son of a returned criminal of renowned infamy came with unearned advantages, which Jack had long been indulging. Prior to Jamal, he was mostly regarded as one not to be messed with, despite no one having witnessed him fight.

To his dismay, Jamal became wise to this.

Capitalizing on the fact that he lived on the main drag of St. Charles Avenue, Jamal's bullying began as mere taunts whenever Jack happened to pass his house. They started indirectly enough but intensified until there could be no doubt as to who he was talking to.

---

"Ya daddy got you walkin' around here feeling like a bad dude," Jamal had shouted from his porch, "but I bet you a pussy. I put a stack on it." Continuing past, Jack stared back when he realized Jamal was talking to him.

Some of the onlookers told Jamal to stop, but he would not.

"This fraud got all y'all trippin' and I'm gonna prove it." A furrow formed on Jack's brow as Jamal continued his threat. "Sooner or later I'm gonna expose you, Jack Boniface."

Breaking eye contact and feeling humiliated, Jack maintained his composure as he turned his back.

Jamal guffawed loudly. "See? He not even gonna do nothing!"

As soon as he got home, Jack approached his father for advice, being sure to detail Jamal's weeklong series of vague provocations culminating in his act of direct intimidation.

"I feel for you, son," Josiah had responded, "I really do, but you have to think long and hard on this. Only you know what your *discernment* is saying, and that is all you have to go by. If it tells you to engage, win or lose, then go nuts. But if it tells you that you will regret it, win or lose, then you better be able to stand down." Jack anxiously clenched his jaw as he watched his father calmly assess the predicament. "Damn sure can't go by what you imagine others would do. To arbitrarily assume they would obey what it's saying to them is unwise, plus, it is unlikely their *discernment* would echo your own."

Jack was unsure what to make of that, but he knew he was not angry enough to hit Jamal, so he decided to avoid him from then on and take the long way home the next day.

However, upon quickly being informed by Josiah that this would only serve to embolden his aggressor, increasing the chance of a fight the next time they meet, Jack bravely returned to his regular route.

Just as his father predicted, Jamal sprang to action upon seeing him, the hums and murmurs of the various onlookers standing by alerting him to Jack's presence.

"Yeahhh," Jamal began, his voice lively with anticipation, "I heard you took a detour the other day. What happened?"

Though Jack felt more annoyance than fear, he knew it was not enough to keep the fight short and prevent himself from getting injured. After all, Jack was of a moderate build, tending toward the lean. Jamal, however, looked like he had been curling weights since diapers.

He would undoubtedly have to shock the imposing bully into abandoning their brawl, convincing him it was no longer worth it.

Jamal aggressively came down from his porch, having

noticed Jack had stopped and was now glaring at him. Stopping in front of his prey, Jamal got in his face, locking eyes.

Jack's glare remained unaffected, seamlessly intimating his contempt. He noticed a flash of reluctance move across Jamal's face and realized the requisite anger for a fight was not coming.

*Damn it, man*, he thought. The glare left his face while he defiantly maintained eye contact. *All I can do now is ensure I don't flinch.*

On cue, Jamal moved with a start, pretending to hit him.

Jack was unresponsive, still as a statue.

Seeing that Jamal's efforts were apparently insufficient to even trigger a blink, the onlookers erupted with jeers and howls of mockery.

Jack groaned inwardly, instinctively knowing what would be coming as a result. *He's gonna hit me for real now.*

For a moment, Jamal's face showed a mix of surprise and embarrassment before he bit down on his bottom lip in outrage.

Eyes still fixed ahead, Jack watched the rapid windup of the incoming blow. *This is going to be the first time I feel a real punch from someone who knows what they're doing. Even if he decides not to pull his punches, maybe it won't hurt that much?*

*WHAM!*

Jack's vision became slightly distorted as he received a strike to the side of his head. Determined not to falter, he reflexively returned his head to its original position upon feeling Jamal's fist follow through across his face.

Though it felt like his eyes were rattling in his head, outwardly, it appeared as if he had never looked away despite the blow.

The swiftness of this recovery, combined with Jack's blank expression, was rather unsettling.

"What the?!" someone exclaimed. "Yo . . . he didn't even move."

Jack could see a brief wrinkle of concern form on Jamal's

forehead. As the initial shock wore off, he received the answer to his musings from a moment earlier.

The punch hurt.

A lot.

Normally, he would have felt some sense of satisfaction from Jamal's brief look of reluctance, but all of Jack's focus and attention was on ensuring he did not display any sign of the ensuing pain.

The tactless onlookers weren't helping either.

"Damn, Jamal, he just ate that."

"He mad skinny too."

Jack wanted to scream at them to keep quiet, but it did not help the situation. He still could not muster the emotion to fight back.

He felt afraid.

He was not afraid of Jamal in the truest sense, as Jack was fairly certain he would be able to permanently injure the brute if necessary. The element of surprise alone would give him an opening, and he would only need one.

Rather, his fear was linked to the potential consequences that came with his "going nuts," and though Jack was not entirely convinced that this was not cowardice, the concern effectively nullified his wrath.

He had no choice but to valiantly take the beating until something gave.

As Jack suspected, when subjected to the endless stream of smack talk from the crowd, Jamal's pride compelled him to strike again.

The muscle-bound menace weirdly kept his eyes on Jack as he punched him, intently watching for any reaction.

Somehow, Jack returned from this strike even quicker, his cold expression unchanged.

"This dude a robot."

Eyes now wide with indignation, Jamal grabbed Jack by his shirt and hit him again.

Though he was fairly certain this was not the most painful experience of his life, Jack had difficulty recalling what was.

Somehow maintaining eye contact, he could see Jamal's determination begin to crack and quickly understood that this had become a battle of wills. His assailant was determined to make him submit, unaware Jack had already come too far to falter.

He readied himself, knowing his continued defiance would only cause things to escalate.

Continuously whipping his head against the repeated strikes, they had become noticeably less painful, leading Jack to wonder why. *Maybe I've become brain damaged?* Deriving genuine amusement from this thought, he unwittingly smiled upon his attacker.

Jamal stopped and stared, open-mouthed and winded.

Jack found Jamal difficult to read and was uncertain if the guy even understood his *own* emotions. He watched Jamal prepare another strike, displaying a complete inability to conquer the compulsions of his learned behavior.

Jack began to laugh as the pain in this next blow was almost nonexistent.

Tears could be seen forming in Jamal's eyes as he stared at his grinning adversary. Whether the waterworks were due to rage, fear, or sadness, Jack could not tell. Additionally, since the beating drew no blood and bruises had yet to form, he appeared no worse for wear.

Their loudmouthed audience fell silent, astonished.

Jack stood upright and removed Jamal's hands from his shirt. "It's enough, man."

Everyone watched as he turned away and departed. It took

everything Jack had to maintain his stoic demeanor the rest of the way home.

Naturally, his beating became the talk of the town, and though the assault was undeniably one-sided, no one could say that Jack lost the fight.

This inevitably sullied Jamal's reputation and seemed to take a psychological toll on the once-feared menace. He had gone from being an ever-present fixture on his block to a near recluse. Most suspected this was due to his pride being damaged by Jack casually brushing off the beating.

Josiah, however, theorized that it was much deeper.

"Such is the trade-off that comes with being feared," he explained. "Especially to those who revel in it."

Jack shrugged his shoulders, wincing slightly at the pain radiating from his neck. "Seems pretty silly since he lost nothing."

"You sure about that?" Josiah asked. "By standing your ground against that beating, you inadvertently snatched that boy's heart right out of his chest. And since fighting was his self-proclaimed métier, you may have very well taken his manhood along with it."

Jack continued massaging his neck as he spoke. "Maybe you don't have an accurate picture of what happened, but I got my butt kicked, Dad."

"Son, I can figure that out just by looking at you. My point is that by appearing fearless while getting your butt kicked and ultimately laughing in that boy's face, you confirmed the very thing he sought to disprove. This would invariably cause his thoughts to run wild with doubts and second guesses, ultimately leading to a profound sense of fear."

"Profound fear, eh?" Jack said. "Stemming from what exactly? Some kind of maladaptive mechanism created by traumatic events he forgot about? Something like that?"

"No need to complicate things," Josiah replied. "The fear

is rooted in mere instinct, like the fight or flight response children learn about in grade school: If you put your all into making someone hurt and it does nothing, your next thought is going to be what that person is capable of come their turn."

The swelling and bruising from Jack's beating had become quite extensive though no one knew as he had not left his home for several days. Feeling pity for Jamal and his dwindling reputation, and knowing it was partially due to his injuries never being seen, Jack eventually took a stroll around the neighborhood to display his injuries for all to see. Though many seemed impressed and intimidated by Jamal's handiwork, his reputation never truly recovered. And due to the vicious nature of the injuries and the townsfolk suspecting it to be a sore spot for him, the event was rarely brought up in Jack's presence.

Jester, however, knew the truth:

Jack couldn't care less.

Jester glanced at the still-chuckling Jack before continuing defiantly. "Too Good don't care no way," he continued. "Y'all acting like it was a legit L or something. Nah, he *allowed* McMullen to beat on him."

Jack let out one more chuckle at Jester's final comment before maneuvering past him and continuing on. "It's not a big deal, guys," he said, "I'll just walk."

Various sentiments expressing goodbye and good luck bubbled through the group as he departed.

Still facing forward, he held his free arm high above his head, waving to those behind him. "I'll be back."

---

By the time he reached the terminal, Jack was thoroughly soaked with sweat.

While en route, he stopped at a local bakery to refresh himself. Determining he was just shy of halfway to the station, he decided to put some finishing touches on a few class assignments.

Having barely sat down, Jack noticed several of the staff members shooting him disapproving looks and, feeling embarrassed, he quickly ordered some beignets and a bottle of cold milk.

He enjoyed the establishment's air-conditioning far more than he did its pastries. They were dry and "lacked soul," as his father would say when characterizing the various fashions, foods, and entertainment offered by businesses attempting to replicate New Orleans culture.

Jack only managed to finish one, having to force the poor excuse for a dessert down his gullet with copious amounts of milk. He left the three remaining pastries in plain view as proof of purchase and brought out his books to begin finishing up his assignments. Having ensured his written answers contained as many big words as possible, Jack delayed putting the books away and sat impressed by the quality of his work.

He took a quick glance around the bakery and was struck by what he fancied a dignified sense of superiority after realizing he was the only patron not on a cell phone. Relishing this, he kept his books on the table and pretended to still be in the midst of diligent study.

All for show.

He maintained the facade for quite some time, his gaze alternating between his books and the window, and it was not until he overheard a customer mention New York that he remembered he had someplace to be.

Cursing his ostentation, he packed his belongings and headed out the door, hurriedly making his way to the station.

Encumbered by his luggage, Jack was forced into an awkward

run. Although he had just left the comfort of air-conditioning, his armpits began to sting with sweat as he made his way to the station, well over a mile away.

Arriving exhausted at the New York departure gate, Jack felt both annoyed and relieved. The disgruntled crowd informed him that their bus was delayed.

Jack accepted his fate with a smile and found a relatively unpopulated spot, save for several people immersed in conversation, and started to pat himself dry with a towel snatched from his suitcase.

Jack could not help but eavesdrop on the heated discussion behind him and realized they were locals who evidently had co-opted this portion of the station, turning it into some middle-aged hangout.

Their debate was ignited by the routine news intermission in the mood-setting jazz that flowed from the area's speakers. The content of the report was essentially identical to that of the newscast from earlier.

This was typical. The city's alleged crime rates seemed to have become the media's sole focus of attention for nearly five years. The apparent shift was something Josiah mentioned often and, while intently listening to the locals' conversation, Jack surmised the man would fit right in.

"They got no choice but to keep the trick goin'," one local replied.

"Who got no choice?" the other asked. "The people or the new—"

"Dammit, Lou," the first man said, suddenly irritated, "the news, of course! Can't fault them none . . ." He paused at the assorted scoffs and cackles given by some in response to his statement. "If we bein' honest."

One of the men continued cackling, apparently offending

his friend. Jack could not blame him as he, too, found his laughter exceedingly shrill and off-putting.

"I don't know what you laughin' at, Coach!" the local exclaimed. "This ain't no joke!"

Coach's laughter began to subside. "Of course, it's a joke, brother," he replied, grinning out his last bits of amusement. "Bottom line, you sayin' the news can't be faulted cuz they got no choice." His cackling began anew. "Only problem is, they lyin'! The fault is always gonna fall on they head before anyone else's. You sound crazy as hell, man."

The local did not respond, retaining his indignant posture.

Jack nodded in reluctant agreement. *Fair play to you, sir.*

Lou began speaking again, redirecting their conversation to its original focus. "Everyone knows it's all lies but—"

"No!" a woman interjected. "Everyone *don't* know. The news got most of the city bamboozled, no different than Solomon's congregation of the dead. They hurryin' to get bulletproof windows even though don't none of 'em know someone who been shot within the past decade damn near."

"You right, Gracie," Lou said, "but I meant everyone here." She nodded in acceptance, allowing him to continue. "All right now, so we know it's all lies, but what we was gettin' at, before Byron's crazy ass came defendin' them, is: What they lyin' for?"

"It's because there's too many Negroes here," a new member of their cohort stated confidently.

*Why am I not surprised?* Jack thought. Rolling his eyes, he could see the Greyhound pulling into its section. There were quite a few people waiting to board so he stayed put, shaking his head as the man continued.

"The white man always want the Black man to think less of himself—" The man paused and turned toward Lou. "No offense, Louie, I know you one of the good ones."

"None taken."

"Now I ain't sayin' that's impossible, Lyle," Coach began, "so don't be callin' me no Uncle Tom, but it gotta be more to it than that."

Lyle gave a short shrug in response. "No it don't."

"It does. Too many cogs workin' for good ol' bigotry to be the fuel keeping things goin'." Coach patted his friend on the shoulder. "We not that important, sorry to say."

"It ain't racism," another said, "Lyle blames that for everything. He don't got the gumption to see the big picture."

"And what's that?"

"That it's just business."

"What you mean by that, Reggie?" Gracie asked, her tone genuinely curious.

"It's just about money," he replied. "They lie to get paid and they get paid to lie because the bigwig companies profit from the lies."

Thanks to Josiah, Jack fancied himself an intellectual and, as such, thought himself much more informed than this group of middle-aged chatterboxes. He resented the casual manner with which they treated the overall premise, as if a lying media was a certainty to be taken for granted. The city *was* being ravaged by crime, just as the news claimed. The idea that it was all just a lie was offensive to him.

But he still could not help but feel intrigued by the discourse.

"How that work?" Lou asked. "How they manage to get greased off that?"

"Cuz the bigwigs don't gotta worry 'bout no competitors." Jack let out a hum of pleasant surprise, impressed. "Nobody with deep pockets fool enough to invest in a place that got unending crime. So, the news gonna go on and tell the lies that keep the competition at bay and the bigwigs of the city pay them kindly in return. It ain't hard to see."

A few of his listeners vocalized sounds of agreement and amusement.

Jack, however, found himself gnawing at his cuticles as he considered the man's argument.

*Could that be possible?* he thought, feeling humbled by the hypothesis.

"All right now, Reggie!" Gracie said. "Can't nobody call you ignorant."

The man nodded with a smile, graciously accepting the temporary praise.

Lou shook his head, albeit smiling just like the others.

"What you shakin' your head for?" Coach asked. "You thinkin' different?"

Lou pursed his lips as if hesitant. "Can't deny it's damn clever," he replied. "But it ain't enough."

"Go on, brother, make your case."

"Kinda like how Lyle's bigotry stance lacks the meat to feed all the gullets that got the beast movin' the way it does, it's the same with Reggie's competition angle. If deep-pocketed competitors really wanna set up shop, no way they gonna lack the means to discover the scam. They not stupid."

Jack let out an audible sigh. *Yes*, he thought with relief. *Yes, of course.*

The group fell silent, pausing to ponder Lou's statement.

"So what you thinkin'?"

"Wicked spirits," Lou replied, "it's the only explanation."

Jack sneered as he finally turned his head, directly looking at the group. He watched as they all, having given it careful consideration, collectively began to show signs of agreement and support for the idea.

He was disappointed that they did not share his contempt for it. Of all the theories posited, that one was the dumbest.

Jack finally left for the bus, having no interest in hearing Lou's reasoning. *I should've known*, he thought. *At the end of the day, no matter how smart they can be, this city always makes people default to stupid.*

Having lived in New Orleans his whole life, Jack was no stranger to voodoo and the superstitions that came with it. However, he found it far too primitive and backward for someone as intelligent as himself. His father, though never sharing his son's condescension toward their heritage, always showed patience and understanding whenever it came up.

Jack felt a strange sense of abandonment as he watched the locals passionately continue their discussion from his seat on the bus. Certain that people as ignorant as them could never be reached, he let out a sigh of pity.

*The world is so much bigger than the one they trap themselves in, and they will never know.*

---

The slamming of his suite door caused Jack to come to himself, startled by the sudden noise.

Warren turned on the light and saw Jack sitting upright on his bed.

"Oh crap!" he began. "Sorry, man, I didn't know you were here." He quickly shut the light back off. "You must be exhausted."

Not wanting Warren to sense anything amiss, Jack had already moved to wipe the tears from his face. He was prepared to deflect Warren's attention by finally bringing up his hallucinations from earlier but noticed that his face was dry, and the overwhelming sadness that had him pinned to the bed was now at least bearable.

*Finally, some relief.* The respite enabled him to don a somewhat normal disposition. "Actually, I feel pretty good, considering."

"HA-HA-HA!" The exuberance within Warren's guffaws was at a level wholly unwarranted.

*He's stoned . . .*

"That daymare you had in class had me thinking you were never gonna go to sleep again."

Unconcerned with his friend's teasing, Jack's eyes widened as he recalled the dream from the lecture hall. He felt the spark of an idea go off in his mind followed by the irresistible urge to see it through.

He tried to flex his sixth sense, on the lookout for any sensory feedback confirming that it was real.

*Is it still there?*

Eyes still wide, Jack pursed his lips together upon feeling the indescribable appendage dutifully responding to his psionic commands.

"You good, bro?" Warren asked, looking uncharacteristically concerned.

Jack pressed his lips tighter to hide the extent of his excitement before composing himself. "Yeah, I'm good, man."

Warren stared as Jack hopped down from his bed and began putting on his shoes. "How's the park looking?" he asked, tying the laces. "Was it packed?"

"N-nah," Warren replied warily, "not anymore, at least. Apparently, some birds were migrating or something, then just suddenly up and left." He noticed Jack staring at him, seemingly confused. "I don't know, man, it's weird. Anyway, yeah, everyone freaked out so the park is basically empty."

Jack headed out, the single-mindedness serving as a distraction from his grief. "Good."

"Why? You tryna smoke?"

"No, never again."

Warren opened the door and moved to the side, his confusion compounded by the weed in his system. "For what then?"

"Just testing something out," Jack replied, hastily exiting the suite. "I'll be right back."

# CHAPTER 5

The Lwa of the void, Bossu Koblamin, glared at the spunky mortal standing before him.

At first glance, Jack Boniface had seemed to be the most poorly suited of all the humans who have served as host throughout the millennia. The boy's disposition set him at odds with the supernatural world. His mind favored consensus and arbitrarily determined proofs, whereas the supernatural rewarded autonomy and discernment.

As if that was not enough, the stripling had seemed utterly destitute of any of the latent affinities that would offer hope. His only connection to the supernatural was Josiah.

Despite all this, the ageless entity, who had long forgotten the feeling of genuine surprise, could not ignore the implications held in the tiny frame staring up at him.

This same Jack Boniface, exuding a mix of sadness and confidence, had performed the unprecedented act of self-summoning. And while Jack was also the first human to be given the Lwa's proper name so quickly, that alone could not explain what the mortal had just accomplished.

Bossu had claimed that the reason he gave his name to Jack was due to some hidden potential within him, which was not entirely untrue. However, his primary goal was to establish dominance. Based on the boy's memories, this method could have been effective in guiding Jack through the customary rules of engagement. However, Bossu never imagined the rascal using it so resourcefully.

Normally, whenever a host uttered the Lwa's name, it gave them the opportunity to engage with Bossu, who would then take further action, whether it was related to combat, reconnaissance, or outright rescue.

While the majority of Jack's predecessors knew Bossu only as "Shadow" and were thereby restricted to a more laborious summoning process, the Lwa's *true* name opened up a direct line of communication.

Without any preparation or basis, Jack intuited that the line of communication was, in actuality, a psychic gate into the void dimension where Bossu resided. Acting on what could only have been instinct, Jack thought his appendage through the breach and began grasping for whatever could serve as a stable hold, quickly latching onto the immovable yet confounded Lwa.

Manipulating his appendage like some kind of retractable cord, the boy drew himself inside the void with a mighty pull.

There was no way a mortal could have achieved such a thing through mere chance. Bossu knew Jack could feel him scanning his mind in search of an explanation, but his expression remained a mix of smug and sorrowful.

There was nothing, not a hint nor word of knowledge nor even a hastily formed plan. Just a continuous series of reactions.

He did all that by chance?

It was not possible. Bossu must have missed something. "How did you do that?"

Jack's face perked up slightly like a small child unexpectedly receiving a gift. "Do what?"

"What do you mean?!" the Lwa barked. "You are here, are you not? What else would I be talking about?"

He felt Jack's appendage swat him off his memories.

"How I got here, you mean?" Jack maintained his look of innocent confusion as the Lwa glared at him in silence. "Well, I thought that's what I was supposed to do. You told me your name, so I called it. What else was I gonna do? My mental arm thing felt something open up . . . like a draft from an opened door or something, and I just started playing by ear after that."

Jack's expression livened some more as the Lwa remained silent.

"Impressed?" he asked teasingly. "Well, get over it! There is work to be done, and if you're already feeling defeated over a bruised ego, then we're in dire straits!"

The giant behemoth lurched slightly as it released a single exhale of amusement.

"Josiah . . ." he growled.

Jack could not tell if the Lwa was smiling or grimacing but decided on the former. "So," he said, beginning to pace in front of it, "what is this work to be done? It's obviously related to my dad."

"Very well," the Lwa replied. "Josiah was the Shadowman—"

"Shadow because of this void, eh?" Jack continued speaking before Bossu could respond. "That's the title of the enforcer you told me about last time? I figured working on behalf of the Lwa was the reason my dad wasn't around much."

"Obv—"

"But what I don't get is why that would change?" Jack interrupted again. "I'm assuming that this role was filled by my grandfather and his dad before him and so on. I find it difficult to believe something that existed for so long would suddenly become obsolete only to be needed again by you guys at the worst time possible. Something must have happened." Jack stopped pacing and looked at the Lwa. "What happened?"

"Very good, Jack," he breathed.

Despite his mouth being in an inexpressive state of permanent gnash, Jack could tell the Lwa was pleased. "Thanks, I guess."

"You are welcome."

Jack started feeling uncomfortable as the sincerity of the statement hung in the air.

"So," Bossu knowingly began, "I will address your statements in reverse order. First of all, we are not, as you say, *guys*."

Jack shot the behemoth a look of confusion. "What?" he said, pacing about the void again.

"The term you used regarding your father's services." Jack gave a slow nod of acknowledgment. "It would be wise to refrain from viewing me as part of the voodoo pantheon. I am not."

"Why not?"

"My answer will differ from their own. In addition, it is not pertinent at this time. Your attention is required elsewhere."

"Fine."

"Eight years ago, the Lwa Erzulie Freda and Baron Samedi were wed. This union affected the mortals of New Orleans by creating a period in which all death and bloodletting were ceased."

"Ceased?" Jack said with a scoff. "Yeah right."

"Specifically, those based in violence."

"Violent deaths and bloodshed came to an end?"

"It was temporary."

"Temporary or not, it would've been nice to live through that."

"You are . . . well, you did."

"Are you kidding?"

"I do not kid."

"Well, I just figured you were."

Bossu's tone changed as if primed for a punch line. "Why?" he asked. "The essence of violent death and bloodletting is crime . . . you are aware of this, right?" Jack was looking up at the Lwa with incredulity as he listened to its condescending speech. Examining its hideous facial features, he was certain he detected a smile somehow forming at the ridged corners of its skeleton mouth. "The statement that you experienced the cessation of crime is factual. What makes you doubt it?"

"What makes me doubt it?" Jack bellowed as he flailed his arms. "You're talking about crime, right? In New Orleans?"

"Correct." Bossu's reply was short and abrupt, keeping his tone from the imminent fever pitch.

Jack pointed toward the void at his back. "Have you been living under a rock, my guy? Crime is rampant! Just turn on the news—" Jack stopped dead.

"BAH HA-HA-HA!" At his host's sudden realization, Bossu unleashed his long-held laughter, manifesting as irreverent guffaws that roared throughout the once-silent void.

He attempted to compose himself, but upon seeing Jack still catatonic with astonishment, the monster tossed its head back and laughed all the more.

While he waited for the titan to tire of laughing at him, Jack's thoughts were on his recently revisited memory of the terminal. The locals had seemed so unsophisticated to him. It was just as the monster forewarned.

Indeed, Lou's ridiculous theory was the most accurate, despite what Jack's hubris led him to believe.

*So*, he thought, his mouth agape in the dark, *I was the*

*ignorant one? But that means my confidence was baseless . . . there was nothing legitimate about—*

Jack was unable to complete the thought, it was all too humiliating.

Sputtering out an anxious breath, he remembered how he was going to boldly interject himself into their conversation.

How pitiful would he have appeared to them?

Jack felt like he had been tricked into becoming what he had prided himself on being so different from. It seemed so unjust as he did everything to avoid it and yet, he could not deny the Truth.

Although he thought it impossible, he was ignorant.

*But . . . how could I have known?*

He thought about his father and their countless discussions. Jack winced at all the times he had confidently spewed forth nonsense, but Josiah never made him feel stupid despite knowing the Truth.

Before allowing any feelings of resentment toward his father's seeming refusal to set him straight, Jack sensed a self-effacing Truth floating just above the multitude of rationalizations vying for his attention.

Unlike the other explanations, this silent revelation seemed unwilling to assert itself, as if it did not care to be noticed.

*You wouldn't believe him anyway.*

As Jack examined the thought, he sensed the throng of rationalizations fall away into the implausible.

*It's true*, he said to himself. *There was no way he could have convinced me and probably would've wound up being viewed with the same derision I had for the geezers at the terminal . . . damn.*

This humbling revelation immediately turned his lurking resentment into something else. He was moved with regret as his thoughts shifted down a new path.

His father was unwilling to subject their relationship to any further strain and knew any attempt to dispel Jack's illusions outright would only widen the distance between them.

That was the reason behind the restraint with which he spoke to him.

With new eyes, his father's patience seemed limitless in retrospect.

Jack thought back to all the times he spoke so matter-of-factly about their "superstitious" culture, and his father would always respond with calm and calculated understanding.

As if handling something fragile.

Cracking a smile, Jack recalled the short discussion that took place in his room before he left for NYU. Josiah knew the Truth, and yet, he sought only to place Jack on the path that led to it.

Though Jack was currently filled with a newfound sense of shame, it was offset by an equally new reverence for his father.

Jack looked up at the still-laughing Lwa and took a deep breath before pretending to look at a nonexistent wristwatch. While he definitely was not offended, he still didn't think his humiliation was *this* funny.

As he continued watching the Lwa, Jack began considering what it must have been like from the Lwa's perspective.

Jack had already cut his mind off from any further telepathic probing, rendering his subsequent thoughts private.

This forced, or perhaps permitted, Bossu to watch the unfolding of his young host's humiliating epiphany like a normal person would. He did not know what was going through Jack's head and was left to go by the look on his face.

And to the Lwa's delight, the highly anticipated expression did not disappoint.

Thinking back to how he felt at that moment, Jack could

not help but snort out a laugh or two. *I guess it* was *pretty funny, but damn . . . look at him go.*

Bossu's eyes were shut, totally oblivious to Jack, who had long since recovered his dignity.

Jack shuddered as he imagined the kind of existential crises he'd be left to suffer through if not for his father's provision. Though he had not realized it at the time, he had made a brush with this terrifying state when rationalizing his hallucination at Carmen's as a contact high.

Shaking his head, Jack tutted three times as he remembered Bossu's rebuke. *Sacrificing the intellect on pride's altar. If it's done even once, then follows a dumb commitment to nonstop concessions.* He began biting his nails as he pondered further. *And the delusion becomes more difficult to renounce after every new concession.*

Jack was convinced that if Bossu had not made contact that second time, he would have believed his experiences that day were merely the result of Warren's presence, regardless of how implausible.

No doubt, his intellect had been fated to make another sacrifice when stumbling on the Truth about New Orleans, since there was no way he would have been able to accept it.

Spitting out the bits of his nails, Jack began to fully appreciate the gravity of what he had been spared from. Calling it an existential crisis was not hyperbole.

*Because of Dad, I was able to accept the Truth.*

Recalling Josiah's admission of failure, Jack felt the corners of his mouth drop as the words his father told him to remember suddenly echoed through his mind.

*Giving up my life to ensure you become more than I can ever hope to be, that is my greatest accomplishment.*

As gratitude and sorrow threatened to burst forth, Jack steadied himself against the ensuing torrent of emotion, unwilling to let Bossu see him cry. He relieved the pressure through short bits of controlled whimpering, wearing a look of sadness more expressive than any clown's.

He heard the Lwa let out a deep and heavy sigh as its mirth finally relented.

Jack remembered the monster's passing comment about his father; it was too accurate a eulogy not to be seconded.

Who better to do it than his own son?

"Well played, Dad," he said aloud, laughing a bit as he wiped away the tears.

Bossu, having fully recovered, finally looked down.

"You're making gains, whelp," he breathed. "That's two paradigms that have been destroyed. Perhaps you are fit to live in reality after all."

The Lwa was obviously misinterpreting Jack's tears.

Jack smiled, causing him to abandon his teasing. "Why are you looking at me like that?" Bossu asked.

Still smiling, Jack didn't move a muscle as he stealthily reached out with his appendage and grasped the Lwa, reestablishing their telepathic link.

Sensing the hold, the bemused Lwa continued to stare. "What are you doing?"

Unsure how to direct his memories forward, Jack left it alone, but the smile on his face remained.

"Has your mind been torn asunder?" Bossu asked, seemingly concerned. "Or is this some desperate prank to save face?"

Jack sensed him beginning to probe his psyche. "Far from it."

Bossu continued his psychic rifling. "Oh?"

"Yeah."

"Interesting."

Initially, Jack had been trying to observe as Bossu perused through the thoughts he missed during his bout of laughter, but the Lwa was too fast for Jack. Seeing as the entity had not been trying to evade him and it was just his natural pace, Jack decided to relax his focus and merely wait for the probing to be complete.

"Hmm," Bossu began, as like the closing of a book, the probing stopped. "Hm hm . . . well played, Josiah." He hummed through an exhale. "Well played, indeed."

Jack released the psychic hold and, like a statue coming to life, clapped his hands together. "Indeed!" he said. "So . . . that's why it stopped. I get that, but what made it start up again?"

Bossu stared, confused.

"The crime!" Jack hastily clarified. "Your statement about my living through its nonexistence was past tense, so it's back up again?" Seeing Bossu beginning to reply, Jack quickly moved to finish his statement. "Also, that period coincides with my dad becoming full-time, which makes sense, I guess. That makes me the next Shadowman, right? You kept implying that time is of the essence, so how do we get started?"

Speechless, Bossu continued to stare at the revitalized youngster.

Over the millennia, the entity had become certain that he was no longer capable of feeling surprised, but in a span of only a few minutes, this boy had managed to make him feel that very way several times already.

What more was needed?

"Erzulie Freda has gone missing," he replied. "That is why death and blood are soon to return."

"Okay . . ." Jack said, continuing his pacing from before. "So because his woman is missing, Samedi is retaliating?"

"Not exactly, but you are free to see it that way for simplicity's sake."

"And Lwas can go missing? In a kidnapped kind of way?"

"Apparently."

Silently walking to and fro, Jack looked up at Bossu. "You're here telling me Dad died, time is short and all that, right?"

"I am."

"How long after Freda disappeared did my dad die?"

For a moment, the Lwa appeared taken aback by the question. "Josiah died before the disappearance."

Maintaining his stride, Jack immediately snapped his fingers in displeasure. "Damn," he spat. "I was hoping you wouldn't say that."

"And why is that, whelp?"

"Because it means his death was orchestrated and all this was planned in advance, even my being left to fill his shoes."

Bossu nodded approvingly. "Impressive," he replied, "but your underlying assumption is mistaken."

"How?"

"Josiah's death was orchestrated by none other than himself. Your two subsequent deductions are correct, though."

Jack stood still to properly bite his nails. "My dad killed himself?"

"Not exactly, but you are free to see it that way for simplicity's sake."

Bossu looked on as Jack stood in front of him, casually spitting the flecks out of his mouth. "But why?" he asked. "Why would my dad leave me holding the bag?"

"Because he knew what was coming and determined it was beyond his capability. He was correct in this assessment."

*PTTTTOOEYY!* Jack jettisoned forth a piece of fingernail as if trying to land a headshot on the titan.

The Lwa said nothing, the impetuous act apparently escaping his notice.

Jack wiped his mouth. "So if it's too much for him, why leave it to me?"

"You know the answer to that already," the Lwa replied. "Josiah told you why. I saw it. Was that not the reason you started crying like a child, his greatest accomplishment? While it is true he determined himself incapable of standing against the forces about to be unleashed upon the mortal world, he also determined that you would be. He was correct in this assessment as well."

Jack was beaming from the reminder of his father's words. "Why?"

The Lwa hummed with a low growl. "As our being wrong is still a very real possibility, I am wary lest I do you hurt through compliments too high for your immaturity." Jack gave a short eye roll as he folded his arms with a sigh. "You see? Therefore, I will limit my answer to this: Look at yourself."

"Please," Jack began, sounding exasperated, "no transcendental stuff, just keep it sim—"

"LOOK UPON YOURSELF, YOU INSUFFERABLE CREATURE!" Bossu's enraged command echoed throughout the void.

"Fine," Jack said in calm compliance, "I'm looking at myself." He motioned with his hands and arms in an exaggerated manner, though they remained unseeable in the darkness, he directed his gaze as if astonished. "These are . . . hands, these are . . . sleeves."

He stopped his sarcasm as he remembered how he sensed the void in the past. He had no physical form. Back then, Jack felt like he was watching and experiencing things from another person's perspective, someone who just happened to follow his every thought, like a first-person video game. Now, however, he felt like himself.

"This . . . this is my physical body?"

"Your intellect is astounding, Jack," Bossu replied. "Biting your nails and prancing about since arriving and it is only now you realize this."

"Yeah, thanks."

The Lwa continued. "I trust you recall my inquiry regarding your method of appearing in the void? It was because you are the first who has ever gained entry in such a way." Jack seemed to be lost in deep contemplation as Bossu spoke. "That's why I agree with your father."

"That's why, huh?" Jack asked, patting his body. "I guess I can accept that."

"I am relieved."

"It's a bit much, though. This being my real body and all."

"How so?"

"Well, what's going on in the real world? Am I asleep or something?"

"This is your real body," Bossu explained. "You pulled your body into this realm on your own."

"So I just vanished? What if people were around when it happened?"

"If they saw it they would either be forever changed or they would convince themselves they saw nothing."

The Lwa observed Jack's bewildered gaze as he continued to tap his body before suddenly bringing his hands to his sides and smiling mischievously into the void.

"What must I do to become Shadowman?" he asked. "Like officially?"

"As I said, you have performed a feat no—"

Jack gasped excitedly. "So no formal training?"

"In what?"

"How to be Shadowman! I will have greater abilities, like . . . super abilities, right?" The Lwa stayed silent. "Right?!"

"One does not need training to understand how to utilize newly increased strength—"

"That's it?!"

"BE QUIET!!" Bossu roared.

He grumbled and growled as he let the relative silence linger before speaking again.

"Even if there is more to be attained, it is preferable that you learn and discover through doing and understanding. Josiah could have told you how to ride your bicycle, but it would profit nothing. Your being would have no way of anticipating what it would feel like until you actually did it. Indeed, the incongruity between how you *thought* it would feel and how it *truly* feels could lengthen the time you would have otherwise taken had you just learned by doing."

Jack's countenance grew duller and more disappointed as the explanation reached its end.

"Listen," the Lwa began, "I am not making you a veritable god on your first day. A stripling like you will only get yourself killed. If you have something specific in mind, then out with it. I will not open the book for you."

"Fine," Jack began. "That's fair, I guess, no point unlocking the full spectrum for someone who has no imagination."

"Precisely."

"Okay, then what about those creepy crows from last night?"

Bossu hesitated in surprise. "You . . . you are asking about something like that?" he asked. "How interesting."

Hearing this, Jack could see the unforgettable purple lights begin to shine throughout the void, twinkling like stars in the sky. Without warning, the purple-eyed crows flapped into being, bursting forth from the dark. The birds' color was perfectly identical to that of the void, only becoming distinguishable upon swarming their Lwa progenitor.

"These are simple little things," he continued. "Minute extensions of myself and, by proxy, you as well. Care to try?"

"Yeah."

Upon Jack's determined reply, the sound of the flapping suddenly ceased and was followed by one akin to scattering sand. Jack could see the swarm crash to the floor in front of Bossu, exploding into vapor.

"Yeah?" Bossu immediately repeated, tickled by his host's confident tone.

"Mhmmm."

"How exactly do you plan on performing such a summons? Granted, crows are on the lower scale of difficulty, but you are inexperienced."

Brandishing his appendage, Jack visualized the crow. Blocking out Bossu's distracting commentary, he slowly brought the mental image to the forefront of his thoughts.

He gingerly felt about the image, rendering it tangible as if it was delicate. And then, like pulling out a strand of hair, he manifested one solitary crow into the void.

Motivated by the Lwa's stunned silence, Jack hungrily thrust the appendage into the area where the crow had been extracted. Like a thief hastily gathering loot, the appendage began sweeping out countless crows from within.

Looking up at the gnashing Bossu while wearing a grin almost as toothy, Jack continued to summon more, ensuring they surpassed the Lwa's in number.

With one last sweeping motion, he drew out the remaining crows. The resulting cacophony of flapping wings was so boisterous that Bossu, though far from angry, was forced to raise his voice.

"You know, Jack," he said as the murder of crows continued swirling around them, "showing off does not suit you."

# CHAPTER 6

The Ghede had assembled within the throne room of the mansion.

Nearly all the members of their branch stood before the baron and his primary wife, Gran Brigitte, as they sat on their respective thrones.

Without the presence of any non-Ghede Lwa to serve as a repellent, the various demons and monsters of the realm began meandering their way to the Manse Ghede, attracted to the assembly of their various overlords all in one place. The ones bold enough to draw close would periodically peek through the windows, doing their best to stifle the snarls and growls that were the inescapable byproduct of their eternal resentment and regret.

The Lwa ignored their nosy thralls. Seeing as the baron was both intrigued and concerned by the information given to him, they were far too occupied with the matter at hand to pay them any notice.

Josiah Boniface, the Shadowman, was dead.

Nibo was the first to break the silence following the

revelation. "Maybe it is just a coincidence?" he sang with an infantile shrug.

Some within the immortal congregation responded with various sounds of irritation while others remained silent as if they did not hear.

"Don't annoy your father with such foolishness," Brigitte commanded.

The woman glared at Nibo over the pince-nez glasses resting on the bridge of her nose. The Ghede queen's red hair began to bloom as if given rise by a gentle current of air, signifying her growing anger.

Nibo quickly bowed his head for pardon, but the queen's rage only intensified. Her porcelain-toned flesh began to fade, slowly shifting to a skeletal visage similar to her husband's but fierce in appearance.

The baron, sensing his wife's wrath brewing, placed his hand atop her own. "Pay him no mind, my dear," he said. "He is wont to speak without thinking." He looked upon Nibo. "Bossu is maintaining his cloak of shadow, rendering him impossible to detect. This means that he is already aware that treachery is at work. No need for him to disappear otherwise."

The baron could feel Brigitte's fury restrained just beneath her skin, feeling its rhythmic electrical pulse through her black lace gloves.

This level of anger was not caused by Nibo's tomfoolery. He just happened to step in its way.

Like her husband, Brigitte initially thought the concern surrounding Freda was a mere storm in a teacup. But since learning the Lwa was taken against her will and that Damballa would essentially be holding the Ghede responsible, she was consumed with rage. The malice currently emanating from her being was reserved solely for the unknown enemy conspiring against them.

Unaware of this, Nibo's assistant, Masaka, moved for damage control, kneeling as he spoke. "And how certain are we of an heir?" he asked, adjusting his headscarf before standing back up. "Perhaps Bossu will cease to exist without one. Who knows the ramifications of an exile such as his?"

Masaka's twin, Ossou, clumsily moved toward him. His exuberant gait sent his rum bottle crashing into the shovel his brother held at his side. Masaka stared at him, rendered speechless.

"There is definitely an heir," Ossou explained, "'cause Bossu still lives. The barrier placed over the home of the woman remains intact"—the polite drunkard covered his mouth with his arm to stifle a hiccup—"which means Bossu still lives, which means there is definitely an heir."

"Your brother, Tipsy," the baron said to Masaka, "though obviously inebriated, is correct. Bossu certainly knows the details behind his host's sudden death and is hidden for both his sake and that of the heir."

Scanning across the multitude, Papa took the opportunity to speak. "Master Saturday," he began, "I implore you allow me a visit to the dead man's wife. It will be but for a moment, and she need not know my identity. I will approach her as a humble pauper and, within that moment, read her mind and gain the location of the heir."

"No!" Brigitte snapped. "Josiah may have placed some sort of charm that will expose you, and then what? It will only lead to escalation, with the resulting fracas alerting our enemy."

"Shadowman has that capability?" Papa asked, directing the question toward the multitude.

"If Bossu decides to give him such knowledge," the baron replied, "there is no reason to think it not feasible. Even regular mortals are capable of it."

The Lwa currently known as Criminel began his address

impatiently. "You all are making it too complicated," he announced. "I will pay the widowed damsel a visit and retrieve the heir's whereabouts the old-fashioned way, charms and incantations are for f—"

Papa cut off his belligerent confrere. "Keep silent!" he hissed.

In defiant response, Criminel heaved his sack o' souls over his shoulder, intentionally displaying his belt of severed heads.

"Dear Criminel has been a rebel since the beginning," the baron said.

Affronted by his subordinate's behavior, his voice was seething in frigid contrast to his relaxed posture. "That is the reason behind his plenteous sobriquets, they allow him to forget his monumental *failure*. He is a goat and, as such, only responds to humiliation. How best to humiliate one who is running from their past? The simple answer is to mercilessly bring it to mind until they are retamed."

Still sitting with his legs crossed, the skeleton lord began wiggling his free ankle as if to provoke. His glowing green irises became visible inside his otherwise vacuous eye sockets. The direction of the two dots of spectral fire removed any confusion as to the intended target of his address.

"Is that not right, *Qayin*?"

Hearing his true name, Criminel's demeanor immediately became distressed. He quickly averted his gaze from the baron's eyes, their glow expressing his displeasure.

Nibo winced and flexed his neck slightly, briefly expressing his pity before taking a pull of his cigar.

Suddenly sober, Ossou stood upright and steady as he spoke. "So what are we to do, my lord?" he asked. "How are we to find the heir?"

"Considering we are no longer bound by my oath, it is once again lawful for our subjects to cross over."

Nibo began tee-heeing excitedly, sputtering out his cigar smoke. "We gonna smoke him out?"

"Precisely." Upon giving his reply, the baron immediately directed his attention toward another. "Babaco!"

An Lwa of a similar appearance to Papa immediately moved forward in response, adjusting his sunglasses as he approached. His confident walk was accentuated by the manner with which he wielded his cane, a subtle lean within every other step. "Yes, my lord."

"I need you to aid your brother," the baron replied, "he will need your assistance to manage the excess souls that are sure to result from our activities."

Hearing this, Papa raised his hat at Babaco as they approached one another. After a celebratory low five, they continued holding hands, jostling their grip in excitement.

"We're back on," Babaco said.

"Seems that way." Still shaking his brother's hand, Papa looked toward the throne. "And what of Bruv? I wager we will need a counter against any meddlesome mortals attempting to cross over."

"It will not yet be necessary," the baron replied. "We must first get things in order for the worshipful mortals to begin acknowledging our actions. Aside from the twins, we have essentially been absent from the Liveside, with little to no influence therein. As such, it is only fair that we regard custom and signify our return through a herald."

Gran Brigitte's frigid countenance finally thawed, making way for a slight anticipatory smile. "So she finally gets to play?" she muttered. "Poor thing. How long has it been?"

"Too long." Having answered his wife, the baron abruptly called for the Lwa in question. "L'Orage!"

The room immediately crackled with the sound of thunder

as a giant column of cloud, unnatural in form, began to manifest toward the rear of the assembly. Within the column were flashes of lightning, its gusts scattering raindrops throughout.

As the wind continued, it appeared to whip the giant cloud into shape, creating a gargantuan silhouette that was unmistakably female. There was one last crack of thunder that seemed to snap the silhouette into flesh, creating a titan in the midst of the multitude.

The towering woman hovered above the floor. The individual ropelike strands of her hair swayed rhythmically, the nature of their floating resembling water more than air.

An otherworldly tunic, sleeveless and extending past her knees, draped about her. It appeared to be composed of the very same tempestuous column from which she was molded. The cloud fabric of her tunic had a movement of its own, causing the shapeless puffs of gray upon the tunic's exterior to float contrary to her every movement.

Billowing just above her black locs was a large scarf, both ends covering her shoulders before wrapping itself about her forearm and wrists. While nearly identical in color to the tunic's fluctuating grayscale, veins of lightning could be seen coursing through it as she addressed the baron. "Is it time, my lord?"

Despite her appearance, the meek and mild manner with which she spoke made her voice seem lower than that of her human-sized cohorts.

"It is, indeed, little gir—"

L'Orage suddenly jerked her elbows and knees inward. "Finally!" she exclaimed. For a moment, her voice became distorted in both loudness and pitch, resulting in a sound that fit her stature.

The baron spoke over the residual thundering of her enthusiasm. "The Liveside must be informed of our imminent return." The titan was barely able to contain herself, nodding fervently as he continued. "To that end, your actions are to be a communication of that fact, they are not to express wrath."

"He means to say be reasonable with the resulting deaths," Brigitte explained.

"Certainly!" The unsettling distortion within L'Orage's voice was gone but the unbridled enthusiasm remained. "Consider it done!"

Her excitement seemed infectious, and the mood of the room began to liven. The Lwa began talking among themselves in anticipation of their return to the Liveside.

The shortest individual within the multitude gestured toward the baron, getting his attention.

"Ah, yes," the baron sighed. "Brother Linto, how forgetful of me."

The diminutive Lwa tipped his fedora in response. It was an uncanny shade of brown and was an exact match to the color of his skin, making it impossible to distinguish where the surface of Linto's forehead ended and the fedora began.

"I am not insinuating that dear L'Orage will be incapable of exercising restraint," he began, shooting the giant a wink, "but shall I go as a precaution against excess?"

"Go," the baron granted with a raised arm. "Feel free to warn as many as will listen. But this isn't the 1800s, you know."

"My lord?"

"I'm saying times have changed. The mortals have various gizmos and gadgets they use to stay distracted. Don't be surprised if they pay you little regard." The baron returned his attention to the congregation. "Now, my Ghede, we find the Shadowman!"

# CHAPTER 7

Jack found himself on a bus headed home for what he suspected to be the last time. Considering recent events, his journalism aspirations had become utterly pointless.

In addition, while Bossu had assured him of his mother's safety, Jack was still unable to contact her, prompting a hasty midnight departure for New Orleans.

Jack's bus had reached Virginia early the next morning and he spent most of the three-hour wait time pestering Bossu about whatever his eager mind saw fit. He was strikingly animated during these conversations with his Lwa, forcing him to wear earbuds and pretend to be on the phone while waiting for the connecting bus.

During the trip to Atlanta, Jack spent time introducing himself to voodoo lore by reading up on the various members of the pantheon.

Periodically inspecting his psyche for any signs of prying, Jack struggled to hide his disappointment when realizing that entries detailing his Lwa, Bossu Koblamin, were remarkably scarce. On the few sites that did manage to acknowledge him, the information provided was only a few sentences.

*I don't get it,* Jack thought. *If the all-knowing internet can't get him right then what hope is there? There's no mention of darkness, shadows, night, or any of that stuff. Which is weird because that's his shtick for sure.*

While reading, Jack noticed that he did not feel tired despite having been up since noon the day before. He had been given a brief summary of abilities by Bossu back at the terminal in Virginia, but was unsure if something like insomnia was mentioned.

Jack would have double-checked with the Lwa, but there were only two ways of doing so and neither seemed appropriate at the moment.

Vanishing into the void while on a bus full of people seemed too extreme, but, on the other hand, mentally conversing with the Lwa was not easy, at least if it was to be done in a way where he felt comfortable.

Jack had come to understand that this psychic connection, by default, allowed Bossu access to his thoughts. Although he was confident the Lwa could not intrude undetected, Jack found it difficult to monitor for nosy intrusions while also paying sufficient attention to their conversation and, all the while, interacting naturally with the real world.

Offering to train him in what Jack referred to as mental ambidexterity, Bossu teased that it was no more difficult than walking and chewing gum. Jack resented that it was the only ability that gave him any significant trouble and vowed to master it on his own.

The only other explanation for his wakefulness was the boundless sense of revitalization that seemed to emanate from the very core of his being, recently acquired through the memories of his father. This was what enabled him to stand when faced with the Truth.

Further examination of his memories revealed that this inexplicable pillar of support was a result of Josiah's master plan, an inherited blessing that empowered his son to succeed where he had failed.

No longer cringing, Jack recalled the moment in great detail while beaming out the bus window. He could still see the hint of suppressed amusement twinkling in his father's eyes.

"Can I ask you something, son?" his father had asked.

"Shoot," the young Jack responded.

"How are you so sure that you're being objective when judging your stance as superior?"

"C'mon, Dad," Jack began, rolling his eyes, "you're saying that a culture focused on pursuing knowledge would be just as backward as one obsessed with superstition?"

Josiah's expression was unchanged as he shook his head. "No, I'm asking what makes you think that the city's condition would improve if its population collectively decided to get 'educated'?"

"Doesn't reality prove my argument?"

"Does it?"

"Well, I'm pretty sure it's a statistical fact that the more educated a community, the higher their standard of living."

"That's not what I asked."

Jack threw his hands in the air. "It's basically the same thing!" he screeched. "Statistics prove that if the city lets go of all the superstitious voodoo crap and focuses on educating the people, poverty will decrease. When poverty decreases, so does crime. It's just a fact!"

"I understand all that, son," Josiah replied, calmly resting his elbows on the kitchen table. "But what if you're wrong? Think of my question as a hypothetical exercise. Literally, what would you do if you were wrong?"

Jack took a deep breath as he considered the question. "Fine, if I somehow wind up being wrong then . . . I guess I'll be confused."

"That's it?"

"And angry, real angry."

Josiah was nodding as a subtle smile formed on his face. "I think you're right about that, Jack," he said. "I'm proud you can predict how you would *feel*, but those are emotions. I'm asking what would you *do*—would you give in to those emotions?"

"No!" Jack replied quickly. "I would have more self-control than that." He paused while gazing at the table. "Most likely, I'd get over it and work my way to finding out why I was wrong. From there I'd just accept whatever the truth actually is."

Josiah suddenly clapped his hands together. "That's more like it, son!" Jack jumped with a start. "That's the key to your success!"

"This-this is just hypothetical, Dad."

Josiah nodded enthusiastically. "Sure, son, sure. The point is, that key will serve you no matter the situation, hypothetical or not. Wish I had it when I was your age. Things would be a lot different, no doubt about that."

Jack turned away from the window and began clenching his fists, still grinning. *Thank you for gifting me this, Dad.*

This gift of assuredness, once acquired, continued unabated, radiating outward to his extremities before returning in a self-sustaining ebb and flow. The excitement he felt while coming to grips with this new state of being had to be what replaced his need for sleep, like a child on Christmas Eve.

Jack was snatched from his thoughts by the sudden frenzy taking place in the aisle of the bus. From the corner of his eye, he could see passengers stampeding their way past him to reach the front.

He stood up and looked toward the rear of the bus to see the cause of the commotion. Three men were hovering menacingly over another, who remained pinned to his seat as they shouted threats.

Jack noticed one person had not fled despite being only two seats away from the ruckus. Casually running her fingers behind her ear to secure several of her braids, the young woman seemed oblivious to the potential fight. She remained relatively expressionless as she briefly locked eyes with Jack as he walked past.

Everyone else, however, was huddled together on the opposite end. They watched in bewilderment as Jack confidently approached the scuffle that was moments from becoming an assault. The mayhem had forced the driver to detour to the nearest exit in order to bring the bus to a stop.

Considering what to say, Jack examined the demeanor of the three aggressors. One of them knelt on the seat in front of the victim while the other two remained standing in the aisle. Their target's eyes were fixed on the back of the seat, seemingly unresponsive. He only broke his gaze to glance at Jack as he got closer.

"I said move over!" one of the men said.

Jack placed a hand on the shoulder of the closest malefactor. "Hey, what happened?"

His voice was calm and concerned, not aggressive.

The man peered at him from over his shoulder. His angrily furrowed brow slightly gave way to confusion as he sized Jack up. The other two didn't even pause their antics, but their victim was quick to speak.

"They're just mad because I won't move over to the window seat."

Curious as to who was being spoken to, the two men looked at Jack. "Is that true?" he asked, scanning their faces.

Incensed, the one Jack had been speaking to turned around, looking down upon him as if to intimidate. "And who are you?" he replied. "The hall monitor or something? Get the hell outta here."

After saying this, he tried to shove him away, but as Jack didn't budge, the force of the push rebounded, sending the man's weight backward into his friend.

Confused by the collision, the malefactors looked among themselves before setting their sights on Jack, who was both smaller and much younger than they were.

"Yeah," Jack said with a smile, "that's me. I didn't know they had hall monitors on buses, but it's okay, I'm whatever you need me to be."

As the three men continued to stare, several feminine titters bubbled from the front of the bus. Jack noticed the resolve touch down on their faces as the newly embarrassed men redirected their aggression toward him. He watched the one who had been kneeling on the seat step down and prepare for their coordinated attack.

"So you a hero, huh?"

Jack's smile remained as the three men tried to converge on him as much as the narrow aisle would allow. "No," he replied. "I'm not a hero yet, I just need you three to get off when the driver pulls over. I gotta get home and you guys are about to delay everything over a seat."

The sound of the young women's laughter emanated from the front again.

Immediately, one of the men threw a punch. Unfortunately for him, this only led to the collapse of his tough-guy persona.

Staring at his assailant with an open mouth, Jack was surprised by how thoroughly painless his attack was.

*That hit felt like a cotton ball*, he thought. *A wet one at most.*

The man mirrored his stunned expression. Apparently

misinterpreting Jack's as one of anger, he promptly apologized. "Sorry, little bruh."

Jack remained in awe for a moment. "Don't worry about it," he said, laughing off the slight. "Just chill out, you could really hurt someone with that punch."

"Move out the way, pussy!"

Undeterred, the second aggressor strong-armed his fellow to the side and quickly sent a jab toward the center of Jack's face.

"Holy crap!" someone exclaimed.

Jack had slightly nodded his head into the punch, bringing the fist into a collision course with his forehead. Several passengers winced and hissed at the resulting crack while the man immediately clutched his hand, mumbling profanities. The apologetic one watched as his companion, newly injured, moved past Jack in an attempt to walk off the pain.

"Just get off the bus, guys."

Hearing this, the first attacker took his eyes off his fellow and onto Jack again. Strangely devoid of the former repentance, he made the confounding decision to attack again.

With his head turned from this new blow, Jack was now facing the final malefactor, who remained standing in front of the seat he had been kneeling on. The original ruffian watched in dismay as Jack began to address his friend, totally unaffected by the strike.

"Do you want to be the first to get off?" Orienting himself within the aisle to give the man space to depart, Jack locked eyes with the one who hit him twice. "I don't want any problems, I need to get home. I just found out my dad died and my mom needs me."

With this, the rest of the passengers began reprimanding and insulting the goons, commanding that they get off the bus. The static of the intercom crackled as the driver prepared to speak.

"All of this is under surveillance," she announced. "I've

recorded you knuckleheads assaulting that boy and already notified the police. Stay on the bus or get out, it don't matter none." She began addressing Jack. "You okay, sweetie?"

Jack turned to see the driver looking at him in her mirror. "Yes, miss," he replied, waving. "All is well."

The driver glanced at the men. "Don't go thinking just 'cause you big for nothings didn't hurt him that it ain't assault."

The one in front of the seat quickly raised his arms as if already under arrest. "I didn't assault nobody!"

"Get off!" the passengers commanded in unison.

Jack moved to the side as the injured malefactor rushed through, still hissing profanities as he shoved past his surrendering comrade.

The other finally broke eye contact with Jack and hastily advanced toward the exit. "I don't got time for this crap," he said. "All over a dumbass seat . . ."

Jack trailed behind the three men as they fled, only to sit down as he came to his seat. He shot a thumbs-up to the relieved passengers as they gave him a quick round of applause while returning to their places. The young man put the earbuds back into his ears and remained peering out the window for the remainder of the trip.

---

It was nighttime in Atlanta, and by then, many of the admiring passengers had noticed Jack never slept. They jokingly exhorted him to get some rest as he stood in the dark parking lot.

Fortunately for Bossu, Jack did not bother him like he did in Virginia.

Instead, he opted to measure his so-called "gains," testing his powers within the shadow of night.

His newly acquired night vision turned the black sky into an illuminating gray.

Not white but brighter than overcast, the hue rendered everything visible and in its true color. The ability was certainly useful, but it was mainly passive, not really needing to be trained.

His shadow manipulation, however, was an entirely different story.

Jack had been engrossed in his growing dexterity with the sixth sense he referred to as his appendage, resulting in any conversation with the Lwa being kept to a minimum.

Pretending to take no notice, Bossu watched as Jack weaved it unseen. He had been attempting to distinguish the passengers in the various vehicles or aircraft that came within range of his ability.

The slightly amused Lwa observed Jack fail repeatedly, and by a large margin. He personally considered it a baffling exercise, too impractical an application toward an objective that was worthless.

Despite there being no evidence of improvement in the face of his constant failure, Jack's enthusiasm remained unaffected.

The Lwa simply could not help but feel vexed at this.

"The way you harness my powers is completely different from your predecessors," he began, seeking a quarrel. "Manipulation of the shadow is purely sensory, but you are unwilling to treat it as such."

Unresponsive, with his hands in his pockets, Jack appeared lost in thought as he continued his invisible antics across the landscape. The ancient entity remembered the pestering he had been subjected to the day before and, seeing as Jack was currently focused on the unproductive, thought it fitting to do the same to him.

"You seem to be under the misperception that it is some

physical extension of you. Why not test that belief before accepting it so blindly? Are you at least envisioning anything when you engage?"

Jack considered the inquiry as he blinked away his night vision and observed the dark as normal. *I guess it's a legitimate question,* he said to himself, *but I can't see what it looks like.* He performed a quick scan through his mind to ensure Bossu was not intruding. *I don't know if this guy is playing dumb or if he really doesn't know all that much about the powers he gives, but it's definitely a physical extension.*

Jack thought back to when he physically pulled himself into the void. The Lwa had not been pretending, he was genuinely surprised. *Bossu was so stunned by that but still believes I have no proof of it being a physical extension? Maybe he doesn't know all that much . . . or maybe every host is different in some way? He did claim I was the first to do it.*

Jack patrolled his mind once more before pondering the Lwa's condescending question. *But what exactly am I envisioning with this thing?* Like a hand in the dark, he could not see the appendage, but he could definitely feel it. *Maybe it's a kind of arm? Its range is crazy, though, I feel like it moves like a frog's tongue sorta . . . a retractable wire, maybe? But that doesn't explain how I can grasp with it.* Flexing the appendage, he activated his night vision once more in the vain hope that he would see something.

*I feel what it's doing,* he thought, moving it about internally and externally, *so even though it's invisible, I should be able to get an idea of its structure based on how I use—*

He stopped short upon sensing that Bossu had finally begun to hover around his cognition. Jack's prolonged silence stoked his curiosity.

Jack silently began manipulating the appendage, attentive

to whether its sensory feedback would confirm the feasibility of attempted movements.

Palpating the darkness around him, Jack felt the imprint of two individuals as they secured the perimeter of a building some distance behind him. Unseen, he turned around and watched as they conducted their patrol. Although his powers allowed him to see in the darkness, evidently magnification was not included.

Because of this, his sixth sense provided much more physical detail about the distant men than his eyes. Like a blind man using his hands to learn someone's face. As they disappeared behind the building, however, so did his perception of them.

Although smiling, a furrow of dissatisfaction appeared on Jack's brow. "That's all it takes to lose me?" he said aloud. "I refuse."

Intending to sense the obscured area behind the building, Jack psionically reached forward and attempted a ninety-degree turn but his mind suddenly registered a distinct expression of denial coming from the appendage.

He thought it was quite similar to the feedback from his arm when he tried to lift weights that were too heavy.

A succinct, yet voiceless, no.

Jack rapidly tried two more times with the same result. Confident that he was doing something wrong, he felt intrigued rather than frustrated. "There is no way I should be eluded by something so . . . simple."

Still smiling, he tried again.

This time, instead of thinking it into a right angle, he visualized a tight curve. Conceiving a bend that stretched around the building, his teeth began to show upon realizing he did not feel the voiceless rejection as before. He restrained himself from a full-fledged grin seeing as he had yet to receive confirmation it worked as intended.

His hesitancy became unnecessary as he suddenly perceived the two guards, with the same intricate detail as before, continuing their patrol along the back of the building while still out of view.

"Yeaaaahhh!" Despite his excited utterance, he maintained his casual posture.

"What are you on about?" Bossu asked.

Jack did not respond and instead directed his senses upward into the air. "So," he began, "you don't do rigidity, but you can bend, huh? Let's see . . ."

He immediately began projecting it into a variety of contortions across the skyline and, sensing no rejection, began reaching it forward with the intent to create the rippling crests and troughs of a wave pattern.

The appendage *felt* like it was doing it.

Jack spun around before excitedly casting the sense far behind him, toward the rear of the building. Not only did he effortlessly relocate the original guards, but also noticed three individuals converge upon them. Correctly identifying the new arrivals as two men and one woman, Jack marveled as he discerned them shake hands. His perception was so acute that he would have been able to read their lips had he the experience.

"Unreal . . ."

As he stood in awe, Jack suddenly felt a spark within his intuition. Its fleeting surmise seemed so implausible he almost dismissed it outright.

"You told me no," he breathed. "Y-you're sentient?"

"Who are you talking to?" Bossu asked.

"I'm not sure exactly," Jack said, finally replying to the Lwa. "I think . . . I think this thing—"

"What thing?"

"The thing you were giving me the third degree about."

"Shadow manipulation! I wanted to know how—"

"How I envisioned it, yeah, always as some kind of an inanimate tool, like an extendable grabber that's controlled by my mind."

"How absurd."

"But my exercise has me thinking it's more like an arm. It's pretty surprising actually."

"I have heard you refer to it as an appendage quite often and yet you are surprised?"

Jack gasped in an exaggerated manner. "So, I was right?" he asked. "Then why were you saying all that condescending stuff before?"

"Do not misunderstand, I still think your interpretation is worth condescension, but that sentiment is now directed at your prior admission." Jack began snickering at the ground, but Bossu pressed on. "Ignoring your statement about it being a mystical picking tool for a moment, the choice to refer to it as an appendage was of your own doing from the very first. You are here claiming that vain exercise of yours has somehow revealed to you that—"

"Yeah," Jack said through a chuckle, "I know."

"—the power you have erroneously termed an appendage is not an inanimate tool, but actually something similar to an appendage."

Jack laughed all the more. "You win, all right?"

"Disconcerting logic and awareness aside, your conclusion remains incorrect."

Jack dropped his smile just before giving an abrupt reply. "Wait, what? I'm not wrong."

Bossu remained silent, given pause by his host's sudden change in demeanor.

"What makes you think I'm incorrect? Because you know

something I don't? Or because no one else perceived it this way? If it's the latter, well, you looked just about ready to crap whatever it is you wear back when I pulled myself into the void, and guess what I used to do that?"

Jack paused his speech to allow Bossu the opportunity to interject but quickly resumed, having sensed the Lwa had no desire to entertain the invitation.

"So yeah, the one based on precedent gets scrapped, which leaves only the former. Sorry to say, but if that's why you said I'm incorrect then you better go back to the drawing board, crystal ball, or anything else you may have, because I'm right."

"Whelp," Bossu began, breaking his silence, "you are overthinking it."

Jack began smiling again as he shook his head. "*Now* I'm overthinking it," he said. "Anyway, what you overheard was my realization that this appendage you gave me is sentient . . . somewhat."

"Only because I'm curious, how does such a peculiarity fit into your arm revelation?"

Though audibly silent, Jack quickly raised his index finger as he answered the Lwa's question. *I said it was more like an arm.*

"That is sentient?"

Jack lifted an eyebrow as he stared off into the distance. *I don't get it, haven't you been around for a long time? Like, you know stuff, don't you?*

"Just explain your sentient arm, Jack."

*You don't think a complex system of transmitters and receptors physically linked to the brain equates to sentience?*

"Hm hm, no, boy," Bossu replied. "No, I do not."

*You don't?*

"I do not," Bossu repeated, "but I can see why you do."

*Care to explain?*

"Considering your previous stance on the inanimate mystic grabber, the capability of the neural network may convince some to agree with you."

Jack's eyes briefly darted from side to side, his smile giving way to a subtle expression of confusion.

Noticing this, Bossu continued. "The communicated message received by . . . let us take the pain receptors, for example. They could be seen as proof of a form of sentience, relatively speaking."

*So you agree?* Jack asked, nodding slowly.

"I cannot fault your logic. However, I would never utter such a statement. You are free to operate under such a standard if you like, as long as you are consistent with it."

Bossu fell silent as he observed Jack process his words, the lad's nodding growing progressively more rapid.

"Are you going to explain your basis for sentience or not? You are suggesting it communicates through the neural pathways, no?"

Jack stopped nodding. "No, it's not like that," he replied aloud, replacing his nods with an equally exuberant shake of the head. "Science isn't my thing, so bear with me, but in a regular arm, the system of transmitters and receptors works through the physical link it has to the brain of its owner. Is that correct?"

"It will do. Continue."

"Right, so this thing here . . ." Jack's eyes slowly moved upward as if he were looking at something ascending to the sky. "It's incapable of taking part in that system as it's not physically linked to my brain."

His incredulity having given way to curiosity for some time now, Bossu observed his host look about the skyline as if tracking something. While he was certain Jack was operating under a false assumption, the confident enthusiasm with which the rascal justified himself compelled the Lwa to hear him out.

Jack's voice was devoid of any doubt as he completed his statement. "It is more accurate to see the appendage as having its own brain that is linked to mine."

"Telepathy? How do you distinguish between that and telekinesis in its application? The distinction may appear trite, but they bear implications that are not the same."

"Exactly!" Jack replied. "The fact that it knows things that I don't is what validates my claim. I didn't know it couldn't move in angles, so when I tried to maneuver it ninety degrees, I was denied. It was kind of like when I try to bench press above my ability, it just won't happen."

"But—" Bossu cut himself off to let out a sound of satisfaction. "Ahhh . . ." he breathed. "I see your way now."

Jack was grinning into the night, cheerfully waiting for the Lwa to continue.

"Since there is no physical connection to the brain, its medium of communication must be altogether different than an arm, which means the intimation of its inability to carry out your directive bears out your claim of sentience."

"You see?" Jack began. "I'm not as dumb as you think."

"Perhaps," his Lwa replied, "and yet I have never seen one interpret the shadow sense this way. Imagine one claiming that their experience of sight is facilitated by an invisible imp that springs forth from their eyes, somehow creates a virtual copy of what is before them, and then returns from whence it sprung, stamping an imprint of the virtual copy within."

Jack left the comment without a response, his gaze having already returned to the sky.

*How should I envision you now?* He began brandishing the appendage across the landscape. *You can't move in angles, so that means you are not freely floating. There is some spectral connection that operates as your tether, but . . .* Jack recalled the appendage and thought it into a coil around his body, surrounding himself with it in the darkness as he spoke. "I can feel myself but I can't feel *it*. Nobody can—"

He suddenly had an idea.

Wasting no time, Jack sent the appendage into the psychical breach and immediately grabbed onto Bossu.

"Eh?" the Lwa grunted. "What are you doing?"

"Bossu!" Jack hissed, failing to contain his excitement. "Do you feel that?"

"I do."

He began gently squeezing the Lwa repeatedly as if hastily giving a massage. "What does it feel like? Please don't throw me off."

"Hm hm, very well." Jack immediately felt the titan begin to wrestle with the unseen appendage, stretching and pulling at it to get an idea of its structure. "Like the rods of a fasces . . . how interesting."

The Lwa paused for a moment before continuing.

"Why did you not think of this before now, Jack?"

"I have no idea," he replied hurriedly. "Check its tether or its tail, not just the business end."

The intrigued Lwa was already way ahead, as Jack felt whatever it was that anchored the appendage to him get pulled with great vigor. Bossu was handling the appendage in the same manner a bucket is drawn from a well.

Suddenly, he felt the massive Lwa extricate himself from the excess winding line of the drawn-out appendage, causing it to recoil mightily in its return.

"So?" Jack asked, mentally wielding it to gain a sense of its condition.

"A hand without a set number of digits," Bossu replied. "They recede into the main portion when seized, quite similar to an eel slipping back to the water."

Jack let out a sound of reflection, forcefully released from his chest. "Hm."

"Yes," the Lwa continued, sounding equally reflective, "the shadow limb by which you are connected . . . it handled like countless strands of supple twine bundled together to form one great tentacle. At least that is how it presents in a relaxed state."

Jack remained silent as his smile began to fade.

"When the tentacle was stressed along its transverse, its tendency was to extend outward due to its countless strands being stretched into repeated side-by-side arrangements, the limits of which would be too laborious to ascertain in this manner."

Jack reflexively glanced to the side as he strove to process Bossu's imagery. "A sheet?"

"Indeed," the Lwa replied. "The tentacle's elasticity seems limitless and while it certainly is not, I cannot think of a scenario in which it could be exhausted. I pulled it in a manner that I hoped you would perceive. Did you?"

His host nodded.

"Take note of how long I was drawing it forth. I had been draping it around myself to the point of near submersion. The tendril never became taut even after the copious excess, it remained slack ever since the beginning."

Jack, who had been gazing toward his side as he listened, suddenly directed his sights skyward. Wielding the appendage upward into his line of sight, he held it aloft against the slightly luminous backdrop of spectral gray sky.

His eyes furiously darted about, scanning for any impression or distortion created by the appendage's presence.

"I know you're there," he said confidently. "So how do I see you?"

Bossu hummed out an exhale before muttering to himself. "Well played, indeed." He returned his attention to Jack. "I was not finished."

"Oh?" he replied, still scanning the skyline.

"Far from it, little whelp." The manner in which the Lwa spoke caused Jack's eyes to still. "For certain, I have felt this before."

"Yeah?" Jack replied with a start.

"Hm hm hm, *yeah*, I know it very well, could scarcely believe it myself. How long have I been here? My my . . ."

"What?"

Bossu's voice lowered to a murmur as if suddenly talking to himself. "Then . . . that means—it can't be. But by the stars . . . it is." He let out a gravelly chuckle, one Jack had not heard before; it contained more surprise than amusement. "Heh heh."

"Don't do this now!"

"Heh heh. Jack, the appendage is your connection to the void, the primordial source of shadow." He raised his voice slightly to silence his host, who already had his mouth opened to speak. "At the same time, it is something I have never seen exhibited by your predecessors, though I know it intimately." The Lwa paused, causing Jack to groan in annoyance. "Heh heh, it is your shadow sense given form."

"Yeah, I thought we pretty much figured that out already."

"Yes and no."

"Oh my God!" Jack bellowed. "Where do you know it from?"

"From when I was first banished to the void."

The tension of his yelp fell from the young host's face. "What?"

"Why do you think a divine entity would subject themselves to entrapment inside a mortal's soul? It is because there is no other way to experience the outside world but vicariously through lesser beings. Such humiliation is inextricably linked to my punishment." The lad remained silent. "The void is my prison, Jack."

# CHAPTER 8

Unresponsive, Jack was left stunned by the revelation and became sidetracked by the long overdue questions and considerations that suddenly began flooding his mind. His mouth moved repeatedly as he tried to voice whatever question was the most prominent, only to abandon it in favor of one judged more pertinent.

Feeling pity for his disoriented host, Bossu resumed speaking. "I am touched that my state is capable of rendering you speechless. You truly are a wonder of firsts, Jack Boniface." The lad appeared deaf to the compliment. "Indeed, as you so assuredly warned me, you were correct. I owe you an apology."

A still-silent Jack jumped with a start as he suddenly sensed his appendage being twirled about the Lwa's finger.

"This artifact . . . this . . . appendage, it is identical in both form and function to the corporeal essence I adopted after being trapped in the void. It has been eons since I shed that form. I had nearly forgotten."

Jack, at last, began to speak. "It all makes sense now," he said. "I chalked it up to more baseless claims, so I didn't mention it."

"Mention what?"

"You probably already know this, but when I researched your name, the aspects mentioned were wildness, strength, and something else, I think. Whatever it was, it wasn't related to shadow, voids, or even darkness in general, which is what I assumed to be your shtick."

"Naturally."

"Which means my shadow powers are a result of your prison. Some sort of assimilation?"

"Heh heh. Rather insightful, Jack," Bossu said.

"But when I explained my thoughts on the appendage you claimed the idea of it being a physical extension is incorrect. Plus, you said I was wrong to treat shadow manipulation as musculoskeletal because it is extrasensory. None of this triggered a memory of your past? It's not like you have amnesia or something—"

"Did you not hear when I said I owe you an apology? Take heed, the hosts in which I have resided are numbered 887, not including yourself."

"Ugh." Jack removed his hands from his pockets and began rubbing the stubble lining his face.

"Yes, now you are beginning to understand. Be aware that I cast aside my said form long before I acquired my first host. I doubt your mortal faculties can comprehend the magnitude of loss over such a vast—"

Bossu stopped himself as Jack politely raised his index finger.

He returned his hands to his pockets. "I get it," he began, "I've forgotten personal details and I'm not even twenty yet. That's what you're getting at, right? The passage of time basically made you forget your past self? That monster I see obviously isn't your true form then."

Bossu let out a sigh. Though guttural, it contained an uncharacteristic hint of pity. "Oh Jack, you truly are a wonder of firsts, all by coincidence . . . and yet . . ."

"Yet what?"

"Heh heh . . . you have presented me with the opportunity to do something new."

"You're old. What can possibly be new to you?"

"So you too, you see it!" Bossu exclaimed.

"See what?"

Jack's question was ignored as the Lwa seemed to resume his internal monologue. "Heh heh. Consent, it can't be coincidence, therefore, it must be you . . . yes, it is evident. Do you not see?"

"I just said—"

As Bossu continued, the tone of his voice would alternate between enthusiasm and desperation in an unsettling rhythm, coinciding with the shift of his speech from discourse to contemplation. "Even if I were to rebel against Fate's injunction and spare you, I alone would bear the loss. Specifically, the loss of something new. And there will never be another who feels the void as this Jack Boniface, I have no doubt. It was all sovereign happenstance, and you stumbled into being chosen, whelp. Chosen to become an unbreakable one."

"What are you talking about?"

The suddenness of Jack's question seemed to snatch Bossu from his stream of thought. "It is just an idea, Jack. Think survival of the fittest, but considered from the perspective of the gods. Imagine an entity being utterly broken only to be made whole again from the midst of its brokenness. Such a process would bring about the aforementioned individual. Yet to be done, however."

"So even the gods are capable of baseless theories. Ha-ha."

"The impossible problem was that immortals cannot be broken, while mortals, though capable of being broken, can never be made whole thereafter." Bossu's prior excitement made a brief return. "But *I* can do it! That great experiment has been entrusted to me by Fate, and you are the orchestrated coincidence that is the bearer of this great news."

Jack folded his arms. "You're acting strange."

"Of that, I am sure." Bossu began delving into his thoughts again, fading in and out within the conversation. "Heh, I think I even feel remorse. Jack, you are weak, you know? More than most?" The Lwa paused his rambling for a moment, restarting just in time to silence his host. "But your exceeding weakness will be . . . hmm. Whelp! Hold on to this and do it well: When all is said and done, I promise you will agree that it was worth it."

"Okay."

"And yet, how dreadful—"

"You think something to be dreadful?"

"—to ordain a mortal to drink from this cup. Such a tender branch at that." Bossu's voice grew slightly louder as he began addressing Jack again. "To orchestrate its being given to one such as yourself, the notion fills me with a terror and joy most . . . *exquisite*!"

"Makes sense, I guess."

"So, you see, I must obey."

"And I'm the unbreakable one, huh?" Jack asked. "Has a nice ring to it."

"You like it, eh? Do you want it?"

"Of course! I'm here, aren't I?"

"Consent again. Perhaps it is best if I begin abruptly."

"Sorry, that sounded brattier than I intended."

"Not at all."

"You asked me if I wanted it, but I thought I already had it."

"Heh, it was made to be received by you alone. As such, it has been yours since its inception. Just like me and this curse, they exist for us alone. It is beautiful in a way too wondrous to be perceived."

Jack turned his head slightly, bracing himself against the sudden breeze of night air. "Beautiful?"

"Fate's relentless cunning," the Lwa replied. "For my part, my imprisonment came with an insidious repercussion the majority of the pantheon could never have anticipated."

"You sure about that?"

"If they did, I suspect my punishment would have been rejected."

"What happened?"

"My confinement caused me to undergo a constant process of deterioration, the essence of my being destined to progressively fade due to the limitations of the mortal constitution."

"So the humans repressed you?"

"How can a newborn baby conceptualize the learned and natural capabilities of a full-grown adult? Relative to a god, even your aged are neonates and since the expression of my essence is subject to my host's turn of mind, I was certain to never experience my true manifestation ever again. And I hated every single one of you for it, perhaps even more than my brethren who cursed me to said fate."

Jack sputtered out an inappropriate chuckle. "I wasn't laughing at that last part," he said quickly. "You basically lost yourself due to your host's lack of imagination."

"You state it that way because Josiah orchestrated your being the exception."

"I'm sorry but that's pretty much what it boils down to."

"I am saying your use of the word *lack* implies the absence of something reasonably expected to be present. Even the most imaginative of my hosts could only conceptualize my essence in the abstract bec—"

"So that's why you denied it as a physical extension of myself? Because everyone treated it as alien."

"Hmm, you are getting it, Jack," Bossu replied. "I didn't just forget aspects of my past self due to time. Rather, I was steadily forced to accept that they ceased to exist."

"And that's why you hated my predecessors?" Jack asked with a newly raised eyebrow. "Because of their limited dispositions? Is that fair? It seems kind of irrational of you to feel that way, especially when you could've just enlightened them for both of your benefits. You're the type to shake a baby because they don't know how to write."

Bossu suddenly erupted with laughter so uproarious that Jack reflexively looked around for any signs of panic in the surrounding area.

"Bah ha-ha! Quite right, whelp, quite right. To be fair, I *did* do something similar to the enlightening you suggested, and it was a disaster. Do you recall what I said to you when you were demanding to know the extent of the powers you are to receive when you become Shadowman?"

"When I become?! I thought I *was* Shadowman?"

"So eager. Be aware, Jack, that once you are transformed, you will no longer be hidden from my brethren. Are you ready for that?"

"I am read—"

"Is Helena? What of your ruffian cohorts?"

Jack's raised eyebrow dropped and joined its twin, a scowl of displeasure on his face. "I had hoped that I'd be able to protect them."

"And soon you shall be," Bossu said. "But to ensure that you attain what I predict to be destined for you, it is best for the process to be conducted meticulously and in proper order. These things I have told you are for your edification." He waited for a sign of acknowledgment from his still-scowling host, who obliged him with a single, impatient nod.

"Good," he continued, "now as I was saying, do you recall what—"

"Yeah, you said I would get myself killed!"

"Precisely, and from then until now, my hatred for humanity precluded me from expanding their understanding. I had no choice but to accept that humanity would never serve as an aid for my revenge on the pantheon. Before long I had developed a ravenous desire to use your kind for ends wholly my own. Unfortunately for them, the mortal mind is nigh impregnable when it is at peace."

Raising his eyebrow once more, Jack let out three tuts of disapproval, increasing his pitch as he did it.

"So, the choice for me was clear, I had to tenderize them with madness. Rather than empower my hosts, I chose to corrupt them."

"Wow, Bossu," Jack responded. "That's awful!"

"Yes."

"And I caught that 'until now' you snuck in there at the start of your horrific admission." The Lwa's deep hums of contained amusement echoed in his mind. As Jack spoke, he simultaneously pondered how the monster could make such a sound without lips. "You intend to do the same to me, is that it? Your knowledge of the process makes it such a sure thing that you can warn me ahead of time, right? Well, like I told you the last time you used your so-called knowledge to doubt me: Better check your crystal ball."

Bossu's chuckle of pleasure intensified somewhat. It sounded gleeful, almost giddy with expectation. "Heh heh heh . . . I *will* do it!"

His host stayed silent but maintained his raised eyebrow.

"Jack, are you aware that the fearlessness you are currently utilizing to speak to me in such a way is my doing? I mean to say, it is not a passive attribute. I control it like a switch."

"Oh yeah?"

Jack could see the man he had rescued on the bus, accompanied by the driver and the young woman. They were exiting the terminal's waiting area and began making their way toward the parking lot.

The Lwa's tone was thoroughly confident, devoid of any doubt. "Indeed," he replied. "And if I remove it from such a tender branch as yourself, you will be quick to collapse. Your relatively meticulous nature will work against you, like triggering a fault line in a rock otherwise indestructible."

"I thought I *was* unbreakable."

"Hm hm hm, you will be. Now observe."

A subtle effervescence began tingling in Jack's chest, dissipating quickly.

"I'm not scared," he announced defiantly.

The Lwa suddenly sounded curious, uncharacteristically so. "Of what?" he asked. "Dying like your dad?"

"Wha—"

For less than a second, the thought seemed like a joke before becoming totally warranted, and long overdue. As if under hypnosis, Jack could not help but examine his father's death from a perspective previously ignored.

How could he be sure that he wouldn't suffer the same fate? He barely survived Jamal.

And what of his mother?

With the rapid onset of dismay similar to realizing that something has been left behind, Jack was immediately beset with newfound concerns.

"Wh-wh-what am I doing?" he said. "This is insane. I can't—"

"Of me?"

Jack froze at this, and although his mind still retained the knowledge that the voice belonged to his Lwa, it sounded different.

Alien.

The sound of the monster's two-syllable question seemed to reverberate forever. Not only had the guttural quality of its voice somehow increased, but it also seemed to bear physical weight.

Jack quickly collapsed to the ground, squatting low as he covered his ears.

Upon doing so, he inadvertently toggled the play button on his once-silent earbuds. He caught the start to his favorite song, "Remorse" by Scattle, before it was promptly drowned out by the Lwa's voice.

He tried to remind himself that it was just Bossu, but that only served to feed the seed of doubt that had formed in his soul, triggering something worse.

Jack felt the Fear, newly sprouted and blossoming with haste. While the newness of this emotion was concerning, what really had him shaken was how utterly incapable he was of stopping it from growing.

"No."

The idea that monsters like his Lwa were real made him afraid. The fact that it had only now begun to do so made the Fear all the more poignant.

Despite the condescension in the monster's remark, it was true. Jack had to be granted the fearlessness of a god just to stand in its presence, and he *still* felt trepidation at the time. But rather than take that as a humbling sign of how dreadful his situation truly was, Jack chose to regard the imparted boldness as his own.

But it was all a lie.

And now he was in for it.

He strove to prepare himself, attempting to steel his psyche by drawing comparisons to past highs gone wrong, but the Fear outpaced him by an order of magnitude. This was going to turn the most traumatic mushroom trip into a forgotten memory, the sound of the Lwa's still-echoing voice guaranteed it.

Jack began pressing hard against his earbuds to try to block it out. However, this did nothing to stop the horror of his new reality from coming into contact with his mind. At last.

There were more monsters like this one, surveilling humanity with impunity and doing whatever they wished.

Privacy?

Knowledge?

Those were just illusions, mockeries no doubt created by the monsters themselves to keep humanity from seeing the true food chain. And Jack was not immune to the infernal hoax. His pursuit of distinction had blinded him from the Truth.

Just like everyone else.

If his fellow humans ever saw the punch line of the cruel joke, that the monsters had flattered them into disbelieving their existence, they would self-destruct for sure.

It was just so cruel, too terrible for humanity to imagine and yet, it was true.

"So much for distinction, eh?"

And the responsibility to protect his people from their devourers was now his alone. At least Josiah was fortunate enough to have been trained from childhood for this. But Jack was nothing more than an entitled brat, too smart to be interested in the terror of the real.

And his father knew it.

Josiah had thought that half-assed plan of his was enough to keep his son alive, but it only worked because Jack had been made incapable of looking at the big picture. The youngster's false confidence had certainly turned him into a fool, but his father was worse.

"Dad," he hissed, "I'm not gonna survive this nightmare. I . . . I hate you for this!!"

"Oh? Is that how you truly feel?" The Lwa spoke with a cadence that forced its every utterance to throb in Jack's head, one after the other. "Or is it just a coward fleeing from his responsibility?"

The panic-stricken host whined pitifully as he felt his appendage being grappled with once more. It felt alien, too.

His shrinking awareness was barely able to recall what it was and, upon recollection, withered away with increased haste.

He could sense his insides recoiling away from the connection's unseen root as the monster vied for his attention.

"Jaaack . . ." its voice rumbled, calculatedly slow.

The appendage willingly gave itself over, permitting itself to be contorted however the entity saw fit. Jack hated the fact that he could perceive these things and hated Josiah for exposing him to them.

Why couldn't he have been fathered by someone else?

Then he would be free to live as he wished, free from the Truth's fetters. If it wasn't for that man, he would never have known the horror of this curse.

This nightmare inheritance.

"Can you see me, Jack?"

Several hate-fueled tears pattered across the grass as the appendage continued to be manipulated in a way Jack never knew possible. Like the hood of a cobra, the tentacle had been stretched to form a sprawling curtain of shadow.

Attempting to dissociate, Jack's eyes rolled white in terrified revulsion as the misshapen tentacle enveloped something unseen, seamlessly transmitting the newly created impression.

But it proved futile, as the Fear merely gripped him tighter. Its squeeze was in grim sync with the tentacle's constriction around its mold.

Unfortunately, Jack's intuition seemed generally unaffected by the Fear's stranglehold, enabling him to identify what the tentacle had been wrapped around. Though it currently hung loose like an oversized cloak of shadow, the most prominent distortions warped in a manner that could only be caused by protrusions within.

Horns.

Desperate to stop himself from beholding what he knew was coming, the fragile mortal clenched his eyes shut, though they had already been rolled past his pain threshold.

Another futile attempt to escape.

Seen through Jack's sixth sense, the image steadily taking shape was the result of the impressions being made within the fabric of his psionically rooted appendage; his eyes played no part.

Though his panicked state made him feel repulsed by the appendage's existence, the forsaken host could not shake the sense of betrayal as he watched it. He heard a strange buzzing as the constriction continued, the pace agonizingly slow, as if spiteful.

But Jack could already see it.

See *him.*

No different than a torture victim with propped eyelids, the Lwa was going to force him to experience the unthinkable. All his prior sources of anguish took a back seat to the dread that coiled about him as he felt his metamorphosed tentacle begin to lose its heavy appearance.

Why was the monster doing this?

He had not become even somewhat acclimated to this new state of Fear, yet the merciless Lwa would subject him to the perfect horror that was its appearance.

The loose shroud of shadow began shrinking itself against what could now be identified as the monster titan's head. Its two lateral horns in conjunction with the two tusks ascending from his chin, stalled the shroud from clinging to his face, creating a harem-like mask from top to bottom that blocked its terrifying face.

To force such a sight on eyes of flesh was beyond a human's capacity to bear, but to make Jack *feel* it through his exceedingly perceptive shadow sense, while being deprived of the fearlessness that came with it, was unconscionable.

Seemingly intent to deprive Jack of any moment of respite, the tentacle betrayed him further, adopting a texture more diaphanous in quality.

Jack was not even able to form another thought before the spectral tether gave one final squeeze. He suddenly felt like a cold stake had been plunged into his heart as the shadow stocking portion of the appendage snapped onto the Lwa's head like shrink-wrap.

"What in the world?"

This statement of shock came from the group of fellow passengers. They had stumbled upon Jack writhing on the grass just outside the parking lot. He was rendered incapable of giving them any regard, completely immersed in the terror that was the Lwa's image.

The appendage made it possible to see the unseeable. Thin as a stocking, it had molded itself around the monstrous Lwa with exceeding detail, even imparting its eyes of crimson glaring at him from the void.

The abominable pig demon's appearance was just as grotesque as before, only this time the petrified youth could *feel* the hideousness.

Being deprived of the numbing effect created by Bossu's

fearlessness caused the sense impression to feel like countless hairy caterpillars performing their stretch-and-pull trudge through his veins. The itchy discomfort was so intense it hovered at the cusp of pain.

The penetrating buzzing sound was replaced by what Jack imagined to be maracas forged in the pit of hell, chattering in his eardrums.

It was the most unnerving thing he ever heard.

Amidst all this, Jack tried to avert his psychic gaze but, seeing as it was no use, ceased his resistance and allowed his focus to set on the monster's face. He breathed sharply through gritted teeth, mimicking the Lwa's fleshless maw that now brought forth speech.

"You see me," it said, "now hear me. The alerting of my brethren is only one consequence of your full transformation. I purposely withheld the other."

Attempting to decipher the Lwa's speech through lipreading was pointless, forcing the young host to block out the penetrating noise from his ears before the words could register. Observing the titan's teeth open and clench in correspondence with its utterances, Jack fought to listen through the mental and physical anguish.

"Son of Marius," the monster began, his tone uncharacteristically soft and encouraging, at least initially. "Son of Julien, son of Maxim, son of Michael, son of Josiah, HEAR ME!"

Jack stopped his writhing and strove to regain himself through the sensory assault. He could hear the address more clearly, albeit with a slight delay.

"Though you are already markedly more . . . unique than these your predecessors, what you will be capable of when you become Shadowman will make your current abilities seem like nothing. However, if you can endure the unspeakable privilege that has been appointed for you alone to be broken, you will be so much more than even that. Your enemies, our enemies, will not see you coming. Heh heh heh, it will be glorious."

Jack understood the words being spoken but derived no joy from them. They seemed trivial and hollow. His being had been brought to the point where the suffering could be put to an end, and he deduced the ability to give up the ghost whenever he saw fit.

Despite this awareness, Jack valiantly strove against it for his mother's sake, trying to stand. But the thoroughly realized Fear continued to overwhelm him, repeatedly gimping his resolve whenever he attempted to rise.

Monsters were real and he had to take them on?

How?

The doubt would just not let up, making the macabre method of escape seem more appropriate by the second. Fortunately, the penetrating nature of the din in Jack's head increased whenever he flirted with the idea. This compelled him to endure and give heed to Bossu's words of encouragement, though he felt certain they were nothing but lies.

Just like everything else.

"Yes," Bossu continued, "this also was orchestrated by the son of Michael, the other side to the coin that was his grand plan. We despised each other to the utmost for so long . . . heh heh. He counted on my being blind to it, so, you see? Josiah was not the irresponsible fool your despair has led you to believe."

Jack managed an utterance from his state of seeming paralysis. "Dad?"

"That is the way, whelp! Shun the method of cowards and acknowledge the brokenness within your mortal frame. Gather the scattered remains of your will and recall how you once stood in the face of the Truth so that you may do so again. Present yourself as one having endured the fearful agony unknown to both gods and men, worthy of the destiny entrusted to you." Bossu paused as he beheld the sorry state of his young host. "And me also."

To Jack, the monster's terrifying gaze seemed to suggest this was all a ruse of the sadistic sort. Its giant mandibular tusk fangs still managed to shine through the mesh-like tentacle, a glimmering promise to gobble him up at once if he made the slightest movement.

"Jack," the Lwa said, his voice now tinged with a tone of desperation, "if I prematurely confer the fearlessness you long for, all of this will be in vain. Therefore, I have devised the simplicity of my instruction to circumvent the need for this to be drawn out any further."

The horror of it all had finally taken its toll on Jack as his mind began to involuntarily dissociate, an act of self-preservation triggered by his subconscious, temporarily freeing him.

Having seen enough, the bus driver began searching for her phone. "This poor boy needs medical attention."

"Do you understand, Jack? All you have to do is stand, and it will be enough. I guarantee it."

No longer visualizing the Lwa, Jack could see himself shuddering upon the ground. The man he had saved hours earlier seemed to be leading a hushed conversation with two others. Though he could still feel the Fear, viewing his torment from the outside made it somewhat less excruciating.

His battered resolve dwindling, Jack was already rationalizing his willingness to concede in order to disguise its true nature.

He looked down at himself. "This is fine."

As if in a sudden rage, Bossu summoned the lad back with a shout, forcing him to return to his body.

The bus driver gasped and dropped her phone. "Did you hear that?"

Jack was unable to disengage. He had no choice but to feel and hear the Lwa's command before his mind's ability to check out was restored.

"I cannot make you whole until you stand!"

The despised suggestion almost made Jack give up, but he was stopped again by thoughts of his mother. He remembered how her personality was forever changed when his dad returned for good. Even as a child, he reasoned the man must have really been something to have such a profound effect on her.

"Dad," he repeated.

Pulling out her phone, the driver attempted to call for help once more but was stopped by the young woman with braids. "Wait!" she commanded. "He's coming to."

Jack was able to turn his psychic gaze away from the monster and onto the memory of his family's final embrace within his room.

His fragmented will spurred his legs to move, and though he was immediately met with the monster's returned visage, the compulsion to remain in a groveling position no longer seemed so insurmountable.

Eyes still white and gnashing his teeth, the broken young man gathered the dregs of his courage and crawled up off the ground to rise into the Fear. His eyes had begun to bleed from the struggle to block out the maracas from hell. Their sound and the piercing buzzing had been raised to a fever pitch.

The bus driver took her eyes off Jack to glance at the young woman. Instead of appearing concerned or dismayed, she looked fascinated.

"Uh-uh!" the driver exclaimed, frantically typing into her phone. "You just fixin' to watch him convulse like that?"

Jack could recall the monster mentioning his father having

accounted for all this. Though he had dismissed it as mockery, nothing was lost if he chose to believe it.

He was going to die anyway.

"Better to die standing . . ." he stated, apparently in a trance. He forcefully hissed this through his teeth, pelting the people from the bus with drops of tears, blood, and saliva.

". . . than to grovel," Bossu said, completing Jack's thought. "Heh heh, well done, whelp."

Jack remained oblivious to his stunned onlookers as he began a voiceless address to his Lwa. *Bossu, please don't lie to me. I don't want to be subjected to all this for nothing.*

"What are you on about?" Bossu spat. "Subjected to what?"

He wiped his eyes free from the gruesome blood tears and set his sights back to the night sky. Jack could still feel Bossu's image, seemingly determined to express his sentiments from the void, staring back at him with artificial contempt.

He started to find it annoying.

*You told me to stand up to your ugly mug and face the fear.*

As he replied, Jack realized his knees were already flexed to rigid extension and he stood upright.

"What fear?" Bossu asked.

Jack scoffed. "What fear he says—"

As his mind processed what was happening, Jack gazed upon his Lwa through his appendage and was certain he could see the corners of his skeleton mouth arch slightly in amusement.

"I did it?" he asked, facing forward.

Noticing the three people from the bus, Jack realized he had an audience and progressively came to understand what they must have witnessed.

"I'm so sorry you guys had to see that," he began, glancing at each of them while doing his best to appear embarrassed. *What the hell?*

Jack almost dropped the facade upon noticing the young woman wearing an expression nearly identical to when he first saw her. This time, however, her demeanor gave way to a muted smile that disappeared as soon as she wiped his tears from her face.

Jack's gaze lingered due to her strange behavior. He averted his eyes to avoid giving the wrong impression.

"My dad just died and I'm having trouble dealing." He paused, confirming a reduction in the alarmed looks of the other two. "I go through bouts of panic attacks semiregularly. They can get pretty bad, so I tried to find a secluded area for privacy." He smiled sheepishly before looking at the ground. "I'm really sorry."

Their countenance switched to relief before they simultaneously offered up condolences.

"Don't you worry about it, sweetie," the driver began. "You mentioned his passing back when you confronted the jerks."

"I did?"

"Yes, you did," the woman replied. "Do you need anything? Water or something?"

Jack politely waved away the offer. "No, I'm fine, just gonna stay out here for a bit and compose my—Oh gosh, is this blood?" He stopped himself before reflexively wiping it with his sleeve after noticing the handkerchief being offered. "Thanks, man."

"Don't mention it, brother," the indebted man replied, "it's the least I can do."

Jack immediately began wiping his face through some sniffles.

"Well, sweetie," the driver began, "we gonna go on and head back. Don't take too long now. If we don't see you when it's time to board, we comin' to find you."

She finished the statement with a wink, prompting Jack

to respond in good humor. “I’ll be there, you don’t even gotta worry about it, miss.”

“I’m Mark, by the way,” the man said as he offered out his hand. “I never got your name, brother.”

Hearing this, the young woman quickly turned to hear Jack’s answer.

Jack shook his hand before replying. “Nice to meet you, Mark,” he said. “My name is Jack.”

# CHAPTER 9

Nibo took another drag from his cigar, the undead horde's ravenous onslaught reflecting off his sunglasses. He had been monitoring the ensuing attack on the denizens of the drug den to confirm it was a success.

One of the panicking victims had a zombie's face buried in her stomach.

Abandoning the struggle to remove the monster from her bowels, and now moments away from crossing over, she finally noticed the fancily dressed man clad in pink.

With the last of her strength, she called out to him in desperation. "Help me!"

Though her plea was barely audible over the screams of anguish and the growls of the undead, Nibo heard it.

He blew out the smoke from his cigar while approaching her. "Sorry, baby," he replied. "We Ghede are obliged to let our return be known to you mortals, the ones paying attention at least. If it helps, consider your death a sacrifice."

The woman threw her head back in agony as the zombie continued eating her with gusto.

"Don't fret, you junkies ain't the only ones getting offered up, there's gonna be loads more. At least till all the dyin' gets the attention of the new Shadowman—" Nibo playfully hopped backward to avoid the resulting splash of blood and guts. "Ehh, you ain't listening anyhow."

The insouciant Lwa pranced around the grisly scene, ensuring there were no survivors, twirling his never-ending cigar as he did it. The cries of those being eviscerated echoed throughout the stairway as he descended toward the den's lowest floor.

Pleased by the macabre sights and sounds, he suddenly stopped in his tracks.

"Everyone is either dead or on their way," he began, "so why am I hearing footsteps?"

Nibo slowly spun on his heels and spied two police officers walking the floor at its far end, the undead too distracted with their meals to give them notice. Tickled by the officers' apparent misfortune, he began marching toward them to test if they could perceive him.

"If you two are human, I reckon you're the dumbest I ever did see." The two men turned to him and silently began to approach. "Nah, you ain't. No human is this dumb."

As if in response, their eyes became lit with a dull yellow, the glow so weak it was barely visible in the dark. The two men began speaking in perfect unison as if they shared a mouth. Their voices, however, were their own.

"Lord Nibo," they began.

"That's me."

"It has come to our attention that you are privy to the whereabouts of the heir. Would you be so kind as—"

Nibo began twirling his cigar as he interrupted them. "Officers," he said melodically, "if you don't mind, please be so kind as to slow it down. Things must be done according to custom, after all."

The cigar suddenly extended at both ends to form a staff. The low-lit eyes of the two men seemed to flicker as the Lwa continued spinning his accessory like a propeller. The wisps of cigar smoke streaming from the staff's tip were spun into rings and intermittently fanned outward.

Satisfied with the quantity of smoke rings, Nibo set the staff's tip against the ground normally. Lazily propping himself against it, he watched the blooming concentric circles as they ominously floated toward the officers.

He continued. "Proper etiquette obliges you to first cough up the manner in which you came by such knowledge well before asking anything of *meee*." As he sang the end of his sentence, the two men shifted their postures at the approaching rings. "How else am I to determine whether you be friend or—"

Just in time, the men leaped away from the nearest ring as it expanded without warning.

Nibo slowly stood upright, carefully observing the unnatural movements of the agile officers.

He tittered as the corners of their mouths cracked open with a grisly noise, making room for the fiendish teeth that appeared. Glistening and inhumanly sharp, they were arranged haphazardly and jutted forth in multiple rows like a shark's.

Their brow ridges thickened, giving an evil arch of wild aggression to their gaze. The demons in disguise stepped away from each other, giving the languid smoke rings a wide berth while they walked in position to surround Nibo.

"I was gonna say foe," the Lwa said, "but I reckon those smiles you shootin' my way can only mean one thing." Bracing himself against his staff, he paused to catch another titter in his throat as his opponents began sprinting in his direction in an ill-conceived blitz. "You must fancy me somethin' fierce!"

Upon completing his taunt, Nibo swiftly pointed his staff toward the slow-moving smoke rings, causing them to react as if startled from slumber. They returned, surrounding him in a chaotically arranged pattern.

The demon officers widened their dim yellow eyes at the sudden formation of the rings into a defensive barrier, the momentum of their attack making it impossible for them to stop themselves in time.

Indeed, rather than seeming to be intercepted mid-pounce, the near-instantaneous movement of the smoky snares made the demons appear to have intentionally jumped into them. The rings shrunk in size, snapping to constriction and holding their prisoners horizontally off the ground.

Nibo leaned back on his staff and watched as the remaining rings vanished to make way for the ensnared demons, helplessly floating toward their grinning captor.

"Please," they began, "don't hurt us." The Lwa shook his head as he brought the unlit end of his staff to his face. "We'll tell you anything!"

Nibo paused what he was doing and held the enchanted cigar in front of his mouth. "All right," he replied, "who is the necromancer I'm talking to right now?"

The two puppets appeared ready to speak but halted before doing so. Closing their mouths in a synchronized manner, they stared at Nibo as his magical torso cuffs brought them even closer.

He kept his eyes on them as he took a massive toke from the enchanted cigar, waiting for the answer that never came.

Scant wisps of smoke escaped his mouth as he began to speak. "Thought so," he said through a smile. "Your deceit is obvious. Now," he finally exhaled, blowing out a disproportionately large plume. "Begone."

Having totally immersed the immobilized pawns, the smoke cloud flashed an electric pink, turning them into heaps of ash in an instant.

Nibo twirled the staff back into its original form and clenched the cigar between his teeth. "Ya think I don't know a puppeteer's thralls when I see themmm?"

He tittered before taking a drag from the cigar. This time, the resulting smoke created a stagnant cloud in front of him. "But I'm certain Maman will want to know the identity of the trickster, so in you go." He kicked the heaps, sending a portion of their scattered bits to be sucked into the awaiting cloud.

Nibo stopped in front of his portal and scanned the gory mess on the floor a final time. "A foolish ruse that was," he announced. "We don't know where Bossu Koblamin's newest victim is, so such a brazen dig for information only confirms that the traitor ain't in our branch. But I'll let the others know y'all are searching for him. They gonna find it interesting for sure."

Immediately upon Nibo entering the smoke, it vanished without a trace.

---

Dark clouds of gray had covered New Orleans by the time their bus arrived.

Seeking to depart without any fanfare, Jack planned to slink off to a secluded area and sit tight for the passengers to go their separate ways but soon realized this wouldn't be possible. Standing in the aisle waiting to exit, he spied some of the passengers lollygagging after retrieving their belongings and knew they were waiting for him.

*Dammit,* he thought.

The driver smiled at him as he passed her. "I'm praying for you, Jack," she said. "You're a good boy."

"Thanks," he replied, "be well."

Grateful he had not brought any luggage, Jack used the crowd as cover and veered off in the opposite direction to find an appropriate area of the bus station to wait. He recognized the makeshift hangout from before and began smiling upon noticing several individuals huddled within, seeking shelter from the incoming storm.

Jack scanned their faces. Though some were new, the original locals were still present. He hurried to the same position he had taken months prior, this time listening in with reverence.

"The wife wants to put an Inicio in the house by any means necessary," one of them said, "and she so damn hardheaded, got a new excuse every time. First, she wanted it to be safe, then after I shut that crap down, she tried telling me that it comes with incentives that will save us scratch come tax season."

This was met with several laughs by the group.

"That's damned stupid."

"Loretta still workin', ain't she?"

"Damn right, she is," the man replied. "And I suspect that's why she so adamant about getting the thing, just wanna be able to tell her friends she got it."

"That's all it is, brother." Jack remembered this man to be Reggie. "Doubt anyone gonna feel safer with it, they just tryna be part of somethin' new."

A woman Jack did not recognize scoffed in annoyance. "So you reckon Inicio won't prevent crime, period?"

Jack smirked to himself. *Oh boy . . .*

"Point-blank period, chéri," Reggie answered. "Crime

already low as is, no criminal fool enough to give it a go now that every house gonna have that contraption inside."

"You crazy as hell," the woman replied. "You think it's all for nothing then? They givin' it out to the most dangerous communities first, after all. Why do it this way if they ain't tryin' to help for true?"

The one named Lyle began to speak, apparently irritated by the shrill woman. "If by most dangerous communities, you mean Negro communities, well damn girl, that should tell you it ain't genuine help they tryin' for. The white man ain't gonna give no Negro first dibs on the good stuff, and even if they did, it damned sure won't be gratis."

"Ain't sidin' with Renee," another began, "but I thought it was made by one of them Chinese boys."

"Same thing," Lyle retorted.

"You gonna stay stuck on race till the day you die!" Renee replied.

Lyle shrugged his shoulders. "You go on ahead believin' the man fixin' to help us, Renee. I ain't gonna argue wit you no more."

Another woman, Gracie, slapped him on the shoulder. "For once, Lyle's baitin' got him on the right track!" she stated. "Whatever Inicio's for, that crazy contraption ain't intended to stop no crime. Probably got cameras in it or something like that."

"Girl, you been spending too much time with these conspiracy theorists," Renee replied. "You don't know that's illegal? Government ain't gonna allow that—"

Jack's shoulders began to quake with amusement as the entire group erupted with laughter. He started to turn around but stopped as he noticed the young woman from the bus driving up to him.

She apparently had grown tired of maintaining her deadpan appearance, now smiling warmly as she rolled down her window. "Boniface, right?" she began. "The hall monitor hero."

Jack laughed, using his leftover amusement from the locals to dilute its disingenuous nature. "I guess," he replied. "Don't think I gave my last name, though."

The woman didn't flinch. "You must have, silly," she said. "How else would I have known it?"

"Good point."

"Pretty much all our group was looking for you at the drop-off. You don't like attention much, huh?"

"Nope."

Outwardly, there was a brief silence between them, but inwardly, Bossu filled this otherwise awkward pause with his guttural expression of amusement and a piece of advice.

"Hm hm hm," he began. "She was bound to make her move sooner or later. Be careful with this one, Jack."

*I can handle a pretty face.*

"We both know that is a lie but, regardless, that is not what I meant. I have seen her before."

Jack surmised he must have made a face at Bossu's statement as he noticed the woman's smile waver slightly before restoring itself.

"Soooo," he stated, consciously smiling at her now. "Did they send you to find me or something?"

This time she flinched.

"Who?"

Still wearing his good-humored expression, Jack raised an eyebrow as he stared at her.

"Oh!" she said with a start. The woman laughed in embarrassment as she brushed her braids from her face. "You mean the group."

"Duh."

"No, I was leaving and saw a cute mulatto boy standing by himself at a decommissioned terminal and thought I'd get a closer look. When I realized it was you, I figured a girl might as well introduce herself."

Jack maintained his smile. "You have yet to do so."

The woman hesitated, and Jack could tell that, like him, her demeanor was fake. Though devoid of any hostility, she was not forthright.

"My name is Alyssa."

"Jack," he replied.

"I know."

Jack animatedly pursed his lips together. "And sorry if I got any spit or blood on you last night. Definitely wasn't my finest moment."

"Don't worry about it," she replied. "As long you're all right now."

"I am." Jack nodded at her reassuringly before abruptly speaking again. "Hey, if I ask you something, will you respond honestly?" Alyssa flinched again, this time at the fragmented crack of thunder. "I didn't plan that, by the way."

The woman's face lit up as she succumbed to laughter, having been temporarily disarmed by his youthful candor.

"Ask away, Jack."

"What do you know about me?"

Alyssa's smile cooled as she observed him, obviously considering whether to honor his request.

Looking away, Jack began shaking his head as he sputtered out the lingering amusement through his teeth.

"As Josiah's son," she replied, "and the new host of the Shadow Lwa by right, you are the Shadowman."

He looked back at her, eyes wide with excitement and

interest. "Such a good guess, Alyssa! But I'm not Shadowman yet." Alyssa maintained her smile as he spoke. "Almost there, though."

"Didn't know it was possible to inherit the Lwa but not the title."

"How could you?" Jack asked. "We look around the same age, so I doubt you were around when my dad first turned."

"You may be surprised. Maybe I'm a lot older than I look."

"Ohhh, so you're like a witch or something? Like hundreds of years old and you suck the souls out of people to maintain your beauty? I saw something like that in a video game, but you don't seem the type. Nothing surprises me anymore, though."

"I'm twenty-three."

"Right, so how do you know about title inheritance? You were correct, though—I'm the first inheritor to go through a freaking probationary period before being made official."

Intermittently tapping against her car, Jack saw the raindrops on the windshield before feeling them himself. He saw Alyssa notice them as well and quickly declined the offer he knew was coming. "And, no offense, but I don't want a ride."

Alyssa showed some teeth, her smile widening slightly as she set her eyes back on him. "Why not?" she replied. "Don't trust me?"

"I never trust a pretty face and besides, you still haven't told me how you know so much."

Alyssa pursed her lips together before reverting to her muted smile. "I suppose it can't hurt at this point," she concluded. "As cliché as it sounds, I belong to a secret organization dedicated to protecting New Orleans from any supernatural threats."

"Wow, that is hella cliché."

She continued, ignoring Jack's comment. "This being our

raison d'etre, it is only natural that we serve as an ally to Shadowman."

"How many allies are in this 'organization' that exists to serve me?"

"Are you Shadowman yet?"

Jack caught the chuckle in his throat. "I'm only asking because there's been no supernatural activity out here for almost a decade. Your cohorts must be super dedicated not to have called it quits. I imagine they've gotten pretty bored, not to mention rusty."

Communicating at the speed of thought, Bossu offered words of advice as his host spoke. "Easy, Jack . . ."

*I know what I'm doing.*

"Whoever is left better be ready for what's coming," he said to Alyssa.

Alyssa's humorous expression disappeared, replaced by a subtle wrinkle of displeasure between her eyebrows. "What's coming?"

"I thought you knew," Jack replied. "You were able to determine my whereabouts to the extent of meeting me in Virginia. There must've been a means and purpose behind doing so." He took in the change in her demeanor as it grew increasingly concerned by the second. "I'm confused. You know my dad died, right? This is just the calm before the storm."

"I was merely tasked with assessing your disposition to determine what is to be expected from you as Shadowman. We aren't aware of any imminent danger. I don't know where you are getting this information or if it's some kind of joke—"

"Bossu didn't give me the details, he only expressed urgency toward my being made ready and capable to withstand the forces fixing to be unleashed."

"To be *unleashed*?" Alyssa began, visibly frustrated. "What are you talking about? And who is Bossu?"

Momentarily silent, Jack was taken aback by the extent of her ignorance. Noticing his expression, Alyssa faced forward and began glaring through her windshield.

Jack took his eyes off her and looked toward the sky. The rain had started coming down harder. "Bossu is the name of my Lwa," he replied softly, ensuring his words were free from any sarcasm. "I'm gonna head home now. I suggest you arrange a sit-down with the other members of your organization. What are you guys called, by the way?"

The young woman remained facing forward as she responded. "The Abettors."

Considering Alyssa's change in demeanor, Jack made sure not to laugh. "Right, meet with them and get yourself some answers. We can meet up again if you want but not at my mother's house, please don't go near—" She put the car in drive and finally looked up at him, still angry. "Uh . . . yeah, it shouldn't be much longer until I become official and I'm sure Bossu knows where to find you. Actually, that's better, don't look for me. I'll contact you when I'm"—Alyssa suddenly took off—"ready."

Jack sighed as he watched her taillights through the rain. "Yeah," he said, "she's pissed."

"Of course she is," Bossu stated, "you just exposed gaps in her knowledge."

"Must be a small outfit if my green ass knows things she doesn't."

"Hm hm, small, you have no idea."

"You said you saw her before?"

"She accompanied the imp in trying to gain some information from Josiah just before he became your 'full-time' father."

"Imp?"

"Fortunately, the answer to that inane question will reveal itself in due time. As of this moment, our sole concern remains unchanged. We have to make haste regarding your final transformation."

Jack had intended to continue listening to the locals, but Bossu's statement had brought him back to reality. There really wasn't any time to waste.

"Why?" he asked, stepping into the downpour.

"My brethren have already begun to cross over," the Lwa explained, "and your human allies know your mother's dwelling."

Determining a leisurely stroll to be inappropriate, Jack began jogging through the evening rain. "I figured that."

"Yeah, but without Shadowman's protection, there is no telling how long they have until they are compromised."

Bossu had to routinely ensure that Jack's focus remained on the task at hand but chose not to hold it against him, seeing as it was a consequence of the lad's state of fearlessness.

Jack, on the other hand, was rather peeved by the constant reminders, judging them as proof of his childishness. "Damn," he said, shaking his head in self-directed disappointment, "how do you know?"

"You refer to the crossover?"

"Yeah."

"Well, I can smell the stench of the devourers already," Bossu replied. "You can too, though you probably do not realize it."

Jack took a whiff and while it was not as pronounced due to the sudden rainfall, he immediately knew the stench Bossu was referring to.

Though detected earlier, he had subconsciously dismissed the odorous mix of rotting flesh and sulfur as just another one of the bus terminal's offensive olfactory byproducts. But now, the scent took on a pervasive quality and seemed to hang in the air with no distinguishable source.

He sneered slightly as he ran. "You're right, they reek."

"Get to your mother quickly, then. The only one capable of wiping them from this plane is Shadowman." Bossu sighed, short and abrupt. "Ah, I cannot recall ever experiencing any kind of anticipation prior to a new host taking up the mantle. Certainly nothing like this."

Jack remained silent in the face of the compliment. Similar to when he was first made manifest in the void, he began paying particular attention to his physiology as he progressed to a sprint.

"Jack?"

Though his focus was directed toward the eventual onset of exhaustion, Jack was struck by his swiftness. It had been some time since he had a good run, but he couldn't recall moving *this* fast. Adding to his excitement was the awareness that this wasn't even his limit; he could go faster.

"Fun, eh?" Bossu asked.

"Not gonna lie"—Jack finally replied, exerting his limbs and core with increased intensity—"hell yeah!"

Jack's modest smile spread into a grin as he sprinted in the downpour, the raindrops seeming to explode into beads of mist as he crashed through them. Both his speed and the ferocity of his bodily movements created a figure that was rather unsettling.

Violent even.

Totally enraptured by the experience, Jack took no notice of the periodic onlookers gawking at his superhuman display. Despite the steadily increasing darkness limiting them to only a glimpse, drivers and umbrella-wielding pedestrians alike were left frightened by the sight.

Driven by pure curiosity, some would instinctively accelerate their vehicles to catch up to the thrashing young man, ultimately freezing in disbelief after gazing at their speedometer. This could have caused multiple accidents, for sure. Fortunately, the number of vehicles on the road was few and far between due to the weather.

Had he been aware of the emotional effect he was having on the citizens, Jack would have stopped immediately. Instead, he pushed himself harder, the sense of awe deepening as he did.

*Bossu*, he called silently.

"Jack."

*Is this normal? I mean . . . like a first?*

"Running?"

The unique logo of the bakery with the terrible beignets flashed across Jack's sights, but being so engrossed with the exhilaration, it took a while for him to acknowledge what he had seen. During his original walk to the terminal, he had determined the bakery was near the halfway point, taking over an hour to reach from home. The animated clock on a digital billboard could be seen shining through the rain, revealing the bus from Atlanta that dropped him off no more than fifteen minutes ago. Jack began to question whether the bakery had multiple locations, hesitant to conclude that he was already halfway home.

*You know what I mean*, he thought, responding to Bossu's sarcasm. *I'm super fast, right?*

"I do not think so."

*Well, relatively speaking.*

"Relative to what?" the Lwa asked. "This speed is not even beyond the capability of natural mortals."

Jack struggled to ensure this fact did not dull his enthusiasm and began to thoroughly exert himself. He became keenly aware of his movements. The momentum of every furious swing of his arms had to precisely complement the subsequent extension of his legs. However, finding this optimal rhythm proved elusive seeing as this physiology was so new. Through a series of twitches and pulses resulting from the strain, Jack felt muscles formerly unknown come to life. His core remained flexed, acting as a taut stabilizer to the flurry of limbs accelerating him. Though not yet winded, Jack sensed the strenuous activity finally begin to take a toll, expressing itself as tinges of pain sprinkled throughout his extremities.

The ferocity with which Jack swung his arms turned them into a blur and yet he felt like they were being drawn through molasses. In addition, his sneakers felt as if they would soon crumble off his feet, forcing him to alter his stride to mitigate the discomfort.

Struggling to regain his rhythm, Jack's grin began to degrade. A fascinated Bossu watched as his host's enthusiasm finally took a hit. Repeatedly clenching his jaw during his sprint, Jack's gleeful expression became altered by teeth gritted in anger.

"You really cannot see this is all pointless?" Bossu asked. Jack seemed to receive this statement as a taunt and pushed himself even more. "Jack, stop. Do you not remember what I said to you back at the parking lot?"

*Nah,* Jack silently, angrily replied. *I was too busy having my mind broken.*

"Truly? You have no recollection?"

*No, not truly.* Jack stubbornly continued his efforts, momentarily ignoring Bossu's silence.

Bossu called out to him as if teasing. "Jaaack . . ."

Jack groaned and ceased his sprint, bringing an immediate halt to his movements as he entered the Audubon district. He stopped so abruptly that his clothes snapped forward, violently wicking off drops of water.

The streetlights turned on, newly activated by the waning daylight.

Jack's attention was drawn to several crates arranged haphazardly along the side of a nearby church. He walked over, sat down on one, and began adjusting his newly battered sneakers. Jack ignored the amused glances of those who noticed him sitting under the streetlight, clothes soaked through. *You said when I become Shadowman, my abilities will make this seem like nothing.*

"Although I did say that," Bossu began, "what I sought to impress upon you was your becoming unbroken will turn you into something even greater than a mere Shadowman."

Jack felt a mix of sweat and rain from his brow fall into his eyes, making it hard to see. Curious, he activated his night vision and gasped in surprise. Though the perceived level of illumination was relatively unchanged, the rain no longer distorted his sight.

A new smile crept upon his face. *I kinda remember that part,* he replied, gazing through a vehicle that stopped in his line of sight. *Don't see the harm in letting me enjoy my new pow—*

"Jack Boniface?!" The voice came from the car in front of him.

"Who is this now?" he mumbled, reverting his sight to normal.

Jack stood up to get a better look inside the vehicle and grinned at the driver, who was leaning toward the passenger window.

"J-Jamal?" he said. "No way."

The driver's look of disbelief was replaced by a smile. "Yeah, bruh, it's me. What are you doing sitting in the rain like that?"

"Well . . . I . . . er . . ."

Jamal reached over and opened the door. "Get in, man," he commanded. "You don't gotta explain."

Jack fought the compulsion to hesitate and immediately got in the passenger seat. He felt the wind pushing the door and slammed it shut.

"Can you close it any harder?" Jamal asked as they drove off.

"Oh, sorry." Jack reopened the door and pulled it with force.

Jamal stared at him as he peered at the dashboard to ensure the notifications had been removed. "Is that better?"

"I was kidding."

"Ha-ha, your delivery threw me off. I swear, I didn't detect any sarcasm at all. My bad."

"Don't worry about it," Jamal replied. Jack glanced at the door's handle and noticed a crack had formed where its upper portion connected to the door. He blocked it from view with his knee as the driver continued. "I guess you on your way to see your mom cuz of what happened."

Jack's attention returned to Jamal as he finished his statement. "Wait, what happened?"

"Impeccable," Bossu muttered.

"What?" he asked, noticing Jamal staring again.

"I heard your dad died . . ."

"Oh yeah!" Jack quickly composed himself, removing the inappropriate amusement from his face. "Yes, yes, that's why I'm here."

Jamal looked at him in confusion. "You good, bruh?"

Feigning an emotional struggle, Jack turned toward the window as if on the verge of tears, subjecting Jamal to the resulting period of awkward silence as Bossu teased him once more.

"You are a rascal, Jack."

"Look," Jamal began, "I'm sorry for what I did to you back then. I have been meaning to apologize for a minute but I couldn't face—"

"You don't gotta worry about that, man," Jack interrupted, still looking out the window. "I never really got my ass kicked like that, so I'm better for it to be honest."

"Oh, aight then."

"And I'm *mostly* good, thanks for asking."

His attention was suddenly captured by what looked to be

some newly erected structure on the comparatively less dark horizon. He thought the unlit obelisk was given the illusion of movement thanks to the erratic cascade of raindrops on the window.

Jack was about to disregard this as a mere trick of the eye but felt compelled to activate his supernatural eyesight.

Having done so, the subsequent urge to shout was extinguished through sheer force of will.

With his sight now free of any possible distortions, Jack beheld a gigantic woman dancing in the distance. Despite being so far away, the behemoth stood tall against the purplish-gray horizon. Her height made the city's skyscrapers appear like toys, as they only managed to obscure her legs.

Watching her exuberant performance, Jack was certain he could feel the ground shake with her every leap. He sought objective proof that he was not imagining her and noticed the windshield wipers tremble as they swept back and forth.

*This has gotta be rocking the whole city!* he thought, observing their immediate surroundings.

In sync with the titan's rain dance, the windows of the various buildings and vehicles quivered like boom boxes. The vibrations caused the people's umbrellas to shed the excess rain, subtle mists rhythmically popping off their membranes.

Despite all these physical signs, everyone continued about their business. Some could even be seen eating and drinking in the downpour, totally unfazed by the supernatural occurrence.

Jack turned to Jamal, who was oblivious to what was happening. The man peered at him from the corner of his eye, either sensing the stare or feeling awkward due to the prolonged silence.

Jack quickly began speaking. "Not gonna lie, though, I do feel like I'm losing my mind a bit."

"Yeah, I feel you," Jamal replied. "Even though I never knew my dad, I know what it be like to lose someone you close to outta nowhere. But damn, that was your pops. It's gotta be unreal."

While not wholly ignoring Jamal, Jack reverted his vision to normal. *No way*, he thought. Once more, he contained his surprise as he was left perplexed by the formerly obvious quaking suddenly becoming indiscernible.

*Bossu, do I have to activate my night vision just to sense the supernatural?*

"I told you," the Lwa replied, "as you are now, you are incomplete. You see the herald of the Lwas of Death gyrating in the skyline and you insist on having a friendly chat with some ne'er-do-well from your childhood."

Jack snorted slightly as he gave Jamal his full attention.

"I don't know if he ever told you but I finally met him a while back—"

"My dad?"

"Yeah, bruh, his words made me feel even more like a piece of shit, but he was a good dude. Knew me better than I knew myself, damn near. The fact he didn't tell you makes me respect him even more."

Jack gave a nod of acknowledgment before noticing the familiar houses and establishments of Black Pearl.

Unsure if it was due to his homesickness or the recent revelations of the supernatural threat, Jack felt a heavy burden fall upon him as he gazed through his darkened neighborhood. Faced with Jack's sudden shift to a somber demeanor, Jamal felt obligated to remain silent, suspecting his mention of Josiah to be the cause.

Jack thought back to the horrifying spectacle dancing in the distance. The fact that such a being existed and was planning death and destruction for the inhabitants of New Orleans was unbelievable.

If it were possible, the thought would have filled him with dread.

"How is everyone supposed to be kept safe?" he said aloud, looking down at his hands.

Jamal turned to him, pleasantly surprised at the apparent change of subject. "Bruh, you heard of Inicio?" he asked. "They say it's gonna change the whole shit out here."

Jack turned to him and gave him a halfhearted smile. "Yeah, thieves and murderers are gonna have a hard time I hear."

"I'm saying though," Jamal began, "what else is there?"

Returning his gaze downward, he emitted a short huff of amusement before being made to jump with a start by Jamal.

"Yo!" he said. "How'd your mom know you were already close?" Jack said nothing, finally realizing they had arrived on his street. "Ain't that her on your porch? She's just sitting there in the rain!"

Still silent, Jack absentmindedly pulled at the door, prompting Jamal to pull over.

"I understand, bruh."

Jack managed to utter some words of gratitude before exiting the car. "Thanks, Jamal," he said, keeping his eyes on his mother. "I'll see y—"

"Yeah, you good, Jack. Just go."

Hearing the slam of the car door, Helena looked up from the ground as her son ran around the vehicle. Though her face was wet with rain and the porch light dim, it was obvious she had been crying.

"Jack, stop!" Bossu commanded, but his host was too moved to give him any regard.

"Oh," Helena began, "my boy has come. I knew you would, I just knew today was the day you would come home."

Having run across the lawn, Jack reached his mother and

hugged her before she could descend from the porch. "You were right, Mom. I'm here now. I'm home and I will never leave again."

"Damn it all!" the Lwa exclaimed.

For only a moment, Jack froze due to the uncharacteristic frustration in Bossu's tone. Sensing her son's sudden stillness, Helena knowingly examined his face.

"Oh my God," she began with widened eyes, "I know that look, you have it!"

Jack glanced down at her, saying nothing.

Clutching his shoulders, the woman immediately broke into hysterics. "You leave my boy alone!" she demanded. "Find someone else, he's too young!"

"Jack," Bossu said, his voice rumbling with contained rage, "you have to calm her down. There is no time for this!"

"I know."

"You don't know, Jack!" Helena replied. "That monster is evil, it will consume you! It did the same to your father!"

"Damn it all! Jack, you—"

"Be quiet!" Jack hissed. His mother flinched and fell silent, causing him to immediately revert to his soft demeanor. "No, Mom, not you, never you. I was talking to Bossu."

"What? Who?"

"The monster, Mom." The panic receded from Helena's face as she released her son. "That's his name."

"It has a name?" she asked. "Josiah never—I didn't know . . ."

"Yes, he gave it to me." The woman was apparently stunned by this, encouraging Jack to explain further. "Consider it a symbolic gesture of loyalty, I guess—" He noticed Helena scanning his expression. "What?"

"You're different."

Bossu rumbled in satisfaction. "Ho ho, a mother knows," he said. "You are unbroken now and she can see it."

Jack looked at the woman confidently as he spoke. "I've been through more than you can imagine, Mom." Though initially disturbed, Helena found herself charmed by her son's childlike grin, ultimately mirroring it. "Don't worry, Dad's plan worked! I can do what he couldn't because he made me better than he was. Remember what he said?"

"But you weren't trained in voodoo," Helena replied, more curious than doubting. "We never exposed you to any of it."

"I'm being trained by the best, Dad made sure of it."

His mother's reaction was not at all what Jack expected. The woman directed her surprise toward the floor. The fleeting expression faded as her confused thoughts transitioned to levelheaded considerations. Her eyes swam to and fro, carried by careful deduction. Unbeknownst to her, no matter how implacable her logic, it remained rooted in hasty supposition.

"You found a doctor to train you," she began. "But it's been almost a decade since they've all lost their connection."

Bossu mentally interjected with a chuckle. "Hm hm hm, see how susceptible they are?"

Helena continued, "If they've taken you under their wing, then that must mean the Ghede have reestablished the connection. But why?" She finally looked at her son. "Do you know?"

The Lwa's chuckles became livelier.

"Yeah, Mom, of course," Jack replied. "Only thing is, I meant Bossu. I'm being trained by him."

"What?" she replied with a scoff her son found somewhat condescending.

"Mom, I told you that Dad made sure I'd be trained by the best and that the Lwa is loyal." Jack began smiling again. "What did you think I meant?"

Helena's controlled calm fell away, shifting to a peculiar expression that was both impressed yet subtly fearful. Her pause complemented the sudden suspension of the downpour, the silence deafening.

"It's okay," Jack said, forsaking notice of the strange occurrence in favor of a renewed hug with his mother. "Dad knew what he was doing."

Helena returned the embrace without hesitating. "I . . . I know."

"How touching," Bossu began, "however, remind her that Josiah told her to stay within the confines of the sigil's barrier until I returned. Why did she disobey one in whom she has such confidence?"

Jack groaned as he rolled his eyes, prompting a look of concern from his mother. "What is it, my special boy?"

"Well, uhh . . ."

"No time!"

"Did Dad tell you to stay inside a barrier?"

Helena looked down as one being scolded. "Yes, I know I should have."

"Yet she is outside."

"But today I just had a feeling you'd come. I just couldn't help coming out to see if my instinct was true. Forgive your mother's carelessness. No harm done, right?"

Bossu continued to address his attentive host. "Take note of the rain's ceasing," he said, "and behold the gyrating giantess."

Already surveying their surroundings, Jack activated his night vision midsearch and noticed his house wrapped in a coil of shadow.

Its perfect darkness was clearly defined against the night. The supernatural binding originated just above the door's lintel and wound itself around the building's entirety. Though intrigued, he sought the dancing Lwa after realizing the rumbling had stopped, ultimately doing a double take upon sight of her.

Jack was immediately reminded of his experience with the crows outside his window. The titan stood still, and her head was turned in their direction.

Despite being miles away, Jack intuitively knew she was watching him.

Staring back at the Lwa, the only thing Jack could feel was the newly boiling blood coursing through his veins. As he clenched his teeth to stifle the seething sensation, he noticed some form of shadow within her vicinity.

Remaining motionless, he palpated the Jell-O–like vicinity with his appendage. Unlike his daylight experimenting on campus, the quality of his grasp felt firm due to the darkness. However, the great distance separating them made the search for a secure anchor point elusive.

His resolve untouched, Jack spied a section of shadow along the distant behemoth's neckline. The shade was created by her blooming attire, though it progressively deepened in darkness due to the sun's hasty departure from her location.

Taking aim with the reckless abandon of youthful ambition, Jack felt his appendage obediently ready itself to be cast toward the target.

"What do you think you are doing, whelp?" Bossu asked sharply.

"She knows where my mom lives," Jack replied, "so I'm going to blitz her and end it quick."

The sound of Bossu's joyous laughter erupted in his head. "HA-HA-HA-HA!" Helena noticed the furrow of confusion appear on her son's brow. "So that is how you are!" Bossu said. "Well now, then Fate has given us yet another reason to hasten your transformation as it is impossible for the mortal composition to survive such a forceful catapulting." He cleared his throat of the remaining dregs of inappropriate delight. "Not to mention, what would you do if you happened to make it to her?"

"So what are we—"

"You simply need to take the amulet off the door."

Jack looked at his house and began to approach.

"Amulet?" As he drew near, he got a better look at the barrier's point of origin and noticed a palm-sized medallion gleaming with a supernatural aura.

"Yesss," Bossu began as his host reached for it, his voice humming with anticipation. "This is the sole portion of my essence your father was capable of stealing away to conceal his woman in lieu of his son's return."

"Sole portion?" Jack paused his reaching and, upon further examination, realized the amulet was the binding's terminating point as well; its appearance akin to that of a fastening construct rather than the power source he had thought. "This is your only link to the land of the living," he continued, directing his deductions at Bossu. "That's why you couldn't complete my transformation."

"And why the crows were the extent of my ability to manifest in your realm. Had I not already dwelt in the heir, I would have been incapable of even that."

Jack clutched the amulet as he examined the spectral bindings, and paused to allow his racing mind to appreciate all the implications brought forth by this information.

"But that means this . . . this is . . ."

"Before leaving for his death, Josiah rid himself of my essence in order to protect your mother, simultaneously ensuring your anonymity even after inheriting his Lwa. It was an exceedingly risky plan and marked a high level of confidence toward you."

Judging the emotions rapidly coming to the fore to be

inappropriate, Jack quickly pulled at the amulet. The binding's tensile strength caught him by surprise, making him lurch forward as it resisted his tug.

Immediately enraged, Jack placed his foot on the door for leverage and yanked the amulet with both hands.

The bindings snapped like a rubber band. However, instead of bounding back against the house, one of its free ends ensnared itself around Jack's wrist in the midst of its recoil, like one of those slap bracelets from his childhood. It remained anchored to him as the other end shot backward, undoing the binding.

Jack watched the whiplike unraveling as Bossu excitedly continued his speech. "Son of Marius, son of Julien, son of Maxim, son of Michael, son of Josiah . . . separated we are weak, but together . . . together we are strong." Rather than dismay, the imminent impact of the furiously spiraling strip of shadow filled Jack with wondrous anticipation. "Truly, this is the beginning of their worst nightmare, how delightful!"

As the binding's free end careened into his body, Jack did not feel the tremendous force he was expecting. On the contrary, the collision was soft, absent of any jarring quality. It barely would have been noticeable if not for it sending him directly into the void upon impact.

Standing within, Jack calmly gazed upon his body as the shadow binding attached itself to him. Winding rapidly around his arm like the hand wrappings of a fighter, its pale purple hue progressively rendered his physical form visible against the impossible darkness.

Before he had time to follow its course, it had enveloped his entire body.

Jack flexed his hands as they emitted a confounding darkness that was nevertheless glowing in the pitch-blackness of the void. "This . . . is awesome."

"Now, tell me," Bossu's voice commanded. Jack finally looked up to see his Lwa looming over him. The monster's excitement caused it to appear even more horrifying than Jack remembered. Its eyes, formerly glaring with a red-hot hatred, were now unsettlingly wide with wild expectation. In turn, the malice contained within the permanent gnash on his skeleton face was subtly altered, forming an expression Jack imagined to be similar to his own as the Lwa continued. "Who are you?"

The two entities faced one another as Jack considered the question.

"*We* are Shadowman!"

Jack noticed Bossu's joyful countenance flicker to one he could not decipher. As the Lwa continued to stare, the young host took the opportunity to test out his capabilities, intuiting they had been brought to new heights.

Summoning the appendage, its feedback confirmed it already knew what he was planning. "Don't stop me, Bossu."

Jack focused on the location of the giant in his mind's eye.

His newly acquired spatial awareness was made manifest through the appendage in a manner similar to a program; the visualized location akin to coordinates stored within its function.

Its directives received, the appendage shot out of the void without delay.

"Jack," Bossu began, noticing the aperture created by Jack's sixth sense.

Ignoring his Lwa, Jack proceeded to wield his invisible appendage, latching onto the shadow just beneath the giant's shawl. Its Jell-O–like consistency proved little consequence as the wormhole's terminal end, made manifest in the mortal plane, appeared mere inches from the titan's head.

Intrigued, Bossu watched as his host went on the attack.

Using the shawl's shade as an anchor, Jack sent himself

through the aperture like a slingshot, emerging airborne right in front of the female Lwa's face.

Already poised to strike with a cocked fist, the superpowered youth found himself holding back laughter. The attempt to focus on the relative speck careening toward her face made the titan momentarily cross-eyed.

Jack swung his fist forward as her eyes widened with recognition. Unsure of the opposing force that would result from a blow to a target of such mass, his body was primed with expectation.

Jack was surprised that, though his strike had followed through, he hit nothing.

The titan had vanished, leaving him immersed in what appeared to be the dew of a dense cloud formation. Jack's amusement was quickly replaced with anger.

"She ran away?" he said with an uncharacteristic growl. "The coward seemed to be enjoying herself not too long ago."

Bossu began chuckling. "Impressive, whelp, very impressive."

"Yeah, thanks." Jack examined his situation, acutely aware of the speed at which he approached the ground. "Can I survive this?"

"Doubtful."

"Damn."

"What are you going to do?"

Jack heard Bossu's statement but became distracted by his appearance.

His long-sleeved shirt was gone, seemingly replaced by a thin membrane, its features identical to the unforgettable black of the apparition he witnessed at Carmen's dorm.

Pinching it between his fingers, he noticed his hands. His skin tone, colloquially referred to as redbone, was no longer visible. His hands had the same perfect dark as his arm, and Jack knew he was gloveless.

*This isn't covering my skin*, he thought. *It is my skin!*

*"Not exactly," Bossu said.*

Jack suddenly sensed an unusual draft at his nether regions, prompting him to look over his entire body. He was naked.

"Where are my clothes?!" he screamed.

"Ground incoming."

Jack could see the former specks of the city lights and people on the ground below had grown significantly in size. "I can't be seen like this . . . I gotta hide."

"Hm hm hm, for your sake or theirs?"

Annoyed by Bossu's apparent disinterest, he sent his appendage into the void and began clutching him with it.

"Oh?"

"Will you sh—" Jack's command for silence was cut off as he suddenly remembered the most easily accessible route of escape.

Yanking himself to his Lwa, he laughed while appearing in the void instantaneously.

Bossu's eyes returned to their default glare as he looked down on his newly appeared host. "How resourceful of you."

"Where are my clothes?" Jack asked, smiling. "Shadowman has to prance around like this?"

"Do not be stupid," Bossu replied. "You are the only one to immediately engage in battle upon first transformation as if there is no need to learn the intricacies of your ability." Jack was certain he saw the Lwa subtly shake its head before continuing. "Your clothes are here in the void."

Jack's night vision was already active as he looked around the pitch-blackness in an animated fashion. "I still can't see anything in here."

"Do you remember the crows?"

"Yeah, of course."

"Where were they?"

Jack began to repeat the question while thinking about it. "Where . . . ?" He scoffed as he came to understand. "You don't have to make it so profound."

"Silence," Bossu said sternly. "What was it you told your mother?" Unsure as to what the Lwa was referring to, but certain the question was rhetorical, Jack gave an impatient shrug. "Ah yes, trained by the best, this is a true statement. As the trainer, it is inevitable that I know both the things that you seek as well as the things you are too ignorant to seek. Therefore, your opinion matters not."

"Fine."

Jack went about retrieving his belongings from the void. Visualizing the clothing, he felt about them in the same manner as the crows and found himself pleasantly surprised by an unexpected change.

During Jack's first act of conjuring within the void, the materialization of the imagery seemed to rely more on his appendage's palpations than mental visualization. Now, however, the process seemed to be reversed, as if summoning the image with mostly his thoughts.

While still able to sense them, his mind's eye immediately lost sight of the clothes upon their materialization. Identifying his lightly tapered cargo pants, Jack began putting them on.

"Meh, I don't need a shirt."

Throwing it aside, Jack noticed that his sneakers were now enveloped in a membranous shadow, repairing the wear and tear caused by his furious sprint. "This is so clutch!"

"Explain."

"As in useful," Jack replied. "I can store stuff in here, right?"

"Yes," Bossu said, letting out a gravelly sigh. "Seeing that you remain susceptible to such trivial distractions, it is evident that I remain obligated to keep you fixed on the task at hand."

Jack's childish enthusiasm fell from his face. "Mom."

Harnessing his supernatural spatial awareness, he visualized his former location at his mother's house, reflexively sensing for any shadows to serve as a means for entry.

Jack marveled at the profound change night's arrival had on the consistency of the darkness. No longer jelly, it felt like wet cement that would immediately harden upon contact. Gently this time, he reeled himself in with the appendage, drawing himself out of the void and toward the anchor point of stabilized shadow.

Recognizing the wormhole's terminal point as the side of his house, Jack emerged from the darkness as one exits a door. He spied his mother exactly where he left her, standing in the faint glow of the porch light.

She stared at the house in calm consideration, unsure as to the reason for her son's sudden disappearance.

Cautiously, Jack scanned the vicinity with his night vision while simultaneously checking for any potential unseen onlookers with his sixth sense. "Hey, Mom."

Helena turned toward the darkened area of her property. "Jack!" she said, hurrying toward the voice. "Where did—"

The woman froze as her son emerged from the shadows, visibly stunned by the change in his appearance.

"What's wrong?" Jack replied. "Oh."

"It's okay, boy." Helena continued her approach. "I'm used to that ugly mug by now."

"That bad, huh?"

"Boy, you ugly as can be with that face." She began examining his outer garments, smiling as she did it. "This is how seriously the new protector of the Liveside takes his role, huh?"

Jack was busy feeling about his face, suddenly noticing it did not feel like his own. "Stop, Mom," he said, almost whining. "What is this thing? Some kind of mask?"

He began tugging at it to no avail and looked at his mother. "You got a mirror on you?"

Helena cupped her hand over her mouth. "Inside, boy," she replied. "You know where it is."

Jack made his way to the bathroom sink and looked in the mirror. "Gross, Bossu!" he said. "I look like you."

Covering the entirety of his face was what appeared to be the front of a skull, pure white in color. While the eye sockets and nasal bone seemed mostly human, its mouth was wholly abnormal. The line of commissure that marked the separation of his lips did not end at the corners of his mouth but instead extended down to his chin before ascending along the sides of his face, their path ultimately terminating at the cheekbones. Jack opened his mouth wide and noticed that, while his true lips retained their position during parting, the extensions formed by the abnormal commissure remained, creating what appeared to be fangs whenever he opened his mouth. Thumbing the pointed ends, he was surprised by their sharpness and began plucking the rest of the mask, left speechless by its stonelike hardness.

"Have you finished?" Bossu asked. "We must be going."

Jack withdrew from the mirror. "Yeah, I'm done," he replied. "Where are we headed?"

"It is time to pay a visit to the baron." Jack felt his body become electrified with anticipation. "So this excites you?"

"It does."

"Hm hm, be advised this will serve as an opportunity to both test your ability and to formally announce our return."

"I'm ready, man. Let's go!"

"And leave your mother without protection?"

"But what about—" Jack recalled what happened to the protective barrier previously established. "Oh, I guess the original one is gone, huh?"

"Get outside."

Jack complied without back talk, hurrying past Helena, who silently turned to follow.

"Instruct her to not exit the doorway until you return."

"O-ok." He turned back toward his mother and moved in for a hug. "Mom, please don't leave here until I get back."

She nodded. "You can do this, my special boy. I know you're not scared, which can be a disadvantage, believe it or not. Just please, don't be careless."

Heading out, Jack gave her a stiff nod and closed the door behind him.

"Return the amulet," Bossu began, his voice emanating a mix of anticipation and urgency. "At this point in time, the best we can do is a beacon."

Jack retrieved the amulet from the ground and immediately felt his appendage begin to resonate in response as he examined it. "Best?"

"Its area of effect is far greater than the barrier of protection Josiah established with the last of his power, but it is far less durable."

"That sucks," Jack hissed. "But you called it a beacon, so I will be notified or whatever if it is activated, correct?"

"Precisely, now bind it to the lintel."

The young host quickly scanned the door, looking for something to tie it with. Seeing nothing, he stood still, having no idea what to do next. He addressed Bossu, growing more impatient by the second. "Am I waiting for something or what?"

"Are you?" Bossu replied. "I provided you with the first step and the overall objective. Besides, what more do you want?" Jack began muttering profanities through clenched teeth. "Just proceed with what you know."

"I don't know anything!"

"While this is mostly true, the little you do know has the potential to shed light on many of the things you do not."

Jack closed his eyes and began breathing through the frustration. *What do I know?* he thought. *The only thing I know is the appendage.* He brandished it aimlessly in the air, still perplexed.

Achieving a state of calm, he looked down at the amulet in his hands. Amidst its whipping and weaving, his appendage vibrated with a faint buzz of recognition.

Jack's face livened with understanding. *So you know this thing, huh?*

He instinctively sent forth his spectral arm, which, to his surprise, was able to physically clutch the amulet. Operating in a manner never seen before, the appendage took the amulet from his hand.

Intrigued, Jack held it in the air. "This is telekinesis," he said. "So my appendage *can* physically manipulate things."

Still slightly grumpy, Bossu hummed approvingly. "To a certain degree, but in the Liveside, it is limited."

"Limited?"

"By requirements, one such example is affinity. The amulet shares it with your sixth sense, hence, its interactions."

"Compatibility. Got it." Jack moved the amulet toward the lintel. "And in the Deadside?"

"Hm hm, the limitations are far less."

Jack grinned mischievously upon hearing this and pressed the floating amulet against his house. Resolving to figure it out for himself, he considered the task at hand. *A beacon*, he thought, repeatedly tightening the appendage's hold around the now-resonating artifact, *to alert me of trespassers*. The amulet trembled forcefully within his invisible grip before releasing a curtain of dark upon the door.

Momentarily pleased with himself, Jack watched as it

unrolled itself from top to bottom before the amulet ceased its movements and became still.

Realizing the amulet thought its job complete, Jack's expression turned to dissatisfaction. *No!* he commanded, his jolting the amulet back to life. *Not just a beacon . . . a barrier as well.*

Aided by the appendage, the amulet repurposed the shadow curtain, causing it to expand across the house.

*Nope, bigger.* The curtain-turned-shroud ballooned off the house, appearing as a dome covering it. *Bigger.* Jack felt slightly winded as the barrier expanded in response, now containing the entirety of the property and a bit of the sidewalk.

The amulet positioned itself a few feet above the front door before becoming still again.

"This is sufficient," Bossu said. "Let us be going."

Jack stepped back and surveyed the entirety of what he had done, bursting with pride. *How do we get there?*

"As you have never done it before, you must first come to me in the—"

Jack vanished as he excitedly yanked himself into the void.

# CHAPTER 10

An uncharacteristically flustered L'Orage loomed over the Manse Ghede, the otherwise imposing structure barely reaching the anklets she wore. Due to her hasty departure from the Liveside, she retained her true size, far too massive to fit in any abode but her own. Listless hordes of the realm's denizens redirected the path of their roaming around the behemoth, like tiny ants continuing their march around an obstruction.

L'Orage had been regaining her composure in order to transform to an appropriate size. However, before she could begin, Baron Samedi appeared without warning.

Seeing the glint of his spectacles, the woman quickly fell to her knees, rocking the landscape and crashing upon the already ill-fated souls wandering below her, their bodies were immediately obliterated, exploding into putrid chunks of undead flesh and fluid. The remaining hordes promptly fled in terror.

The unflinching Ghede lord followed L'Orage's change in position with his head before securing his hat against the resulting shock wave from her genuflection.

"Apologies, my lord," she began. "I—"

"No apologies necessary, dear girl," the baron replied, his tone absent of any displeasure. "I came with haste only out of concern for you. To put it mildly, you seem out of sorts." He paused to further assess her condition. "Did something happen?"

L'Orage lifted her gaze from her feet and set it upon her master. "Shadowman attacked me."

The baron appeared to have no reaction, not moving at all upon hearing her reply. Confused by this, the titan mustered the courage to speak but was interrupted as the skeleton god succumbed to a fit of laughter.

"So you have brought two pieces of good news!" he said, speaking between the cackles.

"My lord?"

"Little L'Orage, don't you see? Not only have you found him, but your tidings also reveal that he is a rambunctious little bugger!"

L'Orage's eyes returned to her feet. "Oh," she replied, smiling weakly. "I see."

The entrance to the Manse opened as Brigitte emerged. Her face bore a mix of amusement and concern as she took in the sight. Her husband continued laughing as she drew near them.

"Why is he laughing like this, L'Orage?"

"I am not exactly sure, my queen, but I just informed him I was attacked by Shadowman."

"What?" Brigitte stated angrily. "How? Tell me what happened."

The baron stopped cackling. "Wait!" he commanded, halting L'Orage. "All you Ghede, appear before me at once!"

Apparently sensing the urgency within the decree, the beckoned subordinates immediately began appearing, one after the other.

Nibo stumbled through his smoke, visibly concerned about

the cause of their summoning. His cohorts expressed similar sentiments as they glanced about each other upon manifesting.

"What happened?" he asked.

The baron motioned to L'Orage. "Speak."

"I found Shadowman." Hearing this, the assembled Lwa shared glances of relief before the titan continued her statement. "And he attacked me."

After the mingled sounds of indignation and stifled amusement had finished, Papa was the first to speak. "I fear I do not understand," he began. "How did this happen? He was able to keep himself hidden to facilitate a surprise attack?"

The baron, along with all the rest, turned toward their gigantic cohort, eagerly waiting for her to detail the sequence of events. Seeing this, she withdrew from her kneeling and stood up.

"No need to downsize, little girl," the baron stated. "Only tell us what transpired."

"Thank you," the titan replied, her voice now booming to reach her tiny cohorts on the ground below. "Regarding Papa's question, I sincerely doubt the sequence of events was the result of deliberate acts of cunning. Having considered it at length, I believe everything that unfolded did so due to mere chance."

"For some reason," Ossou slurred, "that seems even *more* difficult to believe."

"This finna be good," Criminel muttered.

"Precisely," L'Orage continued, directing her response at Ossou. "I struggled with that as well. However, my claim is based on the fact that I was able to identify the heir due to an oversight on his part. He had yet to become Shadowman at that time."

"You lost me, sis," Masaka said. "This was prior to now? When did he attack?"

"The time between my seeing him and the attack was but moments."

"And he had yet to become Shadowman at that time?"

"I witnessed the transformation ritual," L'Orage replied, "or rather, its beginning."

Criminel appeared incredulous. "How can you be sure?"

"He was but a mortal youth prior to being consumed by shadow. My sights remained fixed to his position as I waited for him to reappear and that's when he attacked."

"I must echo the words of my brother," Babaco began, "and admit I still do not understand. The heir was obviously unable to see you standing in his midst prior to his transformation." Despite the woman shaking her head, he continued. "And yet, in mere moments, his nescience notwithstanding, became so emboldened as to attack you?"

Nibo gave a shrug of acceptance. "Seeing as Bruh Koblamin tends to bless his hosts with his fearless nature, it makes sense."

Babaco acknowledged the statement with a nod before turning to his brother. "That is true."

Despite her stature, L'Orage felt slighted as she watched her cohorts treat her testimony as discretionary, choosing instead to entertain themselves with baseless conjecture.

The baron did not command them to silence, choosing instead to address the visibly offended titan. His voice was calm and matter-of-fact as he spoke through the banter of his subordinates. "Prior to his transformation, was he indeed unable to see you?"

"No, my lord," she replied. Hearing this, the assembly of Ghede Lwa returned their attention to L'Orage. "My suspicion is that I actually came under his notice long before he inadvertently revealed himself to me." Raising his ivory-colored hand, the baron suppressed the banter they seemed all too ready to resume. "I say this because immediately after the blunder, he deliberately turned and locked eyes with me."

"And just like that," the baron began, "we are given insight on the heir that all of you lot's premature ruminations would have undoubtedly deprived us of." He returned his attention to L'Orage, the woman now enjoying the vindication granted her. "Now tell us, upon your meeting of the eyes, how far away was he?"

"No less than twenty-five furlongs, my lord."

"What?!" Nibo's disbelief eclipsed his ever-present insouciance, giving way to a tone bordering on protest. "How did he manage to attack then?"

Unlike her subordinates, Brigitte maintained a calm disposition despite her piqued curiosity. "I can't imagine the fledgling host was capable of engaging you at that distance."

The assembly collectively turned toward their master as he cackled once more before L'Orage could respond. They glanced among themselves in confusion while L'Orage seemed to be the only one who was deriving any enjoyment from the display.

Having had his fill, the baron finally began to speak. "Bossu Koblamin has befriended the heir," he announced, the green of his eyes growing brighter as he spoke. "How *exciting*."

L'Orage suddenly turned around, casting her gaze across the distant landscape.

Brigitte scoffed. "But he hates everyone."

"Apparently this newest bugger is the exception."

"But why?"

Deferring his response, the baron knowingly gazed at the female titan just before she let out a gasp of surprise, her back still turned toward them.

"What now?" Nibo asked.

L'Orage quickly faced them. Her locs continued whipping to and fro in front of her grimacing face.

Masaka swung his shovel upward, resting it upon his shoulder. "Don't tell me . . ."

The wrinkling on her forehead more akin to astonishment than anything else, L'Orage set her eyes on her master as she spoke. "He's here."

"*They* are here," the baron replied before turning to his wife. "As to why this bugger is the exception, we will soon discover."

His eyes grew even brighter, and though he was facing Brigitte, it was clear she was not the focus of his gaze.

"What do you see?" she asked.

He hummed to himself. "This one," he began, "is different."

"Master?"

"A lion's whelp indeed, I see why Bruh Bossu took to him so." A raspy tittering began to leak through his grin. "The kid is trying to get our attention."

"How?"

The seemingly entranced skeleton refused to turn his head from his wife, thoroughly intrigued by whatever he was witnessing. "With violence."

Hearing this, Papa crushed the apple he had been eating with his hand, causing it to explode with a loud pop. "He dares do such a thing?"

"It is all right," the baron said, his bony hand lazily beckoning for calm. "He will be taught the formalities soon enough." He hummed once more. "Having the time of his life he is, therefore let us be good hosts and allow him a warm welcome." His eyes came to a calm as he addressed Brigitte. "In the meantime, dear wife, inform my brethren that I request their attendance."

# CHAPTER 11

Using the void as an interdimensional hub, Bossu expounded on how the Deadside could be reached, requiring a description of the void's nature and how it differed from the realm of the dead.

Despite all the concepts and instruction being presented in the abstract, while his sole medium of application was mostly physical, Jack discerned the manner best suited for his sixth sense to accomplish the task. Standing in front of the aperture he formed within the void, he calmly peered into the newly accessible underworld.

Relative to the perfect darkness of Bossu's abode, the otherwise gloomy Deadside appeared bright. Its light entered the aperture but was only able to penetrate the short distance to where Jack stood. "I bet I got the hang of this better than anyone else, right?"

"Such a wager would indeed profit," Bossu replied.

Without moving a muscle, Jack began closing and opening the aperture repeatedly, steadily increasing speed as he did it.

"All that talk about the different realms and how only my world and the Deadside are parallels of one another. And how the void is a pocket dimension somehow existing between all the realms." Like the shutter of a camera, Jack had been manipulating the aperture with such rapidity that it caused the light from the Deadside to flicker within.

"You fancy yourself an idol now?" Bossu asked.

Jack blurted out a chuckle, causing the flickering light to momentarily lose its rhythm. "What?" he said. "I would never condone idol worship."

"No, I mean to say, the ones your era calls celebrities."

"Where are you getting this stuff from, Bossu?"

"It is mere coincidence that your manipulation is creating an effect identical to the countless flashes that dance about them?"

"*Cameras?*" Jack began smirking, maintaining the furiously blinking aperture as he looked about his vicinity. "I see what you mean, but yeah, it's just a coincidence."

"Sure it is."

"What I was getting at was that you could've just said it's like pulling apart two sheets of paper."

Bossu scoffed. "Even you would think it strange if I said something like that."

Jack stopped the flicker, holding the aperture open. "True."

"I cannot overstate how fortunate you are to interpret your shadow sense in the way that you do. It makes things far simpler than they should be. It is almost unfair."

"Ha-ha." The young host was filled with confidence as he walked through the aperture and sealed it behind him. The rapidity of its closing created a small suction at his back. "You mean for my predecessors, right?"

"No."

Jack observed his new environment with an enthusiasm incongruous with the grim nature of the scenery. He breathed deeply in an attempt to reel in his excitement, deeming it somewhat inappropriate.

"Too chilly for you, whelp?"

Only upon hearing his Lwa's taunt did Jack notice the strangeness of the air filling his enchanted lungs with every breath. Though its quality could be expressed as a notable absence of warmth, the sense of cold was not necessarily the kind mitigated by excess clothing.

"It's not chilly," Jack replied, "more lifeless than anything else. Kinda like a corpse."

"Indeed it is."

Jack sniffed the air with delicately drawn breaths. "Smells like one too," he said before coughing into his arm. "This is the same stink from earlier at the terminal." He coughed again, more forcefully. "But without impediment."

The point of his emergence being atop the collapsed remains of some dilapidated structure, he was granted a fairly wide view of his immediate surroundings. His attention was captured by several denizens quarreling among themselves on the ground close by. The snarls and grunts by which they communicated were phlegmy and labored. The intense stomach-churning nature of these sounds was surpassed only by their owners' appearance.

*Damn*, he said silently, addressing Bossu, *and I thought you were hideous.*

"My feelings are hurt."

While it was true that Jack found him to be grotesque, at least the Lwa was *somewhat* humanoid; these monsters were not.

The most animated of the group nearest to him was mostly reptilian in appearance. Its skin seemed to be in the process of shedding. Various areas on its body contained dry sloughs curled back and out. The head, however, held countless eyes that were arranged atop its crown rather than fixed within its face.

Jack cringed at the sight. "This one's like that frog that carries eggs and tadpoles on its back." He began snapping his fingers, summoning recollection. "I forget its name."

"*Cryptobatrachus*," Bossu stated.

"Yeah!" Jack abandoned his brief enthusiasm. "Damn, Bossu, you would've been clutch during exams."

The phlegmy clicking of another monstrosity returned Jack to the task at hand. Just as repulsive as its cohort, this one-eyed fiend had four horns jutting from its head. Two from the top and two from the back, their roots formed various sections of skull. The top two met at the forehead and enclosed the monster's solitary giant yellow eye within a cleft of bone, while the remaining two extended from the rear occipital. Despite all this, the monster's brain could be seen couched within their midst, the horns' roots failing to spread over the exposed crown.

Though repulsed, Jack moved closer to get a better view and began to see more of the realm's wretched minions. They flocked together in various clusters, reminiscent of the locals at the bus stop back home.

He inadvertently dislodged some rubble as he leaned forward, causing debris to tumble down toward the monsters directly beneath him.

The clattering sound got their attention, and the creatures turned from their squabble to trace its cause. Jack readied himself as the creatures finally noticed him positioned above them, but, to his surprise, they continued their bickering.

"What happened?" Jack asked. "I know they saw me."

"So?" Bossu replied. "They do not sense you as human and, since seemingly of their ilk, have no reason to seek a quarrel with you."

"So, it's like a human walking past a group of humans—"

"Rather than a giant cockroach passing them."

"Humans will still attack their own, though."

"This is true, however, the difference lies in the fact that these ones are participants in eternal torture. As such, they no longer retain the sentiments motivating such behavior. Their pride has been utterly stamped out, in other words—"

"They have nothing to prove," Jack said. "Literally." He turned away from them, recommencing his surveillance of the landscape. "Best to leave them be. I kinda feel bad for them."

"That will change," Bossu replied.

Jack found himself morbidly captivated by his surroundings. Though the majority of the Deadside seemed to be in a state of perpetual darkness, scanning the horizon, Jack spied several sectors that seemed to carry the light of day despite there being no visible sun.

"How can you be so sure?" he said. His sights left the horizon as he began peering about the land closer to his own vicinity. "Might change, might not."

He could almost see Bossu shaking his head as he gave his reply. "As you wish."

Jack paused his observations as a sense of familiarity gradually began to assert itself, causing him to stare ahead, stunned. "I know this place."

"Oh?"

"Yeah," he replied confidently, "the structures aren't the same, and the landmasses and rock formations are obviously different, but I know this place."

Intuitively, his eyes moved toward one of the larger buildings in his proximity, its details overlooked during his initial sweep. Climbing to a higher vantage point, Jack could observe its shape—an absurdly impractical tomb-like coliseum.

Jack gestured toward it, pointing his finger with a calm recognition. "That's Caesars Superdome." Jack maintained his position as his eyes darted about the area, quickly identifying several other landmarks based on their Deadside equivalents. "So this really is just a dead version of the real world."

"Deadside. Liveside. Do you get it?"

Jack did a double take as he scanned across a new section of the landscape, the subtle movements of some structure in the distance catching his eye. Unfortunately, while the mound on which he stood was elevated, it was far from the largest thing around.

Whatever caught his eye was positioned so that it was obscured by the abnormally shaped constructions arranged before it, which also ascended against the horizon. Watching his footing, Jack shifted for a better view.

Jack held his breath as if taking aim between the towering obstructions until, finally, he saw all he needed to see.

He began clenching his teeth. "That's the giant from before," he said.

"Indeed," Bossu replied. "I recommend you not repeat what you did earlier."

Jack steadied the already tensed appendage. "And instead?"

"Too ambitious for stealth, are—"

The Lwa was cut off by his host's sudden bellows. "Hey, you!"

Jack remained still as his echo was carried outward, momentarily reverberating against the collection of nearby landmasses and buildings, only to die out long before reaching the imposing edifices of the background.

Undeterred, Jack cupped his hands around his mouth and took a deep breath, ignoring the looks of confusion coming from the various monstrosities surrounding his position.

"HEEEEYYY!!!"

His voice was louder this time but, again, it fell far short of the intended target.

"Unfortunately," Bossu began with a chuckle, "that will not work."

Ignoring the comment, Jack scanned the vicinity in an aggravated search for a solution. He had been unknowingly baring his teeth, releasing his mounting frustration through a sustained and guttural growl.

Of all the denizens available for him to have locked eyes with, Jack managed to do it with the monster that possessed only one. For a moment, he felt confused by the creature's steadily increasing hostility.

"You are aware it interprets your glare as a challenge, correct?"

"I'm not glar—" Jack stopped his response to Bossu, finally becoming aware of his countenance. Unfazed, he maintained eye contact and began glaring all the more, his aggression subsiding only to allow a fleeting grin of excitement.

"Oh?" Bossu began. "You think you can take them on?"

"I don't know . . ."

Though Jack had already come to appreciate his general state of fearlessness, as he sized up his opponents, he was struck by the more subtle changes evoked by its presence.

"You may not know," Bossu replied, "nor do I expect you to. However, I am asking. What do you think?"

Though lacking a counterpart to accentuate the sentiment, the eye of the provoked monster had contorted itself into a look of seething contempt. Spread thin with its corners ascending to the crown of its head, the eye was consequently bent into a downward curve, creating a truly startling expression.

Jack, however, was unable to be swayed by fear one way or the other. He found himself able to assess the situation accurately, his judgment tainted by neither pride nor doubt. He watched as the offended monstrosity began its advance toward him, its slow snarling becoming a disjointed series of threatening clicks.

"I think I can take them," he finally replied.

Bossu hummed in anticipation. "We shall see."

As if prompted by the Lwa's statement, the cyclops suddenly took off, bounding up the mound toward Jack.

Uncomfortable with the rubble's unsure footing, Jack leaped from his position.

The monster halted its advance rather quickly, watching its inexperienced opponent soar overhead before angrily snapping its teeth at him. Jack was forced to awkwardly keep his sights on the creature while airborne, but it was behind him upon landing.

"A somersault would have been more suitable," Bossu said. "The manner of your vault has put you in a disadvantageous position."

Being mindful of the enemy at his back, Jack quickly scanned the demonic audience to his front and found himself pleasantly surprised at the varied personalities displayed on their otherwise hideous visages.

Although aggression was the overwhelming sentiment, some looked confused and intrigued, while others seemed rather disinterested.

Jack quickly peered over his shoulder to see the cyclops sprinting in for a sneak attack. While he had been alerted by the sound of the monster's movement, Jack was delighted at the additional information communicated by his sixth sense, enabling him to perceive what his limited peripheral vision could not.

*It's just like the security guards at the parking lot!* he said silently.

Bossu chuckled as his host faced forward in a bold attempt to test the appendage's precision. "Your timing is impeccable, Jack."

Jack discerned the cyclops winding up its hand in a very human way, preparing to strike. Before he could lament his negligence in determining the physical properties of its hands prior to now, the appendage dutifully transmitted the information in thorough detail.

*Long and thin*—he thought, listing his perceptions to himself—*bulbous at the tips, clenching for attack.* He perceived the amphibious fist as it was sent toward the back of his head and weaved to the side. *Nice.*

Jack threw up his hands as the cyclops stumbled past him, and though filled with confidence, he felt slightly self-conscious as his Lwa began making fun of him.

"*That* is your stance?"

The young host could not help but smile as the monster quickly recovered and attacked again. "It's fine!" he replied aloud.

The communication of his sixth sense fell to the back of Jack's mind as he realized the attacks were easy to read just from sight and instinct alone. He evaded its flurry of punches with ease, alternating between head tilts and footwork based on the trajectory of each attack.

*I'm testing out how fast I've become*, he began, answering a question that he sensed Bossu was about to ask. *Might as well do it now.*

The Lwa replied quickly to his host's preemptive statement. "Just keep in mind that you have an audience." Jack turned his head for less than a second, only to see his onlookers relatively unchanged in both position and demeanor. "And watch that kick."

*What k—*

*WHAM!*

Taking advantage of Jack's momentary distraction, the cyclops took the opportunity to extend a swift kick to his face.

"Hm hm hm."

Jack slipped back to create some distance from the monster

and could hear Bossu's chuckling in his head. But before he could get offended, he froze in awe at how utterly painless the attack was.

*Am I injured? I didn't feel a thing!*

Exhilarated with this newfound resilience, Jack began grinning at the growling demon. "This freak is so pissed!"

After saying this, he reached forward with his arm and began flexing the four fingers of his hand, palm side up.

"Eh?" Bossu voiced. "This beckoning gesture—it is a form of mockery portrayed in your movies, yes?"

*Video games too*, the young host replied, still flexing his fingers. *Not sure if it works on monsters, though.*

"You are not taking this seriously, whelp."

*I am.* Jack watched as the cyclops threw back its head and released a scream of outrage before lunging at him. *It worked! Don't get mad but I want to gauge how strong these guys are.*

With the monster now upon him, Jack began blocking its attacks to establish a baseline of strength. His arms and hands shifted around his body, effortlessly moving to intercept the incoming blows in the most suitable positions.

*Bossu,* he began, *I barely feel a thing!*

"Oh?"

*Yeah, it's not even close to painful.* Jack's eyes darted about as he fended off the monster. *But the freak is slow too. I can see and predict its attacks without even using the appendage.*

"Yes, yes," Bossu said with a sigh, "just keep in mind that these are the bottom-feeders. There are mere mortals capable of besting them."

Jack dropped his guard, allowing the cyclops to strike freely. He received the blows with little acknowledgment while trying to estimate how much more power would be required for the pain to set in.

Seeing another opportunity, the cyclops suddenly crouched before rocketing an uppercut toward Jack's crotch.

Jack abandoned his ponderings and caught its fist, glancing down. "Whoa, nice try," he blurted. "And before your sneaky ass tries anything else . . . mmph!"

Anticipating another attack, he threw a right hook to the side of the demon's head. Tumbling toward its fellows, the force of the blow sent the cyclops sliding across the ground, several of its horns helping to bring it to a stop before breaking off.

"Oh my . . . goodness!!"

Impressed by the distance, Jack had begun cheering for himself, absentmindedly showboating in view of his inhuman spectators. He paused upon noticing them anew. Whatever variation existed within their expressions was gone now.

It was clear the mood had collectively shifted to one of hostility.

*Uh oh*, he thought. *Is hard mode about to start?*

Jack threaded his immediate vicinity with his sixth sense, reaching only the denizens closest to him. Receiving the consequent sensory transmission, he took a deep breath to restrain his deepening excitement. *This whole region is pretty much covered in darkness.*

"Took you long enough," Bossu replied. "Even without access to your memories, it is evident that physical combat is not something that you are used to." His host remained silent as he continued secretly gathering information on the surrounding monstrosities. "Your inexperience notwithstanding, the inherent darkness of the Deadside gives a distinct advantage to any Shadowman, but to you in particular."

Bossu watched as Jack intuitively engaged the appendage in a new manner, and while unsure if his host was addressing him or merely muttering to himself, the Lwa listened all the same.

"It's like those elastic sticky-hand toys from back in the day," Jack said with a blank stare.

"I recall informing you that its elasticity seemed limitless."

Without moving, Jack continued swinging the appendage. With his body at the center, the unseen tentacle spun in a giant circle throughout the space. "Yeah," he replied with a soft grunt, "I know that, but your observation about the tentacle being like a fasces . . ."

Responding to the force in which it was wielded, the tentacle began spreading laterally. Similarly, its distant end increased its outward extension, stretching further the faster Jack swung it. ". . . you know what radar is?"

Bossu let out a chuckle tinged with condescension. "What of it?"

"When I swing the appendage like how it's depicted in the movies, on the little monitors, the rods of the fasces separate a bit—"

"Like a sheet."

"Exactly!" Jack replied. "And I can perceive whatever that sheet covers."

"Your shadow sense."

Jack did not respond, choosing instead to marvel at the intricate detail the appendage provided. Not only was he capable of numbering every individual within the area, but he could also discern their physical characteristics, even their diversely grotesque faces.

Though Jack understood they were preparing to attack, the threat did not faze him at all. On the contrary, whether it was due to a lust for combat or an intense curiosity to experience what he was capable of, every fiber of his being longed for what was coming.

He moved to beckon them as he had the still-sprawled

cyclops, but before he was able to move his hand, they began to charge.

While simultaneously perceiving a collection of the horde moving into position at his back, Jack realized that he could not remain still.

*Bottom-feeders or not, they've got numbers on their side.*

Identifying the first monster to reach him as the reptilian one with shedding skin, he sidestepped its attack and quickly slammed the back of his fist into the top of its head, bursting asunder many of its eyes.

Jack weaved with a rhythm that was disjointed and erratic, partially to avoid the disgusting fluid that erupted from his victim's head, but mostly to remain unpredictable.

*I can see them all.*

The crowd of monsters attempted to descend upon him but their efforts were thwarted as he reflexively danced out of reach, causing those in the front to stumble over the corpse of their downed comrade.

*Am I wrong for finding this amus—Huh?*

Jack's visible snickering was cut short by his detection of yet another monster lunging at his back. Canceling the reflex to evade, he stalled for less than a second, allowing the attacker's momentum to bring it to the point in which a collision would be most devastating.

Bossu suddenly cheered with morbid delight as the creature's face was obliterated by Jack's well-timed elbow. "HA-HA!" The exuberant utterance was more akin to a disjointed exclamation than proper laughter. "That is the way!"

Jack gazed upon the cumbersome blockade of monsters, newly formed only a few feet before him, and saw one of them beginning to separate itself from the pile of chaos. All of its teeth were fangs, and they overlapped each other like a Venus flytrap.

*Oh my goodness,* he said to himself. *If humanity ever laid eyes on these things I don't think they would ever recover.* Jack tilted his head trying to make out exactly what he was looking at. *I mean, damn, just look at how ridiculously gross they are!*

The demon had two eyes and though it lacked a nose, its most hideous feature was, by far, its mouth. Positioned vertically, the fang-filled maw chattered in a manner most unsettling as the creature knowingly taunted him.

Bossu continued his exclamations. "You are getting it now, whelp! Give them no quarter!"

Jack was retrieved from his state of disgust and soon found himself becoming infected by his Lwa's uncharacteristic enthusiasm. "Take it easy, Bossu." Barely finishing his utterance, he darted toward the monstrosity just as it began to extricate itself.

Stunned by the suddenness of Jack's advance, the demon ceased its audible taunting and watched helplessly as its young assailant gave it a mighty punt to the face.

"Mmmmph!" he grunted. "This face . . . has got . . . to go!"

Jack's heel crashed into its fangs, sending the shattered pieces into its throat before completely severing its head as he followed through. It collided with several monsters in the back with missile-like velocity, pelting others with the shrapnel of its teeth as it careened away.

Jack was oblivious to the resulting carnage, astonished by his leg now at full vertical extension. His knee almost touching his ear, he maintained the pose with minimal effort, a feat he was never capable of performing before.

He gazed upon it, smiling from ear to ear. *Wow,* he thought, casually noticing a foolish foe lunging directly at him while sensing an ambush attempt from behind. *This is awesome!*

Without warning, Jack's leg came down like an axe.

His foot intercepted the ensuing tackle, falling upon the

monster's head before bringing it face-first into the ground with a crash.

Using it for leverage, Jack could feel the back of the monster's head pop from his weight as he leaped backward, daring a somersault this time for Bossu's sake. From his inverted position, he could see the monsters who failed in their surprise attack. Their collective anger seemed to be giving way to something else.

*They don't seem so hyped anymore*, Jack thought, assessing the situation upon landing.

His enemies' attempt to surround him apparently proved more difficult than anticipated, the shift in their morale now palpable. Though there remained some reluctant stragglers, the majority of the monsters had been successfully corralled in front of him, putting them in full view.

*Hey, who's that back there?*

Set in the rear of the ranks, Jack noticed a cloaked monster raising its arms in a ritualistic manner. Shining beneath its hood were three eyes arranged in a pyramid shape. Its hands began glowing with the same spectral blue of its eyes as it performed what appeared to be some kind of pep talk.

Noticing Jack, the monsters cautiously moved to block their hooded cohort from view.

"They look worried," Jack said.

"Yes," Bossu replied, "but do not allow yourself to become overconfident, and never drop your guard."

Jack scoffed dismissively. "I'm not overconfident, it's just a fact that these guys are no challenge!"

Waiting for a reply, he folded his arms and watched as the multitude of demons continued arranging themselves to hide their hype man, ignorant that Jack could still perceive their actions through his sixth sense.

Bossu's prolonged silence sparking a tinge of concern, Jack

felt the need to defend himself. "They're not doing anything, man. It's all—"

As he uttered the words, he was caught off guard by a giant blue light appearing directly next to him. He swiftly retreated a few steps back to observe.

*Now what?*

Seemingly in response, a hulking brute emerged from the light. It looked around the area as if confused before ultimately setting its sights upon Jack.

"Oh," he said, noticing several other lights beginning to bloom throughout the vicinity. "They're calling in the big guns."

Jack evaded as the monster's fist slammed into the ground, becoming lodged wrist-deep within. He glanced at the resulting rubble and immediately took off toward the blue-eyed summoner. *Yeah, that's definitely gonna hurt.*

Despite its cohorts' aid, the summoner's obscured location was revealed thanks to the appendage, prompting Jack to begin sprinting to the position.

The monsters desperately clawed at him as he leaped on them, one after the other. Jack periodically checked on the steadily forming lights to sustain his efforts, but the sound of the brute lumbering toward him proved useful as well.

"Get out of my way!" he commanded.

Though they were weak, their numbers made his task annoyingly difficult. When one was dispatched, another came grasping in its place.

"Running out of time, whelp," Bossu said. "Use what you know."

"I am!" Jack replied angrily. "That's how I know where the summoner is!"

"While you are indeed utilizing your shadow sense, you are being passive. You must be active!"

Hearing this, Jack began wielding the appendage and felt the summoner standing in position, overshadowed by the phalanx created by its allies. Palpating the area in which it stood, the ground somehow felt flexible.

*What?* he thought. *It's bouncy. Like a trampoline.*

Unsure of what he was feeling, Jack pressed against the membranous sensation with his appendage and saw the still-clambering monsters rise slightly.

"Oh yeah," he shouted in relief, "it's in shadow!"

Sensing the brute had arrived, Jack leaped high over the makeshift phalanx and simultaneously forced the shadow within upward with a mighty push.

He watched with glee as the summoner broke through the dome of protection and rocketed upward into view.

*Look at his face. Ha-ha. Oof!*

For a second, Jack was able to see the airborne wizard's expression of confusion right before it was hammered back down by the brute it had summoned.

The attack being meant for Jack, the monster swung its clasped hands like the stroke of a hammer, colliding with the summoner and countless others before liquifying them against the ground.

Jack watched with relief as the giant lights immediately vanished.

"Disaster averted," he said with a sigh. "This was about to turn into hard mode real quick."

"Not done yet," Bossu stated.

The young host glanced at the brute. "Yeah, I know."

Having estimated it to be nearly eight feet tall during his prior glimpse, Jack turned to get a better look at the formidable monstrosity.

A primitive loincloth was wrapped around its waist, partially obscured by a massive gut. Though muscular, its legs seemed burdened by the sheer weight of its upper body. Due to the knees' constant flexion, the monster appeared incapable of standing upright and moved in a slightly crouched position, back hunched.

The monster returned Jack's gaze as it wiped the entrails off its thick arms. The orange glow of its eyes gave its demeanor a certain intensity, but otherwise seemed expressionless. It lacked lips, causing the large and misshapen teeth arranged along the perimeter of its mouth to be constantly exposed. Various protrusions could be seen at the top of its head, too pronounced to be mere bumps though too dull to be horns.

"I trust I do not have to tell you—"

"Yeah," Jack replied, predicting Bossu's advice, "don't get lax."

Seeing the monster get even lower in preparation for its advance, Jack acted first and sprinted to meet it head-on.

Taken aback by his boldness, the monster tried to ready itself but apparently was too slow due to its size, leaving it wide open to attack. Unwilling to pull his punches, Jack threw a hefty right hook to its face. He watched as the hulking brute fell on bended knee, slightly dazed from the blow.

Shocked by the lackluster effect, Jack failed to follow up with another attack, instead looking on as the monster gave its head a light shake. "That's it?" he whined.

With a swiftness incongruous to its size, the kneeling enforcer suddenly struck with a straight punch, leaving the bewildered youth barely enough time to block it.

The force of the attack sent Jack's small frame flying, tumbling toward a group of onlooking bottom-feeders.

"You just do not take heed, eh?" Bossu asked.

*I screwed up*, Jack silently replied amidst his tumbling. *It's tougher than I thought. Faster too.*

Still fully aware of his surroundings, he could hear his assailant already in pursuit. He instinctively recovered from his roll through a series of back handsprings before swatting away the monsters poised for an ambush.

The brute was already upon him and tried to hit him with a front kick. Jack sidestepped the attack and proceeded to strike with several counterpunches before fleeing from range.

He watched as the monstrosity shook off the attacks. *I'm gonna need a weapon.*

"I know of one," Bossu replied.

Jack gasped excitedly. *Okay so—*

"But I will only arrange your getting it if you defeat this foe."

Growling in frustration, Jack readied himself as his opponent came at him once more. "I need it now!"

"You do not, you merely need to be resourceful."

Jack failed to respond, thoroughly determined to avoid being struck again. He could feel the pressure generated by each of the narrowly avoided blows.

Forgoing further attempts to counter, Jack instead focused primarily on dodging the brute's continued assault in order to form a plan. His tactical retreat brought his back against a wall, forcing him to watch as the monster advanced, while several resentful bottom-feeders could be seen gathering to witness what was coming.

While emotionally immune to fear, Jack intellectually felt like he was out of options, and judging by the casual manner in which it approached, the monster shared this sentiment.

*What can I do?*

As if responding to his mental plea, Jack felt his appendage gently tug at his mind.

*That's right*—he began, watching as the brute entered the darkened perimeter created by the wall's shadow—*I always have you.*

Jack could palpate the weight of the monster as it lumbered through the shadowed ground. Appearing helpless, he looked up at it as it drew back its gigantic fist for what it assumed to be a final blow.

Interrupting the attack, Jack quickly yanked the shadow underneath its foot with the appendage and darted out of the way as the brute slipped as if on ice. While the monster stumbled into the wall, Jack was already sprinting toward a horned onlooker.

Newly frightened, the relatively small demon froze in place.

Without any delay, Jack seized the bottom-feeder by its two horns and heaved it over his shoulder, smashing it into the ground. Maintaining his grip, he pulled the screaming monster closer and stomped on the base of one of the protrusions, breaking it off. As he moved on to the other, he shot a glance toward the brute, confirming it was still recovering from its collision.

Mercilessly beating away any attempts at a struggle, Jack bludgeoned the shrieking victim into submission with its horn before promptly cracking off the other.

Seemingly offended by Jack's trick, the brute released a deafening roar and began thundering its way toward him.

Jack brandished the two horns, gripping them near their tips, and watched patiently as the monster attacked in the same unthinking manner as before. *Thank goodness it's stupid.*

All too willing to capitalize on its blinding rage, Jack abruptly sprinted toward the monster as in their initial clash. Once again, the monster was caught off-balance and left open for the incoming assault.

Jack leaped in with an overhead swing and clubbed the top of its head with one of the horns, destroying most of it in the process. He resisted the urge to laugh as several of the protrusions on the monster's head receded into its skull from the hit.

*Whack-a-mole!*

The orange glow of the monster's widened eyes grew brighter. But before it could cradle the source of pain, Jack smacked the side of its face with the jagged edges of the horn, ensuring they tore through its flesh as he swung through.

Jack was on the lookout for signs of injury but made sure not to let up. *Gotta tear you up, freak, sorry.* Still spinning from the force of his swing, he caught sight of the grayish-green blood that seeped through the monster's fingers as it covered the fresh wound.

Resembling the backhand of a tennis star, Jack swiftly clutched the remaining horn with both hands as he completed his turn and smashed it into the exposed teeth of the monster, blasting them off its face.

*A lot of these guys got inconvenient bodies,* he thought as the monster's teeth clattered across the ground like hailstones.

These three simple strikes had the brute laid out on its back, too injured to defend itself. Unwilling to allow any further surprises, Jack threw himself onto his foe's chest and drove the still-intact horn into its throat.

"Mmmmph!" The monster instinctively grabbed at it but Jack firmly stomped it into the ground underneath before leaping to a safe distance. "And stay down."

Expecting exhaustion to set in, Jack fell backward onto the ground and watched as the brute tried to free itself.

Struggling against the horn that had its neck pinned like a tent peg, it gurgled out its last breath. Its sputtering forced out the blood that had pooled its way into the hollow stake, visibly erupting from within like a mini geyser.

Seeing that the brute had been defeated, the bottom-feeders started to flee.

"Wow," Jack began, watching their frenzied flight. "I'm killing monsters and I'm not even winded."

He took several deep breaths only to marvel at how unnecessary they were.

The area suddenly echoed with a strange clacking. Though the rhythm was indicative of applause, its quality seemed too hard, almost brittle.

*What the heck is that?!* Jack thought, scrambling to his feet.

Upon seeing the source of the sound, his expression transitioned from alertness to surprise and then, finally, amused intrigue.

Standing before him was a fancily clad skeleton applauding him. Though dimmed by old-school shades that were somehow still fashionable, shining green eyes could be seen glowing behind them. Their brightness seemed to intensify by the second, accentuating the enthusiastic display.

The hardened fang-like extensions descending from the mouth of Jack's mask did little to conceal the childish expression on his face.

Noticing the smile, the skeleton's enthusiasm became mingled with a curiosity that was obvious. Quickly recovering, the raucous nature of the renewed applause rose to inhuman levels before suddenly ceasing, the final clap being the loudest of all.

Its ivory hands remained clasped together in front of its clearly grinning skull. The skeleton pointed them toward Jack as it began its address.

"And he is good-humored to boot," it said. "To the newest inductee into our world." The skeleton removed his ornate top hat and brought it to his chest, revealing black hair that was surprisingly fine in texture. "I bid you welcome, Heir Boniface."

"Thank you," Jack replied. He gave a respectful nod of the

head before abruptly shifting in demeanor. "Wow! The mythical Baron Samedi, in the flesh! Well, sorta."

Still cradling his hat, Baron Samedi lurched forward and immediately began laughing.

Inwardly, Jack remained wary, watching attentively as the tickled skeleton seemed to derive an inordinate amount of enjoyment from his quip. *Was it that funny?* he said silently.

"No," Bossu replied.

Jack's eyes darted around the vicinity as the prolonged cackles seemed to generate various spectral singularities around their position.

"Whooo boy," Samedi began. "That's good stuff!"

Returning the hat to his head, the skeleton composed himself, sighing out his amusement. As he did so, an assortment of individuals began appearing through the singularities.

The last to materialize was the titan from the storm.

Her arrival was identical to her disappearance and lacked the prolonged forecast of her cohorts. A large column of mist had taken shape, followed by her immediate appearance in its place. As they exchanged glances once more, Jack noticed she still did not appear overtly threatening.

*She seems more cautious*, he thought. *Even kind of childlike.*

"Do not be afraid," Samedi said. Jack nodded as he smiled back, secretly amused by the suggestion. "These are my subordinates, eager to do my will. They mean you no harm."

Turning around, the skeleton briefly moved his hand about the air as if conducting an orchestra.

*I bet he's summoning a portal*, Jack said silently, addressing Bossu. *What are the odds it's a trap?*

"Not likely," the Lwa replied. "You are probably the only person he has no reason to conspire against."

Jack remained still and watched the predicted wormhole

form in response to Samedi's quick gesture. Its perimeter manifested as a bright green ring, large and cracking with energy.

Before entering, Samedi looked back at his guest, seemingly keeping his distance. "Come, now that you are here, we have work to do."

# CHAPTER 12

Jack obliged, quickly joining his host to stand in front of the awaiting portal.

Initially an opaque haze of green, the wormhole steadily increased in clarity as he approached, to where it now resembled a trembling wall of water.

Standing before the threshold, Jack could make out what seemed to be the lightly furnished interior of some building. Although his field of vision was limited, he could tell that the space was exceedingly large.

The few windows in view stretched high enough to dwarf the mysterious silhouettes stationed within. While most of these unnamed entities seemed to be standing patiently in expectation, Jack noticed a few of them floating about in an obviously inhuman manner.

Filled with curiosity but unwilling to openly inquire, he silently addressed his Lwa as Samedi passed through. *Who are they?*

"My brethren, of course."

*Great.*

As Jack stepped into the quivering wall, Bossu's tone transitioned to one of seriousness. "Remember the treachery that has brought you here," he said. "No one is above suspicion, so be sure that you remain circumspect with all things. Take heed, the less informed you appear, the better."

Jack nodded in response as he crossed over. The distorted imagery immediately cleared away, revealing what could only be described as a dimly lit ballroom.

Fighting the urge to stare at its impractically high ceiling, he directed his gaze forward only to realize Samedi had his back turned to him.

Standing with pocketed hands, the Ghede lord positioned himself between his young guest and the collection of entities that were before him.

The first to get Jack's attention was one clothed in bright white garments, positioned near the ceiling. The entity floated up high as if to separate itself. *The lightbulb god, I presume?*

"Take heed, whelp," Bossu began. "The life you once led in which jokes and frivolous banter were acceptable is over. It is for your own sake that I am imploring you to take things seriously, for if you do not, you will certainly wish you had."

*It was just a joke*, Jack replied, willfully averting his gaze, *an inside one at that. You want me to be a dried-up curmudgeon like you. Outwardly, I get it, but in my private thoughts, too? You're buggin', dude.*

Unfazed by his Lwa's sudden austerity, Jack was intent on tallying all of the entities present but quickly realized the way they arranged themselves would make his efforts too obvious.

Nevertheless, he found himself staring at a small preteen boy standing among the otherworldly beings and was careful not to smirk. *See? I'm holding back my laughter.*

"That very statement is a testament to your puerility," Bossu replied.

Jack had been staring at the preteen Lwa. Wearing a mischievous frown, the child seemed to hold what appeared to be a bottle of liquor in one hand and a banana in the other.

While fully aware there was more to him than met the eye, Jack could not resist the consequent swell of amusement. "Aren't you a bit too young to drink?" he asked.

Bossu let out a gravelly sigh. "Our manner of conversation has spoiled you," he said. "You can brush aside my counsel if you so wish, but you cannot be so aloof with these people. They are proud and demand adherence to proper etiquette. Consider the fact that they have no reason to aid us."

The childlike entity aggressively bit off the top of his unpeeled banana. He maintained his stare as he chewed through its woody stem and bitter skin with ease.

Seeing as the masticating Lwa's glare remained despite its cheeks being swelled comically past their limit, Jack moved for damage control. "It was a joke."

Jack felt something like relief upon hearing a sound of amusement from the group and, seeking the source, he locked eyes with a being that had the head of a leopard. His chest was bare, and while a seeming leopard-skin skirt was wrapped around his waist in a manner similar to Roman pteruges, the rest of his body seemed human.

Jack's examination was cut short by a high-pitched grating as another stepped forward. "You ignore the heir's casual attitude, Samedi?" the unseen deity asked, and while its cadence did not seem angry, Jack thought it unreasonably loud. "He's too familiar."

As the speaker emerged from the crowd, the unmistakable glint of a blade caught Jack's eye. Glancing at the machete, he spied a chain of great bulk wrapped around the deity's left forearm. The Lwa dragged the excess in his clutches as he moved, creating a piercing grinding sound.

Samedi took a step forward, blocking his young guest from his cohort's line of sight. Though his hands remained pocketed, the Ghede lord's tone was nevertheless conciliatory. "Brother Ogun," he began, "I beg you to overlook the youth's offense just this once. He has yet to learn our ways. This is all new to him, after all. Give me but two days and I will have his rambunctious attitude thoroughly removed."

As if for emphasis, the skeleton turned around upon saying this.

The spectral green of his irises was still visible despite the darkened shades. Noticing one of them suddenly go out, Jack was forced to look at the ground as the smirk he thought he had conquered made a sudden comeback.

Bossu grumbled knowingly just as his host began to address him. *Did you see that?* Jack asked silently as Samedi turned back around. *He just winked! In a situation as serious as this, even Baron Samedi keeps his sense of humor.*

The skeleton waited as the muscular Ogun considered his request.

"Seeing as he is immortal," Bossu began, "he can afford to play the fool."

*True,* the young host replied, *but why are they just staring each other down like that? And what's that sound?*

The pause in Samedi and Ogun's conversation caused Jack's attention to drift toward the noises within the space. The distinct sound of water met his ears, its calm nature similar to that of waves rhythmically cascading to and fro upon a shore.

Jack's gaze fell upon its source almost immediately, but he remained unsure of what he was looking at.

Visible from only the waist up, two entities could be seen

surrounded by a subtle distortion. The periphery seemed to fluctuate, making it difficult to ascertain its nature.

Although they were sitting, the couple's height was not remarkably different from that of those standing. Their eyes appeared aquamarine, the same color as their hair, but shimmering like a sun-kissed sea.

A bejeweled diadem sat upon the man's bald head, and he wore a rivière of equal brilliance around his neck. The hefty necklace consisted of gems fashioned into the shape of seashells that steadily increased in size, ultimately leading to the large conch resting on his chest.

The woman wore a diadem as well, but rather than a complete circle, the portion at her forehead extended down to form a point just above the bridge of her nose. Her formfitting blouse seemed to be made of scales, each glinting a shade of red slightly different from the other before collectively swapping tints in waves.

Having moved slightly to get a better view, Jack felt even more confused.

Far from seeing any physical form of support for the seated entities, there was only the mysterious outpouring of water intermittently crashing on the floor beneath their visible upper bodies.

*That explains the noise, but how—*

Jack's thoughts came to a pause as he noticed distortion encircling them. Water was being spewed forth in steady intervals from the portion hovering just above the floor, allowing Jack to fixate on the transient contour.

*So that's what it is*, he thought. *These two are viewing from a portal.*

Though its perimeter was not as defined as Samedi's, the leaking water served as a point of reference by which the portal's overall shape could be traced.

*They're not even here.*

"Obviously," Bossu stated with a scoff. "This is none other than Met Agwe and his wife La Sirene."

*Silly me . . .*

The Lwa continued, ignoring his host's sarcasm. "Neither is fond of this place but Agwe is particularly averse." He snorted loudly in fleeting amusement. "Intolerably sepulchral, was how he described it."

Jack gazed into the aqueous portal, finally able to contrast the background environment contained within the fluctuating periphery from the gloomy ballroom in which he stood.

*His domain is just as dark as this one, I couldn't even tell the difference at first.*

"Agwe's is an underwater kingdom," Bossu replied. "As such, its present state of drear is nothing more than nightfall's effect on the depths."

*I get it now, this portal is more like a window than a gateway. That's how it's keeping the contents of the deep at bay.* He glanced again at the water leaking onto the floor. *For the most part.*

Jack continued examining the periphery but halted as he noticed the faces of the two Lwa within looking directly at him. While Met Agwe appeared to be in a state of stoic observation, the woman at his side was smiling.

La Sirene, having recognized the telltale confusion on Jack's mask, proceeded into a full-on grin before quickly turning to her husband. Agwe's eyes remained fixed, but a subdued expression soon took shape at the corner of his mouth as he relented.

At this, La Sirene immediately spoke. "Be gentle, Ogun," she said. "There are times when austerity is best but, alas, this one is but a child. His whimsical nature is clearly evident. He means no harm."

Samedi gestured toward her with renewed enthusiasm before continuing his appeal. "You see?" he began. "Full of grace and insight, the queen of the sea speaks sense!"

"See to it that your assurances prove true," Ogun replied. "The mortal has inherited a burden that has little time for instruction in etiquette."

"You ain't lyin', brother," Samedi stated, visibly pleased.

Ogun peered over the chuckling skeleton, setting his sights on Jack. "Come forth, child."

Jack obediently stepped forward as Samedi moved to the side, as if granting passage.

"Are you ready for what is required of you?" Ogun asked, locking eyes with him.

Though his manner was aggressive, Jack could tell Ogun was not trying to intimidate. He maintained eye contact with the Lwa as he replied. "Yes, sir, I believe I am."

Echoes of condescending laughter suddenly filled the ballroom. Their shrillness forced Jack to wince as he watched the responsible entity scamper forward. Having caught sight of her, his irritation gave way to a look of surprise before being ultimately replaced by revulsion.

Initially, Jack imagined the advancing entity to be someone in a bird costume but quickly understood the reality to be more grotesque. This Lwa had the body of a giant bird, but while her ankles and feet remained terrifyingly avian, she had no wings.

An unsightly fusion of human and bird, her arms hung from the feathered tufts at her shoulders. The abnormal length of these scrawny limbs was made all the more striking by her clawlike hands, their appearance evoking memories of the prehistoric creatures Jack fancied as a child.

The woman suddenly jutted forth the hand he was gaping at, breaking his inappropriate trance. Jack finally took a good look at the Lwa's head. Although it was the only thing about her that appeared fully human, her face was twisted into a sneer of outrage.

Far from feeling threatened, her intensity filled him with curiosity.

*Why is she so mad?*

"Your pride is offensive," she began. "Do you even know why you are here?"

Jack feigned discomfort before speaking his lie. "Umm, well, I guess I don't." The bird woman flared her nose at this. "I'm something like a superhero, no? Destined to protect humanity from the forces of darkness . . . or something?"

The space fell quiet as the various entities within simply stared at him. Even Samedi seemed to lose his sense of humor, slowly turning to look at Jack in silent disbelief.

"What?"

Bending at the waist, the skeleton lowered himself to Jack's height before responding. "One of our kin has gone missing," he began, suddenly sounding weary. "You are to discover what has happened to her." He paused once more, examining Jack's reaction. "I'm surprised Bossu has neglected to apprise you of the situation."

"Who's Bossu?" Jack asked. He ignored the gravelly titters that immediately sounded in his head as he continued. "And, don't get mad, but if one of your gods has gone missing, wouldn't that mean the culprit must be another god? Like, one of you?"

Jack kept his eyes off the assembly, not wanting his statement to hit harder than was necessary.

Samedi laughed slightly before standing upright. "Well," he said, "this might take a bit longer than I thought."

The childlike Lwa raised his bottle of liquor. "Cheekiness notwithstanding," he began, "the heir is right." Unprepared for the sound of his voice, Jack's posture became rigid from stifling the outburst of laughter now primed in his bowels. The baritone Lwa looked among his fellows before continuing. "Is it not so? This one has only expressed something we all know to be true."

Thoroughly intrigued, Jack took several glimpses of the immortal assembly. Despite the otherworldly power and spectacle contained within their natures, the discomfort they currently displayed was strikingly human.

"Look at them, Jack," Bossu said. "Do you not find such timidity to be unbecoming of deities?"

Jack gave a slow nod as the leopard-headed Lwa broke the silence. "Be that as it may, Pierre," he began, "what are we to do?"

One of the airborne entities groaned loudly before joining everyone else on the ballroom floor. Jack noticed the Lwa shoot him a knowing glance before turning to the assembly. His eyes seemed to house some form of unstable energy that crackled violently from his face.

"Is it not obvious?" he shouted. "We are left to suspect ourselves endlessly, doing nothing."

Bossu suddenly unleashed a series of guffaws. While such behavior was generally out of character for the Lwa, Jack had seen him exhibit this level of amusement once before. He snickered in a reflexive response as the conversation continued.

"On the contrary, Brother Sogbo," Samedi said, placing his ivory hand on Jack's shoulder. "I will be leaning on the heir extensively. His introduction is the reason behind our impromptu reunion, after all."

"Apologies, Jack," Bossu began, having ceased from his hilarity. "Sogbo has always been able to make me laugh."

Though Jack's ensuing scoff was exceedingly soft, it remained audible against the strange quiet now filling the space. *I don't get it*, he replied. *After lecturing me about seriousness and stuff, you bust out laughing at something that wasn't even that funny.*

"He is my brother," Bossu said. "As such, is it not understandable that I find his sense of humor particularly amusing? Regardless, this is no reason to hold him above suspicion."

Though Jack was surprised by this revelation, his attention was hijacked by the tense atmosphere brought on by Samedi's statement. "Huh?" he breathed aloud.

"What is it?" Bossu asked.

*All of a sudden these guys don't seem so composed.*

"Oh?"

Jack began eyeing two Lwa who escaped his initial notice. *Yeah, less composed, more . . . hostile.*

Making their way to the front of the assembly, the pair's appearance was so preposterous that Jack wondered how he had missed them. Despite the absurdity of their dress, there was no discernible correlation between the particular stereotypes they each portrayed.

*What?* he thought. *Why are there deities that look like this?*

The first caricature nailed the 1800s plantation owner look, a seemingly prehensile leather whip coiled diagonally across his chest, fastening itself to his formerly loose-fitting cotton shirt as he approached.

"We gods are mere stars in the sky," Bossu explained. "Our outward mien being nothing more than the whim of He Who gave us form. They appear to be influenced by your human ancestors, but, in truth, it's the other way around. Idolatry never changes."

Jack was completely baffled as he took it all in, now glancing at the second Lwa who took the form of a young woman. *This one is in cosplay too,* he thought, covertly eyeing her up and down. *But from an entirely different era. What the heck is this?*

A silk kerchief was delicately wrapped around her neck, its color matching the long white gloves on her hands. These

two fashionable accessories complemented her elaborate pink dress. She brought it all together with hair arranged in a style reminiscent of the 1950s. Nestled within the meticulous coiffure was her last accessory—a pair of dark sunglasses set above her blonde hairline.

Though Jack knew the dress was objectively beautiful, it was comically out of place. A smile spread across his face as he watched the drama unfold right beside him.

The woman outstretched an aggressive index finger as they confronted the awaiting skeleton. "For introduction?!" she screamed, her gloved hand trembling with rage an inch from his ivory forehead. "I have no need to meet the accursed one's newest vessel!"

Samedi shrugged, unaffected by her histrionics. "That may be, Mademoiselle," he replied, "but the introduction wasn't for your sake."

The anger immediately left the woman's face but she retained her pose as if stunned. Her partner calmly took over. "What's that supposed to mean?" he asked.

The leopard-headed Lwa let out a deep growl before speaking. "Is it not obvious, Dinclinsin? Samedi intended for the heir to see our faces."

Samedi nodded approvingly, nudging the dumbstruck woman's finger several times before she withdrew it. "Thank you, Charlotte."

Ignoring her scowl, the baron redirected his words to the assembly. "Indeed, seeing it was inevitable that Freda's disappearance was enacted by conspirators within, I thought it good to ensure my agent gets a good look at every one of you and the auras you emanate."

*For what?* Jack said silently. *He's treating this like a supernatural whodunit or something.*

"How conniving," Ogun said.

Samedi shrugged again. "Scant as it may be, it's *my* ass on the line. The sky father made sure I understood as much."

The lightbulb Lwa joined the conversation at last. Landing like an angel, he breathed a sigh of gentle disappointment. "There are better, less insulting ways to do this, Samedi."

"Unfortunately, I have time for none of them, Obatala," the baron replied. "Besides, that wasn't the only reason I requested y'all's presence."

"Out with it!" the bird woman commanded.

"As you know, seeing as Freda is missing, I am thrust into obligations I hadn't anticipated."

Another entity, even smaller than the preteen, hopped out from behind those keeping him from view. Jack looked at the approaching Lwa's face and was immediately reminded of the dwarven race from popular folklore.

*Fairytale creatures,* he began silently, *they're real?*

"Yes, Jack," Bossu replied. "Ti Jean is indeed a dwarf."

Jack noticed the dwarf had only one leg, but despite this handicap, his movements were unnaturally swift.

The dwarf, Ti Jean, stopped his succession of rapid hops upon reaching them. "Out with it!" he said, repeating the bird woman's command.

Samedi held a defiant pause before ultimately obliging. "This was also confirmed by the sky father himself, and I quote, for they have assuredly anticipated the rescinding of your oath of inactivity, seeing as her absence effectively releases you from it."

Jack flinched as the angelic Obatala shed his placid demeanor, seemingly disturbed by this information. "No!" he shouted.

"Yes."

"But you can't!" Obatala continued, frustrated by the cavalier response. "What of the children?"

"What of them?"

Obatala gasped in shock before his face slowly shifted into a glare.

Jack, who had been turning his head between the two, began staring at the floor as his mind processed what was said. *This is what you were talking about*, he said silently. *The peacetime is ending.*

"Correct," Bossu replied.

"That is quite the look you're sending my way!" Samedi began. "The Liveside has been free from the Deadside's influence for a long time now."

"Yes!" the bird woman said excitedly.

"Marinette approves!"

Jack silently watched Obatala's expression grow increasingly more hostile. *The lightbulb god has a personality disorder or what?*

"Perhaps," Bossu replied.

Despite knowing of him for only a few minutes, Jack found the shift in Obatala's countenance unsettling. "Meaningless rot!" the Lwa said, now snarling at the Ghede lord. "She is made merry by the prospect of letting her hounds loose to feast."

"Approval just the same," Samedi replied. "And besides," Jack suddenly felt a bony hand clasp his shoulder. "This one will see to it that the mortals' numbers aren't dwindled to nothing. Isn't that right?"

Jack turned to see Samedi already leaning forward and quickly turned the rest of his body so that the bowing Lwa was now directly in front of him. The skeleton's spectral green eyes twinkled as Jack gave his reply. "It is."

A momentary hush had fallen within the space as they stood face-to-face, only to be ended by someone's giddy laughter.

"How fascinating!" La Sirene said excitedly.

"Not now," Obatala muttered.

The goddess giggled as she finished her statement. "But the mortal was correct after all!"

Jack's eyes stopped on the bird woman, Marinette, looking at him as if pleased. Somehow, he thought this smile to be even more disconcerting than her sneer.

"His reason for being," she stated knowingly. "Destined to protect humanity from the forces of darkness." She paused, grinning wildly now. "Or something?"

Samedi let out a dry chuckle as he stood upright. "I stand corrected."

"You have all gone mad," Obatala said. "You truly believe him capable of that so early?"

"Not sure if I believe it," Samedi replied, "but I'm confident he will put on a damn good show regardless."

Obatala groaned through his teeth before speaking. "All this while somehow discovering Freda's whereabouts?" The agitated Lwa pointed at Jack. "Him?!"

Pursing his lips together, the young host tried to portray an exaggerated look of melancholy despite the mask before averting his gaze to the floor. *No need to be mean.*

Bossu hummed a chuckle. "It would be wise to take note of this one."

*Duh.*

Samedi clasped his hands against the back of his skull, his elbows flexed outward as he arched his back to stretch as Obatala continued. "How much time has passed since his introduction to our world? Has it not been but a day?"

"Not even," Samedi replied with a light grunt. He returned to a normal posture and motioned toward Jack. "But he seems to think he can." The Ghede lord suddenly began marching in place. "He thinks he can, he thinks he can, he thinks he can." Ending the spectacle, the animated skeleton gazed down at the mortal by his side. "Don't you?"

Jack remained silent, responding with a slow yet confident nod.

Obatala sucked his teeth before swatting the air with a dismissive backhand. "That is merely a result of the accursed one's influence," he explained. "Unbeknownst to him, it is this wild disregard for consequences that has sent countless of his progenitors to the grave."

The dwarven Ti Jean entered the conversation. "And Bossu to the void, if I'm not mistaken."

Jack almost cringed at the explosive sound created by Obatala, striking his hands in agreement.

"Precisely!" he said.

*Wild disregard, huh?* Jack asked.

Bossu grumbled his reply. "So *they* say."

Once more, Samedi responded with a shrug. "While it is true that Koblamin's fearlessness is certainly at work, this heir is different. If only you saw him earlier. Provoked a horde and took 'em on all by himself he did."

Obatala watched helplessly as the leopard Lwa approached them, his interest in the conversation apparently restored. "Truly?"

"C'mon Agassu," the skeleton replied, swiftly pointing at various spots on Jack's body. "You see all the entrails and goo, dontcha? Where do you think it came from?"

The beastly entity gave Jack a once-over before turning to Samedi. "And only a day old?"

"How long until you renege on your promise?" Obatala spat.

The Lwa assembly collectively turned to Jack as he spoke. "The monsters have already begun crossing over," he stated. "I could smell their stench earlier today." Preparing to make his exit, he gave a nod to the noticeably less angelic Lwa. "Just tell me how you want me to go about it, and I'll get started. Like I said, I'm ready."

Just as he was about to pull himself into the void, he was stopped by Bossu. "Stop!" he commanded. "Do not do that in their presence."

"*Why?*" he asked, withdrawing his appendage. "*I'm sure the giantess already told—*"

"Just do as I say."

While some of the Lwa began vanishing, Samedi kept his eyes on him in careful observation. "Ready to go?"

"Yeah."

As the skeleton turned around, Jack briefly lost his cool, expecting an inconvenient entry to his previous location in the same realm. "Oh! But t-to the Liveside though."

"I see ya," Samedi replied.

He motioned his hands through the air to summon the portal before continuing, his voice now lowered beneath the various sounds created by his fellows. "Tell Bossu I said howdy." Jack pursed his lips together, saying nothing as he approached the newly formed gateway. "Think yourself slick, eh? Good for you, junior, good for you."

"I don't know what you're talking about."

"Anyway, since I doubt you even know where to begin, the best place to start would be your *helpers*, seeing as they have something that belongs to you." His eyes flashed bright for a moment. "And as luck would have it, now would be a perfect opportunity for you to drop in. Consider this a little meet n' greet arranged by Fate. Meet me at my mansion when you're finished."

# CHAPTER 13

Jack found himself standing at the front of a street he did not recognize.

Behind him was a railroad. The crossing sign was in relatively good condition, suggesting the tracks were active. The street that stretched before him had what looked to be warehouses on one side and residential buildings on the other.

"North Rampart Street," he said, glimpsing at the distant street sign. "Why did—"

His ears suddenly picked up the noise of suppressed gunfire emanating from the house right in front of him. He checked both sides of the darkened street before sprinting toward the sound. "Super hearing wasn't on my list of powers, was it?"

"No, it was not," Bossu replied. "And while it is not enhanced to any supernatural degree, it is not incorrect to claim it as apex-human. If you are curious as to why the gunfight has gone unnoticed, it being the dead of night may be your answer."

Jack barely felt anything upon crashing inside, his charge making short work of both door and frame. Resisting the temptation to celebrate, he dutifully scanned the vicinity and quickly experienced an array of emotions after stumbling through.

Not yet having turned around, three police officers stood a few feet from the newly wrecked entrance. Assuming they were hopelessly engaged with a supernatural threat, Jack was pleasantly surprised by the concern Samedi displayed by sending him to aid these everyday mortals. Setting his sights over their shoulders with the intent to quickly dispatch their foes, his resolve was extinguished upon locking eyes with one of them.

Time seemed to stand still as he found himself sharing a wide-eyed expression of disbelief with none other than Alyssa.

Uncertain of what to make of the situation, Jack promptly returned his sights to the cops, who turned around within the second that transpired. He sensed something amiss in their manner. It seemed too choreographed, resembling the rehearsed movements of backup dancers.

Beholding their faces at last, Jack's confusion was immediately replaced by hateful anger. Their mouths took up most of their faces, and the corners of their heads were misshaped to account for the inhuman spread.

"There you are!" they said in unison. Their demonic visages did little to hide the genuine surprise in their voices.

Jack flashed an inappropriate smile as he watched them speak. Their teeth were similar to some of the monsters he had fought not too long ago, but their placement was so thoughtless, almost silly.

Their demonic brow lines, set in a thick arch above their yellow eyes, lessened a bit due to a subtle shift in expression.

Jack glanced at Alyssa and saw her watching him from behind a large, overturned couch. He avoided locking eyes with her and noticed a silver-haired man peek out from the makeshift cover before quickly moving to another position.

Although his body was obscured, he was too nimble to be crawling. Before considering any possible explanation, the inhuman police officers began speaking, having reverted to their aggressive demeanors.

"Something funny, boy?" they asked.

Jack shook his head, still smiling. "You wouldn't be amused," he replied, pointing above his head. His gaze remained fixed on the officers as he addressed Alyssa. "Alyssa, shut off that light."

She remained unresponsive, staring at him as if daydreaming.

Tickled by her state of silence, the demons in uniform erupted into laughter, each individual guffaw and cackle in perfect synchrony, creating a sound quite unsettling.

"Now!"

Alyssa casually raised her firearm above her head. Her robotic reaction had apparently caught the demons off guard as they promptly stopped laughing. They silently watched as she shot out the ceiling light.

Far from sending them into pitch-black shadow, Alyssa's destruction of this one light resulted in merely partial darkness due to the illumination emanating from the rest of the house. Though their space was dimmed significantly, the lights of the surrounding rooms provided more than enough visibility. Upon witnessing the presumably lackluster result, the officers immediately resumed their laughter.

Jack ignored the demonic cacophony as he weaved the imperceptible appendage through the room. *Is this dark enough for you?* he thought, silently addressing his appendage.

A grin formed at the commissure of his bone-like mask as the feedback from his sixth sense confirmed the shallow darkness suitable for what was about to go down. *Nice!*

Although the cops had a clear view of Jack's visage, his mischievous look was insufficient to deter them from their incessant mocking. "HA-HA, you think a moderately darkened room gives you the advantage?"

Apparently skeptical of Jack's confidence as well, Alyssa suddenly fired into an adjacent room, attempting to shoot out the only other fixture visible from her position. While her shot was impressive, the light was not completely destroyed.

The space in which they stood rapidly fluctuated in darkness due to the resultant flicker.

Jack gave her a thumbs-up. "Thanks so much," he said. "You guys can leave now, though. I don't want them taking you hostage or anything once I start kicking their asses."

Alyssa immediately complied.

Having had enough of Jack's bravado, the cops' laughter came to an abrupt end. "The heir is a proper fool."

Jack finally got a good look at the silver-haired man as he came out from cover to pursue Alyssa. He was uncommonly short in stature, dwarfish like Ti Jean, but obviously human.

"No!" the man began. "We can't leave him!"

The demons in uniform separated themselves into position around Jack. "Look, boy, your allies are desirous to see your end."

"They're gonna be disappointed, then."

As if on cue, the flickering light in the background fizzled out, making the space even dimmer.

"Enough from this dead child."

Jack readied himself as the three demons lunged at Jack in a coordinated attack. *This is it.*

The cop who remained in front rushed him head-on while the two others went for his head and legs, respectively, but Jack had already engaged his sixth sense. *I can still perceive everything they're doing!* he thought. *This is gonna be cake!*

Acutely determining the distance of each, he took a perfectly timed lunge toward the enemy in front, putting him just out of range from those at his back.

*Those two will miss but I can't evade this one.* He used his appendage to feel for the area beneath the one rushing him head-on and felt a rush of exhilaration upon realizing his palpations had unwittingly reached the enemy's foot. *Looks like I don't even have to!*

He gently tugged at the foot, forcing the rushing attacker into a brief stumble.

This momentary loss of control was all Jack needed to commence a counterattack.

*Gotcha!* He caught the stumbling demon's hand and yanked it close before seizing its whole arm. *And now you're done.* Capitalizing on the demon's forward momentum, Jack lifted it into a shoulder throw, putting it on a collision course with the ones behind him.

The ensuing engagement had gone unnoticed by the silver-haired man who was still arguing their need to stay. "We can't leave," he said. "Jack hasn't been trained!" The man shot a hasty glance behind his back to check what Alyssa was staring at before continuing. "He isn't ready . . . ?"

In disbelief, the man turned fully to catch the end of the violent maneuver. Heaving the cop over his shoulder, Jack sent its flailing legs into the face of the other that leaped into the air. In less than a second, the thrown cop was slammed upon the last one, interrupting its intended ankle grab and pinning it to the floor with an impressively loud crash.

*Out for the count.*

Just as Jack was about to release his victim, Bossu suddenly began scolding him. "Do not stop!" he commanded. "This is not some trivial street fight."

The young host immediately reaffirmed his hold and looked

down at the disoriented foe. *I have no clue what to do from here.*

"I do not recall such difficulty during your earlier skirmish," Bossu replied. "I was actually impressed."

The demon officer who was struck midleap had begun grumbling incoherently from the floor.

*I have no choice but to make it harder for them to keep fighting.* Gripping his foe by the wrist and bicep, Jack quickly lifted the limb toward his knee before hesitating. *But I might obliterate the whole arm.*

"You mean to say the enemy need only don the trappings of humanity, and just like that, you are compelled to show them mercy?" The two witnesses watched in silence as Jack's formerly fluid movements came to a sudden and unnatural stop, unaware of the telepathic upbraiding he was receiving. "Truly?"

*Oh man . . .* Jack ended the moment of hesitation by hoisting the demon up by the arm. Bracing its limp hand against the side of his chin, he made the limb straight before crashing into it with his knee.

*CRACK!*

Jack could feel the breaking limb reverberating against the side of his bone mask while the house echoed the sound, startling Alyssa but causing the older man to smile.

Bossu continued. "It is imperative that you become relentless in your warfare, Jack. Do not behave as if your fight is with flesh-and-blood humans."

Standing on one leg, Jack released the limb before suddenly performing a swift somersault. "Whoa!" he exclaimed, surprised by his own reflexes.

Alyssa gasped as the demon officer that was pinned to the floor suddenly swiped at the spot where Jack's other foot had been. The lad came down from his brief front flip and landed upon the outstretched hand before grinding its wrist with a sharp turn of his heel.

It all happened in less than a second.

Jack took a step back as the three officers aggressively got to their feet.

"Ow!" they cried. "That almost hurt!"

The two that were at his front swung their mangled limbs in a forceful motion as if wicking off water, supernaturally undoing the damage.

Bossu hummed with a strangely lighthearted vindication. "You see?"

Jack was still in awe at his unintentional counter. *You win*, he replied silently. *Won't happen again.*

The cops began moving into position, though this time, all three remained in view. "Beginner's luck," they stated. "Or perhaps underestimation."

"Oh gosh," Jack began, rolling his eyes, "rationalizations? Really?"

The demons chuckled. "Irrespective of the cause behind that fluke, it shall not happen again."

*I have to keep those two out of harm's way.* Jack began walking toward the demons while gesturing with his hand, rapidly bringing his thumb and fingers together. "You guys talk too m—"

Without warning, the cops launched into their attack, which now consisted of a series of supernaturally coordinated strikes.

Jack leaned backward, dodging the first that was aimed at his face. *This is just too easy!* He immediately weaved his head out of the path of an incoming claw swipe before bending forward at the waist to evade the hook sent toward his upper body.

Jack's face lightly touched his knees before he snapped back to an upright position.

For a moment, a fleeting look of astonishment formed on the faces of the three demons before they resumed.

*Don't get too cocky,* Jack said to himself. *There's always the chance of things going bad like what almost happened in the Deadside.* He noted the two Abettors still observing the skirmish. *Only now there are potential casualties.*

Although the demons managed to form a triangle around him, Jack's sixth sense made it impossible to exploit any presumed blind spot, thereby allowing him to continuously maneuver around their varied attacks, one after the other.

"WHAT?!" they screamed.

Showing no signs of being winded, Jack watched the cops prepare another go at him.

Responding to his provocative gawking with glares of scorn, they huffed and puffed as they paced around him into the desired formation.

With two now directly behind him, Jack repeatedly took his eyes off the one in front to nervously glance over his shoulders. The scheming demons stepped back and forth, adjusting themselves accordingly to remain unseen by his peripherals.

Easily perceiving their actions, Jack snorted a chuckle toward his chest, unintentionally dropping the farce. *They have no idea.*

Though slightly more than a minute had passed since being encouraged to leave, Alyssa and the old man had not moved, bewildered by the fledgling Shadowman's prowess. They continued watching as he presciently sidestepped a dropkick aimed at his back and immediately ducked under the perfectly timed lariat that followed before springing into the air, seamlessly avoiding yet another ankle dive from behind.

Having rebounded into a scrambling regroup, the cops immediately resorted to a flurry of punches and kicks, hitting nothing but air.

Jack struggled to compose himself, covering his mouth while maintaining the rhythm of his swift dodging. *Gotta . . . stop . . . laughing!*

"HOW IS HE DOING THAT?! ARGH—" The enraged hollering of the demons suddenly stopped as one of them made contact at last.

Jack appeared as a posing statue, having stopped the enemy's foot with a raised knee. "Beginner's luck," he replied. Before they could respond, he snatched the demon's leg, swinging the imposter toward the other two.

One was sent crashing through the entrance, the position of his body adding further damage to the wrecked doorway. The second had stumbled backward, clumsily avoiding the path of Jack's swing. Continuing through the miss, the young host spun another revolution and cast the demon toward its already departed fellow with a hammer throw.

Jack sensed the one who managed to dodge his attack stumbling his way uncomfortably close to the two humans. *I knew they were gonna try eventually*, he thought, angrily lunging at the demon. *But it's not happening!*

Jack glanced at Alyssa as he clutched the demon's collar. "Kill the porch lights."

Upon saying this, he immediately darted toward the gaping entryway with his victim in tow, jostling the demon violently in order to stifle any attempts to break free.

Surprisingly, the two previously jettisoned foes had already removed themselves from the wreckage. Anticipating them to be lying in wait, Jack instinctively engaged his appendage but was confused by the resulting feedback.

*Everything's all marred and murky*, he thought. *I need Alyssa to cut that light ASAP so I can see what the fake cops are plotting. But I can't wait because this one won't stop freaking fidgeting.*

Crossing the threshold, Jack stalled for less than a second upon hearing the sound of gunfire. Several bullets struck the panel set into what was left of the adjacent wall, successfully disabling the light outside. *Nice, Alyssa, now where did—Oh, wow.*

Alyssa's shots came not a moment too soon as Jack's newly accommodated appendage revealed the two demon cops to be just out of physical view, their fists already flying at him from their positions on both sides of the porch.

At the last moment, Jack lifted the monster for protection but was perplexed by the nonexistent impact against the demon he held aloft. *What?* he thought. *No way they missed.*

His appendage dutifully confirmed that they had halted, somehow stopping themselves from striking the third in the nick of time.

Without delay, Jack tossed their fellow forward and waited for the catch before swiftly crashing into all three with a well-placed dropkick.

The demonic trio made an agile recovery, already shuffling into position as Jack arrived in their midst on the front lawn. They immediately resumed their method of attack, viciously sending forth a consistent barrage of strikes.

This time, however, he would abandon his fluid weaving for blocking, switching up with an unpredictable rhythm while seeking an opportunity to redirect any incoming blows.

Jack was carefully observing the demons and soon realized their attacks had not become clumsy. *Hey Bossu,* he said silently, *don't people start slipping up in combat once frustration sets in? These three are getting more pissed by the second, but . . .* He remained stationary, using only his elbows and hands to deflect a series of incoming strikes. *I can't get them to hit each other!*

The Lwa responded with amusement. "Hm hm hm," he began. "Mad?"

*No, I'm genuinely curious. They seem incapable of striking themselves.*

"Well, for one, they are not *people*."

Jack stepped away from a kick rising toward his face before deflecting another's punch, a maneuver that put both demons in each other's way. *You know what I mean.*

Though it had all occurred in the blink of an eye, the two cops' movements came to a halt. Their limbs stopped right in front of their unintended targets, forcing them into a contorted position that seemed impossible to hold.

*Being aware of your surroundings is one thing.* Jack halted for barely a second to behold the strange sight. *But this?* He suddenly started moving again, sweeping the legs out from underneath the two immobile demons while simultaneously ducking under the third's swipe at the back of his head. *This is something else.*

"They are not human, I said," Bossu replied. "You do not understand?"

"I do now," the young host replied aloud. "In that case . . ."

Sensing the orientation of the third cop as it continued reeling from its missed swipe, Jack rose from his leg sweep while continuing its spin and turned into the falling foe, striking the demon with a rising hook to the head.

The strength of Jack's blow, coupled with the weight behind its fall, spun the demon's head around several times. The total rotations achieved could be counted by the grisly rungs of contorted flesh twisted through the imposter's neck.

Although the body landed with its chest to the ground, the revolving head had already stopped in a position opposite to the norm, causing it to face upward despite the body's overall orientation.

Jack's eyes widened with dismay as he looked down. *Oh no, this is what I was afraid of! Bossu!*

The cop had lost all his demonic features. His face reverted to the original human appearance, revealing just a regular guy, albeit in the throes of agony.

"It hurts!!" he bellowed.

Having already attained a suitable vantage point, Alyssa and the man looked at Jack standing defeatedly in the dark, as if petrified.

"Help me, please!! It-it hurts, oh God!"

Before Jack could fill his head with thoughts of regret, he was subjected to yet another telepathic reprimand as Bossu began barking at him. "THEY. ARE. NOT. HUMAN!"

Jack gnashed through his doleful expression with clenched teeth, truly understanding Bossu's statement at last.

Seeing this, the once-distraught cop began grinning, its face suddenly shifting into the demonic. "Puss—"

Its taunt was cut off by a rage-fueled punch rocketing into its mouth.

"Shut up!" Jack screamed, forcing his fist into the demon's throat.

Anticipating a sneak attack from the remaining two foes, he had already sent his appendage whipping about the area. As it did so, its feedback reported another presence lodged within the victim on the ground before him.

"What the hell is that?" Jack growled. "Sit up!"

He seized the demon's hair with his free hand and lifted it up by its head, ignoring the unnatural orientation of its body.

Operating on pure instinct, he homed in on the concealed aura. *And what do we have here?*

Flexing his digits rigid, Jack thrust his hand farther down the demon's twisted gullet. The signature of the otherworldly presence radiated like heat from a lightbulb. Using his fingers to confirm it as the source, he clutched what felt like a densely fibrous root before yanking it out.

His enemies in the background were preoccupied with a confounding tussle against the shadows. Their efforts to pounce on him were hindered by his appendage, which was now greatly strengthened by the pervasive darkness.

"What in the world?" Jack held up the extricated root to look at it while the two cops struggled at his back. "Ecckh!"

Irritated by its constant thrashing about, he steadily tightened his grip and slowed it to a squirm until its agony prevented any further movement.

Situated at both ends of its cylindrical body, he noticed rings of sharp teeth, crowded together like those of the demon cops. *A hookworm from hell.*

Jack looked back at the body it was pulled from, its demonic features unchanged. The cop remained in the posture he had held it when rooting out the parasite.

Keeping his eyes on the catatonic foe, Jack suddenly gave the hookworm a death grip and squished it to pieces. *You die now.*

The yellow eyes of the cop went out like a light before its body immediately decomposed into dust and tufts of hair. Even the uniform disappeared.

"So they're just puppets," Jack said, rising from his crouch.

He twiddled his fingers free from the gooey remains of the parasite as he untangled the two cops behind him.

"Indeed," Bossu replied. "Most likely their primary function is reconnaissance."

Jack turned and began approaching the newly freed adversaries, passively detecting the different locations in which their parasites were hidden. "Yeah, remote viewing basically. Now it's time to end these freaks."

He evaded the opening punch of the first while tripping

him with an extending foot. Like a bully, he pushed the second backward before immediately descending upon the one he had tripped.

Grabbing the back of the demon's collar, Jack dragged it toward the raised edge of the walkway cutting across the front yard. In one smooth motion, he threw the demon on it before leaping high into the air.

Jack landed on the back of his foe with a crushing weight far greater than what his slight frame seemed capable of, and pulverized the parasite nestled against the demon's spine.

The force with which Jack landed destroyed the parasite so thoroughly that it looked like he disintegrated the demon with one mighty stomp.

Undeterred, the third and final demon had already begun sprinting at Jack as he crashed down.

*No fear, eh?* he thought. *Well, I guess that's easy since you're not actually here.*

Quickly spinning on his heel, he sent up bits of debris and mummified hair before impaling the advancing demon with his hand.

"Gotcha!" Clutching the parasite within, Jack pulled it out from the imposter's bowels and destroyed it the same way as the first.

He turned around as the body collapsed into a heap of decomposition.

Scanning the vicinity for potential threats, Jack noticed the human onlookers staring at him from the wrecked front door and raised his arm. "Hello."

The two Abettors hurried over upon seeing his salutation.

Jack began walking over to meet them, watching as Alyssa tempered her enthusiasm by slowing her approach. As she averted her gaze to holster her pistol, the old man overtook her.

The man grasped Jack's newly outstretched hand with both of his own. "So this is the heir," he began. Pausing his exuberant handshake, he leaned to the side to look at the piled remains of their assailants and, having done so, continued shaking his hand all the more. "Damn, it truly is a pleasure to meet you, Jack. My name is Alessandro Paradojo del Verdad, but please call me Dox." He ended the handshake in order to run a scratching finger down his head. "I am left with an endless list of questions regarding how you got so good in such little time. I'd be scared stiff if it weren't for Alyssa already meeting you."

Jack thought to return the smile but, realizing he was still wearing a mask, suddenly began questioning the accuracy of its expressions.

"R-right," he replied, awkwardly feeling about his face. "I met her like once, though."

*Bossu, how do I take this off?*

"You see?" the Lwa began. "You are still a small boy, just look at how flustered you have become." He let out one of his gravelly chuckles. "Did I not speak true when declaring your claim a lie evident to the both of us?"

*I don't know what you're talking about. Can you help me or not?*

"Apologies, I cannot."

Dumbfounded by the lad's fidgeting, Dox glanced at Alyssa. Meeting his gaze, she gave a quick roll of her eyes.

"I don't think it can come off like that, son," Dox said.

"Yeah, I think you're right," Jack said, ceasing his efforts. "So . . . uh . . . what happened here? Why the cops?"

"They were looking for you," Alyssa replied.

"For me?"

Noticing his surprise, she folded her arms. "You didn't know that?"

"No," Jack said, feeling slightly peeved by her incredulous expression that was all too familiar to him. "Why would I?"

Scoffing, she rolled her eyes again before Dox motioned to her with his hand. "Take it easy, Alyssa." He looked up at Jack. "Not that I'm ungrateful, as you came right on time but, ah, how did you know to come here?"

"Oh." He could hear his Lwa's lipless chuckle as he considered how to respond. "That comedian Samedi brought me here."

Alyssa unfolded her arms. "Baron Samedi?"

Silent, Jack gave her a rapid up-and-down glance before nodding his head.

"Why?" Dox asked, expertly containing his shock. "I mean, what was his reasoning? I doubt the baron sent you here to save us."

"I'm not sure. They were talking about my role, and, oh yeah, Samedi said you had something that belonged to me."

Alyssa looked down at the man, evidently clueless as to what Jack was referring to. Dox, however, bore an expression indicating he knew exactly what Samedi was talking about.

Staring blankly into the distance, his handlebar mustache curved evermore upward as a knowing smile formed underneath. "You must be one hell of a prodigy, son," he said. "The baron is known to send people to their deaths. For him to actually aid you speaks volumes."

Jack shrugged his shoulders. "Maybe that was his intention," he replied. "He did send me into an ambush."

"Your attempt at modesty is appreciated," Dox said, turning toward the house, "but no, his intent was a rescue. You dispatched the demons too easily for one as perceptive as he to think them capable of ambushing you."

"Aww, shucks."

"As far as the aid goes, come, follow me."

Jack watched as the man began returning to the destroyed entrance. "Sorry about the front door," he stated, following behind. "It's a relief that the ruckus didn't wake anyone, but still, I imagine this is going to be difficult to explain to your neighbors."

"If there were any neighbors to speak of," Alyssa began from the rear, "obviously they would be checking to see what's up?"

"Okay?"

"The Abettors own this entire street," Dox explained. "Within every house resided one of our members."

"I'm sorry for your loss," Jack replied knowingly.

"Thank you, but it's all right. It's been almost a decade since they lost their lives. That was the battle in which all of hell seemed to fall silent. No sign of any threat that big since. And it's a good thing too, since we're all that's left."

Entering the house, Jack was led past the room destroyed in the fight. "Yeah, I figured."

He was left standing in the middle of the next room as Dox made a beeline for a bookshelf on a distant wall. Briefly watching the man's actions, a piece of machinery caught his eye.

Glowing with a gentle green light underneath a windowsill, he furrowed his brow as he stared at it.

"Afraid it'll make you obsolete?" Alyssa asked. Jack looked at her, brow still wrinkled. "Don't tell me you don't know what that is."

Jack glanced at it once more before looking back at her. "A fire hydrant from the future?"

"It's Inicio," she said, finally smiling.

"Oh, that thing? Why would you guys even bother?"

"Well, gotta be state of the art, right?"

Bossu's voice suddenly entered his mind. His tone carried an unfamiliar exuberance.

"Tell me, Jack," he demanded excitedly. "Do you feel that?! Do you?"

Jack approached the piece of machinery, pretending to examine it while waiting for Dox to return. *I guess.*

"The real reason is that supposedly, the more people in a community who have it, the more effectively it works. Not having one would just draw unwanted attention to our street, so it just made sense to get it and avoid the nonsense."

"Yeah, I get it," Jack said. He sensed something was off as he paced around the glowing beacon. "It's weird that it didn't detect anything or send for help this whole time."

Alyssa fell silent for a moment as Dox made his way back.

"Yeah," she began, "that *is* weird. Maybe because they were dressed as cops?"

"Or weren't of this world?" Dox said, holding a case of some sort.

"Does that make sense?" Bossu asked as Jack began reaching toward the machine.

The air seemed to vibrate around his hand as it approached until suddenly, Dox brought forth what he was holding, offering it up toward the entranced young man.

Jack turned away from the machine to see the saxophone case. "No thanks," he began politely, hiding his irritation, "I don't play."

Bossu's rumbling sigh of exasperation rang out before falling utterly silent.

Dox watched as Jack turned back to Inicio. "You don't understand," he said, opening the case.

Jack felt his appendage react immediately upon hearing the pop of the latches, wildly resonating with whatever was within the case.

He reflexively turned toward what he thought to be the

source of the disturbance and found what appeared to be an unassuming metal rod nestled within. Jack stared inside for a moment, unsure what to make of it before gasping in surprise.

The rod suddenly triggered a memory he had blocked out, taking him back to his childhood during the period when Josiah's visits were intermittent. He remembered playing with this very same piece of metal after finding it in his father's belongings.

His father's immediate reaction upon discovering his small son would prove to be the only time he had displayed any true signs of anger. It would be several months before Josiah appeared again and Jack could not fathom why his father raged at him so.

Dox glanced at Alyssa after seeing the consequent frown form on his face.

*This is what got Dad so pissed?* Jack thought, taking the rod from the case.

As he did so, he noticed Alyssa take a cautious step backward.

"What is it?"

Still holding up the case, albeit defensively now, Dox raised his index finger toward the rod. "Press that button."

Jack noticed a silver nub near the top and pressed it without hesitation.

Several telescoping rods sprung forth with a snap. The last of these contained a shard of curved metal that swung out from its length before immediately ejecting several others with a similar upward swing.

Each shard of metal was connected to form a hook.

Jack stared at the deadly weapon, its crescent-shaped blade reflecting the room's light against its edge, and immediately understood his father's outburst and the prolonged absence thereafter. *Sorry, Dad.*

He clenched his eyes shut as he felt them beginning to sting.

"Are you okay?" Alyssa began, but she was interrupted by an abrupt shushing from Dox.

Jack failed to respond. Silent, eyes still closed, he suddenly saw the image of the weapon. He watched as something began stretching forth like a slender tendril from an unseen vine, darker than the black of his eyelids. It gently touched the staff before creeping along its length and then, like a caduceus, began wrapping itself around the weapon's entirety.

Feeling the edges of the blade as it became enveloped, Jack gasped upon realizing he was witnessing his appendage at last. He could sense the physicality of the weapon within his psyche. He released it with his hands and heard Alyssa let out a gasp of her own. His eyes still closed, Jack beheld the weapon, remaining horizontally aloft. He opened his teary eyes to see it airborne and unmoving before sending it into the void.

"Yeah, I'm fine," he replied with a smile.

# CHAPTER 14

Despite Dox urging him to stay longer, Jack hurriedly took his leave from their home.

"I would," he said, making his way to the hole in the front of the house, "but Samedi told me to meet him once I'm done here. Don't worry, I'll be back."

Jack made his way outside and immediately sprinted down the darkened street.

Bossu scoffed. "Running again?" he asked. "Have you forgotten your abilities already?"

"No," Jack replied, entering the shadows. Determining himself to be thoroughly concealed, he swiftly warped himself into the void and appeared standing before Bossu. "I just don't want them to know what I'm capable of. Not yet, anyway."

The Lwa growled approvingly. "Very good, Jack."

Bossu watched as his young host quickly opened an aperture and stepped into the Deadside, appearing at the front of the Manse Ghede. "You do not trust them?"

Jack approached the front door, giving it a hurried knock. "I don't *not* trust them," he replied. "Just erring on the side of caution."

He fidgeted impatiently as he waited for an answer and, receiving none, moved to knock again. Just before his knuckles struck the door, however, it swung open and revealed Samedi standing some distance from the doorway. The skeleton lord casually shrugged his coat to a proper fit on his shoulders while tightening his pants.

With no hat atop his skull, the flesh form in which he had apparently just inhabited continued its recession down his neck, progressively revealing his body of bare bones.

"Forgive me, kid," he began, continuing to adjust himself. "You were finished a bit sooner than I anticipated."

"It's my bad," Jack replied. "I kinda rushed over here because I want to find Freda ASAP and just get it over with."

Like a magician, Samedi held out his hand to the side, causing his hat to warp into his grasp. "You're a proactive one," he stated, looking down at Jack while positioning his hat. "Unfortunately, the situation we find ourselves in prevents us from being proactive."

Jack remained silent for a moment, processing what he just heard. He stood still as Samedi began making his way toward the wingback chair set at the far side of the room.

He gave an agitated shake of the head before replying to the Ghede lord. "I'm not sure what that means."

"We wait for the conspirators to make the first move," Samedi explained. "For you this means fending off the forces of the Deadside, as you assured my fellows just moments ago."

"Killing demons will lead us to Freda?"

"In a roundabout way, yes."

Jack rolled his eyes before suddenly pacing around the room. *Is it just me*, he said silently, *or does this guy not give a crap?*

The tall skeleton halted his footsteps, apparently puzzled by the lad's anxious display.

"He certainly does," Bossu replied. "The threat of Damballa's wrath guarantees it."

Jack came to a stop, unwittingly positioning himself in front of the chair. "There's gotta be something I can do to speed things up."

"You got some reason for seeking alternatives on your first day?"

Jack childishly threw his hands in the air. "For all we know, your plan may wind up taking forever!"

Responding with fake vexation, Samedi sucked his teeth forcefully, resulting in a loud and drawn-out chirp. Jack covered his ears as the Ghede lord extended the piercingly high-pitched inhale to the point where it was nearly intolerable before bringing it to an end. His ears were still ringing as Samedi gestured for him to step aside with the wave of his ivory-colored hand.

Jack watched as one of Samedi's subordinates walked into the room. He quickly uncovered his ears after seeing her irritated expression.

"Who did that?!" she shrieked.

Jack reflexively pointed toward the baron.

The woman's red hair rose ominously as her furious gaze remained fixed on their young guest, prompting him to gesture more aggressively.

"Gird yourself like a man," Bossu began. "Brigitte is merely teasing you."

The words coincided with Samedi's address. "Be nice, my dear."

Hearing this, the phony anger immediately left the woman's face as Jack dropped his arm to his side, staring at her.

"You're making fun of me?" he asked.

Brigitte made her way to the newly seated skeleton king. "I am."

Jack followed her with his head as she walked to her

husband, ultimately stopping at the arm of his wingback.

"Jack boy," Samedi began, "you gotta believe that I know what I'm doing."

He paused as an irritated Jack took a deep inhale through his nose. *Jack boy?!*

The Ghede lord continued. "You're smart enough to have figured out that I'm the only one you can trust, ain't you? After mommy dearest and Bruh Terror, of course."

Jack nodded reluctantly. "Yeah, I figured that out."

"Glad we're on the same page." The skeleton reclined into the admittedly comfortable-looking chair. "Now, while I appreciate your gusto and all, there's no way you gonna get to the bottom of this by sleuthing or dusting for fingerprints. You see, the conspiracy has been orchestrated in such a way that our every move must be one of calculated intent."

"Why do I feel like your hands are tied?" Jack asked.

"Because there is precious little to go on."

The young host shook his head. "All you guys are so ancient but you still—"

"Mind your tongue," Bossu commanded.

"Never mind."

"What is it?" Samedi said.

Jack sighed in exasperation before speaking. "Have you ever seen how detectives operate in my world?"

The baron let out a grunt, seemingly amused at the thought. "If I'm in the Liveside, then it's for enjoyment's sake, and watching mortals solve crimes ain't how I have fun, ya dig?"

"You can stop right there, thanks," Jack replied, cautiously glancing at Brigitte. Noticing how totally unbothered she was by her husband's statement, he continued. "Anyway, I wouldn't be surprised if there's actually a lot we have to go on. We just have to recognize it when we see it."

"Look, my king," Brigitte began, "the lad thinks himself wise."

"I didn't say that."

Brigitte continued. "Shall we indulge him?"

The seated skeleton began quaking with amusement as he looked at his agent. "I think we shall, my dear," he replied. "Maybe then he'll finally get it." He casually beckoned Jack with his hand. "We merely have to recognize it when we see it, you say?"

Jack nodded. "That's what I said."

"And how do we do that, detective?" Brigitte asked.

*Are they always this condescending?* Jack asked.

"Jack," Bossu began, "you are not blameless. To think these ancient ones can learn something from mortals . . . hm hm hm. And have you forgotten the condescension you had for Lou and the others? It was not too long ago."

*I forgot about that.*

He looked at Brigitte. "By starting with the precious little you know for certain and work your way from there."

"Go on, detective, don't stop now."

Jack remained unfazed. "Well, we know Freda's missing. We only need to figure out why. I'm thinking envy."

"What is your basis for that?" Samedi began. "Not saying you're off base as of yet, but why would anyone be jealous?"

Jack looked at Brigitte with exaggerated suspicion, managing to move the area of the mask where his eyebrows would be. "Your wife wouldn't be jealous of you being with another woman, would she?"

The two Ghede immediately burst into laughter.

*I guess not?*

"No," Bossu replied. "Not in the slightest."

The two Lwa had been facing each other while laughing. When it was all over, having finished, the skeleton returned his sights to Jack. "Next."

Brigitte placed a hand on Samedi's shoulder. "To be fair," she began, "most of us were somewhat envious of Freda, or at least her worship."

"Well, my dear, if that is a motive, we're in big trouble."

"What?" Jack asked. "Why?"

"Because that suggests it's us against most of the pantheon," Samedi replied. "Thing is, it ain't possible for so many hands to be involved and still not get the attention of those that are neutral."

"Yeah," Jack said with a sigh, "that makes sense." He folded his arms across his chest. "So nothing else?"

"Let me try again," Brigitte stated. With pursed lips and an upward gaze, she pretended to be in deep thought.

*She's not gonna stop, is she?*

"Doubtful," Bossu replied.

"How about . . . the Ghede falling under the sky father's condemnation!" Having said this, Bridgette beamed at her husband before excitedly turning to Jack. "That counts, right?" Jack stared back at her in silence, maintaining a look of boredom as she continued. "Damballa himself implied they were sure to have anticipated he would be held responsible."

"You got enemies among the pantheon, boss?" Jack asked.

Elbows resting on the wingback's armrests, Samedi brought his hands together in front of his face. "After giving it some ponderin'," he began, "I wager it's more likely the sky father is just a consequence they couldn't avoid, not a true objective of their plot."

The commissure of Jack's mask obscured his sudden smirking. "I can think of one."

Samedi tapped the fingers of both hands against each other in a wavelike rhythm. "One what?"

"A true motive." The young mortal quickly answered the

question that was sure to follow. "The rescinding of your oath was definitely a motive."

"But . . . why?" Brigitte asked.

The Ghede queen had turned to the sitting skeleton before she completed the question, suggesting that it was meant more for her husband than their guest. However, the Ghede lord remained pensive, allowing Jack to continue.

"The possibilities are vast," he said. "Could be to extinguish humanity or to make you Ghede look bad. Could also be an objective we are not privy to."

Samedi lowered his praying hands. "Or it could be to get an inexperienced Shadowman out in the open."

"I guess," Jack replied, shrugging. "But for what? They already killed the last one. All this just to do it again?"

Samedi and Brigitte looked at each other once more, this time devoid of mirth.

"Josiah Boniface killed himself," Samedi stated. "Bossu didn't tell you?"

Jack's arms remained folded as he gasped, prompting Bossu to take action. "Jack," the Lwa said, "do not forget what I told you regarding your father orchestrating his own death and ridding himself of my essence. Josiah killing himself is no revelation for you."

Jack exhaled to gain composure. "I already told you," he began, "I don't know any Bossu. But regarding my dad, I guess I kind of always knew deep down that's how he went out." He began nodding as if in recollection, though he was in a silent struggle against the rekindled thoughts surrounding his father's death. "You just confirmed it for me, is all." His head stopped moving while he unfolded his arms. "So damn, getting their hands on an inexperienced Shadowman *is* a valid motive then."

Brigitte watched the baron as he stood up from his chair.

"There you have it, Jack boy," he said. "You simply gotta accept that your elders know what they're doing. No point takin' the long way just for ego's sake."

"I'm not sure I follow."

"Well," Samedi replied, "you better learn how, and fast too. All that detective work only comes full circle to the same recourse that I said at first."

Jack shot a look of confusion at Brigitte. "But you said fending off your forces and killing demons all day will lead us to Freda. How is that related to my inexperience?"

"Hm hm hm."

Jack could hear Bossu's contained chuckles as Samedi stared at him.

"What?" he asked, addressing both Bossu and the seemingly perplexed skeleton.

"How is it related to your inexperience, you say?" the skeleton asked. "Tell me, how would you go about becoming experienced?"

Jack scoffed at the question, but before he could perform the accompanying eye roll, he suddenly understood. "Oh."

"Consider it a direct order," Samedi stated. "Get experienced, at once!"

# CHAPTER 15

Two days had passed since Jack had been formally introduced to the Abettors, or what remained of their guild. And true to Samedi's word, the denizens of the Deadside had begun to cross over through interdimensional breaches known as blights.

Jack had an innate ability allowing him to detect the moment one of these began to form. However, this awareness was relegated solely to the blight's formation, requiring clever use of his other senses to determine its actual location.

Fortunately, the blights only seemed to appear in the remote bayous, where their appearance would go unnoticed by the general populace. Nevertheless, Jack always made sure to send a crow from the void to keep watch over his mother's house.

Jack, Alyssa, and Dox had made it a habit to routinely patrol the affected regions come nightfall.

"How heartwarming of Samedi to be so considerate with these things," Jack had said, slicing through the latest cluster of undead visitors with ease. He had only grown in proficiency since his first fight in the Deadside, easily capable of taking care of the blights on his own.

Unfortunately for their otherworldly visitors, restriction enchantments weaved into the barrier between worlds by Baron Samedi himself prevented them from retaining their horrific forms when crossing over. Instead, they became swathed in an unsightly guise of rotting flesh, slightly human and less grotesque than their original forms, but not by much.

This facade put them at a further disadvantage, utterly stripping them of the agility displayed in the Deadside. Their minds and reflexes seemed to be intact, but their forms encumbered them.

Jack would often be seen chuckling during the skirmishes with the undead. Their eyes would betray an awareness of some incoming attack, but their bodies prevented them from doing anything about it.

"I doubt it," Dox had replied, his hands flickering with an arcane power, incapacitating the foes seeking to flee. "Most likely, a more public display would only serve as a reminder of how superannuated he has become."

"What's that mean?"

Seeing the several undead that had been paralyzed by her adoptive father, Alyssa shot their heads off in quick succession. "You don't have a phone?"

Leaving the blade hovering in midair, Jack patted the seamless membrane of void material lining his chest before checking the pockets of his cargos. "Shoot," he replied, "I left it in my other pants."

"He means that nobody would care. They would probably just think it's a festival or something."

He laughed as he sheathed his weapon, sending it into the void. "Yeah, but what happens once the dying starts? You can take that one."

Alyssa fired a round into the last foe. "I don't know. We're just talking hypothetically, you know that, right? I imagine come daybreak everyone will just say it was a bunch of costumed psychopaths."

Jack paused, considering the suggestion. "That's stupid."

Alyssa locked eyes with him before firing into the already liquifying foe.

Dox informed Jack that his recently acquired weapon was a type of blade traditionally called a sengese. This particular one was a deadly keepsake passed down through his predecessors known as the Shadow Scythe.

Jack considered questioning the accuracy of the weapon's name since its bladed portion was clearly sickle-shaped, but he held his tongue.

Whether it was due to its design or type, the prowess Jack displayed with the weapon seemed innate, shocking even to him. Additionally, the sengese exhibited an affinity with his appendage that was nothing short of remarkable, enabling him to wield it with a level of telekinetic dexterity that Bossu himself found impressive.

"You sense it, do you not?" he had asked, proudly watching his host conduct his self-imposed training.

During the day, Jack frequented the Deadside to hone his skills, sometimes seeking fights with the denizens and other times practicing skills and abilities not possible in daylight.

"Sense what?" he replied. "That this isn't the extent of what I can do?" The Lwa began his gravelly chuckle as his host continued. "Yeah, I can feel it. I just don't want to spoil it for myself too soon."

Before long, Jack began to experience diminishing returns on his training method. Within only a few days, the modernized denizens of the Deadside had somehow become wise to his scheme, and this knowledge, when coupled with his weapon proficiency, seemed to sap the fervor and bloodlust they exhibited in battle.

Jack frowned at a group of departing monsters. Some grumbled in disinterest before submissively turning their backs, while others simply sprinted away on sight. As he watched them flee, he recalled his conversation with the baron and realized that enemies such as these would only serve to hold him back.

"I'm gonna ask Samedi to show me where the apex monsters are," he said aloud. "What do you think?"

"I think you should just get on the bicycle and ride it," Bossu replied. "Don't ask how to do it."

"So you agree?"

Realizing his Lwa was ignoring him, Jack took one last look at the fleeing monsters before departing for his mom's house. In an instant, he vanished from the Deadside and reappeared at the home, emerging from the shadowy areas of their darkened basement.

Jack retrieved his balled-up T-shirt from the pocket of his cargos and shifted off his suit of void fabric and mask. Hearing the rush of water from the kitchen sink, he began calling out to his mother as he put on his excessively wrinkled shirt. "Mom, it's me. I'm coming up the stairs."

Jack could hear his mom shut off the faucet before he opened the door at the top of the staircase. He exited the basement and saw his mother smiling at him from the kitchen.

"Hey, Mom," he said, walking in for a hug.

Helena gave her son a tight squeeze before stepping back and holding him by the shoulders. "Welcome home, special boy. It ain't been but two days, and you're already busy as can be."

Jack seemed slightly puzzled as he looked at her. "What makes you say that?" he asked, smiling.

Helena maintained her grip on his shoulders as she spoke.

"Clean clothes that have been creased up like this"—she gave her son a swift once-over—"can only mean one thing."

Jack reflexively looked down and huffed lightly as he rolled his eyes. "Oh my goodness, Mom," he said.

Bossu suddenly began addressing his host. "Her assessment is incorrect?"

*Well*, he replied, silently reflecting, *I guess not.*

Jack hurriedly followed after his mother as she made her way back into the kitchen. "Actually, Mom," he began, "you're right, ha-ha."

"I know, my boy," she replied. "Now go on and tell your mother why you so busy."

Jack stopped in front of the kitchen table. "I've just been easing my way into my responsibilities as Shadowman, I guess."

"You done so soon?" Helena asked. "I love seeing my special boy and all that jazz, but I know how you get when you fixin' for a goal, you don't miss nobody." She moved closer to him as she continued. "So why you here? Tell me what's happened."

No longer capable of feeling frazzled by his mother's aggressive style, Jack's delivery was unwittingly upbeat. "Nothing yet," he replied. "But I'm going to try and convince Baron Samedi to direct me to subjects of his that are more . . . capable, I guess?"

Helena held a pregnant pause while giving her son another once-over. "You gonna go on and ask the god of the underworld to provide you with monsters." Jack was nodding along, attempting reassurance as she formed her words. "And you reckon this will make you stronger?"

"It's called farming, Mom."

"But how will it work, is where my thoughts gettin' bogged. The strength of your punch is the strength of your punch, ain't it? I don't see how seeking a trap from Samedi will make you hit harder."

"No," Jack replied, "it's like the threshing floor that the preacher is always talking about." He waited for a sign of understanding from his mother. "You get it?"

Helena shook her head.

"My hope is that experiencing fights will give me a better understanding of my powers, which can only make me more effective." He paused, again checking if his words were registering. "I wasn't trained to know how any of this superstitious voodoo stuff works, remember? I gotta improvise."

Helena nodded abruptly at Jack as she broke her silence. "How you feelin'?"

"How do I look?"

"I've been through this already, son," she said. "Your dad would return home without a scratch on him, but"—her expression transitioned into a focused glare as she leaned forward—"in the eyes is where it's at."

While he was able to maintain a brave face back at Samedi's, voiceless suggestions surrounding his father's death troubled him.

Was he eaten alive or merely beaten to death?

The fact that his father willingly offered himself up on his behalf made considering any scenario too torturous for Jack.

*No way I'm telling her*, he thought, calmly staring back at his mother. The relative ease with which he was able to defeat the demonic hordes made the untroubled facade easier to maintain.

However, it was not enough.

Helena extinguished the intensity on her face, having recognized what she was looking for. "What is it?" she asked. "Something's troubling you."

*Damn.*

Jack reflexively cast his gaze downward. "I just don't know if I'll ever be strong enough," he lied.

His mother placed her hand on his shoulder. "It ain't going well?"

"I'm winning," he replied. "So it's going well enough for now."

"So why you troubled? You mentioned the threshing floor making a way to learn more about your powers. You don't think that finna happen or what?" She released her grip on his shoulder. "Boy, you ain't lying, is you?" She watched her son roll his eyes, his skyward gaze a telltale sign of sudden ponderings, not rudeness.

"I should've said I don't *feel* like I'll ever be strong enough."

"You winning, ain't you? If snatching up victories at the start of your journey ain't proof you got what it takes, then I don't know what basis you using for *feeling*."

Jack quickly summoned a new excuse. "I need new abilities, is what I meant."

Helena swatted at the air as she sucked her teeth. "Boy, please!" she exclaimed, turning to walk away. "You hungry or what?"

"Yeah, I can eat."

"Sit while I fix you a plate."

Jack obliged and immediately put his head on the table. He could hear the clink and clang of the kitchenware.

"Obsessive turn of mind, I reckon," Helena stated. "You did the same madness with your schoolwork."

Jack looked up from the table and watched his mother set the plate of food before him. "Yeah," he began. "Only then I knew what my goal was and how to get there. I don't know any of those things now. That's why I have no choice but to turn up the OCD and do any and all things I can think of."

Helena took an adjacent seat as her son began shoveling rice into his mouth. The noise of his cutlery clashing against his plate quickly filled the room.

Similar to sleep, Bossu's presence greatly reduced Jack's need for food, but far from inhibiting enjoyment, his taste buds seemed to be enhanced. Much like the stimuli from his strolls through Washington Square, food always felt new.

"You know what your father would say?"

Jack heaved the bolus down his throat, his buoy-like Adam's apple returning to its position as he shook his head.

Suddenly speaking with proper pronunciation, Helena's heavy accent was no more. "First things first, boy."

Jack began grinning at his raised fork. Switching her speech to one exceedingly articulate made for an impersonation of his father that was so accurate that he found it bordering on mockery.

As had Josiah.

Leaning her back against the chair, Helena continued. "Complete the first task within the list of possible solutions. If it fails, move to the second. If it works, even partially, you have your standard by which all the rest within the list will be judged."

"Yeah," Jack said, "he *would* say that. In exactly the same way, too . . . *if* it applied to me." He returned to his food and was chewing a bit before noticing his mother staring at him in silent disagreement. "But"—he protested, quickly using his hand to block the grains escaping his mouth—"how though?"

Continuing her gaze, Helena remained positioned against the back of the chair. The woman's body suddenly jostled a bit, as if trapping a small hiccup. Jack's eyes followed her as she leaned in to hold his shoulder.

"When you came on in here talking about getting stronger—hear me now, my special boy." Even though she was now smiling warmly, her voice's command for attention stilled him, compelling him to smile back. "I asked you about Samedi's monsters and how you reckon they could make you stronger."

"Hm hm hm."

"You said something like more fights means more learnin' of your powers."

Jack nodded along. This time, the gesture gave a certain smugness to his smile.

"This is what you reckoned to mean getting stronger, right from the start. And you just said you winning. Ain't that something that turn of mind o' yours should be focused on? At least before investing in something that might not work as good." Using her hands, she swept the dribbled rice grains from the table and made her way to the garbage. "If at all."

Her son remained seated as he processed her words. *Yeah, that makes sense*, he thought. *Makes things a lot easier, too.*

"When did new abilities come to mean getting stronger?" Helena asked.

Jack unwittingly began running his finger along the fork's handle like a caterpillar as he tried to think of an explanation.

"I seen that before too," she said, noticing his fidgeting. "Must be something downright awful if you actin' like that."

Jack's finger froze as he looked up at her. "I just want to be the best," he replied. "It made me start overthinking things I guess."

"By the stars, whelp!" Bossu suddenly began, his voice bearing a mix of amusement and disapproval. "Forsake this foolish lie already!"

Helena started moving to the sink to wash her hands. "Sounds like you bamboozlin' yourself into a wild-goose chase that won't prosper none," she said. "You tryin' to be Merlin when that ain't your style. From now on, stay in your lane. Whatever's workin', that's your lane." She gripped the faucet and turned toward her son. "Don't get all defensive now."

Jack smiled resignedly, his demeanor devoid of any snark

or insincerity. "I'm not, Mom. I knew you were right back at the part about investing in inferior options or something. Yeah, you win."

"That's my special boy," Helena replied with a nod. She faced forward and turned the faucet. "Stick with what you know. I just want you to be wise for yourself, is all. The same way a dog be on his squeaky toy, that's how you gotta be from here on out. Oftentimes, it be our reliance on the things we know that put us on to the things we don't."

Jack's shoulders began to quake from his sudden amusement, mirroring Bossu's chuckles that had been sounding in his head.

Helena spoke over her shoulder as she rubbed her hands underneath the water. "What's so funny?"

"Yes, do tell!" Bossu said.

At first, Jack intended to just deflect the question, but his Lwa's statement made him decide otherwise. "I honestly don't know how you'll take it," he began, "but since you asked, I figure I might as well." Having shut off the water, Helena grabbed a towel to dry her hands and turned around to listen to her son. "So yeah, it's just that Bossu gave me advice crazy similar to what you just said."

Jack looked up to see his mother patting her hands dry, staring down at him, before immediately setting his sights on his plate to resume eating.

"I'm touched, whelp."

Jack ignored his Lwa as he addressed his mother. "It's just funny to me, Mom."

Helena let out a sigh before responding. "Well, if the monster is giving you advice on par with your mother's, then I guess he ain't all bad."

"How insightful she is today!"

Jack had been rolling his eyes at Bossu's statement when his mother suddenly held the sides of his head with her slightly uncomfortable, cold, and wet hands. "Can he hear me?" she asked.

Jack nodded, unable to hide his confusion as she spoke. "Motherly advice be damned, when dealing with him . . ." Helena paused to lean in toward her son's face and although this movement was not overly dramatic, her countenance had shifted to one of utmost seriousness. "*Be circumspect.*"

---

The sun was just beginning to rise by the time Jack left home. Seeing as he had nothing better to do, he returned to the Deadside, much to the dismay of its inhabitants.

Jack kept his eyes on the now-fleeing monsters. "I guess I should stop beating around the bush and pay a visit to Samedi."

"Still?" Bossu replied teasingly. "Hm hm, why?"

Jack folded his arms while still gazing into the distance. "You know why," he said. "These are all fodder and I need some of the brute class to get stronger."

"Brute class?" he began. "To what end, Jack?"

"For practice, duh."

The Lwa performed his gravelly titter before addressing his host's statement. "Hm hm hm . . . you got it all wrong," he said. "Practice, you say?" He tittered twice before clearing his throat. "No, whelp, that kind of thinking will not do."

"What do you mean?"

"There is no practice for you, for *us*. That is for petty disputes and competitions when it is understood that both sides will live afterward. The intent to kill operates differently, it is not improved by the *practice* you speak of."

Jack began walking to another vantage point. "Eh?" he voiced. "I don't get it."

"In essence, you are a terrible fighter. That is why you seek conflict in order to prepare for true battle. The trade-off is that you may prove to be an excellent *killer*, but there is a problem that I sense may become a severe weakness if we fail to cast it out."

"And that is?"

"You are thinking too much." Jack stopped moving. "Violence is about instinct, feeling, discernment. Remember what you said about inconvenient bodies? That is obvious in creatures such as these, but recognizing such inherent vulnerabilities in all opponents, *that* is violence."

Jack sensed validity in Bossu's words, and if the Lwa's analysis was accurate, he would be a fool to not take heed. "So what's the solution?" he asked. "I'm only human after all."

"You have to let your old self die."

"I have."

"No, you have not, Jack."

The young host cast his gaze downward. "After everything?" he asked. "How are you so sure?"

Bossu's analysis was deft, cutting through any distractive sinew in order to highlight the evidence of his claim without fostering any emotional pushback. "You fight in the same manner you used to think. Your old paradigm is still unchanged, which is proof that you have yet to be born again. You rely on what you think you know rather than examining it to confirm it can serve as a support *first*."

Despite the Lwa's best efforts to avoid emotional backlash, it failed. "I *am* examining it!" Jack protested. "That's why I said I need more."

Bossu paused as if astonished.

"Hello?"

"Did you mean what you said?" Bossu asked. "At your mother's, I mean. The excrement you were spewing about wanting more powers."

Jack hesitated before responding, unsure of the truth. "Honestly," he replied, "I'm not sure. I guess I had to be on some level."

"Fate has a funny way with you," the Lwa said. "Your mother, although her words of encouragement were based on your deceitful deflection, they were, nevertheless, on the mark."

Jack folded his arms again, appearing to be unconvinced. "In what way?"

"In essence, she was stating that what you *know* or what is *inherent* to you will always prove to be a more reliable resource. At least in the context of defeating your enemies, and by proxy, attaining the experience Samedi commanded of you."

"And that's because?"

"The thought that you need *more* is based on a supposition you have deluded yourself into accepting as knowledge. As usual, relying on what you think you know."

Jack's forearms remained interlocked across his chest as he shrugged impatiently.

The Lwa let out his gravelly sigh. "What *more* do you want?"

"Duh, more powers."

"*Whose* powers?"

"Yours!!" Jack exclaimed. "The shadow!"

"Very well, now hear my words." Bossu paused again, this time as if to take a breath. "Why do you ascribe the void to my *self*?"

"Who else should I ascribe it to, man?! You're the Shadow Lwa!"

"Am I?"

Jack's mind began to race as he felt the familiar discomfort that usually preceded a humbling experience. His tone changed as he began to sense that he may have missed something. "Well, I guess technically . . ."

"Who told you I'm the Shadow Lwa?" Bossu asked.

"Umm . . ."

"Don't you see? No examination."

Jack remained silent, unable to think up a defense before his Lwa's voice suddenly boomed in his head.

"I am not the Shadow Lwa," he roared in anger. "I am Bossu Koblamin . . . *the Lwa killer*!"

Having capitalized on the perfect moment to shock his host with this otherwise obvious revelation, Bossu returned his voice to normal. "I would have thought you figured this out already. After all, you were able to notice the incongruity between my purported identity and my presence in the void all by yourself."

Jack was confused by the sudden sensation forming at the corners of his mouth. It compelled him to smile as the Lwa spoke on.

"Where do you believe that anger you choose to resist comes from? You are admittedly proficient with the void but you took no notice of my true nature, the one I've freely given."

The young host stayed silent, smiling with charged excitement as Bossu ensured he was paying attention. "Jack?"

Though he intended to respond mentally to his Lwa, Jack spoke his reply aloud. "Yesssss."

This was it; the little detail that he had been missing the whole time.

Bossu Koblamin.

"What am I?" the Lwa asked, invitingly.

*Wildness, strength, and—*

"You must remember," Bossu interrupted, his voice humming with anticipation, "for it is the key forged for you at last."

Jack thought back to when he was reading the final aspect of his godhood. He could recall being struck by how out of place it seemed for the characterization of something like a god. How could he have forgotten?

"It is the missing piece that will create me anew . . . in yo—"

Unable to control his excitement, Jack mentally recited the word as it was retrieved by his mind, unintentionally interrupting his Lwa. "*Violence.*"

# CHAPTER 16

Since the conversation with Bossu, Jack had undergone yet another shift in perspective. Not only did it grant him a unique sense of appreciation for his role as Shadowman, but, like the revelations surrounding Josiah, it also created a newfound respect for his Lwa.

It was only due to his father's foresight and meticulous planning that the terrifying Lwa had taken a liking to Jack. Bossu had made it a point to mention this quite often but, like a child too ignorant to fear a fall from a great height, the lad would routinely blow him off. But upon learning the unspoken truth about Bossu, Jack was permanently changed.

The young host was the only person to ever be given the revelation regarding Bossu's banishment. The pantheon kept it secret out of pride, and Bossu would not tell simply because of his contempt for all.

To Jack, this could only mean the pantheon was just a bunch of fakers. Seeing as they all knew the Truth but ensured no one else in the universe did, this conspiracy permitted them to pretend to be things they were not.

It was all just a massive hoax as usual.

Jack's sudden lack of respect for the pantheon made it all too easy to abandon his obligations to them. If not for the fact that he truly desired to elevate his skills to the uppermost, he felt certain Samedi would not see him for a very long time.

However, he also deduced how critically important it was that he took this Truth to the grave. A secret hidden this well for this long was sure to be a death warrant for anyone deemed unfit to know it.

So, although Jack had been completely changed, Dox and Alyssa knew nothing. He resolved that it would be this way for anyone he came into contact with, mortal or otherwise.

Presently, the trio remained on standby in an area where the blights proved wont to manifest. Despite the forecast promising a clear night, it was starting to drizzle.

"Don't lie, guys," Jack said, slapping a mosquito dead against his neck. "You wish the blights were in the city."

"No bugs in the city, I suppose?" Alyssa asked.

"Of course there are, they're just not to the degree of a freaking swamp."

This particular hotspot was located within Bayou Boeuf, and was the only one that seemed to get invaded at around the same time on a consistent basis.

"Less likely to get nabbed by a gator too, I suppose." Dox was smoking a cigar while making his way to his car idling nearby. "You kids keep an eye out, all right?"

"Found one!"

While Jack had been *mentally* alerted to the presence of a breach, he barely had to move to ascertain its location. The tell-tale scent of the Deadside had only just begun to leak through the developing tear, but he was able to *feel* the blight before he smelled it.

Unbeknownst to the others, he had cast his sixth sense far and wide, furiously weaving it across the area like the rotor blade of a helicopter. The radar-like appendage detected the blight's spatial displacement slightly before it took shape.

Indiscernible at first, the blight formed a curtain of space-time that appeared to be drawn open by the putrid invaders slowly making their way in.

Dox put his phone away and hurriedly waved the lingering cloud of smoke from his face. "Thought you were talking gators."

Alyssa started looking over her shoulder at Jack while securing her body cam. Her glance was prolonged because he was in plain clothes, casually leaning against a tree.

About to comment on his showing off, she blinked, only to see him clad in his void material suit the next instant.

Jack was staring at the blight, his night vision enabling him to number the arriving undead with ease. "Three, aaaand . . . that's four." He quickly pushed himself off the tree and made his approach toward the visitors before suddenly stopping short.

*Bossu*, he began, *what's going on?*

"The escalation we have been preparing for," the Lwa replied.

Jack watched in confusion as the blight remained open, his eyes capable of distinguishing between the general darkness of the surrounding area and the newly exposed deep black of the Deadside from which several more monsters emerged.

Unable to see exactly what was happening, thanks to the dark and dense foliage surrounding them, Dox and Alyssa found Jack's uncharacteristic behavior somewhat disconcerting. "What is it, kid?"

Alyssa immediately took out her flashlight in an attempt to illuminate the area but was beaten by a bolt of lightning. The sudden flash revealed what Jack had been looking at.

A group of eight devourers stood in a seeming daze, stunned

by the change in their appearance. They swayed like drunkards, each one eyeing the other as the interdimensional breach began sealing itself like a zipper behind them. Jack caught a glimpse of the countless eyes glowing within the deep blackness just as the portal closed.

Dox began speaking again, keeping his cool. "I'm counting seven, am I seeing this right?"

"No," Jack replied, summoning the sengese to his hand. "There's eight."

He casually swept it across his front despite being well out of melee range, and for a moment, its upper portion remained unseen as if becoming temporarily sheathed.

The unmistakable sounds of tearing flesh briefly ripped through the air one after the other as Jack's swing followed through. His subsequent flourishes revealed the weapon to have been made whole, its sickle portion glinting amidst the twirls as a weighty tumbling could be heard along the ground.

Alyssa's flashlight followed the decapitated bodies as they collapsed and caught sight of their severed heads rolling toward them.

"Damn, kid," Dox said. "That's a neat trick."

Jack punted the head of one of the undead just as the audible bubbling of their liquefaction started. "Yeah, thanks."

Dox continued, attempting to keep the mood light. "I don't know what's more deserving of my attention, that or the amount of visitors who just walked through that blight."

Ignoring the light that Alyssa currently had fixed upon him, Jack repeatedly clenched his jaw while staring silently into the dark. *Why the change?*

"It could be many things," Bossu replied.

Jack was not concerned about demons, undead, Samedi, or pretty much anything at this point. *So what's with this feeling?*

The sound of drizzle intensified into an unexpected downpour.

"Eight demons?" Alyssa asked, raising her voice over the rain crashing into the leafy canopy above their heads. "Was that a fluke or what?"

"I'm gonna check on my mom, guys," Jack said. "Give me a moment."

The mention of Helena caused a shift in Dox's voice. "Is everything all right?"

"Yeah, just doing this for peace of mind."

"Okay, kiddo, we'll keep watch."

Jack sat on the ground, leaning his back against the car's exterior, and prepared himself to link with the crow stationed at the house.

The crows were inconvenient in that they required his full attention when being controlled, which was very different from his sixth sense. The appendage communicated through mental signals and passive feedback loops, adjusting itself based on past experience so as to place little burden on Jack's mental real estate. Conversely, the crow on standby had to actively be put into position at his house every night.

Additionally, in order to determine if anything eventful was occurring in its eyesight, Jack would have to view it from the crow's perspective. This meant he had to stop whatever he was doing and take direct control of it, inconveniently blocking his own vision and replacing it with that of the distant creature.

"All right," Jack announced, "I'm gonna check now."

"Copy."

Alyssa and Dox watched as his eyes adopted the electric purple hue of the crow he was remotely viewing through. He performed a quick sweep of his surroundings and could see the barrier over his mother's house was still intact.

"Looks all good here," Jack said aloud. "I just had a bad—"

Just as he was about to sever the telepathic link, something farther down the block caught his eye. He willed the bird to take off from the trees lining his mother's front yard and began flying it toward the area in question.

"What did you see?" Alyssa asked.

"I'm not sure, it looked like a big ass water balloon exploded or some—"

Having controlled the crow to the area, Jack's vision caught the gruesome sight of intense slaughter, causing him to momentarily fall silent.

Dox could immediately tell something bad was happening.

Apparently steeling himself against whatever he was watching, Jack's face was taut with a wince so strained that his visible teeth extended past the fang-like extensions of his mask.

"No!" he screamed.

Dox tugged at his arm. "You're all right, Jack, we're h—"

"It's not all right!" The electric purple of the young host's eyes flickered away as the connection ended. "There's a werewolf slaughtering my neighborhood!"

"What?!" Alyssa shrieked. "A werewolf?"

Jack scanned the shocked faces staring at him and quickly realized they were unable to help. *How am I gonna get there?*

At this thought, he felt the appendage tugging against the void, creating sensory feedback he was immediately able to identify.

*The amulet*, he thought. *Of course it shares an affinity with you.*

"Bossu," Jack said, "they're gonna have to see it."

"Go, whelp."

Visualizing his mother's house, Jack reflexively conjured an aperture within the void, its terminal point forming at the front door.

Clutching the amulet with his appendage to confirm its stability, Jack pulled himself through and disappeared in a shadowy wisp.

Reappearing in the midst of the downpour, he landed silently in front of his mother's house. Jack inspected the barrier with a quick once-over while simultaneously swinging the appendage in wide arcs, his mind instantly registering the numerous corpses just before perceiving the beast responsible.

It rested on its haunches, eating with its hands. Jack felt the wolf's physical appearance in detail. Its razor-sharp claws fingered their way through the gristle of a corpse. Exceedingly sensitive to movement, its ears flapped independently from one another, causing the monster to aggressively turn its head one way and then the other for its next potential victim.

The werewolf stopped playing with its food and did a double take to see Jack staring down at him, having utilized the beast's shadow to teleport into position. It remained still for a moment, holding a piece of human flesh in front of its mouth.

It suddenly went on the attack, springing forth from its hunched position.

With a swiftness too fast to see, Jack summoned his sengese, and grabbing it by the handle, pulled it through the leaping lupine with a downward stroke.

"You should not have killed it so quickly," Bossu said.

Jack stepped back as the split beast landed with a thud. "For what?" he asked. "Did you want me to interrogate or something?"

Examining the houses on the street, he expected to see their front doors destroyed and their windows smashed, but to his surprise, none were damaged.

*It didn't enter anyone's house?* Jack said silently. *Why?*

"You should not have killed it so quickly," Bossu repeated. "Nevertheless, I presume it came here for Helena."

*Yeah, I figured that, but still.*

Jack resumed sweeping his appendage across the strewn bodies, swiftly examining them in detail. Corpses with faces that seemed to have been chewed through and dismembered limbs that appeared to result from a machine accident more than anything else, the state of these corpses would be difficult to explain away by the authorities or media.

Regardless, the fact these people were torn to pieces while their neighbors remained totally oblivious, pouring rain or not, was something the neighborhood of Black Pearl would be unable to recover from.

Jack pursed his lips together behind his mask. *If I leave the bodies, there's no telling the kind of trauma it would cause once everyone else comes outside. But to just dispose of them in the void or Deadside seems too callous, evil almost.*

"This is crazy," he whispered.

"What are you going to do, Jack?"

His appendage still weaving about the vicinity, Jack paid careful attention to the location of all the corpses and far-flung limbs before quickly vanishing to commence his grim work.

Immediately swiping several oversized tarps from an Army Corps building nearby, Jack hurriedly warped through the affected area of Black Pearl. Bit by bit, he gathered the remains of his neighbors and began securing them in neatly covered groups. He would arrange them along the main road in a steady fashion before proceeding to gather the rest.

"Dammit!" Jack hissed his pain away with a forceful grimace upon warping to a corpse he immediately recognized to be Jester. "Oh fuck!"

Unable to look away, Jack began stammering as he took in the young man's final state, memorialized in a wide-eyed expression of horror. "This-this—This can't be happening!"

"Gird yourself, Jack," Bossu stated sternly. "This is only the beginning." The Lwa's voice was without condescension or impatience, merely matter-of-fact.

"Y-yes," Jack replied, "I understand."

He noticed the light from Jester's phone shining through his pocket and retrieved it. Jack looked at the screen and saw it was all set and ready to upload a recorded video to Jester's social media.

*The sneaky bastard managed to capture it?* Jack thought.

He activated the displayed video and saw that Jester had, indeed, recorded some moments of the werewolf.

*Fuck yeah, Jester! This is gonna change everything!*

With all the necessary sign-ins and passwords set to automatically fill upon logging in, Jack hurriedly uploaded the video to Jester's social media, weakly thanking his young friend for his absentmindedness. Upon completion, Jack returned the phone to the pocket and transported Jester's corpse to the remaining piles.

Unwilling to be discovered in the midst of this act and deemed responsible, Jack continued gathering the rest of the bodies until it was over. The two pieces of the werewolf, however, were left untouched.

Now holding his own phone, Jack reappeared on his mother's front lawn and called the house.

"Please leave your message for—"

Jack abruptly pulled the phone away from his head upon hearing the impersonal voicemail that in no way belonged to his mother's thirty-year-old landline.

"Mom?" he called, having teleported inside.

Most of the lights were on and he could hear his dad's saxophone mixtape playing over the sound system he had bought them a few years back.

"Jack?" Helena replied, sounding pleasantly surprised.

Seeing his mother's happy expression as she peered into the hallway, Jack shifted off his mask and emitted a groan of relief.

Helena's look fell to one of concern as she watched her son take deep, meditative breaths. "What happened?" He looked at her in silence, unsure what to say. "Jack?"

"Does the phone work, Mom?" he asked, walking over to it.

"I don't see why it wouldn't."

Dropping his phone on the table, Jack held the landline's receiver to his ear and began dialing his phone number. He heard the voicemail prompt immediately but with no sign of an incoming call on his phone. "Please lea—"

Jack placed his mother's phone down gingerly, struggling against frustration already brimming.

"What's wrong, baby?"

Jack pursed his lips into what he thought was an encouraging smile.

Seeing her son look as though he had been forced to chew a lemon, Helena suddenly began to scold him. "Boy, you think I'm new to this or something?!" Jack dropped the strained expression and stared at her. "I asked what's wrong!"

Suddenly remembering his mother was married to the last Shadowman, Jack blurted out his response. "There was a werewolf attack outside."

"Is that all?"

Jack moved to walk away, unamused by her reply. "Mom, stop."

Helena playfully blocked his exit with a raised arm swiftly repurposed into a hug. "I'm sorry, my special boy," she said. "Forgive your callous mother, I've been doin' this since before I birthed you."

Jack stared down at her, incredulous yet frustrated by the

smirk threatening to appear on his face. "People died!" he said. "Jester, our neighbors . . . they all got eaten!"

Helena's countenance switched to solemnity as she began to approach one of the windows. "So what are you goin' to do?"

The tickle of amusement at the corners of his mouth rightfully dissipated as a plan took form in his mind. "Go after the person responsible."

# CHAPTER 17

Jack appeared at the Manse Ghede, this time letting himself in.

"Where is this freaking guy?" he said, noticing the empty wingback.

Jack turned around and began marching away to search elsewhere but immediately heard Samedi's voice behind him. "You don't know how to knock?"

Samedi was suddenly seated in the wingback with his praying hands positioned in front of his face and legs crossed.

Jack was nevertheless unmoved. "Where do I find her?"

"You're gonna have to explain," Samedi breathed, visibly annoyed.

"The bird woman with the RBF."

"RBF?" The skeleton paused for a moment before his bones began rocking with tempered humor. "Ha-ha-ha hmmm"

Jack remained silent as he stared at the Ghede lord.

"Ohhhh, Jack boy," he murmured. The skeleton paused once more to look up at Jack before shaking his head. "Marinette."

"Yeah her," Jack hurriedly replied.

"What seems to be the issue?"

"Her werewolves."

Samedi did not immediately respond, choosing to gaze at his agent who seemed to be vibrating in place. "What exactly is your plan?"

"I'm going to kill her," Jack replied.

"Hm hm hm."

Jack ignored Bossu's chuckles as he continued to stare expectantly at Samedi.

Although the Ghede lord carried himself like a man in his early forties, he was staring in a manner Jack had always associated with old people. Glasses set low, gaze aimed high, the skeleton accentuated a particular type of silence that never failed to make him feel self-conscious.

Jack stared back at the eye sockets, and as expected, could make out the green of the skeleton's irises positioned above the upper rim of his sunglasses, pointing directly at him.

Samedi stood to his feet. "Let me give you a glimpse of what you're asking for."

With the wave of his ivory hand, Samedi opened a portal.

Jack was about to dart inside with reckless abandon but was held back by a swift raise of Samedi's arm. Peering through, Jack saw a castle covered in something that looked like blood.

"That's her abode, called the Bloody Palace for obvious reasons—" The skeleton paused to observe the young host preparing to enter.

"Unfortunately," he said, snapping the portal closed, "I'm not convinced you're ready for that place."

Jack willed his indignation down with a forceful swallow. "I am."

"Well, seeing that you are my agent, I can't just take you at your word and go sending you to pursue personal vendettas in the domains of my brethren. The kind of foes you'll find in the Bloody Palace aren't the ones you're used to."

"It doesn't matter," Jack replied. "You think I'm confident because I've been wrecking bottom-feeders?"

Samedi curled a bony index around his chin. "Hmm."

Jack patiently paced about the room, eyeing the various artifacts decorating the walls while waiting for the skeleton to complete his impromptu ponderings.

"I know!" Samedi said with a snap of his fingers, the piercing clack summoning a portal behind him. "Follow me."

Entering the portal first this time, Jack was transported to an area engulfed in what appeared to be daylight and instantly recognized it as one of the places he had seen from afar when first arriving to the Deadside. His intake of the scenery fostered within him a state of whimsy that replaced his vengeful state of mind.

Immediately, his eyes set on the structure looming before him.

*A suspension bridge*, Jack began, his gaze darting throughout its design, *contrived by a mad person.*

Instead of stretching parallel toward their respective towers, the structure's main cables crossed each other's path to reach their opposite posts; the point of their intersection coincided with their sag.

The pattern was weaved continuously between the unending rows of towers lining the abnormally long road, stretching across the immediate landscape.

*Trying to recreate the I-10 High Rise. Ha-ha.*

Averting his gaze from the preposterous replica, Jack continued his inspection of the region. Scattered throughout, he spied various mobs of monsters that were undoubtedly much more capable than the bottom-feeders.

The excitement for violence welling within was immediately

dampened by an unexplainable discomfort set within his body, and he felt compelled to look skyward. Colored a uniform orange, the resulting pseudo-daylight was not as affecting as that of the Liveside but still took a toll.

"Damn."

Jack observed the vicinity again as he carefully considered his chances of success. Reaching out to his side, he summoned the sengese.

Disturbed by the unprecedented delay, Jack turned to look at his still-empty hand just before the weapon warped in. He let out a low exhale in response to the winded sensation that briefly bloomed in his chest and continued staring at his outstretched hand.

For the first time, the sengese felt off-center within his grip.

Struggling to find its center, Jack watched as the Ghede lord corrected the teetering weapon with a gentle nudge as he walked past.

Samedi spun on his heel to face the unsettled youth, setting himself before the otherworldly spectacle in the background. He returned his index finger to his chin before flinching a resolute nod.

"You are brazen enough to think yourself capable of surviving the Bloody Palace," he continued, almost scolding. "You don't realize you've been slicing and dicing to your heart's content only because Fate determined you to be a bit above average Shadowman fresh out of the box?" The skeleton god set his sights forward, eyes now ablaze. He was wearing a grin so wide it repositioned his cheekbones. "Why not succeed at something worth giving a shit about?"

Staring speechless at the emerald flame glowing behind the Lwa's shades, Jack's bewildered expression calmed into the slightest beginnings of a smile. The tempest of an invisible aura emanating from the Ghede lord contained an excitement he had perceived only once before.

The window for consideration having ended, Samedi's gaze intimated the intense seriousness within the measured cadence of his speech. "Are. You. Ready?"

Jack gestured in the affirmative, the pace of his nods deliberately mirroring Samedi's delivery.

The skeleton's enthusiasm rose all the more. "If defeat draws uncomfortably close, you're free to leave." While the words themselves seemed encouraging, they could not overcome the portentous quality of the tone with which they were wrapped. "Just remember when you do, you receive an F."

As soon as the words left his mouth, the Ghede lord appeared in front of the nearest cluster of monsters that were congregating near the edges of the flatland below.

*CRACKK!!*

Arms swung to his front, the landscape seemed to vibrate with the echoes of the baron's fearsome clap.

Though he had managed to rouse the attention of those relatively far off, the monsters directly at his back were immediately annihilated. Their chunks were streaked into the distance as if blown away by a mighty fart.

Samedi's ivory hands, still pressed together, gestured toward Jack with his thumbs and forefingers. "Tear him limb from limb!"

Bossu's gentlemanly chuckle was audible just beneath the war cry of countless monstrosities, electrified by the sudden presence of their supreme overlord.

Undeterred, Jack ran out to meet them.

He was forced to halt his advance, however, reacting to the fast-approaching Chiclet teeth of the frog-like demon opportunistically lunging for his head. He held the sengese out to his front, bracing its staff against the ground like a flag as the demon unwittingly dove into the blade.

For a moment, its face and protruding incisors appeared to fit neatly into the sickle's inward curve until a split-second nudge by Jack forced the blade through the monster's teeth.

The momentum of the demon's body bifurcated it into ribbons that peeled forth against the blade's cutting edge.

*They're definitely spirited*, Jack thought, spinning his sengese free from the entrails before taking off.

The enemies proved to be little else as he began slaughtering them with ease. Just like his first outing, there was no need for him to engage his sixth sense. Counterstriking using only his sight and instincts produced mounds of demonic corpses in his wake.

And as much as Jack had been looking forward to the brutes, they were not challenging either. He managed to kill several before feeling the need to catch his breath.

Jack rotated the sengese to block the headbutt of a rhinoceros-faced demon. Calmly maintaining the staff's horizontal position, he kept the horned creature at bay and thought about his present dissatisfaction.

*These guys are the most formidable I've faced so far.*

As the ferocious monster continued pressing its face against the staff, Jack spied another fiend conspicuously separating itself from the nearest horde. Poised for an opening, the demon swayed its prehensile tail from side to side, displaying its countless needlelike projections. These loosely attached spikes formed a precarious-looking halo at the tip of its tail, resembling a giant dandelion.

*But I feel like I'd have a harder time facing a horde of demon cops. Even though they were technically weaker, they had supernatural levels of coordinated tactics.*

With the stampede of monsters now only seconds away, Jack glimpsed at the dandelion demon as it flexed its tail. Moving with blinding speed, he suddenly shoved the rhinoceros off the staff before thrusting the blunt end through one of its still-glaring eyes.

Jack withdrew the weapon before the skewered demon collapsed, and turned just in time to see the dandelion demon jettison countless needles with a sadistic flick of its tail.

*These guys don't have that, though.*

Although the sheer volume of projectiles produced by the halo was far more than he expected, Jack remained calm. He began twirling the sengese in his front before dexterously utilizing his invisible appendage to accelerate the weapon's rotations, like hand propping a plane.

Successively deflecting the shower of projectiles with his furious twirling, Jack redirected them into the horde now at point-blank range. Spinning the staff relentlessly, he riddled the demonic throng with the copious spray of needles, killing them many times over.

Jack began stepping back as the shower abated, setting his sights on the dandelion demon through the fanlike twirls of his staff.

The stunned creature watched as the irreverent mortal began moving his spinning weapon from side to side, swatting away the last of its needles. The vigor had diminished from his movements as Jack casually began bouncing one solitary needle against the slowly weaving sengese. Before the demon could react, its needle was swatted back and sent clean through its forehead. The shocked expression remained on its face as it dropped to its knees and fell forward.

Jack turned toward the two remaining brutes from the horde, undeterred by his deadly performance. *These clumsy goofs are too easy*—he continued as one of them threw a punch—*all I gotta do is keep baiting them into killing each other.*

Continuing to do just that, Jack gently used the hook of his sengese to ensnare the wrist of the brute and guide it toward the face of the other. As soon as the fist made contact, he pulled the weapon clean through the monster's wrist before mortally slashing both of their throats.

Jack landed atop the resulting mound to see the rest of the howling demonic legion hungrily converging on his location. "Not enough," he stated confidently as he released the sengese. "This was getting too heavy anyway."

"Do not—"

Bossu tried to warn him, but it was too late. Jack had already sent the weapon away. This time, his harnessing the appendage left him gasping violently for air.

"Oops," he said, clutching his chest. "I . . . forgot."

"Indeed."

*But why do I feel this spent physically?* he began silently. *It's like all the energy that I used decided to take its toll all in one go.*

"It would be much more severe if this were the Liveside by daylight," Bossu replied. "Now get ready."

Jack exhaled with his cheeks as he sped from the mound, attempting to increase the distance between himself and the vicious mob. He continued struggling to catch his breath as the legion descended upon him, forcing him to reconsider his likelihood of succeeding.

The intensity with which the monsters fueled their strikes and tackles seemed to be without end. Unlike Jack, they were relentless rather than winded. He soon found most of his energy being devoted to not getting swarmed. Using the dregs of his stamina to corral the hordes into one manageable mass, he planned to dispatch them all in one go.

Unfortunately, summoning the sengese this time took Jack to a whole new plateau of exhaustion, significantly worse than what he previously endured. He held his breath as he swung the weapon at the multitude, running it through as many of them as he was able.

No longer did it feel like a hot knife through butter, but every sinew of flesh seemed to sap his strength when cutting through.

Holding his breath to kill off as many as possible, he could see Samedi with the woman, Marinette, walking through the bits of his dismembered denizens while observing him amidst the chaos.

Just as his heart felt like it was about to burst, Jack ended the spectacle, propping himself up against the weapon as the entrails littered the area. He could make out one more demon advancing toward him but was too exhausted to do anything about it.

*WHAM!*

The attack was enough to make him release the sengese, sending him tumbling toward the bridge. Jack quickly scrambled to his feet, readying himself for the demon's follow-up.

Though he had his hands up and could see the enemy's movements, Jack's body was unable to move with sufficient speed.

*This must be what the undead from the blights feel like.*

The monster struck him freely without suffering any counterattack.

Meaning to duck under a blow he thought he had seen coming, Jack instead bowed into an uppercut. He stumbled away from his assailant. The pain from the head strike seemed to be rebounding through his entire body.

It was the first time he had felt a punch more painful than Jamal's, and to make matters worse, the monster was fast.

"No way," he panted, retreating to a column.

The demon let out another battle cry as it watched Jack hobble toward the makeshift underpass.

Upon entering, he was consumed by a profound restorative feeling, like coming up for air just before drowning. It was not a moment too soon as the foe had already bounded toward him.

Eyeing his weapon, sticking from the ground a few yards away, Jack thought to summon it to him. But having only just caught his breath, he decided otherwise and counterpunched the demon.

Though slightly surprised by its opponent's sudden burst of energy, the monster remained undeterred from its pursuit. Fortunately, the succor Jack was receiving from the shadows enabled him to stand his ground against the dogged attacker.

His relief turned to dismay as he heard a scream, similar in sound to the demon currently fighting him, being belted out by yet another.

Wielding his appendage, Jack gingerly directed it toward the sengese as if stealing something. In response, he immediately felt the energy begin to leave his body, forcing him to release the psychic hold.

Bossu, who had been intermittently vocalizing an assortment of reactions since the fray commenced, let out a three-syllable tone of pity while the appendage recoiled like the weapon was hot. "What are you going to do, Jack?"

As the demon shook off the impact from his light cross, Jack prepared himself for the second, who had just arrived. Watching them seemingly join forces with a shared glance, Jack returned his appendage into the void in a hurried attempt to palpate some crows into form.

*I might get DQ'd if I step inside.*

"There is no *might*," Bossu replied, "only certainty that you will."

Just like before, Jack continuously swept the birds forth from the walls of the other dimension until he could hear the flapping of their wings resound in his head.

He did this while simultaneously defending himself from the last two foes who had begun to progressively demand more of his attention. His intent was to abstain from unnecessary movements so that his revitalization occurred quickly, and then wait for the opportunity to land a killing blow.

However, these two seemed tailor-made to thwart his efforts.

*So*, Jack began, *think you can send some crows out here?*

"Do you truly want me to intervene?" the Lwa asked. "After all, this is something you can do for yourself."

His host sucked his teeth.

Though these definitely were not brutes, they were not bottom-feeders either.

Jack initially attributed their overall capability to his exhaustion, which was currently abating thanks to the shadowed area beneath the bridge. But as he continued to fend them off, he realized that their attacks were not the recklessly enraged type he had come to expect.

Due to their tactics, Jack was compelled to intermittently flee from the shadows or engage in bursts of prolonged skirmishes to buy moments of recovery.

It was clear that they had an unspoken plan to wear him down.

"What's you guys' prob—" Jack paused his outraged inquiry as he finally took the time to notice the two demons' appearance. Far from the random variety of characteristics displayed by the diverse denizens of the Deadside, these monsters complemented each other.

They both had fur lining most of the unclothed parts of their body and appeared feline.

The facial proportions of the first were rather normal, aside from its mouth. Its pupils appeared as orange slits, vertically cut across the smoky orbs couched within its eye sockets. The demon's muzzle was in a permanent state of spread necessitated by its unnatural array of teeth—a saber-toothed tiger with all sabers.

The fur of its arms ended just above its elbow while the rest seemed to be composed entirely of bone.

Unlike the forearms of the baron in which the ulna and radius remained visible, these bones were like a vambrace. This macabre armor *covered* the wrists and hands. Jutting from the elbows were sharp projections that rose toward the upper arms. Though bipedal, the demon's calves presented like the hind legs of a giant cat, causing it to appear to be standing on its toes.

The second demon had a similar facial appearance except at the mouth, the lack of teeth allowing for a wiser and more dignified demeanor. The fur of its body continued through its arms, with no bone covering to speak of. Its hands were humanoid, but clawed and somewhat oversized. It also stood on raised feet, but the physiology was more demonic than feline, like those of a gargoyle.

Jack's observations were abruptly ended by their advance.

The first darted toward him with its two fists pressed against one another across its chest, the flex of its elbows extending the projections outward. Despite the relatively fixed position of its upper body, it managed to remain fleet of foot.

Its partner ran more traditionally, swinging its arms like fierce pistons in conjunction with its muscular demon legs.

The first started the assault by spinning forward with its elbow spikes jutted, as if trying to dance its way to the young opponent. The second soon followed with, to Jack's surprise, a frontal attack. It clawed at him with its oversized hands before trying to snatch his head with the downswing kick of a front flip.

Jack thought he saw an opening with critical blow potential, but he was unwilling to commit to the maneuver, so he let the opportunity pass and shuffled away.

Jack thought, addressing his Lwa, *I need the crows to distract them long enough for me to get the sengese. How do I do something like that from the outside?*

Still observing the combatants, he noticed that the one with the elbows would never brandish them when the other was near, preventing them from being weaponized against its teammate.

"How do you do it?" Bossu said. "There are many ways to explain it *theoretically*. But since you have already *done* it, the easiest advice is this: Fancy yourself an idol."

The young host rolled his eyes despite coming to an immediate understanding.

He stepped from the shadowed area in order to enact his plan and saw the demons move to attack, apparently pleased by his decision.

The second decided to give the first a wide berth by delaying its approach by some seconds. Seeing this, Jack established a firm hold upon the void and began opening an aperture right above its position.

The first demon resumed throwing elbows. Spinning like a top, the assorted hues on its body turned into streaks of color due to the ferocity of its turning.

*I can't lose sight of the other one*, Jack thought, before commencing a series of backflips. *But I can't risk this one noticing me look, either.*

While vaulting away, he managed to subtly maintain his sights on both opponents by glimpsing at one and then the other in rapid succession. Jack tracked the first demon's advance by glancing at its feet before eyeing the crows emerging above the second.

He noticed the circular shuffles of the first demon finally coming to a stop. *He's just about finished. One more flip should put me out of range from that killer elbow's final turn, and back into the shadows. Ha-ha . . . Oh sh—*

While his spatial calculations proved spot-on, it was impossible to anticipate everything. Instead of bringing around its right elbow to complete its counterclockwise spin, the demon flexed the arm into a haymaker. Its reach now extended, the foe's surprise attack struck Jack's head.

Hard.

Standing in awe at the crows that had been flowing from the mysterious hole torn through space-time, the already bewildered second demon became all the more so as the murder of crows suddenly glitched.

Jack rebounded from the blow, though still seeing stars from the impact, and instinctively grappled the demon's arm in the middle of its follow-through.

Quickly locating the elbow, he clutched the base of the bony protrusion and in one smooth motion, ripped it out, peeling it along the monster's forearm and down its hand before tearing off the pinky. Once removed, the hardened vambrace that once lined the demon's forearm instantly lost its rigidity and reverted to a texture no different than any other skin.

Having processed the pain of having its arm degloved like shucked corn, the demon took a deep breath and cried out to its entranced companion.

But Jack reacted too quickly.

Immediately leaping into the air following the bloody grapple, he violently plunged the still-hardened elbow protrusion down the demon's throat before stuffing the rest of the arm's newly socklike skin into its mouth.

Simultaneously discerning the condition of the crows while

gagging the demon, Jack realized that the unexpected blow to his head had triggered a change in how he perceived his mental connection with the crows, enabling him to compartmentalize the various communications and feedback that used his sixth sense as their medium.

While psychically maintaining the glitching murder, Jack telepathically commanded three birds from within to retrieve the sengese, directing them to fly it to him before the demon returned to its senses. Snatching the staff from their beaks, he thrust the blade into the shadows of the underpass.

The staff's business end, just immersed in shadow several yards away, immediately reappeared, emerging from the spot of shadow created by the crow swarm. The sengese jutted into the demon's throat, rocketing upward behind the chin and through the jawline before descending back into the dark just as fast as it came forth.

Jack pulled the weapon from the shadow, having cut off the demon's face in one stroke.

He heard the familiar, too hard, almost brittle clacking as Samedi stood in the midst of the dead bodies, clapping with a crazed enthusiasm. The bird woman had been walking about, assessing the quality of the lad's bloody work before advancing toward her celebrating cohort.

Noticing Jack watching him, the mad skeleton clapped with increased vigor, his eyes glowing with more intensity as his applause began bursting the corpses asunder.

He sustained the clapping a bit before finally ceasing. "Don't be ashamed, boy," he said, "you did well."

"Jack Boniface!" Marinette began, cheerfully calling out to him from afar. "The baron told me something that I had to come and confirm for myself. Were you seeking the chance to kill me?"

Jack suddenly remembered the incident in Black Pearl, causing him to nod at her with renewed anger.

"CA-CAWW!!"

Seemingly unable to control herself, the woman erupted with an animalistic cry of excitement before transitioning into a witchlike cackle. The exceedingly shrill giggles continued to echo as the woman resumed her speech.

"I didn't send any of my pets to the Liveside," she explained, "not yet, anyway."

The landscape became strangely silent as the two Lwa waited for a response from the young host.

"Doesn't look like he found it funny," Samedi stated loudly.

"Cheer up, young Boniface," Marinette began. "We will eventually identify who is responsible for your current state of woe."

*Whatever*, Jack thought, *all you Lwa are freaking liars anyway.*

Blood had seeped from the mouth of Jack's mask and began to drip from its fang-like extensions. Jack stared at the skeleton in silence as he wiped it away.

From across the field, Samedi pointed at the lad's injuries. "Look, your wounds are already healing, so do not fret. Soon you'll be as good as n—" The skeleton god stopped short as Jack suddenly vanished from their presence. "Awww."

# CHAPTER 18

The day after the attack, Jack had been riding through the neighborhood of Black Pearl accompanied by Dox and Alyssa. The mayor of New Orleans, Eric Goodwill, was scheduled to give a press conference about what had transpired in front of the military base on the outskirts of the neighborhood.

Jack had told Dox and Alyssa what he had done to prevent the discovery of the corpses by the town's residents, a decision they agreed with.

"Why didn't you get rid of the werewolf though?" Alyssa asked.

"I wanted it to be found," Jack replied. "It's the only way I . . . I mean we, will know what we're up against. Samedi wasn't behind it, which was known, but Marinette claimed it wasn't her either, and I kinda believe it."

"How do you know she's not lying?"

"She just wouldn't," he stated, shaking his head. "If she was behind it and you didn't know, she's the type to tell you herself."

The car fell silent as Dox stopped by the collection of police and media vehicles to let the two youngsters out.

Jack and Alyssa made their way through the steadily forming crowd and positioned themselves close to the temporary podium albeit off to the side.

Jack stared at the vacant area and leaned over to Alyssa. "This should be interesting," he said softly. "It is reported that a werewolf attacked the neighborhood of Black Pearl." He mimicked the mayor.

Alyssa put her hand to her mouth to stifle a giggle. "That's assuming it didn't shift back to its human form a little after you killed it."

Jack's eyes widened as he quickly faced forward. "Crap!" he hissed. "I didn't think of that!"

"That's what teammates are for," Alyssa replied, no longer stifling her amusement. "It's not a big deal, you took care of the more important st—"

"Excuse me, ma'am." Alyssa gasped before setting her eyes on the blushing officer. "Sorry, miss," he said sheepishly, "I didn't mean to scare you. It's just that the mayor will be arriving shortly, and we may need this path to the podium."

Jack watched from the corner of his eye as Alyssa successfully concealed any signs of annoyance and smiled.

"I'm sorry, officer." She made like she was headed out but stopped, her abruptness catching the man's attention. "You said this is the way he'll be using to get onstage?" she asked, her voice singing with innocent curiosity. "Because I think I see him."

The cop looked where she was pointing and watched the mayor approach the temporary podium. "Shoot! I stand corrected, there he goes." He flashed Alyssa a farewell smile but did a double take as he glanced back at the podium.

The mayor's assistants were a ways behind him, advancing along in awkwardly moving pairs. As they neared the podium, the source of their teetering came into view. Each pair was lugging along an Inicio.

The cop reacted immediately upon seeing them. "Oh no!" he groaned. "Not these friggin' things!"

Coming to himself, he shot Alyssa a nervous glance and let out an awkward chuckle before addressing her. "Whoa hey!!" the man began, seemingly startled by her presence. "Don't tell anybody I said that. He-he . . ."

Smiling, Alyssa responded. "Your secret is safe with me, officer. I hated those things way before you even knew about 'em, most likely. I actually used to have one, believe it or not."

The cop, who had switched to a wide-eyed look of worry upon noticing her voice change, let out a visible sigh of relief. "Whew!" he replied, pretending to wipe sweat off his forehead. "Good, so you understand . . . Still though—"

"Yeah, I know."

"Thanks, sweetheart." The cop hurriedly shook her hand. "All right, I'll see ya. I gotta get in formation so the optics can sell the bullcrap."

"Stay strong," Alyssa said as the officer left.

"Good job," Jack muttered. "I knew you could handle him."

The two of them watched the man approach the podium and proceed to do exactly what he said. He and several others took up positions behind Goodwill's shoulders. Alyssa laughed as she saw his new, intensely serious expression.

She was still laughing as Goodwill began to speak.

"We are here to honor and pay respect to those who lost their lives last night in yet another mindless act of violence that seems to be getting increasingly more common. We are here to show support and stand in solidarity with the families, friends, and loved ones of those we lost. And forgive me, I know you all are probably tired of hearing me say it, but things are escalating to a point that something must be done, so I think this bears repeating.

"This tragedy is just another example of why all communities, but especially ones of color, must have Inicio operating as their basis for crime prevention. Communities of low income, low standards of education, and higher rates of poverty have been left behind the growths in technology for too long."

Alyssa spied the cop glance at the mayor and then at her before returning his gaze forward. It all took about a second, and he never broke character.

Goodwill continued. "Now, it is a great sin for one to actively try and profit off of tragedy. That is something I think we all know in our hearts. However, there is something that needs to be said for those who see the potential danger and actively choose to protect themselves and those they love, for that is the very essence of responsibility!"

The sounds of support grew louder, seemingly coming from nowhere and everywhere at the same time.

"I have heard many of the things people say against Inicio. Let's just be honest, we all have, am I right? They may think they're edgy, hip, badasses, and patriots. It doesn't matter. The fact is, they're just slow! We must not be like the slow!"

Jack immediately sputtered out a chuckle.

"We must not allow the thinking of the slow to infect those who don't know any better! That's why it is imperative that we urge our fellow humans to not be slow but instead get Inicio!"

The cop seemed bewildered by the enthusiasm that now neared a fever pitch due to the mayor's impassioned delivery. "*Don't be slow, get Inicio! Don't be slow, get Inicio!*"

They started chanting.

Jack and Alyssa looked at each other, both of them confirming what they were thinking.

Goodwill attempted to pump his fist to add emphasis, but the rhythm in his delivery made it impossible for him to do so without looking silly. Initially, the cops behind him seemed unwilling to join the chant but this changed as he glanced over his shoulder, prompting them to lip-sync along in shame.

*"Don't be slow, get Inicio! Don't be slow, get Inicio!"*

---

Jack, Alyssa, and Dox were at North Rampart Street preparing for the evening's hunt, still struggling to believe the spectacle from earlier that day. While Dox and Alyssa seemed to think what transpired was thoroughly hilarious, Jack's amusement was tempered by suspicion.

"Why the scowl, son?" Dox asked.

"They're hiding the supernatural aspect of the murders and using them to generate further demand for Inicio," Jack replied. "That doesn't come off as strange to you guys?"

Alyssa continued her soft chuckles. "He was expecting the mayor to reveal the existence of werewolves to the public, even though there may have been no evidence of one."

"No," he began, rolling his eyes. "I'm say—"

Just as he was about to defend his stance, Jack remembered that he had uploaded the clip of the werewolf attack onto Jester's social media account.

Alyssa eyed him as he pulled his phone from his pocket and frantically began navigating to the desired profile.

"What is it?" she asked, watching him shake his head with a smirk.

Jack turned the screen toward her face.

"Video banned for offensive content," she read aloud. "I'm not following you."

"My friend recorded some of the attack before he was mauled," Jack replied. "I uploaded the video."

"Yeah," Alyssa replied, "but the internet probably has some algorithm that censors that kind of stuff." Bossu hummed with amusement as Jack stared incredulously at her as she attempted to conjure an explanation, his mouth opening more as she continued speaking. "Plus, it might've been too violent."

Jack dropped his exaggerated expression, choosing to raise his eyebrow at her. "There was no violence in the clip," he stated. "It was just a video of the werewolf arriving."

"Then they're censoring the supernatural." Alyssa watched as Jack turned to Dox. "I'm not saying it's acceptable or anything but just . . ." She trailed off.

Jack looked back at his phone and began searching for a different post. Silently, he held up the screen for her to see. Alyssa watched a feed showing countless purple-eyed crows lining some trees and grass and reflexively jerked back as they all suddenly turned their heads.

"What is that?!" she exclaimed.

Concerned by her reaction, Dox reached for Jack's wrist to view the recording. It took only a moment for his face to light up with recognition.

"That's you?" he asked, smiling at the screen.

Jack nodded, pocketing the phone.

The two Abettors watched as Jack began staring into the distance, a look of anger forming on his face.

"What is it, son?"

"I just remembered something," he said, pressing his lips together. "I called my mother's landline, and it went to a fake voicemail. Then I called my phone from her landline, and it played the same fake voicemail." Jack turned to face them. "Can anyone explain that? Please?"

There was a deafening silence that filled the space as Jack held his breath, hoping one of them would say what he had already discerned.

"They're in on it," Dox whispered.

Jack whimpered out his exhale, a mix of relief and woe.

"This is it, Jack," Bossu said.

Jack glanced between Dox and Alyssa, beholding their wide-eyed expressions, and quickly shut his eyes. "Mayor Goodwill . . ." he began, his body immediately adorning itself with his suit of void fabric.

He heard his Lwa's gravelly hum of amusement while Dox and Alyssa began voicing their concern.

"Calm down, Jack," Alyssa said.

"Killing a human," Dox began, "whether they be good or bad, it ain't something you can come back from easily."

Jack opened his eyes, his confusion obscured by his mask. "What are you talking about?" he asked, scoffing. "I'm not gonna kill him. I was asking if he's doing another press conference tonight."

"Yeah," Alyssa replied. "I remember him mentioning it. What are we going to do?"

Jack inhaled as if he was about to reply but stopped himself. *Can I trust her? I'm going to need help locating the mayor after all.*

"Is she a betrayer?" Bossu began. "No, I think not. But if the tormentors get ahold of her, she will talk. Do not tell anyone of your plans, Jack. Stand alone. You already have Helena to worry about. Leave these ones out of it, trust me. You can do it all yourself."

Weighty considerations surrounding what to do, who to trust, how to protect, how much to care, they all suddenly seemed to be of the utmost importance. Attempting to address even one immediately turned Jack's thoughts into a jumbled mess.

*I can't!* he replied, feeling the frustration rising in his chest.

Sensing this as well, his Lwa was forced to take action. "Whelp, you must stay calm. The answer is already within your reach, just stick with what you know and stay in your lane!"

Jack's mind suddenly went to his mother, the memory of their conversation helping to subdue the chaos in his mind. *Yeah . . . yeah, you guys are right.*

The resulting smile obscured by Jack's mask would have remained indiscernible if not for his eyes. Despite their lack of pupils and an overall hollow appearance, they could not repress the warmth emanating from within, ultimately betraying the inexplicable levity that had taken hold.

Contentment.

"Not gonna get defensive, Mom," Jack said aloud. "Just misplaced my squeaky toy for a second, is all."

He began wielding his appendage. "Besides you, I don't know much else, but like Mom said, the little I know can uncover the things I don't."

"It was I who said it first!" Bossu retorted.

Jack let out a childish gasp. "That's right!" He composed himself against the rising excitement as he continued to unpack his revelation. *The crows, how could I have forgotten?*

As he uttered this question in his mind, its answer soon followed.

Up until recently, these summoned creatures had very limited utility because they required his full attention when being controlled.

But things were different now.

During his fight with the feline demons, Jack's mind had become altered after receiving a blow to the head. At the time, he had been preoccupied with creating crows, maintaining an aperture, and sweeping the crows into the Deadside.

Engaging in these psionic activities spread Jack's mind too thin, creating an unforeseen effect when he was struck by the demon's haymaker. The resulting shock wave of pain crossed from the physical into the psychical, manifesting as a visible distortion in the murder of crows he had summoned.

This trauma-induced glitch signified an alteration in his telepathic link to them.

The trunk-like pathway upon which all the birds' feedback collectively converged was shredded into countless branches, each designed to serve as an individual pathway for every potential summon. This compartmentalization enabled him to communicate with the crows independently, one from the other.

At least, this was what he intuited at the time. Though he reached this conclusion under the pressure of battle, he subsequently forgot it and never truly tested it.

He remembered how he used them to retrieve the sengese. Back then, Jack gave mental directives to only a portion of the overall swarm. While this feat had been unprecedented, the transmission of mental directives to a select few was not the same as directly controlling many one by one yet somehow at the same time.

Jack shook his head, somewhat shaken by the fact he only now was recalling these things. *So many details to be missed*, he thought. *How can I prevent it?*

"Remain unbroken," Bossu replied. "That is what gives you the capability to pass through the snares that degrade your thinking. As long as your thought pattern remains clean, it will provide you with all the answers you need. As it has just done now."

Bossu growled a sigh before continuing. "Alas, you have taught me something once again."

Jack began reaching into the void, paying particular attention to what his Lwa was saying.

"While I have been pleased with your overall progress, I subject it to scrutiny based on my own expectations, which are not valid. The growth you receive is decided by Fate. As such, your progression from glory to glory is on a set schedule, sovereignly determined. I have alluded to this before but let me affirm it now. Unless prompted otherwise, I will not interfere with the lessons Fate has decreed you learn for yourself."

The youth had been psychically sweeping out an innumerable host of crows from the void. Their clamorous wings served as background noise while the conversation continued.

*A silent observer*, Jack replied. *What if I'm in deep trouble?*

"Then Fate will see to it that you either have a revelation or, most likely, place the words on your tongue so that you may ask it of me."

*So I guess my asking for more power is somehow different.*

"Has not Fate already explained to you, proving through different speakers no less, why such a request is imprudent?"

Jack nodded silently, looking through the window as the conjured aperture took shape in the sky. Thanks to his night vision, he could confirm its formation, but as it was otherwise indistinguishable against the backdrop of night, it would have gone unnoticed by most. He watched the birds emerge into the sky, descending from the void like a dark cloud.

Without any prompting, his glitched mind had marked each crow the moment they were plucked, automatically compartmentalizing these unique identifiers within the back of his mind with machinelike precision and making them available for recall.

Curious to see his companions' reaction, Jack willed the crows close.

He watched as the chaotic shoal swirled its way to the building before surrounding it like a tempest.

"What the—" Dox began.

While the unnatural sight had initially taken both Abettors by surprise, Dox's surprise was short-lived as he quickly deduced the explanation behind what he was seeing. Observing the countless birds, Alyssa apparently found their glowing eyes of purple too unsettling to ignore.

"What's going on?" she asked, withdrawing her gun from its holster.

"Don't worry," Dox said. "Jack's just showing off."

Jack was mentally readying himself to control the crows. Up to this point, all he had done was form them, open an aperture for their exit, and impart general directives regarding their flight pattern.

Relatively easy stuff.

However, testing his hypothesis required success in things he formerly considered impossible. After all, assuming control over just one crow was jarring enough. What could he expect to suffer when engaging a multitude?

Unwilling to get stuck in a cycle of worst-case considerations, Jack boldly seized upon the numerous links of communication, visibly cringing in anticipation of the consequent psychic shock.

Far from ripping his mind asunder, the plethora of feedback registered softly in his psyche. Rather than perceiving them in some linear presentation relegated to the passage of time, each telepathic link operated more like an inward thought.

Each individual crow was not only mentally accounted for but intimately known, and this allowed for the lines of communication to be established via the identifying mental markings.

Though he found it regrettably inappropriate, Jack could not help but feel pleased at how intuitive it was.

The moment a particular crow, or multitude thereof, was thought of, their field of view was immediately registered in a manner akin to a fleeting memory.

*I can feel them all, Bossu,* he said silently.

"Indeed."

*Not only that, but I can see what they see.* Jack mentally called on the entirety of the swarm. The cognitive recall of the unique identifiers accompanied by their respective feedback took less than a second. *All at once.*

His Lwa let out a hum of acknowledgment before responding. "Well done, I suppose," he said. "So what will you do?"

*The possibilities seem endless,* he replied. *But since time isn't exactly on our side . . .*

Consciously maintaining his direct hold over the swarm, Jack began sending them off in pairs. As they were beckoned, so they responded. Each pair broke from formation and headed toward the region assigned to them in search of the mayor.

He marveled at the ease with which he was able to psychically account for them all. Whether departed or still swarming, none managed to escape his awareness.

# CHAPTER 19

A set of the crows had found Mayor Goodwill's press conference at the New Orleans Ernest N. Morial Convention Center fairly quickly.

The level of surveillance capability granted Jack by the crows, his appendage, and his night vision, all operating in tandem and through independent routes of perception, was something he had never thought possible.

Though presently residing in the void, Jack had an aperture opened above the Mississippi River through which he observed the mayor's speech.

A handful of his crows were circling overhead, feeding him visuals that his unmagnified eyesight could not. His appendage kept track of the mayor and those surrounding him, palpating the opportune moment for Jack to take him.

"Greater than the sum of its parts, no?" Bossu commented.

"It's crazy." The young host felt the seated audience collectively rise to their feet as he replied to his Lwa's question.

Immediately directing several crows to set their eyes on him from afar, Jack could see the mayor begin moving with his retinue.

He began pacing back and forth within the void in front of the flooding illumination of the aperture. Jack had been trying to determine the location of the mayor's vehicle in advance to ensure he could be taken without anyone noticing.

His crows spied the vehicle in question pulling up in the manner of a celebrity's limousine sans red carpet. They watched as Goodwill's attendants fell away to the side, allowing him private entry into the vehicle as the driver stepped out to open the door.

Jack had been placing particular focus on the feedback of his appendage as it swept through the vehicle's interior; he could feel the intact partition between the front and back seat. Confirming the absence of any passengers, he stopped his pacing and formed an aperture within the limo floor.

His body tense and at the ready, Jack watched the mayor step into the vehicle and immediately fall into the awaiting aperture just before the driver closed the door behind him. He caught the frantic mayor as he fell into the void before they both exited, emerging on one of the more poorly lit docks arranged along the Mississippi.

Jack stayed ominously silent as he dropped Goodwill on the damp wood, though there was little he could do in the way of intimidation that his mask could not.

Mayor Goodwill regained his composure, now liberated from the sense of free fall.

Jack watched him begin mumbling as he stood. Though Goodwill's back was still turned, the young host could not help but feel the man should be more shaken considering what had just happened.

"I told these muthafuckas to stop taking me to the middle of—" Goodwill stopped speaking as he turned to see Jack quietly watching him. "Oh shit, I didn't see you there, boss. As a matter of fact, I don't think I've ever seen you before, period. You down with the Brethren? Of course you are."

As Jack's mind rapidly processed the implications of Goodwill's behavior, it proved to be quite fortunate that his mask obscured the various emotions on his face.

"So tonight's the night we activate Inicio, correct?" he asked expectantly. "I hope so, because I've been shameless in my pitchin' of that shit."

*What did he just say?* Jack thought, his legs nearly giving way. *Activate Inicio?*

He felt a flood of emotions collectively prime themselves in his heart, milliseconds away from making a geyser-like surge into his head.

But before they could launch, he willed them to be still.

*Wait, wait, wait,* he thought, talking his body down from a visible reaction. *Just see this through. It's probably the only chance to find out what is actually going on.*

Jack feigned knowledge, with every passing moment a test of his resolve to remain dead to his emotions. "Indeed," he said, putting on a fake voice, "I've been sent by the commanders to ensure that you remember all the details regarding Inicio's launch."

Goodwill paused for a moment. "I guess you must be pretty low on the scale if you in the dark about this. Only been in the works for damn near a decade." Jack bit his tongue so hard he thought it was bleeding. "We done put enough around the city's buildings and within family homes that once the demons are in position, they gonna cross over directly into people's dwellings and public spaces."

Jack's blood ran cold. "O-oh, I see, and ju-just to make sure you've been paying attention, what was the intent behind this whole plan?"

Goodwill stood tall, his chest nearly bursting with pride. "And I quote, that bastard Baron Samedi rigged the whole process causing the demons to degrade once they crossed over, making proper copulation impossible." The man sucked his teeth through a smirk. "Some messed up shit, to be honest."

Jack felt himself slipping. It was all just too much. "What the fuck did you just say?"

"Copulation, man," the mayor replied. "Can't spawn Nephilim without f—"

"Control yourself, Jack," Bossu said, attempting to rein in his host.

But it was too late. "What's wrong with you?!" Jack screamed, cutting Goodwill off. "You're human!"

Goodwill was temporarily stunned silent, staring at the skull-faced entity who seemed just about ready to explode in anger. "Oh shit!" he suddenly shouted in dismayed surprise. "I know who you are!"

He quickly pulled out what looked to be some kind of talisman from the inner pocket of his jacket. "I need your protection, my lord. That muthafucka you warned me about is here, but he's smaller than I thought he'd be, so I wasn't paying attention. What's his name . . . oh yeah, fucking Shadowm—"

Before he finished the words, a large portal began to form and revealed a large, sharply dressed demon stepping its way out.

"There he is!" the monster boomed happily. "Shadowman fun size!"

The monster shook the dock with its every step and when Jack saw it, he immediately knew that this was the entity behind the three demon cops.

The demon suspended its taunting upon seeing Jack glaring at it, the lad's rage creating slight visual distortions in the air.

"Remember, whelp," Bossu began, "your anger fuels your

strength, and your strength fuels your violence. That's what it will feel like, but the truth is they are one and the same. Therefore, control your anger. Do not stifle it, but *control* it. Listen and understand, as it must not be indulged unless necessary."

*Why?* Jack asked impatiently, his gaze still fixed on the demon.

Bossu's gravelly tone became more pronounced as he replied. "Because when they see it, they will fear."

This time, Jack's response was audible. "Good," he said, speaking through his sneer.

His Lwa reacted with amusement before continuing. "Hm hm hm, whelp. In truth, do you know why it is not good to be feared?"

"I'm listening."

"Because it guarantees that everyone will be plotting against you, *always*."

Jack processed the Lwa's words, calmly intuiting their sobering import despite his overwhelming anger. "I understand."

Sensing the reverberating distortion, Goodwill fell backward in fear. "Th-th-that bass in the air!" he said. "That's you, right, my lord?" The man looked over at the demon, whose fang-packed grin had fallen. "Oh shit," he continued in realization, "I'm outta here."

The demon maintained eye contact with Jack, although it was losing confidence by the second.

Jack began shouting. "You think you can just walk away?!" Goodwill kept on fleeing, unwilling to acknowledge the address obviously meant for him.

The demon watched as Jack thrust his arm toward his side as if punching at the air, resulting in a pained yelp that echoed through the vicinity.

"GAH!!"

The demon broke eye contact with Jack to see Goodwill cradling the side of his face, clumsily attempting to stumble back to his feet.

"*Now* you can walk away!" Jack stated, his eyes still on the monster. "And after I'm done killing this twisted knot of shit in a suit, I'll be listening to how you explain away that broken jaw."

The sounds of Goodwill's whimpering began to fade as he hobbled away.

"So," the demon began, "you're a fe—WHAT?!"

Unwilling to engage in small talk, Jack warped the sengese to his hand and with three strokes, each one disappearing into the darkness before making contact, removed the white suit from the demon's body.

"That's what I thought," Jack said, scanning the demon's newly exposed physique.

Countless of the hookworms from hell were wound together to form its body. From a distance, Jack plucked one off the body and crushed it beneath his heel.

"Y-you are too arrogant!"

The massive demon lunged forward, attempting to break Jack's concentration and create an opening to seize him. But Jack was not only physically quicker but was also able to read the demon's movements and react accordingly.

During the demon's unsuccessful tackle attempt, he had removed several more twisted pieces of its body.

The monster suddenly stopped swatting at the ephemeral blade of Jack's sengese and began laughing boisterously. "Ha-ha-ha! You're a fool! To think you plan to pluck me asunder. Ha-ha—Huh?"

Jack waited for the monster to toss its head back to guffaw once more before forcing it through the newly opened aperture with a sudden shoulder tackle. They both emerged on the other side, roughly tumbling into a conveniently positioned group of the realm's demonic denizens.

"What are you playing at?" the monster screamed, reflexively scattering several of the demons with one blow.

"These guys don't take kindly to interlopers," Jack explained, casually extricating himself from the crowd. "And I can tell from your smell that you're not from around here."

The monster's pairs of eyes lost their aggression as it listened to the departing lad. "You were right though. It would've been pretty stupid to pick you apart myself. But these guys will be able to do it pretty fast. Bye shit-knot!"

"Wha—What the—?"

The monster watched in disbelief as Jack ran away but was unable to keep its eyes on him for long as the mob of demons began to grow in number, each one hungrily joining the fray for an opportunity to feast on its flesh.

Jack, however, observed from afar, knowing it was only a matter of time before the monster would either get devoured or flee. He summoned one solitary crow and willed it to fly unseen as he lay in wait.

"That sneaky little bastard!" the monster roared, still fighting for its life.

Jack remained in his position, watching the monster's humiliating defeat. At this point, it looked to be only thin wires of flesh and sinew with a giant head, and the devouring hordes were continuing to come from far and wide.

"Master!!" it cried.

"This is it," Jack said, causing his crow to hover at the ready.

"I've been outsmarted by your enemy, forgive my foolishness and rescue—"

It stopped pleading as a portal formed in the midst, its

light causing the hordes to flee. The emaciated fiend hurriedly clambered away, but just as it reached the portal's threshold and began to voice its gratitude, Jack's crow suddenly careened into its upper back like a kingfisher.

"Thank you, Mas-*hrgk*!"

The crow lodged within its body, and the demon stumbled through the portal, causing it to immediately snap shut.

Bossu's chuckles of impressed satisfaction echoed in Jack's head as he went about establishing a mental link with the crow. "Ho ho ho . . . *whelp*!"

Jack said nothing as he readied an aperture at the crow's coordinates, willed his appendage to the location, and anchoring himself against the dense darkness on the other side, began pulling himself through.

Stalling his emergence from the void, he could hear the monster still whining. "Master! Forgive me! I've been tricked again by the young Boniface. He's not like those who came before him! He likes *tricks*!"

"We have met Jack Boniface," a familiar voice stated, "and he is but a foolish youth."

"No, you must—"

"The Inicio machines have already started to facilitate the crossover," the voice continued dismissively. "The invasion will commence. Nephilim will be created and the oblivious heir will still not know we are the ones that—"

"He is not a fool, is what I am telling you . . . for he is here!" The space fell silent as the monster rushed to complete its warning. "You must hide yourselves so that—"

Not wanting to miss the opportunity, Jack abandoned his caution and warped out of the void into the cavernous haunt apparently belonging to the Lwa conspirators now before him. He shook his head in disbelief before suddenly picking up the emaciated monster and casually tossing it through a new aperture leading back to the Deadside.

"No, ple—"

The aperture vanished as Jack set his eyes on one of the Lwa. "Obatala, right?"

Not waiting for a response, he continued to peer through the space. Against the wall was a seemingly unconscious woman pinned beneath an arcane sigil. "Erzulie Freda obviously, unbelievable."

Jack's eyes beheld the only other woman present, La Sirene. She was no longer smiling. His gaze lingered a bit before he shook his head again. "So, it was all just an act, is that it?"

He turned to look down on the final Lwa. "You drunken little shit!" he said, sneering at Pierre. "I should have known you were involved somehow."

"Jack," Bossu began, sounding slightly urgent.

The young host's sights fell on someone he did not recognize. Despite the individual's lack of melanin and his aquiline nose, Jack could immediately tell he was not what society would identify as white.

The unnamed man initially looked shocked but suddenly transitioned to a wide-eyed expression of joy. The onset of this strange change in demeanor coincided with Bossu's uncharacteristically urgent address.

"JACK!"

Instinctively, Jack opened an aperture beneath his own feet. He was able to hear assorted screams of panic and rage echo above his head as he fell through to safety.

# CHAPTER 20

Plummeting into the void, Jack telepathically corralled the prepared swarm of crows from within before continuing on through to the Liveside.

Though surrounded by a swirling multitude of crows too plenteous to be numbered, Jack had never felt more alone. For the most part, his traumatized psyche had revived despite having uncovered the horrifying intent behind the otherworldly conspiracy. And while he was resolved to confront the imminent tragedy head-on, his intuition picked up on yet another disturbing truth.

*"Be circumspect."*

The moment his cognition processed Goodwill's explanation regarding Inicio, those last words from his mother immediately passed through his mind.

And with good reason.

There was no way Bossu could have been ignorant of the machine's true nature. Jack only hoped he had guarded his psyche before the Lwa detected his realization.

Now, however, his primary focus was fixing what he had so ignorantly permitted to unfold.

Arriving in the Liveside, he was immediately met with the unfiltered stench of the Deadside's demons while his appendage suddenly started the unprecedented transmission of spoken words.

"Jack?" his mother began, her voice registering directly into his mind as she spoke into the amulet. "Can you hear me, my special boy?"

"Oh no."

Jack spoke this plea out loud upon realizing the means she was utilizing to communicate.

From the midst of the murder, he focused on the speech-turned-psychic transmission and froze at the disturbing sounds in the background. The growls and gnashing of some unknown monsters could be heard interspersed within the human screams of terror.

Jack composed himself as he replied. "Mom?" he began, calmly speaking over the noise. "Is everything ok—"

Alyssa impatiently interrupted his mother. "Werewolves, Jack!" she hissed, her voice bearing a tone of uncharacteristic panic. "In Black Pearl. We couldn't reach you because no phones work. S-s-so we came to your mother's house!"

Jack felt the familiar tempest of emotion materialize in his chest and immediately begin its upward surge.

Committed to the task at hand, he redirected the white-hot fury before it could reach his head and affect his thinking. His body temporarily immobilized by this outward burst of pressure, Jack began communicating with his surrounding shoal.

Operating at the speed of thought, he willed the sentient reconnaissance drones to his besieged town just before the furious shock wave caused them to explode off him.

Jack shook off the residual bodily tremors while taking a moment to consider what to do. Far from feeling worried, his steadied rage somehow carried within it the promise that he would reach them in time.

He could feel his appendage swaying in anticipation. *What are you going to latch onto though? Mom is holding the amulet now and it's not like you can just grab street signs and houses and stuff. You don't have an affinity with*—Jack suddenly remembered the crow he had stationed at his mother's house. *Of course you share an affinity with the birds, but . . . can I pull myself to them?*

Jack hurriedly moved for confirmation. However, the intrinsic properties of the spectral creature circumvented the need to visualize his destination. The appendage seamlessly transmitted the coordinates of the distant crow. Preparing to shortcut via the void, he formed an aperture that would serve as both an exit from the dimension and an entrance back into the Liveside, positioning it just underneath the perched bird.

The psionic transmissions felt more automated than he remembered. The appendage went through the void and back out again, confirming its hold on the distant crow.

In an instant, the young host slingshotted himself into the void and out through the other side.

Upon emerging, he was joined by several additional crows that were deftly snatched from the dimension as he passed through, two of which were immediately directed to assess the town's condition.

Jettisoned high above his mother's house, Jack took the opportunity to ensure its spectral barrier remained intact while utilizing his spatial awareness to scan about the surrounding mayhem. The two crows and his appendage simultaneously began marking areas fit for tactical advantage.

Beginning his descent, Jack spied a monster giving chase to one of the townsfolk.

He was unsure if saving them was feasible but remembered

the extra pairs of eyes summoned for this very reason. He vanished from the air and reappeared in the shadowy area where the monster had pursued its victim.

The werewolf was about seven feet tall and agile, and despite her effort, it left its fleeing prey no hope of escape. It had closed the gap and sadistically maintained its stride.

Enjoying the sheer terror the woman had given herself over to, the werewolf opened its maw and slowly began to bow its head forward, intending to bite off its victim's head mid-sprint.

Jack had planned to use the appendage to grasp the monster's foot but froze as his mind suddenly registered a distinct request coming from it.

A succinct, yet voiceless, wait.

Met with a sense impression he had experienced only once before, Jack marveled as the appendage suddenly bloomed itself wide, like the hood of a cobra.

*What are you doing?*

Time seemed to stop as Jack perceived the appendage hovering above the werewolf that was just about to clamp down on the woman's head.

Jack recalled the terrifying moment his psyche was subjected to the torture of Bossu's image but began grinning in satisfaction.

*So that's how it is.*

In an instant, Jack willed the appendage to constrict itself against the sprinting werewolf like shrink-wrap. Aided by the darkness, it completely halted the monster's movements, forcing it to freeze in place.

Still grinning, Jack noticed how different the constriction felt on his psyche now that the Fear was removed; a numbing coolness pulsated through his veins, replacing the maddening itch he remembered.

The calming sensation enabled him to focus on the physiological signs of panic emanating from the werewolf. Jack's eardrums became filled with the sound of the monster's frantic heartbeat as it strained to draw breath against the squeezing pressure of the enveloping appendage.

The stunned monster was watching its prey escape when it sensed something in the shadows. As Jack approached, he could see it following his phantomlike silhouette with panic-stricken eyes.

Sensing a sudden rise in its massive chest, Jack intuited some kind of battle cry to be incoming and swiftly chopped off its head.

Still maintaining his remote surveillance from the shadows, Jack could hear the residents screaming with terror from within their homes as the Trojan horse–like Inicios fulfilled their sinister purpose.

But outside was no better.

The town was an infernal mess. The pack of werewolves was merciless in their slaughter. The chaotic manner in which the beasts handled the bodies, dead or alive, spread the remains in such a way that it was difficult to determine just how many people had been killed so far.

In addition, the werewolves were exceedingly cruel.

Dead set against leaving any human alive, they would hastily disable their current victims in order to pursue those who managed to flee. The beasts would then handle them in a variety of violent ways, all deeply injurious.

Jack saw one of the wolves seize its fleeing victim by jamming its claws into the top of his head, causing the man's movements to come to an immediate halt.

With claws nearly knuckle-deep in his crown, the man was dragged back to the general area of slaughter, where the powerful monster whipped him around like a nunchuck. The velocity of its swinging increased until its claws became dislodged from the victim's brain, causing him to be tossed like a rag doll.

Still not finished, the beast advanced on the corpse, squatted low, and began gnawing at the lifeless legs until they separated from the rest of his body in full view of those not yet dealt with.

Jack could hear people screaming what he assumed was the name of this recent victim, and quickly realized the man's loved ones had been watching the whole thing.

Having thoroughly assessed his soon-to-be battleground, Jack suppressed his analytical mind, preparing for his emotions to set in. He quickly took roll of the crows that were in the vicinity to double-check the safety of his mother and the Abettors. Once confirmed, his emotions immediately took over.

And he was furious.

Holding the head of the slaughtered werewolf, Jack emerged from the shadows and into the area that had become a killing floor. His appendage revealed a group of townspeople trying to hide themselves nearby. Initially, the monsters were only able to make out his slight frame, but as he drew nearer, they noticed the head of their cohort.

The pack responded with a mix of howls and roars, creating a disturbing cacophony of fury that bordered on lamentation. Their collective echoes were still in the air as they suddenly bounded toward the shadowy interloper.

Jack took off with equal quickness, leading them away from the collection of survivors.

As for the pack, the immediacy of their reaction, despite the sudden and abnormal nature of the young hero's arrival, was a testament to their combat capability. Though it could not be denied that they were exceedingly vicious creatures, Jack observed their nonverbal preparations for a coordinated attack and determined them to be monstrosities of a more disciplined sort.

Sensing their impromptu foot race along the deserted street was coming to a close, Jack noticed the monsters flex for the kill and did likewise, psychically gripping the sengese from the void.

The werewolf that had positioned itself directly behind Jack made the fateful decision to swipe at his ankles. Jack leaped into the air and tucked in his knees, ensuring his feet would be out of the path of the beast's oversized hand.

As his momentum carried him into a front flip, Jack was given a clear view of his attacker still flying forward as a consequence of its missed attack.

He summoned the sengese as he rolled through his somersault, warping it into position beneath the airborne foe, and held it tight. As expected, the werewolf's body forced the sickle's tip into its chin and throat the same moment Jack landed his flip.

Jack pulled at the blade's handle from an overhead position, acting against the beast the moment its weight had fully fallen. Drawing it out in a forward-facing arc, Jack surreptitiously returned the sengese to the void a moment after his follow-through.

The remaining wolves continued to enact their plan, assuming their adversary's one-second flip to be nothing more than a flashy dodge.

The swiftness of their formation slowed as, one by one, they caught the scent of their fallen fellow's blood. Halting in disbelief, they collectively examined its condition, beholding the clean split from its throat through the top of its head.

Jack quickly began to move against the four remaining monsters, forcing them to abandon their battle plan. Since they remained oblivious to how their fellow was killed, suddenly being coerced into defensive tactics did not serve them, as all their movements were accompanied by second guesses.

Now on the offensive against enemies that had no idea what to expect, Jack was able to make quick work of them. He warped the sengese in and out however he wished, sometimes faking them into thinking a blade was coming when he was empty-handed. The incensed youth swatted at them without ceasing until each lay thoroughly dismembered.

Dismissing the sense of victory, Jack hurriedly scanned the entirety of the town's houses and gnashed his teeth at the copious amounts of demons already invading them. Despite the culminating regret, Jack felt a much-needed sense of relief upon perceiving his appendage resonating with each, revealing its capability to anchor itself to all of them.

Without hesitation, Jack pulled himself to the first Inicio, causing him to warp inside like a ghost. The demons within, sensitive to Jack's scalding aura of fury, paused their acts of unspeakable wickedness to see the hero staring at them in wide-eyed disbelief. Before the demons could react, either to attack or flee, they were cut down.

Determined not to weaken his resolve by consoling the traumatized victims, Jack clenched his eyes shut and followed the quicker-than-thought impressions transmitted to him by his appendage.

He warped from house to house like a vengeful spirit, cutting down the demonic invaders while destroying the infernal beacons they had used to gain entry.

Having disabled them all, he at last entered his mother's house. He found her, Alyssa, and Dox huddled together in his room, preparing for the worst.

He shifted off his mask as he spoke. "Mom!"

Helena turned and immediately ran to embrace him.

"My special boy," she began, whimpering into his shoulder.

Already looking in his direction, Alyssa's face immediately livened with relief. "Jack?" she said. "Jack!"

"It's okay," he replied. "They're gone but I—"

"You have to go," Helena said knowingly.

Her son nodded.

"So it's true," Dox stated. "Inicio is a gateway."

"Yes."

"My God."

There was a desperate silence that temporarily filled the room before Jack moved to reassure them.

"Dad knew this was coming," he explained. "And he knew he wouldn't be able to succeed." He looked at his mother. "But he knew that I could—"

Helena completed her son's statement, suddenly remembering what her husband had said in the very same room. "Succeed where he failed."

A warm expression of acceptance came upon her face as she looked into her young son's eyes. "Go, my special boy," she commanded. The woman grasped at Alyssa's hand and held it tightly, stopping her from speaking. "Do what you have been appointed for."

The beginnings of a smile began to form just before Jack's stonelike mask reappeared, its coldness still unable to repress the warmth emanating from within.

Without uttering another word, he warped himself outside.

The stench of the demons invading the city was overwhelming but rather than breaking, Jack felt unwavering determination as he prepared himself for the task Fate had given him.

He seized upon his innumerable crows, inviting their feedback into his psyche. One by one, yet altogether, their individual fields of view swept across his memory, giving him a holistic and detailed vision of the city within moments.

Jack felt his anger achieve a new baseline as his mind recalled the presence of blockades that had been strategically implemented along the outskirts of the city.

The resulting isolation was due to what the signs declared to be a state of emergency, a ploy enacted by the human traitors to ensure the invasion would occur privately. Jack quickly deduced that all electrical forms of communication must have been disabled as well.

"Which was why Mom's phone didn't work," he said, gritting his teeth. "Black Pearl was just their test run."

His memorized vision of the city's interior had provided him with his next priority.

The demon hordes seemed to be centralized in the French Quarter.

An ogre-like demon, no less than ten feet tall, had established something like a throne in the center of Jackson Square. Symbolically set atop a high mound of countless corpses, the lesser demons would transport the humans here, where they would be given their final destination based on the whims of the overseeing brute.

Its primary responsibility, however, was to guard the spire.

The crows revealed the spire to be an arcane piece of machinery that enabled the demons to cross over the space-time fabric while retaining their overpowered physical forms.

It seemed to function as a beacon, drawing the demons' essence to it as they were transported through the fabric and enveloped in the protective shield of Inicio's energy, meticulously designed to temporarily negate any inherent properties that resulted specifically from Samedi's spectral signature.

As such, the baron's enchantment that had devastated the demons' overall capabilities upon crossover from the Deadside was undone.

*This doesn't feel like it comes from Lwa*, Jack thought. *It feels scientific and more . . . human.*

Having observed the process in detail, Jack intuited that

this counter-equivalent energy was the product of a mind that naturally resonated with this kind of stuff but was also obsessive in its pursuit for perfection.

Naturally, the spire's tactical value was evident even to someone as inexperienced as Jack, who immediately resolved to destroy it.

Jack willed one of the many crows already monitoring the square to get closer to the lounging brute, planning to use the distant summoned creature as an anchor for his appendage.

Confirming the summoned bird had reached a more suitable position for his surprise attack, Jack slingshotted himself to the distant location and straight toward the slouching mountain's face.

With frightful agility, the brute stood from its slouch and threw a punch at the speedily arriving Shadowman, Jack just happened to block it.

Jack's surprise was visible as he eyed the changed position of his staff's edge. The sense impressions of his appendage triggered a reflex at the last second.

The ogre's follow-up was backed by a force Jack estimated too much for him to stand against outright. He tried to vault over the attack but its momentum kept him pinned, stifling his attempt to tumble away.

As Jack struggled to orient himself, he considered how surprisingly strong this monster was. *I could only imagine how many people lost their lives trying to play hero against this thing.*

Although its body type suggested clumsy and cumbersome, the reality was different. Not only was the ogre able to detect the subtle repositioning of Jack's crow, but it reacted fast enough to strike him from the air the moment he appeared.

Bossu used this as an opportunity to break his conspicuous silence.

"Why did you doubt, whelp?"

Taken aback by his Lwa's sudden speech, Jack dawdled in his recovery from the grazing blow, allowing himself to be sent into the church positioned right in front of the spire.

Careening through the building, Jack seized the former crow anchor with the surrounding rubble still falling around him and, without exiting the Liveside, slingshotted himself back to the brute.

The ogre once again proved itself an exceedingly skilled combatant by deflecting Jack's blitz with another blurry counterpunch.

Jack had surreptitiously arranged more crows to act as disparate anchor points, hoping to catch the monster from an unexpected angle, to no avail.

In terms of both its footwork and striking, the ogre was just too quick.

Like shadowboxing an obstinate hornet, it reacted to Jack's zipping to and fro by swiftly pivoting its body and throwing inhumanly precise jabs to parry the repeated attacks.

"Why are you fighting like this?" Bossu asked, abrasively curious. "Attacking it in a straight line while not even utilizing apertures to throw off its timing? It is too strong for that kind of attack to work. Can you not see?"

As if timed to prove the Lwa's point, another ogre appeared as a bolt summoned by the lightning rod–like spire.

"ENOUGH!!!" it roared.

Barely missing Jack as he zipped by, the agile mountain began swatting as many of the sneaky standby birds it could reach, bringing that method of attack to an end.

"Do not permit yourself to be disheartened, whelp. Most certainly, this is the Deadside-equivalent overseer, beckoned to defeat you once and for all. We shall dispatch them both at once straightway."

By now, most of the lesser demons in the immediate area had taken notice and began gathering to witness the impudent terror of the Deadside finally meet his doom.

As Jack pondered how to respond to his shady Lwa, the other ogre struck him and sent him crashing into the local museum.

"The time of your race . . ." Having sprinted inside, the second ogre was upon Jack before he could react, batting him deeper through the building's infrastructure. "Is over." The monster started raining blows on Jack who, despite acute awareness of what was coming and how to counter, did not.

With his mind filled with doubt toward his Lwa, Jack could not help but suspect the timing of his renewed speech and put an inordinate amount of focus on monitoring his inward thoughts against intrusion.

The ogre stood over him confidently, continuing its boasting. "Your women," it began, winding up for a kick, "are ours."

These words got Jack's attention, just in time for him to receive the faster-than-expected kick to the gut, sending him through the floors above and rocketing through the roof.

The overwhelming pain from the spine-breaking foot seemed to fuel Jack's outrage at the demon's words, but the overwhelming uncertainty left the emotion with no outlet.

His Lwa let out a gravelly sigh. "And so?" he asked. "For that reason, you will let this overconfident excrement kill you? Have its way with your kin?"

As Jack reached the top of his ascent and began free fall, the ogre's twin appeared behind him and clobbered him back down to the earth. The shock wave of his crash landing brought great joy to the onlooking lesser demons.

"EVEN WHEN YOU HAVE THE ABILITY TO RIP HIM LIMB FROM LIMB!?"

Jack could see shards of his newly broken mask embedded in the ground as Bossu's enraged reprimand echoed in his head. Drowning out the pain, it rekindled memories of their past conversation.

"Remember whelp: Your anger fuels your strength, your strength fuels your violence. That's what it will feel like, but the truth is they are one and the same. Therefore, control your anger. Do not stifle it, but *control* it. Listen and understand, as it must not be indulged unless necessary."

"Why?"

"Because when they see it, they will fear."

"Good."

As Jack felt himself get kicked toward the spire, he sensed his body engage in recovery against the momentum of his flight. As he did so, he could see the same ogre sprinting toward his flying body, preparing to strike once more.

The agile mountains were so annoying.

Feeling the elusive outlet for his rage finally fall in line with the swelling geyser already primed within, he thought back to his conflict with Jamal and recalled his father's prophetic advice on engagement, given for such a time as this.

The young hero could make out the ogre hesitating in its advance as his discernment began to speak to him, somehow reciting the instruction in the voice of Josiah.

*Go nuts.*

Suddenly, it was as if the wall he had first sensed against Jamal that kept his rage nonexistent had been breached.

To Jack, it was almost like Providence had predetermined Bossu to be the key needed to dismantle it, though they had not even known each other.

Nevertheless, here Jack stood, a slow burn of fury sizzling just beneath the surface. And judging by the changed demeanor of his demonic opponent, this volatile emotion was outwardly visible.

Apparently affronted, the monster attacked quickly, sending thunderous blows to Jack's partially exposed face. Each one was so loud that the audience of undead fell silent. The mountain's twin finally touched down and gazed from afar, awaiting the cue for its turn.

However, what it could not see was that its partner's mighty shots were being shrugged off. The broken mask revealing portions of his altered skin tone, Jack's seething expression remained unchanged as his head returned from each strike progressively quicker.

Like a robot.

The audience of lesser demons quickly shifted from disbelief to terror. The ogre apparently shared this emotion. Its eyes widened with uncertainty as the renewed bass of Jack's anger began rocking the air with a fever pitch.

The brute threw another strike, only to have it stopped by Jack, once and for all.

"Yes, whelp, yesss," Bossu began excitedly, "show them . . . *violence*!"

The confused monster noticed its massive forearm stuck in the maw of its small opponent. Jack had opened his mouth inhumanly wide to accommodate the limb, causing the intact fangs of his mask's commissure to dig in as he stood upright.

Wincing in discomfort, the monster helplessly watched as he continued working his jaw into its flesh, glaring as he did so. Maintaining his clench on the ogre's limb, Jack took a short leap back before suddenly jerking his head to the side.

*"Hhhrgghh . . ."*

The monster groaned in shock and pain as it hobbled backward against the base of the spire, staring in confusion at where its shoulder used to be. It looked up to behold Jack standing with its gargantuan arm in his mouth.

The demonic horde watched with unbridled terror as Jack casually grasped the limb from his mouth and, holding the arm as if giving it a handshake, fell upon its original owner and proceeded to beat the monster to death.

The flayed flesh and tendons of the ogre's upper arm gave way to the hammer-like head of its giant humerus, increasing the lethality of the already top-heavy club.

Jack was mercilessly flipping and spinning his body in assorted ways to make the most of each strike.

But before he could give the killing blow, the overseer's Liveside equivalent interrupted Jack's vicious overhead stroke, attempting to tackle him from behind.

Already primed for the immediate collision, Jack instinctively recovered by planting his feet firmly on the ground to brace himself against its massive weight, surprising the brute and momentarily slowing it. Baffled by the stance, the imposing demon began jogging against Jack's low grapple.

Taking advantage of their size difference and the momentum already in his favor, Jack tightened his grip on its oversized waist and moved for a suplex.

The ogre snarled a laugh, apparently amused by how ineffectual the maneuver would be on level ground. The laughter was cut short, however, as they began to pass through the ground instead of making contact with it.

Suddenly appearing within the New Orleans nighttime skyline, the airborne combatants were accompanied by a cluster of newly summoned crows that steadily grew in number.

Teleporting them from the ground into the sky above, Jack had utilized the momentum from his furious throw to accelerate their plummet toward the tiny dots illuminating the distant street below. Jack's strength, coupled with the acceleration from their descent rendered the monster helpless to break free from his hold.

The upturned fiend peered at the ground below as they sped toward it.

"We will both perish, you fool."

Jack silently maintained his grip through gritted teeth; the fiend could only stare at the incoming ground, shocked by the youth's suicidal intent.

Seeing the ogre clench his eyes shut to prepare for impact, Jack repositioned himself, swiftly appearing upright with his foot firmly established beneath its jawline.

Unresponsive, the ogre had been timing their fall, waiting for the right moment to wrestle free from the position and avoid a disastrous landing. Unfortunately, it did not anticipate Jack teleporting them once again, this time to the Deadside.

Swiftly scanning the vicinity upon entry, Jack marked the location of the realm's equivalent spire and the countless demons preparing to cross over. Some of the assembled denizens caught a glimpse of him and the ogre plummeting from on high, but before the horde could make sense of the sight, it had vanished.

Not only had Jack returned both of them to the Liveside, but they were now much closer to the earth than their rate of free fall would've otherwise brought them, making the ogre's precise timing useless.

Sensing something amiss, it opened its eyes.

Immediately understanding its predicament, the ogre set its newly terrified gaze on Jack just before they collided into its twin, still incapacitated against the base of the Liveside spire.

Jack obliterated the ogres into soup as he crashed into the infernal machine, causing it to explode in a violent burst of arcane power. The surreptitiously gathered murder of purple-eyed companions that had been waiting for his telepathic directive exploded through the area upon his crash down.

Jack reappeared in an instant, walking away from the toppling structure, totally unscathed. Scattering in a manner all too familiar, he watched as the innumerable throng of lesser demons desperately tried to escape what they already knew was coming.

The screams of one, in particular, happened to meet his ears, its shrillness standing out against the sound of the murder already flapping throughout the vicinity. "That is no Shadowman," it cried. "That is none other than Bossu Koblamin!"

Reaching out to his side, Jack summoned the sengese. "Let's try this again."

Bossu let out a gravelly titter. "Hm hm hm, very well."

In the same manner that proved fruitless against the overseer, Jack began slingshotting himself between the haphazardly positioned crows, cutting down any demons unfortunate enough to have gathered to witness his death.

Ricocheting faster than the speed of thought, he cut through the multitude like a reaper sent by Fate Himself, leaving no survivors.

# CHAPTER 21

Having received a detailed visual report, Jack was embittered by the condition of the besieged city. Not only was its infrastructure broken beyond repair, but so were its people, with many seizing the opportunity to commit crimes against their fellows—men, women, and children.

*Not now*, he urged himself.

Warping to the Deadside, he was surprised by the arcane energy still cracking in the distance and immediately went about drawing forth a company of eyes.

The crows had enabled him to realize the obvious. Though Inicio was mainly used for invasion, it could also be used for kidnapping.

He froze at the sound of a woman's screams, and warping to a nearby dilapidated rooftop overlooking the area, could not believe his eyes.

A woman desperately hung on to the intact portions of her clothes that the demons evidently had attempted to strip away just before dragging her through to the Deadside.

Their incessant pulling caused her to fall forward. She stared up at the six monsters that had taken her captive, the exceedingly grotesque features of their individual bodies burning into her psyche.

Noticing the subtleties within the woman's pitiable countenance, Jack personally understood what she was going through. The terror of the real had robbed her of the ability to speak.

She was only capable of emitting disjointed squeals that were barely audible.

Her pursed lips were sealed due to an inordinate amount of horrified cottonmouth, only made worse by the Deadside's bone-dry air.

The more she beheld the monstrosities, the wider her eyes became, growing close to bulging like some circus act. But this woman was not a performer. She was someone's daughter, possibly a sister, a wife, or a mother.

As she tightened her hold over her clothing, Jack felt the rage again, only it was not directed toward the six soon-to-be dead demons surrounding her.

The woman began trembling violently. The hands that had been used to secure the clothes began to betray her, jostling the coverings loose through their dread-convulsions. As her paralysis began to set in, the corners of her mouth began to droop as if someone suddenly made her sad.

But it was dread.

Only evil could have known something like this was on the horizon yet chose to remain silent. How many more people like this one were unable to be saved?

No matter what, the damage was done and nobody could take it back. So the judgment would remain unchanged regardless.

Jack could not ignore it any longer.

His dark ponderings were interrupted by a sudden ripple

within the leg muscles of one of the demons, prompting Jack to cut them all down before the intended step could be taken.

He removed his mask just before turning around to face the woman. "You are okay," he said, speaking slowly. "I got rid of all these baddies so I'm going to take you to my mom's house, okay?"

The wide-eyed woman nodded rapidly, prompting Jack to calmly reach for her shoulders.

"I'm not going to hurt you," he said, smiling. "It's just weird because normally, regular people just don't come here. That's why I'm coming off awkward, you know?"

She nodded frantically again, glancing at his hands as they clasped her shoulders. "Makes sense," she replied, clenching her eyes shut.

"Jack?" Helena asked. "Is everything okay? Who's your friend?"

Helena, Dox, and Alyssa looked at the newly arrived young woman.

"She was on the other side, Mom," Jack explained. "She's in shock. Put on the television or something. I don't know."

"But—"

"I can't right now, Mom."

---

After destroying the Deadside spire, Jack had planned to pay Samedi his overdue visit, but he could not delay a confrontation any longer. If Bossu was a liar then it was best to confront him sooner and minimize the chance of intrusion.

Just as the thought entered his mind, he had another light-speed inkling, a compulsion to double-check for intrusion with his appendage, sweeping in a direction opposite the norm. Before Jack could think about the idea twice, he did it.

Whipping the appendage over his psyche, he felt it make contact.

*There!* Jack thought, maintaining his calm exterior. *He read it! I just grazed him!*

The focus necessary for Jack to hide his surprise was substantial, forcing him to struggle to prevent his mind from delving.

But he was too weak.

*He just follows the movement of the appendage so that I never detect him.* He almost smiled. *So he's been doing this from the beginning, only faking incompetence. Oh my goodness.*

Under different circumstances, Jack may have found this revelation funny, but the idea that his Lwa had always known about Inicio made that impossible now.

Maskless, Jack stared off into the Deadside's bleak horizon, racking his brain for any possible alternative before committing to what he was about to do. Unfortunately, every time he would get close to letting it go, that woman's look of utter dread compelled him forward.

Before the remorse could set in, Jack willed his rage to the fore and warped into the void.

Once inside, Jack already found it difficult to control his culminating anger. He reached out his appendage to grasp Bossu but, for the first time, latched onto nothing. More irritated than curious, he began swiping at the dark, never making contact with anything.

Jack ceased his efforts upon hearing a progressive tapping sound, like footsteps making their way to him in the darkness.

"Where are you?!" he bellowed.

"I am here, Jack."

Finally, Jack felt his maddening anger abate due to the perfect confusion that now consumed him. The voice that emanated from the dark was not Bossu's, it sounded youthful.

Almost human.

The footsteps' owner became more visible. Their purple hue contrasted against the surrounding darkness, causing the silhouette to grow in clarity.

"Who is that?"

"Do not be daft, whelp," the voice commanded. "You called for me and I answered. What are you playing at by asking who it is?" As Jack continued to behold the individual before him, his confusion had risen to a level that made it feel quite similar to fear. "You are aware that this is my prison, are you not? Therefore, who else can I be?"

Try as he might, Jack simply could not manage to speak. This was not due to fear, but rather, all the questions that sprang to his mind became irrelevant the more he stared.

While the young man's physical appearance suggested that his origins were exclusively European, Jack could not deny that the two of them looked quite similar otherwise.

If he didn't know better, Jack would have believed the individual to be from his mother's side, a relative from House LeBreton, and not a distant one either.

But that made no sense.

Regardless, all these ruminations just added to his confusion since he knew without a shadow of a doubt who this person was.

Jack *felt* it the moment he heard his voice.

Looking upon the Lwa's true form, Jack spoke his name, unsure if it would still sound the same. "Bossu."

"Jack."

Hearing his Lwa say his name yanked Jack out of his astonishment, allowing him to return to himself.

"So, what?" he began. "You make yourself look like me for some kind of deep lesson after lying to me this whole time?"

Bossu adjusted the sleeves of his ancient-looking garments,

utterly untouched by Jack's accusations. "Not at all," he replied. "That is just you presuming while missing the true import." He paused his adjusting. "As usual."

A wrinkle appeared across the bridge of Jack's nose as he made eye contact with the insouciant Lwa. "Why didn't you tell me about Inicio, Bossu?"

Bossu scoffed before finally abandoning his sleeve. "For what?" he asked, the casual tone of the response caused Jack's eyes to widen as he unwittingly bared his teeth. "You sensed the Truth when you first came upon the Abettors' beacon. I even amped up the resonance thereof, but you *chose* to ignore it. Had you inquired, I would have told you." The Lwa let out a sigh of fake sympathy. "But you did not."

Jack suddenly let out a roar of frustration, and while it seemed to be projected toward Bossu, its true trajectory was inward. "AARGHH!"

His arms trembling at his sides, Jack's scream seemed to summon the sengese to his hand.

Bossu's countenance perked up at seeing the weapon manifest.

His eyebrows and the corners of his mouth rose as one, resembling a small child responding to the unexpected appearance of something they fancy.

The sight of the woman would not stop tormenting Jack's mind. The intimate features within her state of fear remained memorialized in vivid detail, all thanks to his curse.

"But," Jack began, hissing through clenched teeth, "the suffering!"

"So?"

The single-syllable response of disinterest had barely left the Lwa's mouth before the youth was upon him.

*CRACK!*

Bossu had blocked the blindingly swift blitz with what appeared to be a sengese of a more traditional design, enveloped in shadow.

The suddenness of Bossu's maneuver created no change in his demeanor or tone. He spoke as if nothing happened while his glaring host continued pressing against his staff. "You should be angry at the imp for distracting you."

"Fuck you!" Jack screamed.

"You want to fight me?"

Further incensed by the question, Jack gnashed his teeth as he growled his answer. "What does it look like, asshole?"

Bossu thrust Jack off his weapon, dismissively casting him aside. "So be it."

The momentum created by the Lwa's push was difficult to overcome, causing Jack to travel too far to initiate a successful counter.

The velocity having waned, he performed a controlled fall and realized Bossu had not moved, apparently waiting for him to try again.

"So be it!?" Jack bellowed. "You set me up for disaster and you don't fucking care!"

Jack warped out of the void and then back in, appearing behind Bossu with a prepared strike. Swinging down the sengese toward the back of his neck, Jack had made sure to appear close enough to restrict the Lwa's range of movement and hinder any attempt to block.

*CRACK!!*

Propped up by the Lwa's sengese that had somehow been brought around with enough speed to intercept his nearly instantaneous attack, Jack found himself looking at his sickle as it hovered less than an inch from Bossu's exposed neck

"The issue is that you are not a very good fighter," Bossu

taunted. Jack's face scrunched into a bratty scowl upon hearing this. "That is to say, you fight too much like a mortal. You are too predictable, telegraphed almost. In addition, you do not know how to harness your emotions efficiently. Either too hot or too cold. If I left you to yourself, you would remain bouncing from one extreme to another, never truly in control."

Bossu looked up at him, still balanced against his sengese.

As Jack returned the stare, his Lwa's eyes suddenly shot forth an aura of killing intent, forcing him to move as if seeking cover.

"Where are you going?"

Jack tried drawing forth the raging tempest from earlier, but despite burning fine moments before, it seemed depleted.

Bossu let out a youthful-sounding, closed-mouth chuckle.

While in his bestial form, this laugh triggered feelings of fear. But now it fostered suspicions of mockery.

It was just too much.

*CRACK!*

Colliding once more, Jack experienced an unfamiliar sensation as Bossu put forth a level of force that was meticulously equal to his own. He matched Jack's rapid fluctuations in strain with effortless control, bringing their clash to a perfect standstill as their staffs pressed against each other.

Jack continued glaring through the crossed weapons as Bossu began speaking. "You know the irrepressible persona that you are trying to harness right now?"

He eased up on their stilled staffs, drawing Jack near and quickly morphing into a horned version of himself. His brown slicked-back hair suddenly bloomed, each side unnaturally arching itself into a horn shape as his face tensed upward, bringing forth a snout and fanged smile.

"IT'S ME!"

The words echoed in a high-pitched whisper, far different from the deep and gravelly tones Jack had grown accustomed to.

Hobbling backward, the sight seemed to snatch the heart from Jack's chest, compelling him to look away as quickly as possible. The familiar sensation caused him to wince in discomfort as he stared out into the void and tried to brace himself for the Fear.

Somehow, it felt less severe than what he suspected that woman experienced.

"You could've said something, Bossu."

"I could have," the Lwa replied. "But it would have been folly on my part. Especially since it was unreasonable for you to not have predicted this on your own."

Jack continued his pained expression, unable to respond.

"You moved as one operating under an implicit premise suggesting humanity allying itself with the supernatural to be impossible. This would be easy to overlook if not for conjurers and shamans being common knowledge, not to mention the countless movies and video games you once indulged in."

Bossu had been observing his host maintaining an averted gaze while trying to steel himself against the Fear.

"Furthermore, I would have done you a disservice if I told you outright. Remember your father? Some things must be discovered for yourself. Had I told you outright, you may have been spared the shock of that particular revelation, but there was no guarantee that being force-fed the knowledge would have been enough to *change your thinking.*"

Jack recalled the discussion with Josiah in his room.

Thinking back, it was as if he could perceive some sense impression within the man's demeanor. Though he knew he was incapable of doing such a thing, he began standing upright to get a better look at his father's imagined face.

"And your thinking *has* changed," Bossu continued. "I can see that swift insight of yours making all the connections still unattainable to you even after Josiah's intervention. I can see it in your eyes. You have realized it, the one thing I could never have told you, he-he, tell me what it is."

Jack reflexively uttered what he saw intimated on his father's face. "This world is nothing but lies."

"Yes, whelp," the Lwa replied.

Upon saying these words, the young host felt the Fear vanish from his chest and began scanning about for Bossu.

"Your kin speaks much of facts but rarely of Truth," the disembodied Lwa continued, "and what you just said is the Truth." Jack began patting his chest as if searching for something. "The humbling caused by your monumental failure will become part of you. But unlike myself, your innocent nature will turn it into an instructor, not a torturer."

Bossu watched Jack shift into plain clothes. "You are not done!"

# CHAPTER 22

Jack had warped to the cavern where the conspirators were gathered.

The melanin-deficient man with the bald head was still within. No longer bearing the joyful grin he was wearing the last time Jack saw him, he was now gazing mournfully at the comatose Freda. "What was this all for?"

"I was going to ask that," Jack said, emerging from the shadows.

The anxious man spun around at the sound of his voice.

"Jack Boniface," he began, "I knew your father, you—Oof!!"

While winding up, Jack warped to the man's front and struck him with a right hook before instantly returning to his original position.

"Let's get this over with," Jack stated, pacing back and forth.

The bald albino held his jaw, following his young adversary with his eyes. "You are not interested in the name of he who kills you?" he asked. "And did the same to your father?"

Jack continued to pace, unaffected. "Try harder, man," he said. "Look, I'm going to attack if you're n—"

He watched as several orbs, pulsating with different colors, appeared behind the man's back and rose to position just above his shoulders. They crackled and sparked as if readying themselves, but suddenly, a ribbon of energy shot out of one of the man's eyes.

This streak of arcane power was intercepted by a speed-of-thought aperture, which, after receiving the energy, instantly transmitted it through another aperture that Jack had willed open behind the man's back.

The man's eyes widened with shock upon being hit by his own spell, which promptly paralyzed him. Through his ensuing convulsions, he watched Jack look down at him and shake his head before suddenly disappearing.

The man regretted how proficiently he had designed the paralysis spell. Having been hit without being prepared, he would not recover soon.

It seemed not even a minute had passed before the bastard youth returned with none other than Baron Samedi in tow. He watched as the skeleton bowed over him in the same manner.

The accursed spell had deadened his sense of hearing, making it impossible to understand what they were planning.

He saw Samedi mutter something to the Shadowman before clutching his hat against the top of his skull.

The cavernous hideout was rocked by an explosion of pressure suddenly blustering mightily within. The baron's intricate long coat flapped in violent response to the rush of wind as Jack buried his face in the nook of both his elbows.

The tempest ended as suddenly as it began, prompting Jack to peek through the newly lighted space between his arms. The sudden brightness revealed the entirety of the interdimensional hideout. The torches lining the encircling wall seemed to be unlit by its intensity.

Jack's eyes reflexively traced the near-blinding brightness to its source and widened in response to the sight before him.

*Is that a-a freaking snake?*

His Lwa replied. "Yes, joyously terrifying and not to be compared, the mighty Damb—"

The titanic serpent had appeared as a giant mound of light arranged neatly in the midst of the massive underground arena.

"I can hear your words to that son of man entrusted to you," it said, eyes glowing from their position atop its wrapped body. Its delicate whistling whisper sounded like a subtle hiss was slipped underneath its every word. "But more importantly, Bossu, I know that *you* are aware of this fact, and given that a being such as myself holds no regard for flattering words . . ." The serpent raised its head and began to advance, the scales of its massive coils rasping against each other as it wound its way to them, ultimately stopping at their front while looking directly at Jack. "Be quiet."

Jack felt unable to take his eyes off the creature, its presence demanding a certain sense of woe in the heart of its witnesses if fear was not available. The looming serpent forcefully broke their eye contact to stare down at the paralyzed man with disgust.

"Who is this incontinent one?"

Baron Samedi looked down at him, his face spread into a grimace of pity. "That is Nicodemo Darque, necromancer extraordinaire." The skeleton sniffed the air. "He appears to have crapped himself, my lord."

The snake's white hue suddenly blinked itself to black, as the now-ebony-colored titan swiftly turned his head upward. "Obatala! Sirene! Pierre!"

The serpent's voice was too loud for Jack to comprehend. He merely looked on as the three god-conspirators suddenly appeared, trembling.

"Explain yourselvessss!"

The first to speak was the angel of light, Obatala. "Forgive us, master," he said pleadingly. "We merely coveted Freda's level of worship. It was never meant as a slight against you."

La Sirene, the mermaid ruler, propped herself up on the mass of her piscine rear as she took a turn to make her case. "I was affronted by the unending competition for my husband's affections," she said. "Seeing that she has many husbands whereas I only have one. As if that was insufficient, the mortals have replaced my daughter Ursule with the Erzulies. As punishment, I planned to snatch many of the newborn Nephilim for my underwater nursery. All I wanted was a host of worshipful subjects."

Unlike the impossibly loud shouting of Damballa, Jack understood what the shaken Lwa were saying and was flabbergasted by what he was hearing. *Are they serious?* he began silently. *How can gods be so . . . so lame? They must be lying! Right, Bossu? Bossu? Hellooo, why aren't y—Oops, sorry!*

Damballa had quickly whipped his head to the side, setting its gaze directly on Jack. "Quiet, you."

Jack reflexively pursed his lips together as the sky father returned his attention to the three immortals.

The baritone Lwa Pierre was the last to speak. "Admittedly," he began, "I was in it only for mischief's sake. The drama is enjoyable to the utmost. But had we known you would take offense, we would never have set our hands to do such a thing."

Hearing the justifications given by its three progeny, the black serpent lowered its head to their level. "Good," he began as if pleased. "I know for certain that Lwa such as yourselves respect and honor me." He glided past them, apparently finding something of interest etched into the engravings on the far wall. "You do, don't you? I know the likes of Samedi do not for certain."

The fancily clad skeleton struck a pose suggesting surprise as the giant snake looked upon him.

"He lies, you know," the serpent continued, "and the measure to which someone lies is the greatest indicator as to whether or not they respect you in their hearts. And I do not mean trivial lies. I mean ones of significance, ones in which the person lying is acutely aware that doing so is akin to contempt or, worse yet, mockery. Like you." He returned his sights to the three affrighted immortals. "Implying that your respect for me is the guaranteeing proof that you acted with innocence of heart." He lowered himself once more, placing his giant head flat on the ground directly in front of them. "Yessssss?"

Obatala remained pensive, not yet willing to answer, while La Sirene quickly replied. "Yes, of course, my lord!"

"Never would we have done so, had we known," Pierre followed. "Never!"

Obatala opened his mouth as if suddenly sensing something off, but it was too late.

Hearing their replies, the serpent recoiled away from them. Its swift arcing into a question mark shape obliterated the formerly darkened ceiling to rubble, revealing stars and luminaries furiously swirling about it.

Jack could not look at the display for too long before he felt the overwhelming urge to vomit. However, no one else seemed to be affected in the slightest.

The giant serpent did not miss a beat, continuing the confrontation. "So I will asssk you a question, and do not say you were afraid!" It hissed out its speech with a habu-like sneer. "When Samedi told you I was planning on punishing him for Freda's disappearance, why did you not come forward?"

"Ooop!" Samedi exclaimed, snapping his fingers. "Gotteemm—"

"Silence!" the serpent commanded.

The skeleton immediately adopted an at-ease position, not saying a word.

The three conspirators looked at each other with dread, whimpering at the black serpent's charged silence.

"We were afrai—!"

The titan darted forward with a swiftness Jack could barely perceive. "Foolssss!!" it exclaimed with an ear-piercing hiss, gobbling them up in a line. "And you still say it?!" Their limbs were snapped off with a flick of its neck, as if juggling crumbs. "Maybe five hundred years in my digestive tract will lead you to repent and acknowledge your unnecessary wickedness."

Like lightning, Damballa reverted to his blinding white color. His massive tail suddenly came into view and wrapped the bald man so that his head stuck out like a lollipop in its clutches.

Jack watched as the serpent snapped its giant body upright into an ominous-looking contortion that made his skin crawl.

The serpent looked down at the man, Nicodemo Darque. "You come with me," it whispered, vanishing in a flash.

The echo of its utterance lingered for a moment before the space became a vacuum, making it impossible for Jack to breathe. *This is crazy.*

As suddenly as the suction began, it stopped, leaving Samedi and Jack alone in the destroyed arena.

The skeleton looked at him. "I guess be happy he doesn't consider you worth his time," he said with a shrug. "He's not really cool like that."

"It's fine," Jack replied. "The Liveside is a mess for sure anyway."

Jack pulled himself into the void to depart, but instead of darkness, he found himself surrounded by overpowering light.

Its brightness almost made him squint, but it was unnecessary, his eyes were able to take it all in without discomfort.

"Prostrate!" Bossu commanded urgently.

Without questioning, Jack fell prone, placing his face on the ground.

An entity began to speak, its voice like the sound of many speaking at once and in perfect harmony. "Ask what I shall give thee."

Jack remained silent, thoroughly unsure as to what was happening.

"I know what you desire, Bossu Koblamin, but let Me give it more time to decide. I must determine if all this was truly the heart of repentance or just another one of your cons. As of now, it is asked of you, Jack Boniface, what shall I give thee?"

Jack's mouth began to utter a request seemingly on its own. He did not give any thought to it before speaking.

"I want everything to go back to the way it was," he stated, "but I don't want people to return to their ignorance. I don't want those suffering to have to bear the reminder of the demons' acts against them either."

There was a long silence as Jack tried to think of a solution, but failed.

"I don't know what to ask."

"Very well," the voice began, "because such a desire was in your heart, mercy for the distraught and relief for the downtrodden, and you did not ask power for yourself nor the necks of your enemies, mercy and relief is granted your kin, in the way you had not the mind to utter. I will resurrect those killed during the invasion of your world, but their memories of the ordeal will remain intact. Furthermore, those used to gestate the abominations will have their bodies healed and their memories erased."

"Thank—"

Before Jack could express his gratitude, he heard the voice of Alyssa.

"He's waking up!" she said, standing over him.

Jack opened his eyes to find himself in his room. The television rambled on with its newly restored programming as his mother stood proudly at the entrance.

"We're continuing coverage of the city of New Orleans, just released from its two-day lockdown caused by an unprecedented wave in criminal activity. Mayor Goodwill is scheduled to make an announcement after being hospitalized for a broken jaw he received when coming to the rescue of one of his citizens."

"No," Jack began, sitting up in his bed, "it's all lies."

Helena made a swift advance to his bedside, shushing him to calm. "All is well, my special boy," she said, taking him by the hand. "You did it."

Her son looked around the room in confusion, the vision of Light dripping slowly into his recollection. "I don't understand . . . I . . . I saw a Light."

"It was undone," Alyssa explained. "Somehow, everything was undone."

"Mostly undone," Dox stated as he passed the doorway, followed by the woman brought from the Deadside. "The majority of people remember what happened here, as do those that were resurrected. The only ones that seem to lack any recollection are the women that—"

Jack raised his hand abruptly. "Stop," he said. "I remember now." He set his eyes on the woman he had rescued, now looking much better. "How are you?"

"I'm fine, Jack."

"Glad to hear it," he replied before looking upon the others.

"So what's the plan? How come I see no revolution? Why's that traitor Goodwill still in one piece?"

"All in due time, sweet boy."

"Rather than revolt against the treacherous government," Dox explained, "don't be surprised if the people decide to keep the Truth of what happened secret. At least temporarily."

Jack shook his head, forcibly suppressing his frustration. "Why?"

"To spare the women the trauma."

Hearing her response, Jack looked up at the woman still standing at the doorway and, smiling resignedly, nodded at her.

Jack remained silent as his Lwa began to speak. "I never imagined you would have granted us the privilege of seeing Gran Met," he said, still audibly shaken, "but, as for now, the Ghede branch of Lwa is free to operate once more. Damballa has annulled the sham marriage and has once again removed himself from their affairs. And since the Father of Lights has set everything aright according to His good pleasure, you are made a witness to the extent to which human leadership is compromised." His host continued smiling as he gazed upon his four onlookers. "Remain valiant in your innocence and diligent in your insouciance, as it is only a matter of time before Shadowman must emerge from the darkness again. I trust you know this, right?"

Jack's reply was audible. "Duh."